MW01071717

A POST APOCALYPTIC NOVEL

GHOST COUNTRY

Book Three of the Catalyst Series
by

JK FRANKS

Thank you Morlan !

Published by JK Franks Media, LLC
Made in USA

Ghost Country
Copyright © 2018
J.K. Franks

Editor: Debra Riggle

Paperback ISBN: 978-1-7326144-0-6
Hard Cover ISBN: 978-1-7326144-1-3

v. 8102-913

For Kerry

Thanks Bro for your continued encouragement, support and most of all teaching me the rich and complex art of being a true smartass.

"Success is not final, failure is not fatal. It is the courage to continue that counts."

– Winston Churchill

PREFACE

And so, here begins the end.

Since the solar superstorm and CME almost two years ago, the Gulf Coast town of Harris Springs, Mississippi has suffered from gang attacks, famine and hurricanes in addition to battling a crusading army of religious zealots. Now, they face their greatest challenges: outsmarting a tyrannical president and escaping an approaching pandemic.

The Gulf Coast of Southern Mississippi was supposed to be an escape for Scott Montgomery, a computer consultant for the DHS, hiding from a failed marriage and taking a break from the world. Then, the collapse began. Now, he and the remnants of his community shelter in an abandoned cruise ship knowing their time is running out. Survival has become a way of life in this post-apocalyptic world. A lawless world that seems intent on wiping out humans, or at least their humanity.

The fallout from a breach at an overseas bio-lab has brought a zombie-like pandemic to the shores of America. The pathogen has already wiped out much of Asia and Europe. The genetic engineering of a treatment becomes the last hope of salvation. The country's new president and her rogue government have other ideas, including using the bio-weapon on internment camps full of imprisoned American citizens.

What's left of the US military leaders are beginning to come to grips with the fact that America is being ripped apart at the seams. They must act decisively to give the remaining population any chance for survival, while Scott and his friends come up with a plan to escape the approaching pandemic. Those plans go awry when one of their own is kidnapped.

Scott and a select team of Special Forces must go head-to-head with the enemy in one of the most secret bases in the world. The rescue mission shows every likelihood of turning into an epic battle, one that reveals new heroes and betrayal that may spell the end of humanity. Nothing in this new post-apocalyptic world is what it seems—and the deadliest threats are often the ones you didn't see coming.

A major release in the bestselling Catalyst series, as America struggles after a global blackout, this is JK Franks' Ghost Country.

CHAPTER ONE

HARRIS SPRINGS, MISSISSIPPI

The storm had passed; Scott sat on the smooth sand and stared out at the still pounding waves. The rhythm of the beast that had nearly killed him now gave him peace. He had never thought of himself as a survivor or a leader, but that was what he had become. The community he and his friends had built had survived the worst year imaginable. No electricity, little food, gang attacks, and they successfully fended off an army calling themselves the Messengers. *What's next?*

He knew she was looking at him, he smiled. Then her tender fingers rubbed up his neck and into his hair. It was shorter now because she preferred that. He had changed much this past year, and now he changed for her. Gia leaned in close and kissed his face. She didn't try to put words in this moment. That would have broken it, made it somehow less than it was. All the deaths, the struggles, the violence; it had to equal something, maybe something better, *right*?

After more than a week stranded at sea with his former enemy, Skybox, Scott had found a way to work with the man, and eventually, they saved themselves. Then he had rediscovered the woman he had always been too cowardly to declare his love for. Now she sat beside him looking at the greenish waves crashing just feet away, her fingers intertwined with his. Being smart and finding ways to work together was the key. He was sure of that when all this began the hot August day when the sun spat out its lethal cocktail of plasma and energy directly at the earth. He held on to that principle, time and time again, but returning home to the AG…to Harris Springs, seeing all those bodies, damaged and dead friends and neighbors, it had jarred him. He was no longer sure humans deserved to survive. The cruelty they could unleash on others far surpassed anything the sun had done.

The Navy had spent a week cleaning up and helping dispose of the corpses. Acting Fleet Commander Garret hadn't outright said it but seemed genuinely apologetic for the Navy's lack of response when needed. The faint lingering smell of the burn pits would be the last remnants of the attackers that they had to deal with. The reunion with his friends and brother had been bittersweet. He still smiled remembering their faces as if he had returned from the dead. Seeing how badly some of them were injured, probably none more so than Jack, was more than he could handle. Thankfully, he hadn't had to do it alone. He turned to Gia. "I love you."

She smiled, and he noticed a tear forming in the corner of her eyes. "Always," she said, leaning in to kiss him on the lips this time.

How could life be so excruciatingly brutal and yet so tender and sweet? Maybe the yin and the yang, light and dark, good and evil. One could not exist without the other, and the stronger the one, the stronger the other.

They heard footsteps running down the beach from behind. Turning, he saw his niece, Kaylie. "Uncle Scott, we need you." She was panting as she slowed, her ragged looking running shorts and shoes the only sign of the athlete she had been.

"Kaylie, my dearest, sweetest niece, I was having a moment, you know?"

"That…was a moment? Damn…sorry, Gia, I thought he had gas or something. He was making a face."

Shrugging off the 'moment' and grinning, he began to stand, "What now?"

"Someone is calling for you on the radio." She took in a large breath before continuing, "It sounds urgent."

The three of them turned back toward the white cruise ship moored in the canal behind the old town. "Any idea who it is?" He was reasonably sure it would be Garret or some of the other Navy guys, since nearly everyone else he knew was here.

"It's your friend, Tahir, and…he's in trouble."

~

"Scott, my friend," his voice cut out, then came back in stronger. "Are you there?"

Scott keyed the mic, "I'm here, Tahir, can you please repeat that? Where are you again?"

"I am in a small jet circling what used to be the Biloxi Airport. Need a place to land, I have a fuel problem."

Hundreds of questions ran through Scott's mind. Why was his hacker friend here; how did he know how to fly? All of that had to wait. "How many feet do you need?" he asked.

The response was instant, "Five thousand feet."

"Shit." Scott knew the local airport was well short of that, not even jet rated." *Think, think.* "Tahir, Jackson, Mississippi, or maybe…Mobile will be the closest with runways that long, but neither place is safe. Can you handle a roadway landing? We cleared a stretch of interstate a few months back."

"Can't make those other airports, may have to try it, but an interstate will be rough. That concrete is laid down in sections and not top-dressed like a runway. I'm not sure I could keep it on the roadway but may have to try. I am turning eastward now."

Scott whispered for Kaylie to get Bartos. The Cajun was still acting weird but knew these roads better than nearly anyone. His concussion was beginning to clear, and he had helped the others clear cars and trucks left by the Messengers. The running vehicles would be invaluable in time, so most had been stored in parking lots here on the island. Tahir was still broadcasting.

"BikerBoi, I have news, even if I don't make it, you need to hear this."

"You are going to make it, man, just hang in there."

"I will most assuredly do that, but..."

Scott was distracted by his friend, Bartos, entering the small radio room. He motioned the little man to sit down. Returning his attention to the speaker, he caught, "...Homefront brought them here."

"Wait, what? Say again?"

"The pandemic is here, the Navy's Homefront operation. The ships all returned full of infected from overseas." When the bio-weapon was released in Pakistan after the blackout, it had quickly become an epidemic racing across Europe and Asia. Now, it was a full-scale pandemic.

"Oh, shit." Scott and Bartos looked at each other in horror. This changed everything. How much time did they have? "Tahir...where are they now, where did they land?" He assumed Tahir had left the DC area; if that was where they landed, they would have some time. "Was it DC, Baltimore?"

The response was garbled. "Say again."

"I don't know, Scott, they could have landed at ports up and down the East Coast."

"I hope you guys are just fucking with me," Bartos said, "cause this shit's not funny." Then he started singing a little unrecognizable tune.

Scott was having trouble processing it as well. "Hush, Cajun." He needed to get his priorities down. "Bartos, is Highway 50 clear yet? We need a mile of level roadway with no obstructions or powerlines."

Bartos stopped humming long enough to look quizzically up at the blank wall. "Um, sure, over by the old dam entrance. Flat as a pancake there, and storm surge never got high enough to over wash the highway that far inland."

"Yeah, perfect." Scott relayed the location to Tahir. "Bartos, grab some gear and get out there as soon as you can. Pop a few smoke canisters at the edge once you hear the jet." He still could not get over his friend actually being a pilot. "Roger that." Bartos headed out the door grabbing Kaylie as he went. Scott wanted to go as well but wouldn't be able to guide him in as the portable radios didn't work on the aircraft bands.

Tahir's voice came back, "I am descending to 3000 and should be over the area in a few minutes."

In a few minutes, he began speaking again, "Ok, I am coming over a big cruise ship in a canal behind a town. Well, what used to be a town, lots of debris and downed trees."

"That's it, Tahir, follow the main road heading north. It will be about fourteen miles out before you see a dam and reservoir lake on your left."

"Over it now," came the immediate response.

Shit, he was fast. "Ok, my people won't be there for another five or ten minutes but scope out the road and see if it will work." Scott knew that stretch of highway well and keyed the small handheld radio. "Hey, Cajun," he called.

"Yeah, man, you got him."

Scott could hear the throaty sound of the Bronco in the background. "Tahir is over the roadway now. Once you get there, you need to knock down the road signs on each side and clear any large debris you see. He will let us know which way he wants to come in. Pop smoke at the beginning of the clear area. He's probably going 300 plus, so you won't see him until he's right there. Stay well clear of the flattop. Call me when you are ready."

"It looks clear to me, Scott, maybe a dead deer or something, but I see your people approaching. I'm going to circle once more. The engine is beginning to misfire badly."

There was a pause for what seemed like an eternity. Bartos radioed back that they were ready. Tahir spotted the smoke and began his descent. "Scott?"

"Yes, buddy?"

"There is something else," the fear was evident in Tahir's voice. *Something worse than the possible plane crash about to happen? Something worse than ships full of infected landing on US soil?* Tahir continued to fill him in. *Shit, it is worse.*

CHAPTER TWO

OUTSIDE JACKSON, MISSISSIPPI

Mahalia Simpson sat with her hands on her lap. The old cabin felt more like an extension of herself than a creation of wood and nails. She scraped a bit of the mud from beneath a fingernail; her withered and wrinkled hands shook slightly, but she tried to hide it. She'd lived a simple life, full of family, friends and serving the Lord. It was satisfying and full despite her never traveling more than thirty miles from where she had been born. She'd never been on a plane, she'd never seen a big city, never even dug her toes in the sand at the beach. It was a simple life…until now.

The tall man in the black uniform towered over her. "Ma'am, I have no desire to hurt you or any more of your family." He glanced back at the other men with a look that clearly indicated otherwise. "You will tell us what we want to know."

She sat, silent and stoic, her eyes unmoving from the dark, wet stain across the gray, cracked, wooden floor planks. Blood, Wilson's blood, her sister's firstborn child. She had raised him, raised both her nephews, in fact. Her sister wasn't cut out for it. No shame in that to her, just fact. Mahalia had never forgotten the joy of holding the family's first baby boy. *He was so loud.* She smiled a little on the inside as she thought about him. His dark skin all wrinkled, like an old prune, her husband had said. *He'd always been so stubborn, just like today. Always looking for someone to argue with, someone to fight.* The man's slap knocked her to the floor.

"Get up—it wasn't even that hard," the man said.

Her tired, sad eyes began to water, but she refused to let the man see her cry. She stayed on the floor. "I done told you, I aint got nuttin', and no one else is heah. You people done captured erreybody." She pronounced the word like her parents did. The white men in the uniforms seemed to think she was stupid—they made fun of how she talked. Ms. Mahalia was a lot of things, but stupid wasn't one of them.

"You said that before, then that man, your nephew, you say? He came charging out of that bedroom wanting to do us harm."

"You didn't has to kill him, he didn't have no weapon. Y'all just shot him down like…like he was a dumb animal or something." She scraped more dirt from her fingers. They'd let her go out and bury him in a shallow grave they dug. She'd had to use her hands to put the dirt back. They laughed as they leaned on their shovels refusing to help further. Covering that baby's face with dirt was something no one should ever have to do. Wilson was a grown man, but all she could see as she performed this last act was his sweet face as a baby, a child, then a precocious teen. She prayed for him silently, then prayed they would kill her, too.

"Why would someone live out here like this?" one of the men in the shadows said. "Y'all choose to live like dumb animals, we will be happy to treat you like one." He moved from the shadow into the light streaming through the window. "Hell, you should be grateful, the relocation camp will be a paradise compared to this."

They heard someone walking up the steps, and the front door opened. Another man appeared, this one was also in the black uniform of the National Security Forces. He spoke with authority and with an accent

Mahalia was unfamiliar with. "Wat are you still doing here? Does she have anyone else in hiding or was she hoarding supplies?"

Hoarding supplies, she had been informed when they started tearing up the place, that keeping any supplies was apparently now illegal.

"She had something." The man thumbed a hand to the stove where she'd been making a simple breakfast for herself and Wilson when the soldiers barged in.

The new man walked to the stove and picked up a biscuit and a piece of meat and began chewing. "Pork chop? Nice…good biscuits, too, but I think your flour's gone bad." He picked at a dark fleck in the biscuit's crumbly white interior. He held something up to inspect, then popped that into his mouth as well.

"Lady, do you have a radio of some kind in your home?" He waved a hand around the small dwelling like it was an expansive mansion. "Not a radio for listening, mind you, but one that you can talk to other people on?"

She stayed silent. That man and boy who came through five months ago had left a pack and a radio, but it wasn't here anymore. Mr. Bobby and Tre had worked out how to keep that secret from anyone listening in. They could look all they wanted for that. The tall man slapped her again, and she let out an involuntary cry of pain.

One of them said, "We searched the house, nothing Chief."

The one eating the biscuit apparently was the one in charge. He delicately picked up another and inserted a bit of the fried pork into the middle. "These are quite good. Shame you are too old to be of any use at the camp." He took another bite. "Kill her."

Tremaine Simpson watched from his hiding place as the man had stomped up the steps and into his aunt's house, the house he and his brother had both been raised in. The loose dirt in the front yard confirmed one of his fears already. He clutched at the Bible, the black leather cover hanging on by just threads of material. Silently, he prayed for guidance, for strength, and, as ashamed as he was, he also prayed for revenge.

He wasn't sure who these people were. When he had called Mr. Bobby to tell him about what was going on, he had told him they were a 'fake' military. Some new government police force run by the president herself. He had no idea who the president was, much less that it was now a woman, but these guys looked more like those German soldiers from that old war. This certainly wasn't somebody from his government, maybe not our president anymore either. The two vehicles looked like military. He knew people had been rounded up by soldiers the last few weeks, but he thought they were safe this far away from town.

He went to rise just as he heard his aunt cry out. He paused halfway exposed and crouched back down. Anger and helplessness paralyzed him momentarily. He lay the Bible down atop a simple rock that marked another grave and reached into the pack for one of the other gifts left by Mr. Bobby. This one he hoped never to have to use and wouldn't consider it now except to save others. He'd kept the black weapon cleaned and oiled the way his uncle had always taught him. He inserted the ammo clip and loaded a bullet into the firing chamber. He didn't recall what kind of gun it was, just that it had a lot of bullets. The little bald man who picked up Bobby had spent a few minutes showing him how to use it.

He hefted it into his right hand. If felt wrong, evil, but somehow necessary. He had no moral objections to guns. He and his brother hunted for food every week in fact. But this was not a gun for hunting food. This was a weapon meant for killing. He ducked low and ran to the side of the old cabin. The smell of wood smoke, bacon and other flavors filled the air as he got closer. It filled his mind with thoughts of better days. How ironic the blackout he'd heard about hadn't affected them at all. It was the people, first the Messengers, and now these police guys. How could humans be so evil to one another?

He was just below one of the few windows but wasn't interested in risking a look in. Instead, he knelt down and crawled between the stacked rock pilings that held up the old house. He lay on his back and scooted as quietly as he could farther beneath the old floor. He saw a drip, drip of something dark and thick from one section of boards. Filing that away, he maneuvered himself into position. He just had room beneath the floor to aim the short-barreled gun.

For once, he was thankful for the rickety condition of the house. The spaces between the loose-fitting flooring used to let in the cold air in the winters, the insects in the summer. Now it allowed him to locate where everyone was standing up above. Four men and one woman. He prayed again, this time for the good Lord to shield his aunt from what came next.

He pointed the gun straight up between the shoes of the man closest to his aunt and pulled the trigger. He heard the man get hit, released the trigger and moved to the next position repeating the process. Three bodies had hit the floor when he heard the front door slam and saw legs running down the steps. He fired at the legs and that man fell as well. Blood was spilling between all of the boards now. The pain hit him as he realized he'd been shot as well.

He thought it was mostly a fair exchange... at least they wouldn't go to the camps. The smell of breakfast cooking and memories of his aunt shooing him and his brother out of the kitchen made him smile. Then darkness came.

CHAPTER THREE

HARRIS SPRINGS, MISSISSIPPI

"It's really beautiful down here, Scott. Thank you and your friends for making me feel welcome."

The two friends had only had a few chances to talk one-on-one and rarely to speak privately since Tahir had arrived.

"No problem, man, just glad you made it out of there. Sounds like it was getting a bit hairy."

Tahir gave a sad shrug. "Bad everywhere, but yes, DC was very bad."

"Tahir, I am sorry about your family."

"Thank you, Scott, that means a lot." The pained look spoke volumes. "You know, I was not an easy child for them to raise. I put them through a lot over the years. I regret that now, but I think they were proud of me...at least in the end."

Scott only knew parts of Tahir's story but realized, with his intellect and curiosity, staying out of trouble had likely not been easy. "I am sure they were, friend. You're a good man, Tahir." Scott sat and leaned back on

the grass. "Tell me what you think we are up against. Not the disease…
you know, Catalyst."

Tahir looked at Scott and said, "I think we are likely facing
extinction."

Scott took an involuntary step back. "No, no, don't beat around the
bush, dude, just tell me what you really think."

They both gave a chuckle that was totally absent of mirth.

Scott looked at his friend, "This is about the other thing you mentioned
when you were landing?"

"Yes, sadly so. You read the docs. Those idiots put that whole plan in
play within hours of the CME."

Scott shook his head, "Who are 'they?'"

Tahir gave one of his trademark shrugs as a non-answer. "I have some
ideas, but I could only track it so far. A couple of families coming from
old money—lots of old money. The closest I came was a scan of a document in the Library of Congress' confidential archives. It mentioned a
Council that was instrumental in helping shape the country during the
mid-1800s. One of the men was named Church, the head was named
Levi, and it included others named Warren and Pratt. After considerable
digging, I came to the conclusion that these were simply cover names.
No one in this group used real names."

Scott thought back to his former enemy, now friend, the Praetor
commander called Skybox. He thought about the lack of names used
throughout Praetor. "Did this group become the Praetor forces?"

"Not exactly, no. But, they are connected. Praetor, or the Guard, is the
modern Praetorian Guard which grew from a covert CIA paramilitary
group formed around 2001, primarily to go after Bin Laden. They separated from the official government sanction a few years later and indi-
rectly fell under the control of…well, they have no name. Let's call
them the 'Shadow Council.' It appears this group is still made up of the
same number of people, and whoever they are, they are still using many

of the same familial names, although the spellings have changed over time."

Scott stopped his friend, "But it can't be the same people. Who is this Shadow Council made up of now?"

"That is a question with no answer. I dug deep to find any clue and came up empty. You know how much I love a puzzle, and this one was a doozy. I broke into every computer system that I didn't already have access to and came up empty. What I did find was those files, the Catalyst docs. I did come to the same conclusion that Sentinel did. These people have been running this country for a very long time. Probably other countries as well. Money is no object to them – they print the money. They own the banks, they own the politicians. When they got Praetor – they essentially owned the military."

Scott knew that the elite members of Praetor were embedded into units of every military branch as well as in the command structure. "Tahir, you've talked with Skybox. I've run into other members of Praetor. They aren't the friendliest of people, but they aren't out to destroy the country." He thought back to his conversations with Skybox about the mission of his organization.

Tahir quickly answered, "My friend, you won't find any un-American sentiment with Praetor or the Council. They believe they are doing what is best for the country. They all think they are patriots. Maybe they are, but what they are doing goes far beyond what was in those documents we read."

"Like what?"

"Genetic engineering, or more accurately, genetic editing. They are working on something called forced evolution," Tahir stated. "I am no expert like your girlfriend, but I do know that evolution is not always a straight line. There are ups and downs, twists and turns. DNA doesn't have the secret destination in its arsenal. Instead, it tries different combinations to see which adaptation works the best. This is normally a slow process making incremental steps over thousands of years.

"Now, though, using a tool called CRISPR, they were able to quickly snip the DNA code and splice in something totally new just to see what happens. Like you and I trying out a new bit of software code to see if it fixes a problem or improves the program. With CRISPR, they can quickly and cheaply engineer biologic vectors to introduce this new code into a host to see what will happen. The DNA doesn't even need to come from other humans, they could get it from anything. The goal must be to make the hosts, humans, into something else—something better."

"Huh?" Scott mindlessly scratched at some flaking rust on a railing as he thought. He knew Gia had referred to CRISPR, and Tahir had mentioned some of this earlier, but it still hadn't connected in his brain. "They are making monsters, Tahir—this Chimera virus is not creating better humans, it's killing them—killing…us."

Tahir nodded in agreement, "Yes, my friend. Homo Sapiens' days are numbered, and what comes next is the real question, Scott."

"So, how bad is it…the pandemic, I mean?" Tahir avoided eye contact, something Scott was beginning to realize must be a coping mechanism his friend used when discussing sensitive topics with people.

"Scott, it is very bad, very bad indeed. The Navy's operation to bring Americans home has sped up the infection by months if not years."

"Homefront." Scott said with a gloomy sigh. That was what Lt. Garret and his father had mentioned to them months ago. He rubbed the bridge of his nose. "They didn't know…"

Tahir cut him off, "They were stupid, Scott. They let their patriotic duty overrule common sense. They wanted their soldiers home to their families, and by doing so—they doomed us all. You said your friend, the super-soldier, saw what the virus did to people. The good doctor says there is no cure. I barely got out of DC before the city was overrun."

His friend's voice was pitching noticeably higher as the memories and emotions took over. Scott knew Tahir had lost everyone after the collapse; coming to Harris Springs had been a 'Hail Mary' pass. "Any idea who it was defending the capital? You said jets were making bombing runs on the ships as they ran aground in Baltimore."

Tahir pondered this, his lightning fast brain retaking control from his erratic emotions. "The jets were small, unmanned, I would say. UAVs, so that is likely the Guard, what you call Praetor. They have those, but we must assume the president's National Security Force may have them as well."

"The NSF. His radio contact, Sentinel, had mentioned them before, too. Do you think the Navy may have deliberately done this?"

Tahir thought again on Scott's question. "That would be an interesting theory. Using the infected like a weapon. Unleashing them on Washington to bring down Chambers' presidency." He tapped his lip with a forefinger as he paced the room. "I don't think so…that would give the Naval leadership way more credit than they deserve. Just not that smart to plan something like that, and even they would know there was no way to control the weapon once unleashed. So, no, this was not planned."

Scott nodded in agreement, "Just thinking out loud, considering all possibilities. You saw the infection spread rates from the Middle East and Europe. How long before the infection reaches here?"

"My guess would be six months, but Doctor Colton would probably have a more accurate number. A lot will depend on the number of living hosts it finds between here and DC. Also, we don't know if those ships only landed in Baltimore. If they were headed to other ports on the Eastern Seaboard like Charleston or Jacksonville, well, we could be seeing them here much faster."

"How do we know they will come west?"

"The infection spread pattern appears pretty standard to me. Not unlike the flu, it will radiate in all directions from the initial area. Where it finds more hosts, it spreads faster. Before the CME, 60% of Americans lived east of the Mississippi River. That number was around 180 million. The statistical mortality rate since then is well known. Just about everywhere, the national average has been about 85% death rate. You guys here did much better than that, large cities faired much worse. That leaves around 27 million people alive, spread out over the twenty-six easternmost states. That is still a very large number, but due to the overall landmass, the density is not so great. Assuming Gia is right, and the virus is not being spread by non-human animals, I think six months is about right."

"We can't stop this, we can't prepare for it even—it's coming," Scott said.

"There is one thing we can do, Scott."

Scott looked at his friend curiously.

"We can leave."

CHAPTER FOUR

Jack's mouth hung in a lopsided grin.

"What's your point?" Scott asked.

"Brother, I am just trying to get you to realize the obvious." The man went on, "You are it, if this town…shit!" he said, remembering the obvious, "…this ship has any chance to survive all this, it will be because of you."

Scott shook his head, "Sorry, Preacher."

Jack cut him off, "Not a preacher, not anymore." His eyes fell as he said it. "Scott, look, this, this…" he struggled again to find a right word, "…situation we are in just keeps getting worse. We may have survived the blackout, but then came the gangs, then came the crazies, and now, apparently, comes an epidemic. We can't keep fighting this shit off forever. We have to get ahead of the next crisis, so we can get busy growing food, getting our shit together and hopefully making a life. To do that, we need some long-term strategy. We need your kinda' smarts."

"We need more than that, Jack. We need luck."

"I don't disagree there."

They both wandered down the crackled and crumbling pavement that had been the main street of Harris Springs. The old courthouse was falling in on itself, one more victim of the hurricane several months earlier.

"I hate seeing the old town like this, we should clean it up. Maybe rebuild what we can."

Jack stopped, kneeling to inspect the battered end of an old sign in the road. "Scott, this town is broken, we can't get it back. Shit, we're nearly too damn broken ourselves. We can't save the town, as much as we loved it. It was never more than bricks and boards. What mattered… what made it a town, was the people. Those are all that matter."

Scott nodded in agonizing realization. "I know."

Jack flipped the sign over and gave a stiff laugh. "Shirley's."

The nearly unrecognizable sign once hung outside the coffee shop where the two friends had first met that fateful morning. "God, that seems so long ago now," Scott said thinking of the shared memory.

"Scott, do you realize that we are all still here mostly because of the choices we made back then? That first week? Do you understand how much better off we are than most?"

They walked a bit farther, Scott nodding his head in understanding. "So, where do we go from here?"

Jack shrugged, "I'm not sure, Brother. That is going to be up to you. I'm lost, sadly, so is our friend, Todd. Those of us who aren't lost are damaged or just too exhausted. You are the only one of us who has really grown—you continue to overcome and adapt. Don't get me wrong, man, you have been through hell, too, but you seem to be able to let go of the past and do what is needed."

Scott looked out at the sea, sparkling in the late afternoon sun. Indeed, he'd reunited with his brother and even found the love of his life in the midst of all this. Now, he just wanted to hold onto her and the happiness she brought him.

Jack laid a hand on his shoulder. "Todd asked you to lead this town back then, after Liz…" he faded off momentarily, "…and you did."

"I didn't do it alone, Jack. I had you and Bartos and…"

"You still do, Scott, you aren't alone. Bartos is still a little damaged in the head, but hell, you barely notice another level of crazy with that guy. In addition, you have Angel, Roosevelt. Not to mention DeVonte and Tahir. Use them to help you."

"What about you, Jack?" He knew how hard it had been for Jack. Possibly worse for him than anyone. He seemed to have lost his faith and his willingness to guide or teach with that single act of ending the Messengers' murdering plans.

"I'll be around, Scott, but not like before. I'm sorry, but I just can't." Jack sat down heavily on the steps leading up to a building that was no longer there. "I'm no use to anyone like this. I just no longer have the fire or the fight in me. Thought I might go and check on some of the other survivor colonies, see how many of them made it through the storm. Maybe, in time, we can even get a little trade re-established."

They both knew how unlikely that was. They barely had enough to get by on these days much less any excess to trade. When the Messengers had descended on the AG, they had not just focused on the group sheltering in the Aquatic Goddess. Unknown to those fighting on the ship, others had been raiding farms, taking supplies and killing many of the people who hadn't taken refuge in the cruise ship. They'd even managed to loot what was left in the old hidden freight train they'd been using for emergency storage.

"We got lots of old cars," Jack said smiling.

"True. No gas to speak of, though. At least none that's any good in any of 'em," answered Scott.

"You'll figure something out, Scott. You always do."

"Alright, Jack. I need to head back—Gia is coming back tonight. You coming?"

"Nah, I think I'm just going to sit here a bit, Scott. You go on. I'll catch up later."

∽

Scott could see his brother was about to lose his shit. "Bobby, listen—I get it. They are your friends, and we need to help."

"Scott, shit, man. They saved my life."

The paper he held up was a radio message he had received about his friends. Bobby had left his handheld radio unit with them when his daughter, Kaylie, and Bartos had made a reckless, but brave, trip to rescue him from the grip of the Messengers months earlier. "They were checking in pretty frequent, then nothing—until this."

Scott took the crumpled yellow paper and read it for himself. He let out a long breath. "So, they have cleared out Jackson now." It was a statement, not a question.

Bobby nodded.

Scott handed it back. "Doesn't even indicate who this is from, just that they need help."

"Has to be one of 'em, no one else would know what day and channel to use."

Scott didn't like this, any of it. "I guess that pretty much confirms what Sentinel told us." Sentinel was a seemingly well-connected member of the Patriot radio network, an ad-hoc collection of preppers, militia and actual military that had formed in the wake of the global blackout. The network ran on ham radios and was a useful back channel to pass information along. The man had told them some alarming news a few weeks earlier.

The US military operating on American soil was unbelievable, not to mention unlawful, but so was the illegal capture and detainment of American citizens. Much of the military leadership had been declared warlords or rogue commanders. Huge bounties for the capture or killing of these commanders were being offered by President Chambers' administration. Sentinel had also told them to expect this. Most larger farms were being occupied, and entire towns were now being cleared for the remaining supplies and for conscription into the labor camps. Apparently, the town of Jackson, Mississippi, just 170 miles to the north, had been the latest to fall.

Sentinel's connections in the military had passed along some information. It was widely known that the government had set-up so-called Aid Camps that were, in fact, forced labor farms. The Army had been getting increasingly aggressive about shutting them down and liberating the civilians in outright defiance of a presidential order. Everyone suspected the camps were simply designed to grow food for the chosen people under government protection. Military commanders from all branches were increasingly disobeying orders and even engaging some of the paramilitary troops that the government was using, the National Security Force, or NSF.

"This shit is heating up fast, Scott. Jackson was big, it was a town of 170 thousand."

Scott looked at his big brother; the once robust man was a mere shadow of his former self. The dark cross tattoo on his hand a memory of all he had lost. "I know, man, but that was before. It's been eighteen months since the CME hit. In that year and a half an estimated seventy-five to eighty percent of people are gone. That is just in towns that weren't in the path of marauders like the Messengers. Those guys stripped Jackson bare when they passed through."

"So, what are you saying, Scott? It's not a big deal anymore?" his voice rising as he said it.

"Will you calm the fuck down, Bro? What I am saying is that Jackson probably was down to less than forty thousand survivors. That's still a shitload of people to try and imprison. Others on the radio have been saying they only take the able-bodied. The sick, injured or older ones are left behind. They do take kids, though, not sure why. Maybe for leverage or perhaps just to make sure they have replacements when they work the parents to death. In either case, for them to go after a town that size seems to me to be an act of desperation."

"Desperate how?" Bobby's frown lines were beginning to overtake most of his face.

"This was their plan, all of it. You read the Catalyst documents. Hell, they had PowerPoint presentations on the damn thing. They would scoop the best and the brightest, their elite ten percent — off to the protectorates, small, self-contained villages, to wait for better days. These were supposed to be well-equipped to wait out the collapse when they could then emerge and have the best possible team in place to rebuild society. To shape, customize and build the type of world they envisioned. There wasn't any mention of internment camps for the rest of the country. Nothing about forced conscription or even these damn security forces. Something has gone wrong, or they had a shitty plan. All I know is, these people overseeing Catalyst are fucking desperate."

Bobby nodded in agreement, "So, can we go get my friends?"

CHAPTER FIVE

"This isn't right." None of the others in the room spoke. "This is his town, he deserves to be making this decision…not me," Scott said for the third time.

"Bon ami, you are it, man. Todd is not even part of this council anymore. He has refused to make decisions that affect others. You know that."

Scott did know, he had been one of those ill-fated decisions Todd had made. In agreeing to work with the Navy to help root out a Catalyst lab, Todd had inadvertently nearly gotten him killed. "Still, Bartos, he's our friend…my friend. I owe that man my life, many times over."

The bald-headed Cajun shrugged, "It is what it is. We all have our wounds. Jack won't preach, Todd won't lead, and I am just fucked in the head. Everyone…well, not everyone, you were stranded at sea and somehow survived and got the girl. Not sure how da hell that happened, but whatever…you da boss now, Scott. When dis meeting is over, I'll go light a candle for him, but for now, just get on wid it."

"Well, shit!" After the talk with Jack, he expected it, but he still was hoping someone else would step forward. He really just wanted to let someone else take over. He wanted to ride his bike, make love to Gia and enjoy life. Scott sat at the end of the wooden table and looked around at the faces, his friends, his family. Slowly he began to nod. "Okay then, this is how it plays…for now. Angel, you are in charge of this boat – mayor, chief of the boat, whatever, you are it. Got me?"

She looked stunned but nodded in silent agreement.

"Use DeVonte and Bobby as needed. Recruit others if you want. Now, we have two major topics on the table. First, we need to get this ship seaworthy again." He then proceeded to fill them in on the spread of the pathogen and how long they likely had. "Now, Bartos and Tahir are helping me with a special project, but afterward, we are going to take another look at the ship's systems. To get this beast mobile again, we need engines, steering and navigation at a minimum. I don't want us stuck here at the dock next time." They all knew what next time meant —the infected.

Bartos leaned in, "We're going to need more fuel for that, Brother. If you're thinking what I believe, no way that we would have enough diesel for that."

"Bartos, I just want us to have some options. You know…if the infection…" he trailed off, not needing to say more.

"What about the Navy? Could we get any diesel from them? I mean, shit, this problem is on them anyway."

The younger man at the table, Lt. Garret, spoke. "Afraid not, Mr. Montgomery. I spoke to the fleet commander earlier in the week. They are running out of fuel and already had to suspend ops on some of the vessels due to lack of it. With no resupply available, it's becoming less likely they can even remain on station."

That was not new news, but Scott was hoping something had changed. The Bataan was a mile offshore. Its main mission right now was keeping Gia's lab up and running. His 'special project' was to get the old hydro dam back over on the Black River producing electricity again. That would open up a number of possibilities, including letting Gia move the bio-lab back on shore. Otherwise, Gia would have to go wherever the ship went. It was a selfish reason, he knew, but he wanted to be selfish – *haven't I earned that right?*

He scratched his head and the growing stubble of beard. "What about all the abandoned vehicles around? I know the gasoline has already started to go bad, but I thought diesel was more stable. Couldn't we tap into all the diesel trucks, storage tanks and such?"

Bartos shook his head, "I'd agree wid you, Scott, but shit, then we'd both be wrong. We've already been doing that for months to keep da farm equipment running. Diesel is more stable, it won't go bad as quickly, but we're pushing our luck already. Da tractors will run, even if it is somewhat degraded, but da AG, well, I don't know. I assume this lady likes her fuel fresh." He patted the bulkhead behind him to emphasize this was the 'lady' he meant. "There's a tank labeled 'Bunker Fuel,' though. I have an idea of what dat is. If it can burn dat, then we may be in luck."

"Ok, ok," Scott relented. This is a problem we must solve. Our lives may very well depend on it. In the meantime," he checked the notes in his hand, "I need you two…" pointing at Skybox and then to Bartos, "…you continue as security for the AG and surrounding communities. Lieutenant Garret, I appreciate you staying with us. Could you assist Bartos and his people to make sure the AG stays secure?"

The young man nodded. No one needed to point out that the young Navy officer had been cozying up to a certain young lady on-board more and more lately. He and his dad, the fleet commander, had not been seeing eye to eye since the Messengers' attack. In truth, with the Bataan stationed just offshore now, many of the sailors were now taking leave time here at the AG. Garret was not on leave though; this was a temporary assignment. Part of a passive acknowledgment of the Navy's failure in helping the community in its time of need.

Scott turned to Jack. "The former preacher here is heading out in the next few days. He is going to try and get some of our trade routes back open and see that those farmers have what they need. We have no idea what he may find out there, so be careful, Jack."

"Of course, Scott, you know I will."

Scott knew the man now dreaded being on-board this ship. He blamed himself for much of the death and destruction surrounding the community he loved. What he had done to save it had eaten away at his very soul.

"Now, for the second big question of the day," continued Scott. "Bobby has filled us in on what is happening up in Jackson with the Simpsons. It seems likely that our president's security forces have now cleaned out the town. We need to decide on how to best go up in the middle of that and get the Simpsons."

Bartos started unconsciously humming the theme song to the old animated series of the same name. "Can it, Homer," Bobby said.

Scott went on, "Brother, I owe these people for saving you and Jacob, but I can't vote for a mission to go save them. I just can't put more of our people at risk going into what amounts to occupied territory."

Bobby was pissed at him, Scott could see it in his eyes, but he nodded his head. "They are good people, Scott. They wouldn't have asked if they didn't need help. I do understand your reasons, though."

"Let me finish, Bobby. While I can't ask someone to do this, if anyone wants to volunteer, I won't stop them. Not you, though, Bobby. You haven't recovered enough to be of any help."

"I'll go," Bartos said cheerfully.

"Some of my guys will go, too," the younger Garret said. "They are all a bit stir crazy here. Besides, my dad…I mean, the commander, has been wanting to get eyes on one of those internment camps. He may even let us take a few of his toys to play with if we can manage that."

Bobby began to smile.

Scott nodded, "Sounds like we have a plan."

CHAPTER SIX

"What's wrong?"

Gia didn't answer but rolled close against him, her warmth spreading through him like a fire. Scott wrapped his arms around her slender shoulders. Although new to each other, he felt a familiarity, an intimacy that seemed to have existed forever. He knew she sometimes went quiet while her magnificent brain worked its way through a challenging problem. He tried again.

"Can't sleep?"

"Huh? Oh, sorry, Scott...just thinking about work. I thought we were really on to something. Something very promising, and then, well, today..." she trailed off, deep in thought again. "I just feel like everyone is depending on me, and I just can't seem to beat this thing."

He knew the 'thing' she was referring to; it was the Chimera virus. Finding a treatment to fight the growing pandemic consumed her every waking moment. Now, it seemed to be consuming her resting moments as well. He'd mentioned some of Tahir's ideas and suggested she at least speak to his friend, "Couldn't hurt."

The time they shared together was rushed and infrequent. Early on, she had been able to relax when she was aboard the AG with him, but, increasingly, she seemed to act more like she was hiding from her responsibilities and her work.

Scott often felt the same way with everything he, too, was coping with now. His responsibilities were for way more than just himself, way more than he was comfortable with. The threats and issues the community faced were his daily challenges. But all of that paled in comparison to what Gia was working on. The fate of the entire human race could literally come down to her success or failure. He ached to take some of that pressure away but knew there was nothing he could really do to help. He kissed the back of her neck. "I love you."

She slowly turned toward him and pulled his face close. "Love you, too." Kissing him deeply, she placed a hand on his chest. The feeling of completeness washed over him like a wave.

Their mouths connected again; the electricity surged through him as she pulled at him with a sudden hunger. They had made love before going to sleep, but her appetite was apparently not sated. *How had we ever just been friends?* The thought disappeared as he ran a palm over Gia's smooth thigh. She reached for him, and he was again consumed with the need be one with her.

The lovemaking was, at times, intense and physical and, other times, slow and intimate. They both seemed to know what each needed and when. When they were together, the problems outside their cabin door stopped mattering. Scott knew she was his safe harbor, the place he could always escape to. He wondered how one person could make such a difference in his life.

Still inside her, he felt the rise and fall of her chest. The exertion had them both slick with perspiration. She stroked his chest and smiled, he leaned in and kissed her forehead.

"Scott, where do we go from here?"

The faint moonlight gave the darkened room its only light. He brushed a strand of hair out of her face. He was unsure if she meant the two of them...the community...or was it the world? Should he mention getting the AG ready to sail again? He realized he was over-thinking the question. The answer was the same no matter the 'who.' "We do what we must. We rise-up, battle on…we survive." He kissed her again. *Just one more hill, one more mile*, he thought, the mantra that helped saved him when he was lost at sea. He looked into that face, half-hidden in darkness. That face, that smile helped save him during that ordeal. The chance just to see her again gave him a goal to keep fighting for.

As tired as he was of the fight to survive, he knew they had not yet turned the corner on that. All of the original threats were still there: illness, starvation, clean water and, of course, always the others who wanted to take it away. Add to that the government and the pandemic. It was exhausting for all of them—he wasn't special; he was simply too stubborn in his desire to keep living.

"We just don't quit, we don't give up, hon. We heal, we love."

She nodded and pushed her head into his chest. "If we're suffering, it means we're still surviving—right?" He thought he felt tears against his skin, but he said nothing. At least in the few battles he'd fought, you could usually see the enemy. Hers was a battleground under a microscope. A world that would fit on your thumbnail, filled with deadly creatures more mysterious and alien than anything he could imagine. He held her like that until he felt her breathing soften and her arm fall slack. He moved back to his side of the bed allowing her sleeping head to cradle against his chest. Despite everything he had been through, despite how the world was out there, he fully realized he had never been happier.

Gia was gone before he woke up. This wasn't unusual; the labs out on the Bataan ran on a Navy schedule, so early starts were common. Scott rubbed his face and headed to the common toilet everyone on this corridor used. Supplies and water were too precious to waste, and they found keeping public restrooms working was more efficient. Truthfully, they had only managed to get the ship's plumbing working on a handful of levels anyway. He picked up a wet towelette as he went by the sink.

They had run out of toilet paper months earlier. Somehow, they still had cases full of the baby wipes, but they were rationed as well. Eventually, they would be down to a bucket of wet rags. The laundry detail would love that.

He needed a plan to get to Jackson safely and hopefully find the Simpsons, but that wasn't his specialty. He'd speak to the resident warriors. The AG had to be the only small town around with its own special forces division. Skybox and Bartos were up for it, with Lieutenant Garret, it might be doable. It would be dangerous, he knew that much. While the NSF wasn't regular military, they were already earning a reputation for cruelty.

Scott finished up and went to the sink. He brushed his hair and thought about a shave, but it wasn't his bath day yet, so he decided to wait. He ran a half cup of clean water from the tap and brushed his teeth with that. Toothpaste had also run out. Many people used sea salt or even some of the baking soda from supplies, but that seemed like a waste to him. His breath was probably horrid, but not a lot he could do for it this morning. Besides, he was about to be drinking coffee, one of the luxuries the Navy had helped supply. His breath would smell like ass anyway as the kitchen crew always made it strong.

He left the toilet thinking once more about how easy everything used to be. All the shit they used to take for granted. Admittedly, much of what was gone was only inconvenient—an issue they could deal with and move on. But some things were much more serious, like vitamins. Without a balanced diet, they all needed supplements, but no supplies remained. Fuel was another, and that one was a biggie. They finally had plenty of working cars thanks to the Messengers, and collectively, they had drained tankers full of gasoline, but it was all starting to go bad. They had filtered it, kept it in sealed tanks and done everything they could think of, but it was still going bad. Tahir said the molecular bonds break down pretty rapidly. While older cars had engines that were more forgiving, none would work forever. Bartos had told him that without fuel stabilizers, it would all be worthless to them within the next few months.

Scott's mind went through the list. It was how he started most days. As an analyst, he was accustomed to gathering the data, prioritizing and coming up with solutions. His brain was wired to solve puzzles, but now that it was literally life and death, he found himself struggling. He could still handle the data and see the priorities clearly, but the solutions were taking longer and sometimes did not form. Gia had said it was just that the problems were harder now. *She's probably right.* Still, it frustrated him. People counted on him to come up with good answers, but, increasingly, he felt like a fraud in that department.

CHAPTER SEVEN

Walking into the dining hall, Scott saw Angel and Roosevelt. Grabbing a cup of coffee from the urn, he joined them.

"Hi, Scott."

"Mornin' there, Mr. Scott."

"Hey, guys, am I interrupting anything?"

The older man laughed, "No, no, I just flirtin with this lovely creature here and she was bein' too polite ta stop me."

Angel shook her head, "He's telling stories again, Scott. Roosevelt was telling me he spotted Ghost again yesterday. He was sitting with your friend, Skybox, near the canal. Do you think that means he is getting better? Does he recognize him?"

Ghost was actually an SOF soldier named Tommy who had received a severe head injury from a roadside IED in Iraq. The injury was years old now, but his friend, Skybox, still carried the guilt for the injury along with continued hope for his recovery. "I would like to think so—Skybox seems convinced he does but...I don't know. The damage to Tommy's head is extensive. The doctors don't think there is anything of Tommy still in there."

"Well, das sumpin' in dat boy's head," Roosevelt said. "When he went to work on dem boys dat was 'bout to kill yo preacher, it was unlike nutting I ever seen. Dat looked like a tornado full a razor blades the way he tore through dat bunch."

He was talking about Jack's rescue from the group of Messengers and especially the twisted bastard they called the Prophet. Tommy, who the townsfolk had taken to calling Ghost due to his ability to seemingly appear and disappear almost without notice, had single-handedly rescued Jack. Scott downed another gulp of the bitter, black liquid. "I agree, some part of the warrior that he was is still alive in there, even if he's just running mainly on instinct. Skybox said he had been heavily sedated since the injury."

Scott thought briefly about the chopper crash, seeing Ghost standing in his yard shortly after. Now knowing that crash also had taken the lives of Gia's husband and daughter. It was a subject that she had refused to discuss—ever.

"That poor man," Angel said somberly. "Can you imagine being in that condition? Trapped with a brain that no longer works. Not knowing who you are or where you are. I mean, who knows what he thinks of or even if he thinks? Maybe the killing and stuff is all just instinct. Like an animal or something."

"He's not an animal," Scott said firmly. "I don't know if Skybox can reach him, but he's determined to try. He said this is the most responsive he's seen Tommy since the accident. Being off the drugs may be allowing him to access more of his memories—maybe he can remember who he is. In either case, we owe him everything. His actions definitely saved Jack and may have saved the entire community."

"I know, I know…I didn't mean to say he was an animal, Scott. I just can't imagine anyone suffering the way he must be. He may be in constant agony but unable to let any of us know."

Roosevelt chimed back in, "Dat boy done figured out how to handle dat pain. He done put it to work for him. Lawd help anyone getting in his way when he needs to let it come out." He gave a little chuckle before continuing, "Sides...he knows we are friends. Specially dat SkyFox dude."

"Skybox, not Skyfox, you old coot," Angel said with a grin. "I gotta go to work. You boys have a good day." With that, she disappeared. Both men watched her until the door to the kitchen's prep area swung closed.

"Dat young man of hers better do her right," Roosevelt said.

"DeVonte is a good kid, and he knows what a catch she is. I hear rumors that he may try and convince her to make it official."

The old man's eyes lit up. "Really? Wow, dat gives me hope. It sho do. It would be so easy for us to just give up, ya know? All dis awfulness out in da world. People needs to keep on falling in love, havin' babies, growing old. Dat is what survival really means, not how much beans and rice and guns ya gots..."

The old man leaned over, growing more serious and quiet. "Mr. Scott, I needs to tell you something. Something I been dreading eva since you come back."

Scott panicked, he hoped the man wasn't leaving, going back out to his little farm. Everyone had adopted the older man almost as a wise grandfather. He was sharp as a tack, and his knowledge of...well, everything was amazing. He was well versed in survival, farming, hunting, fishing, but also people. Beyond that was something else, though. Roosevelt Jackson had intuition or some way of anticipating things in an uncanny way. Scott found it awkward at first accepting things on faith, but Roosevelt's accuracy had proven itself time and again. He felt the chill go up his spine as he felt the edge in the man's words. "What is that, Roosevelt?"

"Now listen to me, son, I'm a...I'm jus' an old man. An ole fool as dat girl in yonda said, but sometimes, evry now and den, I gets a feelin' bout something. Sometimes it goes away, and...sometimes it don't. You member me telling you dat you got da signs?"

Scott thought back to the first time he had met the man. "Yes, Roosevelt, I remember."

"Well, ya see, I knowed you would be ok when you was lost out at sea. I just knowed. Even when Mr. Todd said you was dead, I knew betta. Just like I know this other thing. My friend, you about to be tested like never before."

Scott started to speak, but the old man's look silenced him. His friend wanted him to know this was important.

Roosevelt stared at the table for a long moment before continuing, "Scott you gonna hafta face a terrible choice. One...one dat no man should ever hafta face. I can't tell you more, but I do know it will be the mos' difficult thing in your life."

Scott's face must have shown the concern and questions. "Dat's all I can say bout it. Trust yourself, Scott. I know you will know what to choose when da time comes."

With that, the spry old man stood up, patted him on the shoulder and ambled off. *Just what did all that mean?* Scott wondered what the man could be referring to but had no idea. Time for him to go to work, anyway, as he downed the last of his coffee and stood.

Jack had been gone a few days and had taken an old diesel pickup. He'd loaded in a few of the things to trade, like bags of salt, dried fish, and even some coffee. These were the few items they had a surplus of. This was just an initial visit, though, just to find out who was still left out there to trade with. Scott missed the man already, he was more than a friend, and the burden he himself was carrying seemed immense. Jack represented the soul of Harris Springs to Scott and watching him go had pained him deeply.

If Jack was the soul, then the man he was about to talk to was its heart. He found Todd with DeVonte down at the marina. They were siphoning fuel into Todd's boat, the *Donna Marie*. His little sailboat had not survived the hurricane. "Todd, got a minute? I need your help."

"Sorry, man, haven't come up with a cure for stupid yet, check back next week."

Scott laughed, "Asshole."

"Kidding, man, come on down. What's up?"

Scott ran his hand over the polished wood, recalling the same feeling touching the treasured woodwork in his families' old beach cottage, now just a pile of ashes. His friend loved this boat like he had once loved this town. "Todd, we have to leave here."

The older man set the fuel container down and leaned back against the rail, his weathered face filling with unasked questions. Scott went on to explain just as he had to the AG's new council.

DeVonte's face looked ashen at the news. "How long we got, Scott?"

"Maybe six months, but we have a lot to do before then."

Todd looked northward, Scott knew what his friend was thinking. His wife, Liz, was buried on the other side of town. Most of the town was buried there, in fact. He ached for his friend but had to make him understand, they had no options.

Todd looked at him, eyes filling with tears, "Don't make me do this."

Scott walked the few steps and hugged the man, "We have to, Todd, the AG needs her captain."

CHAPTER EIGHT

GEORGIA, SOUTH OF ATLANTA

The major looked out on the scene of utter misery in disgust. The smell filled every pore with the odor of rot, filth and decay. He turned and nearly tripped. He looked down to see what had caught his boot. A small, white curved bone extended above the sucking, red clay mud. A rib bone, human—probably a child's. He slid his foot back and carefully stepped around the small obstacle.

"Colonel Willett, sir?" he said smartly as he approached the Humvee.

The bald-headed man lowered the binoculars, handing them back to an aide. "What did you find, Kitma?"

"It is veery mush what we feared, sir, mush like de others. Worse even."

The colonel spat over the edge and scanned the scene. "So, just like the last one?"

"Oh, no. No, sir. In this one, they had no food left at all."

The US Army drones had been monitoring the camp for months. They had overflights every few days since the black-clad security forces had begun setting them up just after the solar flare. They had seen the sharp increase in the number of dead bodies over the last couple of months. The mass graves had increased daily, and then, they suddenly stopped. No new burial plots had been spotted for weeks. Now they knew why.

"We failed them, Major. We failed them all—they were the America we swore to defend. Fucking bastards. Goddamn 'em. Damn 'em all to hell!"

Kitma knew who the man's anger was directed at. The National Security Forces, those black-clad mercenaries the government was using to keep camps like these filled and productive.

The colonel had climbed down and walked around to the front of the nearby tents. Calling it a tent was giving the flimsy structure way too much credit. It consisted primarily of scraps, several pallets standing on edge with the tattered remnants of blue plastic tarp draped over the top. "Major, rough numbers on survivors and captured?"

"Approximately 1300 survivors rescued and 119 of their former guards in custody"

Willett shook his head. "Thirteen hundred out of, what was our original estimate, 28,000 or so?" His words, laced with bitterness, left much regret unsaid.

"Colonel, there is something else. We questioned the guards. Not all of them are American."

Willett exploded at this discovery, "You have got to be kidding me. They are importing soldiers to help keep our own citizens imprisoned?"

Kitma knew the question needed no answer. The colonel was doing a brave and dangerous thing in making it his mission to free as many of the internment camps as he could. They had sat on the sidelines for too long. Being first ordered to help build the relocation aid camps and then sitting idly by when they saw how they were actually being used was simply too much. He, like many others, could only follow presidential orders just so far. At a certain point, they came to realize the acting president was not simply incompetent; she was certifiably insane.

When many of them in the military chain of command refused, they had been removed. Then, when the replacements also refused, the camps' fuel, food, supplies and even radio communications were cut off. Willett was one of those replacement commanders. He took over after the other commander disappeared. He had initially tried to obey orders from Washington and President Chambers. After proof came out that the former president had been assassinated, though, few in the military would listen to the orders from the high office anymore.

Willett remounted the Humvee. "Release the survivors, let them take anything they want. They can make their way back home eventually. We can't feed 'em either, nor take them with us. Got no fuel to spare." He paused, looking at the ragged line of the survivors in the distance. Most were so skinny, they looked like holocaust victims. "What the hell have they been eating the last few months?"

"Each other, sir."

The look of utter hatred on the colonel's face needed no words. "Those guys," he pointed at the captured camp guards. He got back down from the truck and slowly walked to the assembled remnants of the NSF guards. He walked in front of each man, looked into the eyes of each.

"You people fucking disgust me. You're about as useful as an unwiped ass. How in God's name do you feel justified in what went on here?" None of the men spoke, most held their heads down. "Let me guess, you were just following orders—right? Orders to imprison and subsequently starve American citizens. Innocent Americans that had come to you for help. Had come to you thinking this was an aid camp!" He spat out a dark stream of tobacco juice. "Let me guess, someone gave you a gun, a uniform and just enough authority to make you feel important —right?" The tempo of his condemnation increased with every step he made. "Let me explain something to you, I got those same orders, just like all my men. Against all our training, we refused to obey. WHY? Because it was wrong, reprehensibly wrong, morally wrong!"

He paused at one end of the line of former guards. "Do you smell that? Maybe you've been here so long you no longer notice. Take a deep, fucking breath. That is the odor, hell, the remains of bodies you burned.

Bodies of Americans, of men, of women, even of children. The order to protect those people overrides everything else. Those people are who we serve. You bastards don't deserve to be on the same planet as them!"

He turned away to his men guarding the prisoners. "They are hereby sentenced to death."

～

From the bunker in Mount Weather, VA, President Madelyn Chambers watched the monitors for situational updates. Currently, she was intently following the video feed labeled as Camp 10H3 located just south of Atlanta. The situation was getting out of hand; even she knew that at some point the military was going to question her authority and begin undermining her directives. She had just not anticipated it would be so soon nor the use of military force against the Emergency Security Forces. She knew she would have to pass the information on as well and saw no way to spin it as a positive. *Fuck,* she hated politics. She had only wanted the authority, the prestige, not all this *shit.*

She called her assistant. "Ed, get me an update on all the remaining aid camps. Specifically, any within reach of all former military bases with a non-compliant commander."

He knew what she meant, over two-thirds of the bases that remained were commanded by officers refusing to take orders from her. In her mind, they were warlords setting up their little fiefdoms, carving up the remnants of the country and flipping her off as commander-in-chief. Ed went to the intel room and began pulling up the information and transferring it to his tablet. She had already cut off all food and fuel supplies to those bases as well as jamming secure communications between them, but their resistance was increasing. Her decision to place infected people into some of the camps had been a horrific act of desperation. He was convinced they would all burn in hell for what they were doing.

The phone in his pocket trilled again. Answering it with some reluctance, he said, "Yes ma'am."

"Ed, one other thing. Please get Ms. Levy for me. I need to brief her on this latest development."

"Of course, ma'am." He gritted his teeth as he put the phone away. The only thing he hated worse than dealing with the country's first female president was talking with Ms. Levy. That woman was categorically maniacal. He also never knew where she was. He had a contact number to call, and sometimes she would appear in the offices within minutes, other times it was a short satellite transmission some hours, or even days, later. He felt sure she was well away from the virus 'hot zone.' The infected were already moving well past the hidden base they were in. While the Mount Weather complex had self-contained air, water and food supplies, knowing the pathogen was just outside freaked all of them out.

The return call, this time, was minutes, not days later. He transferred the call to the president's encrypted line. As usual, he listened in covertly as President Chambers passed along the day's events with an unmistakably shaky voice. Her normal confidence collapsed whenever she spoke to Ms. Levy. There was no illusion as to who held the real power. Chambers was losing her very loose grip on the country, anyone could see that.

"Madelyn," Levy said. "You need to be presidential. Act like you're the fucking president for once! Control the camps, control the military and for God's sake keep the people under control. If you can't handle this, I will find someone who can."

Chambers gladly hung up the phone, then launched into an angry fit of cursing that deteriorated into stomach-churning nausea. She rushed to the toilet to vomit. The leader of the free world on her knees in fear. She cleaned herself and donned the mask of authority once more. She had a speech to write.

Several hundred miles away, in a nondescript concrete bunker, a metal door at the end of a dark corridor opened to reveal a lone figure sitting on a metal cot. "Up, prisoner," the guard said. The man stood silently. His hands and legs were already shackled. The guard ushered him out the door which slammed back shut with a metallic clang. The prisoner shuffled his feet in an awkward gait. He asked no questions but took in every detail. The guard had been joined by four others. None of them carried firearms, only tasers, batons and other non-lethal weapons. *So, they want me alive, not dead.* Someone out there knew his capabilities. He'd been here in this former domestic black site for over a year. A supermax prison that didn't officially even exist. From what he knew of the outside world now, he felt somewhat grateful for the accommodations and the regular meals. It seemed like that was about to come to an end, though. Someone was pulling the old man out of mothballs.

The bright sunlight was blinding, they were leading him out of the prison bunker. A sleek black helicopter sat just outside the fence. The noise of the engine obscured all other sounds. Out of the corner of his eye, he saw a large black man signing a paper presented by one of the guards. His restraints were quickly removed. The black man walked around him in a full circle as if he were inspecting a prize cow he might buy. "Good to see you, Archangel. We need to go."

CHAPTER NINE

HARRIS SPRINGS, MISSISSIPPI

The galley area of the AG was immaculately clean as always. Angel no longer managed the meal preparation as her responsibilities were now much larger than that, but, like Scott, she still took several turns each week helping prepare meals and insisted on the galley staying spotless.

"Hey, Boss," came her normal cheery greeting.

Scott gave her a hug. "Don't call me that…please."

The two had always been friendly, but something had changed when Scott had gone missing. Angel was the one who never gave up on him. She had been an outsider. Just a college girl on a summer beach trip when the lights went out. Even though she was just a few years older than Kaylie, he had seen a maturity and wisdom in her, rare for someone her age. Her abilities and confidence were immediately recognized by Scott. There was nothing romantic in their friendship, but it was now more familial in nature. Increasingly, she was more like a younger sister to him.

"Angel, DeVonte said you needed to talk to me."

"I do, Scott, but mainly I wanted to just make sure you were doing ok."

"Yeah, I'm doing fine. Why do you ask?"

"Just seems like so much going on..." she let the thought trail off. "You're not about to go do something stupid again, are you?"

He smiled and shook his head. "Yes and no. I'm going up with Skybox and Garret's team to try and find the Simpsons. I'll be fine."

"But?" Angel asked with a frown.

"But nothing, you are in charge...that's all."

"Does Gia know you're going?"

"Well...hmmm, not exactly, but she isn't here."

"Scott Montgomery, you just can't stay out of trouble, can you? Got a woman that loves you and a ship to fix, but you want to go off and play soldier."

Scott reached across the table and took her slim hand, her brown skin and his tan not that far apart in color. "Angel, you are my second in command. You know this mission is important. It's the right thing to do. Look, this boat is yours to run. That takes a lot off of me. I'll admit the stress of it all is more than I am comfortable with, but good people like you keep stepping forward to help. That is allowing me to look at the bigger picture more. Now, what was it you really wanted to discuss?"

She nodded, but it was obvious that she was moving on reluctantly. "Scott, I have my crew inventorying all our supplies, and I know Jack is out making trades for more, but I'm concerned. Essentially, we just are working with less than a week's buffer of supplies right now."

"You mean food?"

"I mean everything: food, fresh water, cooking oil, salt...all of it. That mess with the Messengers and the hurricane didn't just deplete our stocks, it crippled the farms around here. Barely any of the crops made it. Roosevelt has helped me...pointing us to wild greens and food sources we would have never considered, but that's not enough to build up any surplus."

Scott understood all too well. "I need to see that inventory and your estimates, assuming everyone is on reduced rations. Jack is going to check up near Yokena, you know, those big farms, no one has heard from them in a while."

"Dang...so, how long do we need to plan on for this trip?" she asked. "A week, a month? Will there be supplies at wherever we land?"

Scott rubbed his temples, "We should be able to get anywhere in two weeks at sea. Beyond that, it's just a guess, but we are going to need to land where we can find food. One month's supply is my recommendation. More would be better, but anything more than that seems unreasonable to expect."

"So, one month's food for just us—the regular people here on the AG?"

He shook his head, "No...well, maybe. Some of these people probably won't leave, and we can't make 'em. Also, Jack is offering safe passage to anyone who trades with us, but they will need to bring their own food stocks."

"You better figure some of the Navy guys will want to go as well."

He looked at her in surprise, "How's that?"

"You gotta know, many are starting to look at the AG as home. They have nothing to go back to, and it's common knowledge the Navy is on its last legs."

"Hmm." He looked at the empty pantry shelves behind her. "We have no idea if we can even get this thing moving again...maybe this is all just wasted effort."

Angel started to challenge his comment, then decided to take a new approach. "When is Gia going to be back?"

Scott couldn't quite pin down the vibe Angel was giving but let it pass. "She told me end of the week. Assuming the Navy can get her back from whatever hush-hush place she is this time." Her work over at the lab on the Bataan was now interspersed with more frequent trips to other labs trying to nail down a viable treatment for the virus.

"When she comes back, Angel, I'd like your help if you could…just a little surprise for her."

She nodded. Scott had something to live for; she knew he would do anything to keep that spark alive.

"So, this is it?" Tahir said stepping out of the Jeep.

"Yep." Scott walked up to the top of the old dam and pointed to the equipment on top. "Do you want to see the transmission equipment, spillway control or what?"

Tahir was looking fearfully at the drop to the Black River below, "Um… no my friend. Let's look at the generators first. Nothing matters if we can't get those working."

Bartos already had the access door open. It was a very concealed entrance on the back of the dam. Scott would've never have known it was there if an old worker hadn't pointed it out one day. *That day*, as he thought back now. He had been on his bike and gotten a flat crossing the road atop the dam.

The three men walked into the dark interior, the damp smell reminding Scott of the supplies he had stored here right after 'The Day'. This was his bugout location, it hadn't ever really been used for that, but he kept thinking about all the possibilities here. The town still used it to store supplies and extra fuel as no one had ever discovered the space inside the old decommissioned hydroelectric dam.

Scott and Bartos had told Tahir what they knew about the place, and even though not an engineer, Tahir had been intrigued as well. "So, what all have you tried?"

Bartos spoke, "Scott and me hooked up a generator to the spillway motor. We got it to move about a foot before the circuit blew. Strange you need an outside source of electricity to make a hydroelectric dam work, but, apparently, you do. From there I just mainly cussed at the damn thing. Scott put his little nerdy monkey-brain to work on it. Truth is, he had about as little success as me."

Scott nodded, "Yeah, we never were able to get enough water flow to see if any of the generators would even turn. Without maintenance, I assume rust in the turbine shaft and bearings would be pretty likely."

Tahir was using a small flashlight to inspect the three huge generators. "Good thinking, Scott. The intake impeller or the turbine shaft would be the likely trouble areas, but it appears these were all removed." He peered in closer, "Wait, no…not the impeller, but the main shaft is missing."

Scott couldn't believe he had missed that. As often as he'd been here, he mostly focused on getting the spillway gates to work. "So, the main shaft is gone? That is what turned inside the windings to make electricity – so we are screwed."

Bartos called from a darkened corner of the large room. He was shining the light up at some metal racks. "Hey, brainiacs, would those shafts look anything like these?"

"Perfect!" Tahir exclaimed. "They would have removed those regularly for maintenance as yes, corrosion would be a problem. When they mothballed the place, they just left them out."

Scott was chastened on missing the obvious but asked what, to him, was the obviously harder question, "Ok, so we get the turbine shafts reinstalled. How do we get the floodgate open?"

Tahir laughed, "Easy, BikerBoi," using his old gamer name.

"How the fuck is that going to be easy? I spent months on the problem and came up with nothing."

"Simple, Scott. You were trying to fix what was already there instead of just solving the problem. You don't really need that spill-gate to raise and lower, you simply need a supply of water flowing down to the turbine."

Scott thought about what his friend was saying. "Oh, my God!" How head-slapping obvious the answer was had stunned him. "We could blow the gate off."

Tahir nodded, "Of course, or perhaps cut a hole in it or even just bypass it temporarily with a large pipe from the water side of the dam. If we keep the gate intact, once we are generating power, we could then shut it back down if we needed."

Scott marveled again at his friend's unique intelligence that had examined the problem for mere minutes before solving it. Honestly, he didn't even think Tahir saw it as a problem; the solution was just so glaringly obvious to his sharp mind.

Bartos radioed for Scoots and some of the other mechanical types to come out and help. Installing the massive turbine shafts was going to take most of the day. Clearly, not work that Scott and Tahir would be much help with, so after Bartos ran them off the second time, the two wandered up past the dam and out around the lake.

CHAPTER TEN

Bobby jerked the headphones from his head. "What in the hell?" His look of bewilderment was suddenly matched by DeVonte sitting on the opposite side of the room.

"Who…I mean is that really, is that her?"

Bobby flipped a switch to record the broadcast. Looking at the young man on duty with him, he muttered, "I don't know."

He used a smaller radio to scan other channels. "It has a powerful signal and it's on a whole range of frequencies. Who else but the government could do that? Do me a favor, run get Tahir, he may know more."

As DeVonte left, Bobby picked up the headphones and listened in on the speech. It certainly sounded like the same woman.

"… Let me say that once more. The days of simply surviving are over, it is time to put this country back together. This has been a dark time for the US and for the entire world. If this message is reaching you, then you are in better shape than most. We've all lost, we've all suffered. Casualty reports have been unprecedented. Now it is time to put the grieving behind us and get back to work.

"Some of you will ask if we are even in a position to do that. Do we have the people and resources any longer? The answer is: absolutely! We are a country of doers, we are a people with a rock-solid resolve. Your government took steps—at the beginning of this crisis. Unprecedented steps to make sure our country's future would be protected. It is now time we tap into that plan and begin to take back what is ours.

"Now…let me be clear on this. There are enemies out there who will try and prevent this. People who fear a strong America. These are the threats we've always faced, but now they operate in the open. How do you find them? They are the ones that hoard supplies instead of contributing to the rebuilding effort. They are the ones who steal and believe they are out of reach of our justice system. They hold on to their illegal weapons instead of turning them into the authorities like they were ordered. They are the ones who conspire and plan against your government. They prefer chaos and brutality over order and justice."

Tahir came in with DeVonte. They both plugged in headphones, and Tahir booted up his MacBook which had a cable going to the one digital receiver. Bobby wasn't sure what he was doing, but the guy had a way of figuring answers to questions that no one else would even think to ask.

The president continued, "You may have heard a lot of things. Most are lies and exaggerations, but a few of those terrible, terrible things are true. For one, terrorists have taken over a few small, insignificant US military bases. We are dealing with them swiftly with deadly consequences. Just because they may wear the uniforms of our military doesn't make them our friends. Secondly, the health crisis I predicted years ago is now a fact. A pandemic is sweeping the nation. We urged people to come to the treatment centers in our aid camps, but those are mostly closing now. If you remained outside, you are on your own.

"Lastly, and it is with a heavy, heavy heart I do this, we are reissuing a full travel ban in advance of this pandemic. We simply cannot be having those people who refused to come in when we asked them to now carry the disease to uninfected areas. Our country is at stake. We have closed off both our southern and northern borders. The Coastal Patrols are ensuring our shorelines are safe. Each of you must do your part as well. Radio an alert if you see people in violation of any of the above. People hoarding, people with weapons, people traveling and potentially spreading the virus. We must work together to contain further damage.

"I have authorized Homeland Security to expand the role of its security force due to the collapse of local and state governments and law enforcement. The NSF will take an active role in protecting our citizens. You are required to treat the NSF as my legal authority and obey their requests. Violators of any laws will be dealt with swiftly, particularly those I have specifically mentioned today."

The broadcast went on for several more minutes with more of the same. "Jesus, that woman is insane to think anyone would listen to that crap," Bobby stated matter-of-factly.

Tahir was holding a single headphone to one ear but nodded. "A few will, she is using just enough truth to sound believable. Many will also view this as their last hope." He adjusted the settings on the signal analyzer software. "She is all over the radio spectrum. I guess she really wanted to be heard."

The broadcast finished, but Tahir kept running one of his search programs. "Location was most likely near the East Coast but not going to get any more specific." He slipped both headphones on. His face distorted into a mask of concentration. "That is unexpected," he said as he pulled up yet another program.

"What?" Bobby said loud enough for the man to hear over the headphones.

Tahir ignored him. DeVonte leaned over and saw the frequency he was monitoring. He adjusted his shortwave to match. "It's on the AM free-qs," Tahir explained. He gave him the specifics, so he could tune his as well.

Bobby and DeVonte listened in to the monotonous female voice droning on with a repetitive list of numbers. "That's just one of the Numbers Stations broadcasts. The world could end, and those damn things would keep going. All of the radio operators had heard them countless times. You didn't even need a fancy HAM radio for it, just an ordinary AM one would often do, if you knew where to spin the dial. Bobby had gotten interested in them early on just after getting his amateur radio license. Common theory was it was coded intelligence communications and had been going on for decades. Broadcasts had been plentiful during the Cold War but had decreased somewhat since then. Since there was no way of knowing specifically what was being said, he'd lost interest pretty quickly. It was a novelty to him, certainly nothing worthy of the numerous conspiracy theories. That being said... *Why is Tahir taking notes as he listens to them?*

CHAPTER ELEVEN

Tahir slowly shook his head, "No, Scott…it was no accident."

During his time in the bunker in DC, Tahir had access to the best surveillance and intelligence systems that ever existed. Scott had been pressing him for more details about who put the Catalyst plans together and what had happened with the former president. "Look, friend, I just want to know how our secretary of 'who really gives a shit' woke up one morning as the new president," he fired at Tahir.

"Well, a lot of top government were already dead or missing after the CME. Speaker of the House was killed in a car accident, secretary of state was overseas when it happened and was never heard from again. Many things had to happen for that to go on, Scott. Very powerful people involved. First thing was the vice president's plane went down over upstate New York. The footage I was able to access clearly indicated a surface to air missile impact. Over the next few days, several others in the line of succession died or disappeared. The last five, the ones between our former president and the secretary of transportation, were all together at the presidential retreat. You know, the one in Maryland."

"Umm, yeah, Camp David."

"That's it. Did I ever tell you about some of the crazy shit that went on at that place?"

His friend was beginning to drift. "Focus, Tahir. What happened to the president?"

"Oh yeah, yeah…crazy shit, man. They supposedly were there to discuss a plan for government continuity…ironic, isn't it? No official reports ever entered the system. Someone scrubbed all the normal channels. What I pieced together came mostly from the few working street cams and a couple of secret service body cam feeds that I was able to find in the storage cache waiting to download. So, there are a dozen or so people in the main lodge including the president, the attorney general, chief of staff, treasury secretary and the secretary of defense. The last five of the top successors to the nation's highest office."

"Pretty dumb, yeah, but I guess they felt safe," Scott added.

"It appears that the chief of staff ordered everyone out of the room. I only had video, no audio, but I can do a bit of lip reading. Anyway, everyone filed out except the four of them and the two-man protection detail assigned to the president. From the video, it appeared that the secretary of commerce, you know, the weasel looking, former Wall Street banker. Anyways, he took something from his briefcase, and they all leaned in to look at it. Then a flash, and the video went white. Over-head drone footage showed the entire building was destroyed. Scott, that building was bomb-proof. Steel walls clad in wood to make it look rustic, and the whole thing was gone. Blown apart from the inside."

"Wait, so you are saying the treasury secretary was a suicide bomber? That's crazy, man," Scott shook his head.

"I know…I know, my friend. I can show you the vids. The expression on his face at the end. He knew what was about to happen."

"Holy fuck…what kind of leverage must these people have to get someone like that to kill himself and the president?"

"Scary shit, man…"

"So, someone else is pulling the strings, right?"

Tahir nodded.

"Yeah, that is basically what our friend, Sentinel, has said, and it lines up with what Commander Garret thinks as well." "So, who are these people?" Scott questioned.

"Scott, I've been digging around to find that out most of my adult life. They are always very careful, layer upon layer of obfuscation. I will tell you the little bit I have pieced together, some of it is conjecture, but I feel relatively certain."

Tahir absentmindedly started rearranging the nuts and bolts scattered on the table where they were sitting. "There is a nameless group that has been around since basically the founding of the country. It appears to have been as few as four people and as many as nine but always very small in number. They most likely come from old money—money is never the focus, nor is it an obstacle. They sit on the boards of countless corporations in healthcare, biotech, defense and technology, but their base is always in finance. My analysis suggests they own or influence thousands of smaller companies in an even more diverse portfolio."

"Okay, they have money, we figured that already. Lots of people are rich, and it doesn't make them evil."

"My friend, you see, that is where the problem lies. I would not say this group is necessarily evil. Much of what they have done throughout our history was very beneficial to this country. Have you ever stopped to think about how America went from British colony to a world super-power in just a couple hundred years? It seems they may have been instrumental in paying Washington's Army after the Revolutionary War —the country was essentially flat-broke back then. They helped set up the state university systems and even appear to have pushed the right buttons to end slavery, although they did apparently start the Civil War to bring it about. This group doesn't just have money. They got the laws changed so they could create money."

"They started the Civil War?" Scott asked with incredulity.

"Yes, of that I am quite sure."

"They started it to end slavery?" Scott asked.

"Oh, no, no, that was just a side benefit for them. They started it to collapse the American banking system at the time."

"WTF, Tahir, you are taking too many sharp turns for me to follow. What are you talking about, and how does that all tie into this?"

"Follow the money, Scott. You see, money is a tool, and in this group's hands, they have used it to build and shape the US into what it has become. In the 1800s, there was no real national banking system. Banking was mostly a state-sponsored activity, sometimes even a local one. Some cities even coined their own currency. About half of all banks failed back then. Someone in one state may or may not accept currency from another. It was a cumbersome and weak system, to say the least. This Council knew that had to change for the country to grow, but most likely, the states wouldn't change unless forced to. The states still had too much power for the federal government to affect much control.

"Now, keep in mind, war is terribly expensive, the Shadow Council took steps to profit from the war efforts and to weaken the local banks to the point of collapse. To do this, they supported both sides in the war, and, in many respects, also opposed both. The end result was the states that were opposed, mainly the South and the West, were too weak to fight the changes, and the US then had a strong federal banking system. Wall Street was now the second biggest financial market in the world."

Scott had heard a bit of this before but not quite in this context. "So, slavery had nothing to do with it?"

Tahir shrugged in that damnable way he had, "Scott, from what I know of politicians, none are that altruistic. Slavery had its opponents in the South and the North. The Council simply looked at it as another tool, one that had served its purpose and probably one that would be too costly to maintain for much longer. The slave economy had helped jump-start the US well ahead of most of the world. To keep growing, they had to put on the front of respectability and sweep all that unpleasantness away. The war gave them a perfect opportunity to do so.

"These people play the long game, they play to win, and they are damn good at it. At least until recently."

"What do you mean?"

"Leaving the plans to Catalyst where they could be found, taking out the former president and successors, possibly even allowing that Chimera virus to get loose. None of this is like them. Something has changed for them to be this sloppy."

"Well, shit, Tahir, doomsday happened. Didn't you hear?"

"I am very certain they had contingencies for that, worst case scenarios and such. No, something else is at work. The Shadow Council is losing control, and that scares me more than anything else that has happened."

"This is what is happening with the NSF rounding up people and raiding farms?" Scott asked.

Tahir nodded. "Somehow, they underestimated how much food would be needed, or the level of resistance, or numbers of survivors outside the camps. Maybe even the pandemic, although that one…may not have been unplanned. Either way, Scott, we still have to leave."

They had been making repairs to the ship. Bartos was working on ways to collect and even make fuel, but the idea of leaving the US was still hard to accept. "I know," Scott responded. "It just seems like we are the rats fleeing a sinking ship."

Tahir shook his head, "No, very much not true, my friend. We are rats swimming to a very much still floating ship."

Scott cocked his head slightly. The man had a point.

CHAPTER TWELVE

PEARL RIVER VALLEY, MISSISSIPPI

"Hey, LT," one of the uniformed men in the rear of the Humvee yelled.

"What?"

"Are we really going to engage these guys?"

Garret shook his head. His men, no, not his men, this was the remnants of Commander Ramos' old SEAL team. They were so mission focused, but the idea of possibly fighting against another US based force was inconceivable. Despite the hours of briefing, he was unsure the men would follow orders. "Look, we are just here to make a quick look-see and hopefully rescue that family. We only fight if we are cornered."

Besides the Navy team, Skybox, Todd and Scott were along for the ride. They had Scott's jeep, an armed Humvee and a battered old church van. It had taken longer than expected for Garret to get the green light from command. Bobby had gotten only one other garbled call from someone named Tasha. It seemed like whatever survivors were left had gone to ground and taken refuge farther back, up along the Pearl River.

As they neared Jackson, Mississippi, Garret motioned to them all to pull over. Taking out a large plastic case, one of the SEAL team members assembled half a dozen sparrow-sized aerial drones and launched them into the late morning sky. Each rose to several hundred feet, then sped off in a pre-programmed pattern to map out the route ahead. Scott looked quizzically at the series of tablets showing the camera feeds from the little drones. "These two," one of the men with a name patch reading 'Rollins' said, "they are the ones scouting the route to the Pearl."

"What about the other four?"

Lt. Garret looked at Skybox. "Those were his suggestions. If there is an internment camp nearby, we would like to know where it is. The drones are semi-autonomous, we don't have to wait on them. We can go on with our mission as soon as the route is clear. We can recover them on our way back."

Cool, Scott thought.

The route into Jackson was surreal. It was one of the largest towns Scott had been in since the CME, and the absence of people and the scenes of destruction were overwhelming. They bypassed the main part of town. Too many spots for ambush, and the drones spotted what looked to be buses and troop carriers on several of the major highways. It took until noon to get near the area where the Simpsons were supposed to be.

"I hope they know to expect us," Skybox said. Scott looked out at the group all in tactical gear and nodded his head.

"We'll scare the shit out of them otherwise."

So far, they had avoided any of the enemy forces but saw plenty of evidence that this was an occupied area. The drones had spotted countless roadblocks and encampments as well as what might be regular supply routes as small convoys of trucks were apparent.

The group of soldiers deployed into the deep woods following the crude map Bobby had provided. The drones were no use over the heavy foliage.

One of the men to Scott's right threw up a hand signaling to stop. He whispered, "We got movement ahead."

All of them froze and slowly went to ground. He followed the SEAL's eyes and saw it, too. A flash of black uniform, then another. It appeared to be a full squad of Security Forces moving through the forest. Scott had an earpiece to listen in on the tactical channel. Cryptic and whispered conversations were quickly voiced and hushed. Scott got the gist of it. Stay concealed, but, if discovered, they would engage. Two groups of SEALs moved to the north to get on the opposite side of the NSF squad.

Rollins crawled up next to Garret and showed him the incoming drone feed. Scott eased over closer to get a look, too. "Too many of them." The feed was now in infrared. The heat signatures of the enemy clearly visible.

Garret nodded, "I count at least twenty-five scattered through here. Any sign of transport?"

"Yes, sir, here," Rollins pointed to several faint yellow-orange spots near what looked to be a dark blue curving line.

"Boats on the river. Looks like they are headed back to those. Is there any way to see if they have prisoners?"

Rollins shook his head, "We can go visual on the birds once they are back in the open, but no way we can spot that now. Maybe when they are on the river."

"Do it. Also, tag them to track. Can't the drones do hand-offs? I want to know where that group is heading."

"Yes, sir. I'll route the other birds to pick up the trail when the target enters their sector."

"Mr. Montgomery."

He had told the lieutenant countless times to call him Scott, but the man rarely did. "Yes?"

Garret held out the tablet. "The target location is here," he pointed to a location perhaps a mile away. "We are giving those federal guys ten minutes to clear the area, then we are moving. Would you mind taking the lead? If there are friendlies out here, you look a lot less threatening."

Scott wasn't sure if that was a compliment or not but agreed. He hadn't told Gia he was coming with the rescue team. She would have been furious. Truthfully, it was probably stupid for the community leader to be heading into enemy territory, but he owed the Simpsons for saving his brother. Also, like the Navy, he wanted to know who they were up against, too.

It was mid-afternoon when they reached the area. The Simpsons had said they were taking refuge in a hidden cave system. But Scott's team hadn't seen any caves anywhere. Several of the men searched the ground for any sign of them. Garret and Rollins were watching drone feeds as they searched for heat signatures. Scott walked away from the group to think. He found himself on the riverbank looking across the peaceful looking waters of the Pearl. The family or families had been forced to flee from their homes. *They would need fresh water, and they'd need food…maybe fish. Probably fish.*

His thought process made him start scanning for certain objects. He'd walked almost 200 yards before he bent to pick something up. A scrap of nylon fishing line coiled around a small stick. Kneeling there, he scanned the immediate area. A worn place in the weeds possibly where animals or *maybe* people came down to get water. Then, a faint odor that was out of place. Something of old cooking fires or bacon fat. The mere thought of it made his mouth water. He keyed the mic on his chest. "LT, I believe I see it."

He stood and approached the large bushes. They looked the same as all the rest, except it was much darker behind this group. He got within fifteen feet before seeing the shotgun barrel pointing at him from between the leaves. Slowly, he raised his arms.

∽

The smiling muddy faces of Mahalia Simpson and Tasha as well as five other people looked out of the church van. She had seen the resemblance of Scott to the man her nephew had saved. She lowered the gun and walked out gingerly to Scott with arms outstretched. It had taken them only a few minutes to gather the few belongings they had and head back to where the vehicles were concealed.

Scott and the others helped them maneuver through the woods. "Mahalia, how did you survive all this?"

Someone on the radio had filled Bobby in on the events in the cabin that day. "Honestly, Mr. Scott…I have no idea. The Lord wrapped his protective arms around me, dat's all I knows. Tre was there, I knows it was him firing up into those…those bastards." She spat the word as if it was stinging her tongue.

"He was a man of faith, ya kno, but I didn't think either of us had a prayer that day. Maybe…" she broke into tears. He knew she hadn't seen if Tre had survived or not. "Dey dragged him off, I know dey did. Sister Tasha and the others found me, took us to the caves. She treated me best she could. Dem soldiers been searching for us ever since, though. We know da woods, dey don't. Only reason we still heah. Dat was where the radio and guns wus hid."

"Sorry to hear about your nephews—I know Bobby will be, too. We should have gotten here sooner."

The older woman shrugged, "Wilson was like dat. Wanted to fight 'em all. Tre, he jus wanted to save everybody, specially me, I guess. Reckon he did dat. I am glad to hear yo brother's doing ok, though. And da boy?"

Scott grinned, "Yeah, they are both doing good. Can't wait to see you, in fact. I can't thank you and your family enough for what you did for them."

"It's ok, jus wish we could've done more for da boy's mom. Hated to see her go like dat. Seen a lot more go since den, though. Dem damn Messenger folk got some of us, but dem black uniformed people took all da rest. Dey is some real bastards. Dis right heah," she pointed to the people loading into the van, "dey all dats left of my church. All of 'em...gone."

Scott pointed toward Skybox, "We are working on that, too. Think we may have some ideas on where they took them."

Mahalia nodded weakly. She held her side; a recent wound was leaking through a nasty bandage, and the smell was foul. Garret's medic began to unwrap it and begin treatment. "One of dem bullets flying around my kitchen grazed me. Dat's all."

The medic injected her with an antibiotic and began to quickly redress the wound. "That's no graze ma'am, it punched right through," the medic said.

They were making plans to exfil the area when the radio, now clipped to Scott's vest, made a small sound. "BikerBoi, you there?" The tactical team was all back together, so he was momentarily confused as to who it was until the voice registered.

Scott keyed the mic, "Preacher, that you?"

CHAPTER THIRTEEN

HARRIS SPRINGS, MISSISSIPPI

"Kirk, obviously. What are you an, imbecile? Why would any self-respecting geek even mention Skywalker or any other Star Wars character in the same breath as 'The Captain?' Tahir smiled and

looked away. He was not the type to be upset with the lad, it wasn't totally his fault—he was just an over-educated moron.

"Tahir, listen, Kirk was just a glorified driver. All the real work was done by actual competent officers. He was a glory-hog."

"A glory-hog…a glory…HOG? Um, let's see…maybe something along the lines of Darth fucking Vader maybe. He seemed to like showy shit and stagecraft. Face it, DJ, Star Trek was science, Star Wars was voodoo, witchcraft bullshit. Sorry if you are too smart to see the obvious. You like fairy tales where the hero rescues the princess from the evil witch… stick with Star Wars. You want science…then come over to the Trekkie side."

Tahir was laughing now and bumped the arm against the table. "Oh… oh, oh….that really hurts."

DJ got serious and checked his patient over. "Sorry, man, Kaylie said you were coming over for an X-ray this afternoon, but I don't know shit about broken bones and mangled tendons."

"But you're a doctor."

"Ugh…yeah, well sorta, but dude, I am an epidemiologist, not a GP. Only patients I see are infected with something. Most of 'em are dead. Even then, I am studying the infectious agent, not the person. I spent most of my time looking down the barrel of a microscope. You probably need Bones—he could wave that little swirly light thing over you, and you would be fine."

"Look, DJ, I don't care if you are Scott's future nephew…don't be hating on Dr. McCoy."

The two had gotten to be close in the months since Tahir had arrived on the Gulf, since the week of the massacre of the Messengers and Scott's miraculous return from the sea. Besides both men possessing brilliant minds, both were somewhat obsessed with pop culture. The debate of the moment was pretty standard fare. The sad realization that all culture, pop or otherwise, was a thing of the past was a sad reality to both.

"So, what happened to your arm again?"

Tahir was still rubbing his exposed arm along the edge of the sling, his olive brown skin contrasting with the bright white plaster. "It is a bit of a surprise Scott and I are working on. Bartos kind of let something big slip and basically tried to kill me."

DJ nodded, "Maybe you should stick to computers and leave the real work to the others."

Not yet ready to relent, Tahir offered another verbal jab, "So, we both agree you are not a real doctor, and Star Trek is far superior to every other sci-fi series. Can you at least come up with something that can help this rash? This damn cast is making me miserable."

"I'll need to run some tests, make sure it's not Chimera or some new form of STD. Have you taken on any new lovers lately?"

Tahir raised his middle finger in response.

DJ laughed, "Yeah, yeah…I think you're number one, too."

"DJ, stop being a dick and find me some cream or something."

"Aight…aight, man, cool your jets. Don't want to get your light saber over-agitated."

"Phasers, nimrod. What kind of advanced culture would revert to swordplay? Even if they were made of light—ridiculous." Tahir shook his head in frustration.

Dr. Gia Colton popped her head in just as DJ was finishing up with Tahir. "Hey, Boss," he said without looking up. "What'cha need?"

"Actually, I need your patient if you are done with the x-ray," the beautiful woman said. "Tahir, do you have a few minutes? I need to run a few things by you."

"Absolutely, if I survive this imbecile's healing ceremony, I will be there most pronto."

She smiled. Although still infrequent, occasionally someone from the AG, like Tahir, did have to come out here to the Bataan. While the two ships were only a mile apart, the gulf between civilian and military was wider than just water. Out here, it was normally all business.

"Doctor?" Tahir said knocking on her door.

She pointed to a seat. "Hey, sorry about your injury. Scott tells me you have some timeframes in mind for the disease to spread. I would like to know more about that, perhaps see if I should adjust my own projections."

Tahir nodded and in a very businesslike manner proceeded to go through all of the data he had collected. His recall was perfect, relying on nothing other than his brilliant mind. She seemed troubled by something as she took notes. "If you are correct, then the speed of the pathogen has varied significantly since the outbreak began. I have been using a standard model with a normal escalation based on available population. I projected at least a year before we would see it here."

"Um, yes, no, that would not be accurate anymore. I am assuming something has happened to alter both the disease vectors and some other aspects of the contagion…maybe carriers. Whatever happened, it has sped up considerably."

"You're quite sure about this."

He nodded, "Yes, very."

Gia set her pencil down and flipped back through some older notes. "Overseas, near the origin point where Skybox was, the soldiers were calling it a zombie plague. By the time it reached Europe, the infected were altered. While still hyper-aggressive, they were no longer brainless. They seemed to recognize the need to eat and had more of a sense of self-preservation. All of which made them even more dangerous."

Tahir nodded, "So, more of them survived. More of them to spread the infection."

"That is one possibility, yes. From the rather limited samples that DJ and I have access to, we can see that the actual virus has changed. We can track its morphology almost from inception. We assume it is evolving in response to its environment. Adapting to changing conditions."

"Doctor, I have only basic knowledge in this area, but I have heard mention more than once that this has to be a human-engineered genome. Do you agree with that assumption?"

She looked him in the eye and slowly nodded. "It seems to be a near certainty in my opinion. The genetic makeup is too complex to be natural. It seems to be made up of snippets of genetic code from a variety of other disease variants. This manufactured viral agent was spliced into something truly ancient, something known as Archaea. We don't even know enough about this form of life to properly classify it. Much like viruses, we aren't sure if they actually are a life form or just a very crafty chemical process. This had to be engineered, Tahir. In fact, I think this was an interim step, not a final product. Most likely, a bioweapon was the end goal, and this was just a hodgepodge of genetic material someone put together just to see what would happen. There is a small chance it could have evolved this way on its own. Some of the material resembles material recovered from the corpses of mass die-offs in humans, but it is way beyond that now."

"Have you learned anything helpful?"

"Yes…but helpful would be a relative term. Some of it is more curiosity than cure. Such as how the infected are attracted to certain stimuli like ultra-low frequency sounds and emit a very distinct pheromone when threatened. Some of this most likely are just vestigial responses. Biological relics from ancient parts of human DNA.

"Other findings have been more challenging. While we now have a workable cure for what would have been the first iteration of the disease, it's been totally ineffective against each of the current strains."

Tahir could see her hands were shaking slightly as she made more notes. "Doctor…Gia, will you be able to develop a treatment in time?"

"No…maybe, I don't know. In six months, I really doubt it. Please don't tell this to anyone else, Tahir. We gave up months ago trying to fight this from a traditional standpoint. While we are issuing boosters and antivirals to everyone, all of our efforts turned from understanding the Chimera to understanding what, or more accurately, who was immune to it."

"Like Skybox?"

"Yes, he was our first, but we have learned of a few others that are in other labs. While not technically immune, something in their genetic makeup allows them to keep the more damaging aspects of the disease in stasis while allowing certain rather positive changes from the virus to occur. We first thought this was in the blood chemistry. Some mix of other disease exposures and various immunizations a person may have acquired. In Skybox's case, that was a lot to run down. With him, what we concluded is it was actually his genetic makeup that was at play. His DNA has the genes turned on, not just to resist damage from the virus, but to make use of it. When the virus invaded his body, unlike other victims, his immune system attacked the virus, and it retained some of the virus's genetic code, so it could recognize it again. His body caused the virus to adapt to him instead of the other way around."

Tahir was very intrigued at this. "So, developing a serum based on his blood is not viable. Correct?"

Gia nodded, and he continued, "You are talking about an epigenetic treatment protocol if you can identify exactly which genes are switched on?"

She marveled at the young man's grasp of this complex knowledge well outside his main areas of expertise. "Yes, and gene therapy is a very challenging business even when we had all the cool tech toys. DNA structures are very complex, and we only have a superficial understanding at this point. We can manipulate genes, but often, with very unpredictable results." She recalled Scott's earlier conversation on Tahir's ideas. "It is very much like your computer code, except the code is individual to every computer. We turn one line off on this machine, it may do great, get faster, work forever. Do the same thing on another, and you may kill it."

Tahir didn't like it when other people used analogies to simplify ideas. He rubbed his head. "Yes, yes, I get that. There have been lots of studies on the human genome since it was mapped. Surely, you have enough of a baseline to make some logical progression, though."

"Possibly," she said. "We don't have time for incremental steps, though—we need to leap ahead in our understanding. If your timeline is correct, we have so little time."

Tahir rubbed the itch beginning again beneath the cast. Glancing around, he noticed her workspace was devoid of mementos, photos, personal touches of any type. Like him, she obviously preferred to focus on problems without distractions. "Doctor, one question – what adaptation did the virus make in Skybox?"

She sighed, "That is a very difficult question to answer. You see, human evolution is a constant state of adaptation. Even things we consider as maladies may have been the result of an adaption to solve some other problem. One form of diabetes is now known to have developed a millennium ago in Europeans to help them adapt to colder climates. Evolution also makes some missteps—not every adaptation works. What is complicating this is the Archaea, that is a biological entity that is designed to live in extreme environments. In Skybox, this is what is interacting with his base genome. What we can see right now doesn't make that much sense. His normal body temperature has decreased slightly. His ability to store fluids and fight dehydration is more efficient. Increased stamina, speed and muscle mass seem likely, but since he was in peak condition before, less easily quantified. The man can hold his breath for almost eight minutes. Markers in several other areas have changed as well. Nothing that makes him super-human, but definitely more adapted to something."

She could almost see the wheels turning in the man's head. "What are you thinking, Tahir?"

He stammered slightly when answering, "I…I'll let you know. Something, yes…something."

CHAPTER FOURTEEN

JACKSON, MISSISSIPPI

The former preacher's call had been disturbing, to say the least. "Say that again," Scott asked.

"I'm at the commercial farms near Yokena. You know, the ones you and Bartos got us set up with."

Scott remembered clearly. That was last year when he, Bartos and the boy-man, Abe, had made the first contact with the group of farmers. That was before they knew Abe was actually a Messenger spy. Thoughts of the traitorous bastard still filled him with rage. "Yeah, Jack. Good people up there. What happened?"

"I think they're prisoners now. Bunch of guys running around in black unis with guns. They look like they are making them farm their own lands. I've been hiding out, scoping them out and already saw two of them killed in a show of force by the guards."

"Shit," Scott said in disgust.

Rollins leaned over the seat and showed him and Lt. Garret an incoming drone feed. The screen was in IR mode and showed clusters of bright spots in a confined spot. It appeared to be an enormous herd of cattle. Rollins hit a button and the view changed to normal. *Not cows…people.*

Garret looked up. "Where is this?"

The view on screen was replaced by a Google map view. "Here, sir."

"Hang on, Preach."

Scott pressed the button to expand the view out. The internment camp was on the far side of Jackson. Running a finger along an isolated route, he found Yokena. "I guess that camp wasn't producing enough food on their own."

"Stay put and stay safe, Preach. I'm sending you some help. We need to stop this shit once and for all."

Garret and his men had heard the conversation, and they all looked ready to go charging in. "My dad is going to go ballistic when he hears about this."

His dad, the fleet commander, was in a position to help if they could get him enough specific intelligence on what all was going on. Scott felt sure what was happening here wasn't an isolated incident. The Catalyst plans had definitely taken a darker turn.

Skybox, Todd, Scott and company got the Simpsons safely back to the AG. Bobby and Jacob were waiting on the dock as they arrived. Seeing them brought Tre and Mahalia again to tears. Kaylie came and helped them all into the ship to get checked out and a proper meal. Garret left his men to go brief the fleet commander on what they had found.

Bartos came stumbling up out of the dark. Dark grease and grime covered one side of his face.

"Damn, Cajun, you been wallowing with the hogs?"

Bartos snorted like a pig, "I wish, that would be better than what I've been doing. Been checking the fuel tanks on this old girl," he said looking up at the massive ship. "Just seeing what all she can run on, how much is left and all. How did it go up in Jackson? I see the Simpsons made it."

Scott filled him in on the rescue op and the call from Jack. "So, the NSF is becoming a real problem," Bartos said.

"Obviously."

The National Security Force, or NSF, as they had begun calling it, was getting too close to home. If they were shaking down the larger farms and suppliers for resources, how long before they came calling here?

The Simpson family had told them some horror stories of what these NSF bastards had been up to. Skybox had no idea who these guys were, but they'd heard these were former government security and enforcement employees from various departments now unified under some domestic policing force. That being said, they seemed better organized and had more resources than any other group right now. They might be thugs, but they were the President of the United States' thugs.

"So, when we gonna hit 'em?" Bartos grinned at the question.

"You know, you are just as psychotic as your dog."

They both looked over at the dog curled up on the edge of the dock, head resting on his paws, watching them both lazily. "Solo takes offense with that remark."

"Let's go in, I'm bushed. We can talk on the way."

~

As expected, the older Garret wanted more proof. He was pissed but needed specifics before taking direct action. What was the troop strength, schedules, how often were supply runs made? Where was the food going?

"Sorry, Scott, you know how Dad is."

"I understand, and I would be the same." He knew the commander and respected him despite some of the Navy's failings over the last two years. He always had to remember, though, they wouldn't even have the AG if it weren't for the help the older Garret provided.

"So, let's get a full recon team in place at the farm to support Jack. Drone support and enough manpower to move in if it looks doable. Skybox will probably be up for it as well as a few others."

The lieutenant nodded in agreement. "I'll get right on it. Should I count you in?"

"Not yet, I'm going to stay here with Tahir and Bartos. We have to make some progress on getting this boat moving. I don't suppose your dad offered any assistance with that, did he?"

The man smiled, "Actually...he did. We have a full complement of men and an engineering team to come over as soon as you are ready."

"Hot damn! Wow, that's the best news I've heard in weeks!"

CHAPTER FIFTEEN

Tahir sat in the darkened room lightly tapping a pencil against the side of his head. The rhythm was automatic, almost as autonomous as the way his brain was working, inspecting, analyzing. His conversation with Gia days earlier had stuck with him, and what had originally been a half-formed thought, more nebulous than real, had eventually begun to take shape. His internal dialogue occasionally voiced itself by challenging a thought or offering support for one possibility over another. Today, it was firing queries and possibilities like bolts of lightning.

His brilliant mind loved puzzles and the challenges of complex problem-solving. He had been, still was, a brilliant hacker partially because of the way his mind approached challenging problems. While most people looked for a solution in a logical, analytical and linear manner, Tahir's brain was wired differently than most. When he met a challenge, his cerebral systems erupted into chaos; storming over the problem, breaking it apart with mental outburst, looking at multiple paths simultaneously. As a teen, he had diagnosed himself with a moderate case of autism but found it useful when he was the one directing it.

Tahir had become skilled at solving complex puzzles at the age of three. By six, he was routinely beating adults at games of all types. He became bored very quickly and had to keep challenging himself with increasingly tougher games and tests of his abilities. By his early teen years, he had been referred to as slightly retarded by one instructor in a report that was supposed to have been confidential, and yet another had called him a true savant; potentially one of the most gifted minds of his generation.

As he discovered computers and then the Internet, his prowess really blossomed. Unfortunately, so did his problems. He had the dubious honor of one of the most brilliant and audacious hacks on one of the most difficult computer systems in the world at age fourteen. By the time the authorities finally figured it out, he had learned to stay well-hidden, cover his tracks and, in the process, had become one of the top computer hackers in the world. He was still just a seventeen-year-old kid; the FBI didn't even have a strong case against him. In the end, instead of prosecuting and having a judge likely only giving him a slap on the wrist, they had instead offered him a job. Work as a white-hat hacker and do all his juju cyber-witchcraft with the full support of the US Government.

That was eight years ago; the deal he had with the nameless agency's cyber division had long since been cleared, but his reputation as the best was firmly established. He had later gone on to work for a group affiliated with the NSA before moving to the DOD and then to private government contracting. The result of his early career was that he had an arsenal of information that few people in the world could equal. He had made sure to leave back doors into every system he ever touched, so he could easily access them in the future if needed. Tahir had been at the top of a very elite group for many years, doing his part to keep America safe. But more important to him, was the need to know that which was hidden. On the fateful day, that August, it had all fallen apart. While a master in the cyber world, his skills were much less honed in the physical realm where he now operated.

The theory he had now was bizarre by any standard, but it had to be right. When presented with competing for hypothetical situations, the one with the fewest complications, the simplest answer, was usually right. He had put it together in his head; now to see if anyone else would believe him.

~

"You're completely batshit crazy, Tahir," Scott said.

Gia's lab assistant, DJ, nodded, "I agree. As Yoda might say, 'Knowledge have you, understanding you have not.'"

"Shut up, child. Scott, surely you can see it," Tahir said grinning.

"Tahir, its way over my head, we need Gia. I was hoping DJ might grasp it but go through it one more time. Kinda like you would explain it to a child."

"Why would I be explaining genetic engineering to a child?" He paused for a moment before getting it. "Oh, ok, simple. Hmm…let's see. Ok, you know about the birds and the bees, right?"

"Not that freakin simple," Scott said with exasperation. "Look, Tahir, I have a basic understanding of genetics. Remember, I once worked in a research lab with Gia, and I've read Darwin's *Descent of Man*. I understand that humans keep evolving and adapting to changing environments. What I am not getting is the role you think the Chimera is playing."

"Scott, I'm pretty sure you were the computer jock in that lab, but that's ok. Think of the virus as two parts. One is the actual viral payload – let's just call that rabies. It's not, but it works well for this illustrative discussion."

"It's not rabies, goober," DJ said snidely.

Tahir scratched at his head emphasizing his first words loudly, "FOR THE POINT OF DISCUSSION, let's call the viral side rabies. The other, we'll call side 'B' is the Archaea."

Scott was familiar with the Archaea domain from various discussions with Gia, DJ and even Kaylie. He nodded toward his friend, "I'm with you, go on."

"The B-Side, the Archaea, has the ability to adapt life to extreme living conditions. That's where they were discovered. Animals living in sealed cave streams, cut off from the world above for millennia, or in the ice and snow of the artic and at the boiling, acidic volcanic vents on the deep ocean floor. The Archaea helped adapt these creatures to live successfully in these harsh environments."

"Why is this important, Tahir?"

"It's important due to what it's not good at." He registered the looks of confusion. "The Archaea does not make for a good weapon. From a purely logical standpoint, it would not be a good base to develop a biological weapon system. I know DARPA and military science, they would have never gone down this route. I don't care what country was doing the work in that underground lab. It was not a bio-weapon."

"But someone did," DJ said.

Scott was beginning to see where his friend was going. "If the point was to kill people, it was not the best option, even though it's doing a damn good job of it. Shit, Europe, Asia and probably much of northeast US are gone because of it." He paused. "If not designed to kill us, what was it being designed for?"

"I think that is really the right question," Tahir said. "Gia mentioned that evolution is not always a straight line. Sometimes a genetic marker is activated to see if that modification is a helpful adaptation or not."

DJ took over, "Yeah, basically the human genome has lots of code that is inactive, seems to do nothing. Not only can a gene be turned on or off, but also the degree that any gene can be allowed to express itself can be regulated. So, when a group of humans is under stress, such as with malnutrition, lots of genes may be activated in their offspring. Those descendants that do better will carry the winning combination of new genes. It's less like an intelligent plan for success, but more like try everything and see what the benefit is…or the drawbacks. Those with beneficial adaptations will thrive, those without will fail."

"Precisely, my friend," Tahir chimed in. "Gia mentioned how long Skybox can hold his breath."

"Yeah, the bastard is scary good, I watched him wrestle a sea turtle once," Scott said.

Tahir nodded and continued. "Just before the blackout, I remember reading where researchers from UC Berkley discovered a group of people in southeast Asia who could dive down over 200 feet and hold their breath for up to thirteen minutes. They traced it to a unique DNA mutation that affected mainly the spleen's role in the human body cells' ability to store oxygen. Now, this was natural evolution among a society that depends on the sea for food."

Scott was mostly following it, "But how does that mutation develop, how did it spread?"

DJ offered some insight, "Naturally, aberrations happen all the time. The ones that get the attention are usually because of something external like a birth defect, maybe double eyelashes, but internal mutations happen as well. The first one of these people, um, what were they called, Tahir?"

"Bajau," Tahir dredging the name up instantly from his vast mental repository.

"Okay, the first of the Bajau to have this probably was much better at fishing and providing for his family than the others. He would have likely had his pick of mates and produced descendants that also had the modified gene, and over eons, that gene would have become dominant in the Bajauan people."

"Exactly, DJ," Tahir said. "Now, imagine if the mutation had been for gills or fins. With the Archaea involved, researchers could try genes from other species, not just human. And, in this case, the Archaea is using the rabies, or A-side, as a vector to insert these random epigenetic changes into the host. It is turning on and off genetic markers at each iteration to see what works best. This is why what Gia has been doing is doomed to fail. Getting a handle on the mutations of the Chimera is so hard to follow. That is why the range of victims goes from the horrible zombie-like creatures to those like your friend, Skybox. The Archaea is firing everything it's got. The 'rabies' side simply exists to get it distributed as widely and quickly as possible."

Scott leaned back, "Whoa, fuck, ok…shit…damn, I think I actually get that. So, despite all the damage this pandemic is causing at the root level, it could be that researchers were attempting to manipulate human evolution on a grander scale?"

"I believe so, yes. We still need to run this by your lovely doctor, but this is my belief. Chimera is a Swiss Army knife for genetic engineering. Sadly, whatever manipulation they had planned never got programmed in, so now it is just randomly firing all of its genetic switches, some of which may produce an occasionally beneficial adaption, but many won't. Sadly, the recipients of the A-side mutations will probably kill off many of the other variants, so it may take longer for those that are immune or possibly better to emerge."

DJ was writing furiously trying to get it all down. Tahir wasn't a doctor, but his vast depth of knowledge in such a broad area allowed him to see the distant mental horizon much clearer than most. The young researcher knew his boss would want to hear this as soon as possible.

CHAPTER SIXTEEN

Scott watched his older brother as he approached. He was startled to realize how much he now resembled their father. Bobby had seemed to age considerably in the time since the blackout. Trailing behind him and almost out of site was Jacob. The still silent but ever-present shadow of Bobby. Scott had thought of the boy as Bobby's son in every way, although he had heard the tragic story of their escape from the Messengers and his mother's sudden death. Bobby sat down at the window in the vinyl covered chair. The view overlooking the town and ocean beyond was hypnotic.

"What's up, Bro?"

Bobby didn't answer immediately, instead, he gazed out at the beautiful scene below. "Amazing we are here, Scott. Truly something else what you and the guys managed to accomplish. Dad would have been really proud of you."

Scott had heard as much from him before, and honestly, it made him a little uncomfortable to hear his brother's praises. After a lifetime of picking, fighting and pointy barbs, to know their relationship had matured to this point was a bit sad.

"So, you're not still pissed about the cottage burning down?" Scott said.

Bobby smiled and shook his head. "We've been over that, it wasn't you, and you saved my little girl that day. I have no complaints."

The thugs that had taken over the old family cottage and eventually burned it down were trying to get to Scott and wanted to use Kaylie to draw him out. Bobby's daughter had outsmarted them by hiding in the swamp until help arrived. Losing the cottage had been hard on Scott though. Rebuilding their dad's old fishing cabin into the craftsman style cottage had been a labor of love, and it had been the perfect escape for him after his marriage failed.

"Listen, Scott, thinking of going out with Todd fishing tomorrow. Kaylie's friend, Diana, is going to keep an eye on Jacob for me. Mrs. Mahalia asked if she could have some real seafood, she's never tried it, if you can believe that. You want to join us?"

Scott smiled at the bit of almost normal in the conversation. "Sorry, I can't, trying to pull something together before Gia comes back. How are Mahalia's people doing, they get settled in ok?"

"Oh yeah, they went right to work finding places to help out. She is still healing up. Still hurting for the boys, of course. They are all so thankful. So am I, that was a nice thing you did. Didn't know it was going to lead to all this though."

Scott gave a small nod, "The Simpsons are good people, I'm glad we helped them. I wish we had enough firepower to go after those camps directly. Maybe Tremaine was taken there if he survived. The camps are too well defended to go after, we have to leave that for the military. Garret and his team are up near there with Sky and Jack scoping things out now. We probably should have known the bastards would go after the farms, too."

"Yeah, 'bout that. Been in the radio room most of the night. Sentinel was transmitting some files."

Sentinel was a somewhat mysterious source of high-value information on what was dubbed 'The Patriot Network'. The 'network' was made up of mostly amateur HAM radio operators across America. Most of them broadcast covertly as the signals could be tracked, and fears were that the government security forces were eliminating these as quickly as they were discovered. The man calling himself Sentinel seemed immune to this as his broadcasts were frequent and specific. The intel he passed on could only come from sources in the military. The general consensus was he was either on a rebel military base or under the protection of one of the rogue base commanders. No one was exactly sure of his location other than somewhere in the Southeast. Bartos felt like it was in Florida, possibly Georgia, but the man never indicated.

"So, what did our friend have to say?"

"Nothing, he just sent the file."

Scott was still not sure how you could send data files over radio signals but guessed it wasn't that different than the satellite uplink he and Tahir occasionally used to connect to the few internet servers still operating. His brother handed him a tablet computer with an official looking document open.

"Should I read, or do you want to give me the short version?"

"Both," Bobby said. "You need to read it through as there are a lot of specifics in there. Some more troubling than others. The gist of it is that what's left of the Army is now in open combat with the president's National Security Force. The Army is attacking lots of those internment camps to free the citizens being held. Also, they have been going after C&C installations to get food and fuel."

Scott knew C&C meant Command and Control Infrastructure. "So, we are a country at war?" he asked his big brother.

"Seems that way, but the real bitch is they believe the president may be planning or possibly already has used the infected and the virus as a bio-weapon against them." Jacob eased up between them and sat on Bobby's lap giving Scott a small smile.

Scott watched the boy; even having seen so much, he was still such an innocent. How to keep something of the world for him to grow up in.

Some tiny bit of sanity amidst the growing insanity. "Our president is reverting to terrorist tactics to hold on to power? Jesus, what's next?"

"That's about the gist of it. She is also leaving the camps with no food, and the fuel they are finding has already gone bad. It's some shit. With no media or, hell, any kind of oversight, this woman is just doing whatever she wants. Trampling all over the Constitution and all Americans. They even believe she is starting to hire outside mercenaries, possibly even foreign soldiers to shore up the National Security Force. Foreign security forces holding our citizens in prison camps. Attacking our armed forces on American soil."

Scott shook his head, he had never been one who cared for politics, and now it was almost all they discussed. Politics, the pandemic or the blackout, and they were all connected. "Catalyst."

"Huh?" Bobby said confused.

"It's all about Catalyst." Scott offered. His brother nodded for him to continue. "We often speak of a catalyst as a person that causes a significant event. Tahir reminded me that in chemistry, catalyst is a substance that causes or accelerates a reaction without itself being affected. Both of these fits what is described in the Catalyst documents. It is not the government that is driving this, that has already mostly failed, it was… very much affected by the events. I now believe this group that Tahir has spoken of is the real issue."

Bobby shook his head, "You are still buying into the conspiracy crap, Scott? Some cabal that rules the world? The Rothchild's, or whoever it is this week. Shit, man, we have real tangible threats all around us. We don't need the boogeyman."

"Bobby, you are my big brother, but don't be dense. I'm a lot of things, but you know I am not paranoid. The point is, Tahir is more informed than nearly anyone – he says there is something to this….well, I believe him."

Bobby shrugged, looked at what Scott had been working on and frowned. "So, you are serious about leaving? Starting the engine and just cruising off into the sunset?"

Scott examined his brother; the man was a shadow of who he'd been before the collapse. "Man, you always fought my battles. You remember that kid back in middle school? The one with the port wine stain over half his face that kept punching me and stealing my lunch money?"

His older brother grinned dredging up the memory. "What was that rat's name? Tony something. Oh, yeah, Tony the Rat, wasn't it? Stinking little shit. Man, he was an evil prick."

Scott nodded, "Anthony Ratuzzi, and yeah, he was a total shit, and you broke his nose."

"He was going to hurt you bad one day, I just wanted it to stop. You're my kid brother, nobody gets to fuck with you but me."

"Bobby, the kid was in foster care, he had nothing. Had that messed up face and then a broken nose to go with it. Yeah, he ate a lunch a few times off of me, but big deal. It was more your pride than any real threat that drove that final fight." Scott saw the anger building in his brother. "Listen, you have to know when to walk away. When staying and fighting doesn't equal winning even if you do survive."

Scott's face took on a pensive expression. "Yes, Bobby, we are leaving. The AG will depart from America in order to save us all. Will you help me do that?"

Bobby hung his head, the weariness of the last few years. The things he had seen, things he had done, people he had lost…they all went through his head. He looked at the ink stain tattoo on the back of his hand, at what he had become just to survive. "I like it here, Scott. I enjoy the people and the work. I like being able to see my little girl and now, Jacob, grow up here." At the mention of his kids, the tears came. He gently rubbed a hand through the boy's hair.

He took a long time to continue,, and his little brother didn't press. "If we have to leave to ensure they get to live, then yes, I'll do it. I'll help."

Scott walked over and hugged his brother. "Damn, you are ugly when you cry—stop that shit or we'll leave you behind."

CHAPTER SEVENTEEN

"Please, Scott, stop!"

He reached for her, desperate to calm her now. Her sobs were pitiful and bordering on manic. "I'm sorry, so sorry, Gia."

She was inconsolable, he had inadvertently laid a mental trap and then sprung it on her. What had seemed like such a perfect night was crumbling away. The cake sat untouched, Angel had scrounged ingredients from who knows where to make it. The simple fact that Scott had even remembered her birthday should have surprised her. Just knowing the actual date in the absence of calendars was perhaps even more impressive. While today wasn't officially the day, it was only a couple of days early, and he knew they wouldn't be together on her actual birthday.

He'd worked with DJ to make sure she was caught up on work and would be traveling back to the AG for a long weekend. Angel had gotten the small cake ready, and Scott had prepared one of her favorite dishes, roasted chicken and asparagus in beurre blanc sauce. He'd opened his last bottle of wine and added a nearly white linen tablecloth to the table. The candlelight flickered off the woman's grimace.

How was I to know that Gia's daughter's birthday had been two days before hers?

He had avoided opening the door to those memories so far, fearing what they might unleash. Now they were out there, and it wasn't pretty. The woman he loved had gone through the range of emotions, from anguish to guilt to something he could not begin to interpret. He reached for her, and she stiffened and pulled away. The food sat untouched as did the open bottle of wine he had been holding onto for nearly two years.

How was he so bad at this? Memories of his first wife and how horribly that relationship had been bungled arced through him like a lightning bolt. He thought he was planning the perfect birthday, and yet, all he had done was torture her with bitter memories. He felt the circular band of metal in his pocket. *Shit,* it was definitely not the right time, he knew that.

The fire in her eyes dimmed slightly, and she leaned her tear-stained face in and kissed him. "You are such a good man, Scott. I am sorry, I know you…" Her words were almost lost in a choking sob. "I'm sorry, you deserve better than this."

"It's ok, honey, I should have thought to ask." He wasn't sure what to say or ask. Leaning back, he looked at the sunset streaking orange and red over the deck of the cruise ship. The flickering candles, less for romance and more for illumination, had been one more detail for the perfect night that wasn't to be. The sunset and candlelight gave Gia's red hair an almost unearthly glow. He watched her—taking in her beauty even in sadness. "Do you remember when you took me out for my birthday…back in college?"

She dabbed at her eyes and gave the briefest of laughs. "Oh, my God, that was awful—we drank that piss awful wine, and you talked me into singing karaoke. What on earth made us think that cheap wings and even cheaper wine were a good combo?"

He laughed at the shared memory. "We were broke. We were unpaid lab interns back then. We both got a stipend from the university, but that was laughably small. Besides, the wings were always good at that place. What was the name of it, over on College Street? He tapped on the table trying to remember and was glad the spell of misery seemed to be moving past.

"Gus's Bar, and the wings were awful, especially when I tossed 'em back up on stage in the middle of that song."

They both laughed, and he pulled her close and held her. She no longer seemed as upset, but the coldness of her lost child was still there like a shadowy wraith. Scott was unsure if she had fully dealt with the loss of her daughter and husband in that helicopter crash. He'd feared bumping into their ghosts at every turn. He clearly knew and accepted that some parts of Gia were off limits to him, some memories apparently too much for her to share.

The night was a disaster, but still, she was here. He considered briefly asking about Tahir's ideas but hated to dredge up work talk, no matter how important it was. He leaned down and kissed her. All of that other stuff would wait until later.

CHAPTER EIGHTEEN

The morning broke clear and bright, the seagulls were already diving for morsels in the blue-green surf. *So much has not changed*, he thought, *but…so much has.* He had moved down here to the Gulf Coast of Mississippi to escape. To escape a bad marriage, to escape a city that wasn't home; now it had really become an escape in the truest sense of the word. The issues of the previous night were fading. It was a new day, and he was determined for it to be better.

"What's the matter, Scott?

He reached up and gently touched the hand now resting on his shoulder.

"Nothing, G, just thinking about the past."

"You mean the time before me?"

He laughed, "No, silly, nothing existed before you."

She nodded approvingly. She had returned to the coast the day before after almost a week at another lab. Scott wasn't sure if it was a Navy facility or one of the remaining Catalyst labs. All he knew was she was wearing herself out searching for a treatment for the pandemic. Her actual birthday was tomorrow, and she'd already let him know she would be working.

He sighed, "No, just thinking about how much luckier we are here than most parts of the world, and what happens if we have to leave? And what becomes of our country?

I'm not good as this, Gia, not meant to be a leader."

"Sweetie, that is what makes you a good leader. You want action, you want to do, not just talk or delegate, but mostly because you see the bigger picture."

She took a long sip of coffee and moved over to the rail of the ship, leaning against it for support. "I know you went with the team to get those new people."

Oh, shit, he thought. She went on, "That was reckless and…well, you already know what I'm going to say. You did it anyway. Scott, you are the leader this community needs, hell, you're probably the leader this country needs." She looked down. "Just never forget I need you, too."

He nodded, slightly chastised, but also amazed at this woman before him. He felt the ring in his pocket again, but the moment passed, and she was once again all business.

"I talked to Tahir and DJ. Went over his…" she paused, searching for the right word. "His hypothesis. You are right about him. He does have a brilliant mind, but…"

"But he is completely crazy on this one?" Scott asked hopefully.

A frown briefly crossed her face, "That's just it, Scott. I think he's on the right track. It fits in with way too much of what my team and the other labs have uncovered. We keep trying to pin down the virus, and yet, it always has moved on, changed, evolved….mutated."

"Gia, how does this alter anything, your approach will still be the same, right?"

She shook her head, "If he is right, and I really do believe he is – we will never develop a truly effective treatment for that A-side virus. It's a lost cause. We must go after the Archaea. I have one lab that works exclusively on that. I may need to go there to see what progress they've made."

She let out a sigh that seemed filled with regret. "We don't really understand the Archaea domain yet. Much of it is still very alien to us. The one thing we do now know is that it uses viruses to carry out much of its dirty work. Adapting and modifying life for extreme conditions."

"Yeah, that's what Tahir said. So, the virus is more like a tool for the Archaea. Just another way of getting the genetic coding into a host body."

She nodded and watched as one of the morning seabirds circled overhead. "That is why the mashup is so crude from a design standpoint but also so effective as a killing machine. If this had been something natural, it wouldn't be killing off so many of the hosts."

"If it had been natural, it would have also taken hundreds of thousands of years to develop…right?"

"Yes, the changes would have likely been more gradual. I like Tahir's thoughts that perhaps the genetic payload was not set, and that's why it is firing everything, but I am not so sure he is correct on that."

"Gia, are you going to be able to stop this thing?"

"I have to, Scott."

She said the words with such determination that he believed her, but he also detected something else in her voice. *Hopelessness*, he thought. He reached for her hand. He wanted to give her hope, he wanted her to know better days awaited them both.

She pulled back slightly from his touch, "Scott, you need to get this ship ready to move. Even if we are right, no way I see us having a treatment before the pandemic gets too close. I'll talk to Garret as well, we'll need to move the Navy lab farther offshore."

Scott nodded glumly, "Where can we go, we have to have food and fuel. Can't get that out on the open sea. Where can we find safe harbor?"

"Anywhere but here, anywhere but America, at least until this thing dies out. Right now, just buy me some time, so I can keep working somewhere safe. We are already making plans to move the three other labs off shore. Of those I am the most remote, the safest for now— so no immediate problem, but eventually, even the Bataan will be too close."

"Probably best, if the disease doesn't get us, I am afraid our new president might."

Gia sat the cup down on the rail and looked at him quizzically.

"Sorry, it's nothing you need to worry about, just something Bobby mentioned." He had not told her about Jack's reports of NSF at the farms nor any of the Simpsons' details on the brutality. He really didn't want her thinking about the country's other problems. He stalled, then relented, "Just seems like we may be in the early stages of another civil war. The president apparently has her agenda, and the former military, nor the American people, seem to be part of it."

"What specifically did Bobby hear and from whom?"

"Just one of our contacts on the Patriot Network. You know, the amateur radio operators that pass along messages?"

Her look of concern was obvious. He continued, "Yeah, everything they have said has been accurate. I think this one, Sentinel, has a direct link into some of the military bases' chain of command."

Gia looked like she wanted to ask more, but she let it go and slipped her arm inside of his pulling him close. "We're going to be ok, Scott."

He was unsure if it was a statement or a question.

A bald head popped in the cabin door, then a much smaller head just below it. Bartos called, "Hey, Doc, can I borrow him for a few?"

She smiled, "Morning, Bartos, sure…he has served his purpose to me – he is dismissed."

Bartos smacked him on the shoulder with a grin, "You dog, you."

~

"I thought I saw Jacob with you."

"He is…somewhere. You know how he likes to disappear. I think he could teach the Ghost a few tricks."

Scott nodded, "I don't think he likes me, seems to always vanish when I'm around. Bobby said he gets that way sometimes. Anyway, what's up?"

"Making some progress on our special project, and me and the Navy guys have worked out a few new ways to make fuel."

"No shit, really?"

They watched as Solo padded around a corner followed closely by Jacob. The boy kept pulling at the fierce dog's tail, then running away as the dog playfully snapped his jaws at him. The psychopathic canine killer acted like a goofy puppy around the boy. Scott smiled at the scene; when those two were together was the happiest either ever seemed. Bobby obviously didn't know the dog's well-earned reputation, if so, he would have never let Jacob near him.

"Yeah, I'd like for you to come out and check it out when you can. Just running the numbers, and I have a problem. We are way short of one of the main things we need."

CHAPTER NINETEEN

Bartos' plan for making fuel was two-fold. The first was making fuel from the many tanks of waste motor oil the county had. Every garage, fast-lube shop, and he knew many of the gas stations, had underground storage tanks for customers' old motor oil. The process to convert this to diesel was straightforward. Heat it up, pump it through a series of filters and condensers and at the end, in theory, you had a workable diesel fuel.

The second solution was a bit more complex. That was to make diesel from crude oil. This was the raw unprocessed petroleum. They had one tanker car full of crude from an old abandoned train they had found after the CME blast. If the process to refine it could be found, additional sources of crude were located all around the Gulf Coast.

As Tahir and the Navy guys had said: to distill diesel from crude, you had to go through a lot more steps. Extreme heat and pressure were needed to separate, or 'crack,' the molecular bonds between different hydrocarbons. Chemicals like bauxite were added to speed this along. Then, the temperature had to be closely monitored to extract diesel and not gasoline which is what happened if it got too hot, or kerosene if it was too low. To be honest, you got some of these byproducts anyway. It was a natural part of the process, but Bartos' total focus was to get fuel for the big ship.

The Navy was eager to help also, as most of their ships used diesel as well. Something in increasingly short supply for them. Of course, they also wanted him to make JP1 – jet fuel, or avgas, but that wasn't possible with Bartos' homebrew set-up.

"That thing is butt-ugly, Cajun."

"Screw you, Scott," the man said without pause. "What it lacks in aesthetics it makes up for in performance."

"Where in the hell did you learn a word like that?"

Bartos gave one of his evil grins, "What, 'performance'? Your girlfriend taught it to me."

The men were in a building in what was formerly Harris Springs' mostly failed excuse of an industrial park, one of the few non-tourist industries in the area before the collapse of parts manufacturing for the ship-builders in Pascagoula. "This is the main pressure vessel, Scott. Damn lucky to have found one this strong. See, the oil must be heated to very high temps, over 1000 degrees. That's why we need the electricity from the dam, and why we're so far from town. It really is a lot like cooking off mash to make alcohol…just a, well…a shit-load more dangerous."

"How much diesel fuel do you think you can make?"

"Well," he said, scratching his head, "this one is just the waste oil setup. I'm going to start with the few drums we already had recovered. Scoots tells me there're probably 30,000 gallons of waste oil in nearby tanks. We'll lose a lot of that during the process, but I'm guessing 10,000 gallons. From there, we can venture out farther to collect more, if it all works, that is."

"How much do the tanks on the Goddess hold?"

"A shit-load, nearly 4000 tons of fuel, total."

"Damn, that seems like a lot, Bartos."

The little bald man filed away at one of the welded metal joints. "Well, it is…and it isn't. It'll take us a long time to make that much, but the beast drinks it like water. She gets lousy mileage, man—only about fifty feet to the gallon if I read the charts correctly. Even so, with full tanks, that should be enough for nearly two weeks at sea."

Scott went through the math in his head. "That's over ten times the amount you can make with the used waste oil on hand."

"I know, I know, Scott, but what are our other options? The good thing is the AG can run on 'bunker' fuel. I checked that out, it's still diesel, but doesn't have to be super clean or overly refined. I'm confident we can make that. And she still has some in her tanks. It also appears to be more stable than diesel, but still, we need more. I'm letting the Navy guys take lead on refining the crude. They mentioned possibly tapping into the SOR tanks over in Louisiana. Tahir is working with their engineers to try and get everything we'll need to do that."

"What the hell is the SOR?"

Bartos laughed, "Damn, college-boy, don't you know nothing? The Strategic Oil Reserves, the nation's emergency supply of crude oil."

Scott nodded, that did ring a bell. "Don't you mean the president's?"

"Minor difference," the man said as he inspected the joint. "Navy thinks they can take it, more power to them. It's definitely an emergency situation, no idea what else they would be saving it for."

"Fuck, fuck… Uh, uh, no. Forget it, man, I ain't going near that shit." DeVonte stepped off the yellow tractor leaving it idling. Two of the Navy divers waved for him to finish pulling up the basket of debris. A pale blue arm hung from the jumble of limbs, roots and old car tires. A human arm, maybe a child's—or a girl's.

Lt. Garret walked over to the basket. "Damn, that's like the third one."

Todd leaned in and moved some of the other material away from the corpse. DeVonte was asking if it was anyone they knew.

"No." He let the arm drop. A dark outline of a cross tattoo was on the backside of one hand. "She was one of them." They all knew who he meant, one of the Messengers.

"I don't care, I am not hauling off no more dead bodies!" DeVonte started walking down the roadway to the far side of the dam.

"Fine," Todd said as he climbed up on the tractor.

The debris pile at the base of the dam had turned out to be much larger than anticipated. In addition to the trees and bodies, was all manner of accumulated trash, including two cars. How cars got in the lake and washed this far down was almost beyond belief. The Navy divers were relying on tethered air lines, so they could stay down longer, but it was brutal work. The operation had been going for almost two weeks, but they were beginning to see an end. Most of the intake grille was cleared already. Now, they were just removing nearby debris to form an open radius for the water intake. They didn't need it to stay clear forever, just the next six months or so.

Todd was reluctantly getting the ship back on track. He wasn't convinced it would ever be seaworthy, but everyone was pitching in. The pressure on everyone seemed to be ratcheting up. They all knew the pandemic was getting closer, and Dr. Colton still had no treatment. The AG was still dead in the water, and *oh, yea*h, the NSF was all over the state causing problems. Getting electricity generated would give them some significant advantages, but he knew it would also make Harris Springs an even bigger target.

CHAPTER TWENTY

MOUNT WEATHER, VIRGINIA

President Madelyn Chambers held the satellite phone slightly away from her ear as she listened. This was partially to avoid mussing her hair on that side but mainly to add a fraction more distance between her and the person speaking.

"Yes, ma'am."

That had been the extent of her responses to the irate woman. Ms. Levy was not happy with her pick for the top office.

"Madelyn, dear, let's get one thing perfectly clear. You may have presidential authority, but you do not have mine."

"I'm sorry, the Army, they…" she was cut off again mid-sentence.

The sound of Ms. Levy's frustration was ringing in her ears like a death bell. "Madam President, you are making us look bad when the whole world is watching. We are not going to start a war on American soil. Have I made myself clear?"

"Yes ma'am." She hated herself for sounding weak, but shit, she was weak. No one stood up to Ms. Levy or any sitting member of the Council.

"The point of having power, sweetie, is to never use it. You simply threaten to use it. Now tell me, did you disperse the agent at the aid camps?"

The silence was answer enough. "You fucking bitch! Did you release SA1297 on Americans? Answer me now, or you will not survive the morning."

The president stammered when she answered, she knew the threat was real. "The virus, it's already here. It seemed to be the only deterrent that would stop them."

Them…the US Army, Marines, National Guard…who knew what they were now? The military had refused to follow the president's orders en masse. They didn't accept the legitimacy of her rise to power after the deaths of all those in front of her in the line of succession. They had refused to perform law enforcement duties domestically unless Congress ordered them to. What Congress? Barely half the House and less than a third of the Senate was currently filled. Chambers' hand was shaking noticeably now as she waited for the response from the other end.

The icy silence stretched and stretched as Madelyn Chambers, the first female President of the US awaited word on her fate. The calm voice of Ms. Levy cut through the quiet like a scalpel. "I am very disappointed in you, Madelyn. Our goal is to save the republic, not watch it burn. I am sending someone over to see you. Someone who can help…guide you in your decision making from here on."

~

Ms. Levy sat in the quiet contemplating her next move. Sitting in the small room of the immense underground complex was increasingly causing her to feel claustrophobic. She had plans for everything. The Council spent years, generations even, working out various contingencies. Those that would help the republic and those plans that brought…

other benefits. The Catalyst plans had been in constant refinement for years. The basic outline had been drawn up in the mid-50s.

The concept was simple, use a significant natural disaster to reduce government and lower class elements of society to more manageable levels. Every civilization faced similar obstacles throughout history. Political systems became corrupted. Candidates focused too much attention and money on getting re-elected instead of leading or making decisions that benefited everyone. The soft underbelly of the state, the burgeoning masses on the public handout got more and more and the working class and the wealthy paid the ever-increasing bills. Revolution comes to every society eventually.

At its heart, she found Catalyst to be a humanitarian mission. A total reset on the country. She had not been the architect for the plans, but her father and his father had been. Most of her life she had resisted the pull of the Council, the chair that held her secret family name. Like the Council, the name, too, had changed over the years from Levi to Levy, neither was what was on her birth certificate. When her father eventually stepped down, she had no choice but to assume his role. The other sitting members of the Council were less important but still useful: Mr. Church, Ms. Wolfe, Mr. Adams and the rest. Seven members in total, representing six families and one at-large chair.

A half-filled glass of water and several pills sat on a silver tray in front of her. She was unsure if she would live long enough to see this plan through. The president's blundering was not helping, but the spread of SA1297 was out of her control now. While much of its creation had been her idea, it was simply one of many pet projects she had overseen. Its release overseas had not been noteworthy to her, but then reports that the antiviral was ineffective began to surface. Now, it seemed this virus might rule the world instead of the Council.

She called to her attendant who was stationed just outside the door, "Has he arrived yet?"

"Yes, ma'am, he is on his way."

"Good...very good."

~

"And you are?"

He looked at the outstretched hand before deciding to accept the hand-shake. "I'm the man they call when they need shit done."

Releasing the grip with a sudden iciness, the man took an involuntary half step back. "And do you have a name?"

The pronounced Downeast Maine accent of the wiry man was annoy-ing, "We all have names, probably best you just call me Grey."

"I see. So, um…Grey, you've been out there? What's it like?"

He let the question trickle through his memories. This man hidden away in this camp completely isolated from the real world didn't actu-ally want to know what was going on out there, he just wanted to know he was safe. It never ceased to amaze him how much people were willing to give up for safety. He decided to give him the truth, or at least a portion of it.

"It's bad…really bad. No food anywhere, not many people left. Cities are abandoned. Hardly any fuel, much less anything else of use. The world's gone, friend."

"Sounds like a real Mad Max kind of existence doesn't it?" The man had a nervous grin on his face that was completely at odds with the reality.

The man going by Grey cocked his head slightly, the way a cat might as he watched a mouse. The wiry man had said his name earlier, *What was it again?* "Look, uh…David, is it? It's not a movie and certainly not Mad Max out there. Think more like colonial America. It's a tough life, but people are hanging on. It's just different now."

The man looked puzzled. "So, what about the monsters?"

"What fucking monsters?" his voice rising above what he had intended.

David seemed to retreat at the response and looked like he wanted to hide back in his shell. "We, um…" he stammered. "We just hear things. Stories, you know."

A tap on his shoulder rescued him from the awkward little man. The large black man gave a quick head nod, "This way."

"Do we have monsters? Why do these people even know about the outbreak overseas?"

The black man shrugged his shoulders and kept walking down the dimly lit corridor. "It's here now. People talk, and most of these are whip smart little assholes. Best of the best, you know. Give 'em a few clues and they figure shit out. That guy that was talking to you ran a Fortune 100 tech company before 'The Day.' Had his picture on magazines and gave talks to thousands walking around on stage in his black t-shirt and sandals."

"That guy?" he said looking back to see if he was still standing where he had left him.

"Yep. Pretty standard fare here, though. Did you ever watch the news, get on the internet, anything besides work, Archangel?"

"I was in lockup and…what was the point? I knew you assholes would fuck it up eventually."

"You have a point there," the other man said.

"Tell me, Vincent, why am I here? Why are you based here, with these people?"

Vincent stopped walking and turned to face him. "You know the answer to that. We serve the republic. Right now, this is the republic, or all of it that matters."

"It doesn't bother you? What they are doing here?"

They both resumed walking turning a corner, "Archangel, I do what I am told, I follow orders. That's my fucking job, yours, too. Talking like that is what got you thrown in the brig." They passed two sentries and came to a very substantial looking, nondescript gray door.

"No…shooting the president's dog instead of the president himself is why I was locked up."

Vincent just looked at him. "You disobeyed a direct order just because you disagreed with it. This is your second chance, man…don't fuck it up. I went out on a limb for you." He knocked twice before pushing it open. "Ms. Levy, Archangel-9 is here."

CHAPTER TWENTY-ONE

HARRIS SPRINGS, MISSISSIPPI

Gia Colton was exhausted and frustrated. She pulled her long, red hair back into a ponytail and went through the printouts again. She almost hadn't come back to the AG tonight, she had too much work to do, but Scott was waiting for her. She didn't want to disappoint him, not again. She smiled to herself, he really was such a good man. He almost took away the pain and hurt that was her constant companion—almost.

Tahir had been right about the virus. The new test results proved it conclusively. The updated treatments ignored the virus and went after the gene mutations directly. By using the new treatment protocols, they had been able to somewhat keep the lethality of the viral agent, the "A" side, in check, at least in the testing labs. They were beginning to make real progress. One thing Tahir had not been right on was the Archean not having a genetic payload. Of that, she was quite confident it did. Her lab was doing the sequencing on its genetic signature now. They were getting close, she could almost see an end to this mess.

It couldn't come soon enough; her body was wearing out. The constant work, travel and stress had to stop. She knew she couldn't keep it up;

she looked at her reflection in the bathroom mirror. *Can I save them, save humanity?* She was a confident person, but right now she didn't even think she could save herself. This cabin aboard the AG was her refuge, her escape from reality. How much longer would it be safe harbor? The stack of files by the chair beckoned her to dive back into her work. She made a feeble attempt, but her energy had drained.

Scott walked into their cabin and saw Gia sleeping in the overstuffed chair. He closed a folder she loosely held and set it to the side, atop a stack of other papers and folders. He'd been told she was back aboard, but this was the first chance he had to come see her. She was the most beautiful woman in the world to him, and…she loved him. He was still smarting over the incident on her birthday. She had forgiven him but causing her pain had also hurt him to the core. He knew she was not that fragile, the woman had always possessed a drive that few could match. He bent over and kissed her forehead.

Her eyelids fluttered, then opened. "Hey, you."

"Hi, love," he responded with a kiss.

"Sorry I missed you getting back." She had been gone for days, and he had missed her terribly, but he knew she had to concentrate on her work.

"I know, we made a lot of progress, though. I'm heading out in the morning to Lab 4. I think we are ready to expand some of our trials."

"Really? That's great." He hugged her as she stood.

"It was Tahir, honey, he gave us the jump start we needed." She reached into her bag and pulled out a vial and syringe.

"What is that, more of your vitamin cocktail?" She had been giving him booster shots for weeks along with some antivirals.

"No, this is our latest, it won't prevent the Chimera, but it will keep it from killing you if you get it." She injected it into his tan bicep.

She sat back down suddenly and held her stomach.

"You okay, G? What's wrong?" She was pale. Beads of sweat appeared on her smooth skin.

"I'm, I'm…I'll be alright, I just need some air."

Scott panicked as he slid the balcony doors wide and the sea breeze swept in. She suddenly rushed to the railing and began vomiting. He held her up and rubbed her back as she kept pulling up content to spew out into the night air. His mind raced at the possibilities. She worked with deadly pathogens, but also bad food was a real issue for everyone now. With resources so scarce and no refrigeration, foodborne illness had become a real problem. Her sickness finally eased up, and he ran into the room to get a bottle of water and a cloth.

The sickness seemed to pass as quickly as it had arrived. She seemed surprised and embarrassed. "Sorry about that."

"Are you ok, did anything happen at the lab?"

"I'm fine, Scott. It's nothing."

He busied himself picking up the vial and syringe. The vial had part of a hand-written label on it. "297AV. one dose 15 cc."

"How many doses of this stuff do we need to be immune, and is this really almost the 300th version you've tried?"

"She was wiping her face with the rag. She answered with a weary laugh, "Yeah, at least that many, and none of them will make you immune. Multiple doses are recommended, but one should likely do the job. The treatment is designed to kickstart your body's own immune system into recognizing the pathogen."

He sat on the floor beside her and began flipping through her folders; the notes and diagrams meaning nothing to him. "Are you ready to let everyone know? Does this mean we don't have to leave?" He looked at more of the papers dislodging and falling free from the folders. He examined one, then another, completely lost in the science. Even the few terms he understood seemed foreign: telomeres, chromatids, eukaryotes and thermohaline. The notes were neat and even in Gia's precise handwriting. Some of it made sense to him, some of it raised questions.

"Gia, isn't thermohaline something to do with the climate?"

She looked at the files with a brief look of…something…but shrugged nonchalantly. "We've had to look at a lot of things. Lab-4, in particular, has had pretty expansive research going on."

He began reading the file in earnest now, fascinated by science he could actually understand.

She grew impatient with him to stop and look up at her. She finally placed a hand on top of his and forced the papers to the floor. She left it there until his eyes met hers. Taking his hand, she placed it on her stomach. And just like that…everything changed.

"Scott, I'm pregnant."

～

He woke up to find her lying beside him, watching him, grinning. "What?" he asked.

"Nothing, everything."

They had talked long into the night. Was this the smart thing to do? Bringing a child into a world full of chaos and madness seemed so wrong. An earlier conversation with Roosevelt had played back in his head, *Real survival meant folks fallin' in love and makin' babies again.*

There was a sound, then another. The dim morning light in the ship's cabin was suddenly joined by a flickering glow from the overhead lights, then the blessed sound of air blowing from an AC vent overhead. Gia's face showed an expression that was priceless. "No way!" she exclaimed.

"Yes…way." Cheering could be heard from every part of the ship. "They have been working on it around the clock the last few days. I told them to flip the switch whenever they felt good about it." The overhead light was still flickering slightly but glowing brightly now. This was going to be the start of a very good day. He pulled her close and kissed her. "Gia, please marry me. Not just for the baby, I mean. I've, I've been wanting…"

"Scott."

"Yes?"

"Stop talking."

They made love beneath the glow of a flickering overhead light and the almost cool air flowing across their naked bodies. She lay next to him, their desire somewhat sated. *We are going to be a family*. He reached a hand under the mattress, then offered her the ring he'd been carrying around for weeks. She began to cry, nodding yes as he slipped it on. "I know it's small, but it was all the jewelry store had."

"It's perfect, Scott, just like you. Thank you. Thank you for the ring, thanks even more for this." She rubbed her tummy, and in the light, Scott could now see she was indeed a little plumper than he remembered. She wasn't sure how far along she was, a month, maybe six weeks.

"I love you, Gia Colton."

"Soon to be Gia Montgomery, when are we going to do this?"

"Soon as we can, I've been waiting for you to be my wife for years, so we can't put it off long."

"When I get back we can start making plans. It should be a real party – something special." Gia beamed as she looked at the ring and smiled.

"As long as we are together in the end, I don't care," he said.

CHAPTER TWENTY-TWO

The following day, Gia left early to catch the Navy transport back to Lab 4. Scott had no idea where it was but watched from the top deck as she left. He wanted her to stay, begged her, in fact, but her work came first. They'd agreed not to tell anyone about the pregnancy until she was further along, but soon, everyone would know wedding plans were in the works. The first person he had to tell was his brother. Walking down the ship's corridors, now illuminated by recessed lighting, was an amazing feeling. The few people he passed all had a look of amazement. *How long before electricity will be taken for granted once again?* he wondered.

Bobby's reaction was measured exuberance. He practically exploded with happiness. "Wow, man, that is awesome! Congrats! Did you have to threaten her, offer cash...what?"

"Hush, Big Ugly," Scott answered.

Bobby held up his hands, "Just don't forget Rule #18."

Scott had to think on that one before flipping him the bird. As morning turned to day, everyone on board learned the news. The joy of having electricity just spilled over fueling even more excitement over wedding plans. Angel was the one he most feared telling, although he wasn't sure why. She took the news in stoic silence. He feared he had mistaken something in their friendship, then she burst into a big grin and took him in her arms and danced across the floor. High fives from DeVonte and Bartos, hugs from Kaylie. He would tell Jack by radio when they checked in later, but Todd was sitting at a table when Scott walked over and sat beside him.

"I hear congrats are in order."

"Yes, thanks," Scott said, failing miserably to conceal the huge smile.

"She's a pretty unique woman, Scott, and…she's getting one hell of a guy. The two of you together will be an unstoppable force."

Scott had been expecting a friendly barb from his friend. The show of genuine sentiment surprised him and left him without a response for several seconds. Then he got it, and as happy as he was, his heart ached for the man. He looked at his friend and placed a hand on the man's arm. He could feel the big man was shaking slightly, just barely holding it together. "Thank you, Todd. I'm not sure how to say this, but if I have learned anything since this mess began, it's to let people know how you really feel. You never know if you have another day to say those words. I learned from you, my friend. I watched you love, I watched you mourn, and I watched you struggle to heal. If Gia and I can have a fraction of the happiness that you and Liz had, I'll be one lucky man."

Todd's eyes were tearing up as he nodded.

"So, would you marry us?"

"Huh?" the man said with a start. "Why me, why not Jack or one of the other preachers? I'm not even a captain anymore, that would be you or Angel."

"You will always be our captain. Jack's not here, and he won't do it, I already know that. He refuses to ever step behind a pulpit again. Besides, Gia wants it to be you, and I know you can't refuse her."

The older man had tears streaming down his face in torrents now. "Of course, I will, Brother."

~

Throughout the next several days, people continued to offer congratulations or ask if a date had been picked. The attention Scott got was somewhat unnerving, but he was as happy about it as they were. He tried to recall if getting engaged to Angela, his first wife, had felt like this. It hadn't, he was sure of that. He'd been happy, but more surprised that she had said yes. The entire engagement, he had been afraid she would simply change her mind. Even during the service, he hadn't been sure she would walk through those doors and down the aisle. In time, she had changed her mind, regretted that day, and that hole in his heart that she caused had taken years to mend.

He'd agreed to help Bartos' team this morning make sure the power was off to the old buildings downtown. No need starting fires because an old lamp was plugged in. "I take it no problems with the generators?"

Bartos had been humming the unmistakable theme to "Love Boat" as Scott walked up. "Nope, they are doing fine. Well, the one generator we're using is fine, no need for the other one just yet. Few issues with the substation settings and getting the routing right. Tahir was a big help on that as I was clueless. He says he separated out all the other stations from the local grid. So, no juice headed over to the old industrial park or the hospital. Just to the AG, marina and downtown area."

"That's good, so we could get power to those other places if we wanted?"

"Yep…well, up to a point. None of us are really sure of the amperage we have from that one generator, so we're adjusting water flow to control the power levels. Scoots will be keeping someone out there full time now to adjust flow. Maybe times we just need to shut it down for short periods while bringing other buildings back up or even other substations back online."

"This is amazing, Bartos, you guys did a fantastic job."

The little Cajun smiled, his pride in the work was well earned. "It was your idea, man. You da one that convinced us we could do it."

They checked another building, heard electrical arcing in the back and went to see what it was. A frayed wire from a falling light fixture was making contact with a metal shelving unit. Bartos found the old circuit box and pulled the main lever to disconnect it. "I have a feeling we will be doing this for days."

"It's a good problem to have," Scott added. "So, what are the main buildings getting power?" They had discussed priorities previously, but Scott wasn't sure it had been finalized.

"The shop and the warehouse."

Scott knew that was the old county shop just outside of town and the boat storage warehouse down at the marina. That was where a lot of the vehicles were stored as well as the armory for weaponry and ammo that had been acquired.

"Waterworks in da next day or two, so we can get more fresh water and have some working toilets again. Beyond that, I'm not sure. Scoots and da guys can help do that. I'm going to finish up on da refinery boilers, now that I have power, that should go a lot faster."

The day's hard work briefly took Scott's mind off the fact that Gia was gone and the even more amazing fact that she was going to be his wife. Every few minutes it would occur to him again, and he would find himself grinning like a school kid. Everyone started referring to it as his G-face. "Screw you all to hell," he would say in mock anger.

It was dark when Scott and Bartos walked back to the cruise ship. The cabin lights were shining through many of the windows and portholes. "That's a beautiful sight," Scott said. "Hey, look," he pointed down the coast where several of the abandoned beach houses had lights on.

"Shit," Bartos said. "I'll get some guys down there tomorrow to shut them off. They must be off the same leg of the grid as us."

Scott shook his head no. One of those houses had been the one he and

Kaylie had used up until the hurricane. After that, and her reunion with her dad, they'd never gone back. "Leave 'em on for now."

Bartos shrugged, "Yeah, sure. We got the juice to spare. It does kind of look like old times seeing lights down the coast."

How much difference having light meant was simply amazing. It was a case of man defeating nature, light beating back the darkness. It was a small victory, but in the nearly two years since the blackout, it was a huge triumph for the town. Scott walked through the offices of the ship seeing Kaylie working late in the lighted clinic, Tahir setting up computers in the conference room, and he nearly fell over when he heard the sound of cartoons playing on a flat screen TV in the common area. Angel was there with a group of kids, moms and a few dads. She held up a DVD case as he waved and grinned at her. As desperate as the situation was, a bit of hope had returned to Harris Springs.

DeVonte came out of the communications room just as Scott started through the corridor. "Hey, man, just coming to get you. Skybox is on the radio—looks like it's go time."

Damn, well at least he and the others would get one night's sleep in the air conditioning before jumping into all the fun in Yokena. He knew he should have told Gia what was going on. He also knew she would want him to stay, but it was his friends out there. Those farmers were people he had worked with personally. Despite everything, he knew he had to be a part of whatever went down.

CHAPTER TWENTY-THREE

YOKENA, MISSISSIPPI

The men looked haggard, most had not eaten in days, and adding to the arduous workdays that lasted from dawn until well after dark, most were getting by on only a few hours' sleep. Harsh punishment was dealt out for even the most minor of infractions. From time in a tin covered 'sweat box' to sleep deprivation to good old-fashioned beatings. Sadly, this was not a life in a prison camp…not as such. This was life on the men's own farms. Family land that they had farmed for generations producing some of the best crops, cattle and pork in the country. The Yokena area was the food producer for multiple states, and these men had kept a large portion of the area alive even after the blackout. Now, they were indentured servants, farming the land for the benefit of a bunch of assholes in black uniforms with Security Force armbands. Someone had given them the authority to do all this. Probably someone on the receiving end of where all the crops went. Little of which was winding up on the prisoners' trays.

Jack watched through the night vision goggles and made a sound of disgust as the line of men were lined up next to a communal trench latrine. The farmers were shackled together at the end of the workday like chain gangs of an earlier time. The guards were taunting the men; like normal, they were hoping to provoke some of them into action just to break the monotony. Lt. Garret's voice sounded in his small earbud.

"That is all of them. We count thirty-eight tangos, total."

They had spent weeks covertly learning the shifts, guard rotations, meal schedules and, most importantly, the supply runs. No one left the farming commune to get supplies; instead, the convoys came here. They dropped off what was needed and added whatever crops or meat was ready for pickup. The next run was just a few days away, and they had to be ready. Jack dropped back down into concealment. He knew what would happen next. The farmers would be hosed off and marched off to the barn that was now used as a bunkhouse.

These farmers weren't random strangers. They were friends, allies and trading partners of the AG community. Seeing the abuse they were going through was more than he could deal with. Since the first day he had seen what was going on, he had been ready to take action. Garret and his men showed up a few days later and convinced him of the wisdom in waiting. He hated it but did understand the logic. Now, though, the time to finally free the captives and exact revenge was fast approaching.

"Jack, make the call," Garret said quietly.

Jack silently scrambled down the bank eager to get the rest of the men heading up from the coast. The team here with the younger Garret was tough but small, eight men in total, including him and Skybox, who was off at another location. While they felt confident they could easily take out the relatively small security force guarding the farms, they were not confident in doing it with no civilian casualties. They would wait for the back-up to arrive. The other real need for Scott, Todd and the others from the AG was to lay a trap for the incoming supply mission. If they could capture a convoy of supplies, that would go a long way toward prepping the AG to launch.

He radioed it into Bobby who would pass it along to the others. A rendezvous point had been established well outside the NSF patrols. If all went to plan, the assault would launch in two days, the resupply mission would be here end of the week, so that gave them almost three days to evac the farmers, hopefully, find their families and prep for the ambush. The sudden sound of gunfire let him know, *it will not be going to plan.*

~

As the only non-soldier in the group, Jack stayed off the tactical channel. The chatter coming over the earbud was professional but anxious. Someone had fired; no one seemed sure of which side, but everyone was given the green-light to engage. The angry sound of suppressed automatic weapons cut through the still night, and rounds lit up the darkness of the compound.

Garret didn't lead the SEALs, they had their own line of command, and each moved like a precision machine. "Rollins, bird's up now, feed IR and NV to all goggles." Garret handed Jack his pair of the special optics as he slid back in close.

"We have a target-rich environment, gentleman. Open it up np boys, move, shoot, communicate." the deep Texas accent identified the speaker as the SEAL team commander. From off to the right, an ear-splitting sound erupted as a fixed mount .50 caliber machine gun began unleashing hell on the scene below. The BRRTTTTT came in waves and seemed to suck all other sound away as it fired.

Garret was firing, but Jack couldn't see at whom. The original plan had been for him to work his way down to the bunkhouse and attempt release and then protect the farmers. He grabbed his gear bag and headed down. The NSF troops had mostly been gathered around the large house they used for a mess hall and offices. That was now under a barrage of weapons fire. The barn where Jack was heading had only two guards visible, both taking shelter behind large farm equipment.

A bullet hit the tree to Jack's right causing him to duck down and simultaneously realize two things. One: he'd removed his armored tactical vest when he'd called the AG, and two: his rifle was still slung on his back. *I make a lousy soldier*, he thought.

Through the greenish night vision displaying on the goggles, he saw an invisible light laser briefly land on one of the guards. A splash of darkness suddenly painted the man's face, and he collapsed. The second guard retreated inside the bunkhouse. Jack rose and ran toward the barn. He knew there was another entryway on the far side, so he moved in that direction. Through the earbud, he heard Rollins.

"Hey, Preach, might wanna turn your IR strobe on so we can keep all the players straight."

Shit, shit, shit, shit, he thought as he fumbled for the small emitter on the helmet he was wearing. He had just run right through a battle zone without letting his team know it was him. They had been over this countless times, but in the here and now with adrenaline pumping, he'd forgotten it completely.

He gave a small wave toward the location of the SEAL sniper who was charged with overwatch on this part of the mission. He assumed that was who took out the first guard, but nothing else about the mission was sticking to the script this night. The famous quote about all plans failing once you meet the enemy came to mind...*How true.*

Jack grabbed the door and pulled. *Nothing.* He tried again with the same result. It was secured well, that had been expected, too, they were keeping prisoners inside. He propped the M16 against the wall and lowered his gear bag removing a heavy-duty tactical prybar. The metal tool had pronged forks at one end with a stub sticking out to use for leverage. The opposite end was a modified ax head. He worked his way to the far side of the door, inserted the tool and began to wedge the door open.

CHAPTER TWENTY-FOUR

"Jack, this is Overwatch, be advised, we have no visual on you."

"Yeah, yeah," he muttered as he strained against the wood. It was bowing out, just a little…bit…more. The door frame came apart in a shower of splinters, and the momentum of the now freed tool carried Jack inside the building. He looked up just in time to see two soldiers. One was raising a stubby rifle to fire at him, the other had something in his hand and was racing toward a line of wooden racks. Jack dove to one side as the soldier began firing rapidly. The idiot obviously had it on full auto, and the weapon clicked empty in a couple of seconds.

Jack stayed in the crouch and rushed the man who had stopped fumbling trying to load another clip and instead, swung the butt of the gun at his head. It knocked his helmet off, but Jack ducked and pulled the man's arm holding the gun toward and then past him in one fluid motion. Despite his appearance, Jack was a martial arts expert and had used the skills to kill and maim in the past. He jabbed a fist into the man's throat then looped the strap that was holding the useless gun around the man's neck as he went down. Jack leaned in and braced his feet to arrest the man's fall. All of the soldier's weight centered on the strap around his neck. There was no sound as Jack released the strap and the dead man slumped to the dirt floor.

The other man was doing something near the wooden racks. Not racks, beds, he now realized. Rows of eyes were silently watching him. Jack briefly thought of stepping back outside to get his gun, but the realization of what the other soldier was doing quickly ended that thought.

Jack had been a troubled kid, went to prison, in fact. That was before he discovered preaching and a childhood friend named Todd Hansen who had shown him a better way. What he saw now reminded him of the very worst of prison. A guard who would end it for everyone rather than lose. He recognized the man in the faint light. He was the hard-ass that was by far the most abusive of the black-clad troops. "Hey, you stupid fuck," Jack yelled to get his attention. The man looked up from the padlock. Fear and rage painted the man with madness. Jack's insight into the brutality reached a new low at realizing the man's intentions. The locked cage the man hovered over covered an electrical power switch. Jack's eyes quickly followed the crude wiring which ran to long metal poles running down the entire length of the bunk racks. Each of the farmers was chained to one of the metal poles. After surviving a blackout for two years, they were going to be electrocuted. The universe does have a dark and brutal sense of irony, it would seem.

Jack withdrew the fixed blade Ka-Bar knife from his ankle sheaf and hurtled it at the man. You were never supposed to voluntarily give up a weapon, but he needed to buy time for the real attack. The blade of the knife punched into the man's shoulder and stayed. Jack sprinted faster than a big man should ever be able to do. When he got within ten feet, he launched himself at the guard. Jack pivoted in mid-air and landed both feet against the man's chest.

This should have ended the struggle, but in the dimly lit building, he'd failed to realize the sheer size of the guard. Jack lay on the ground, panting to regain his breath as the other man stood back up and grinned. *Shit.* "You know, dude," Jack said wheezing, "you don't look that big from a distance."

The soldier erupted from the spot enraged. Thankfully for Jack, he was too angry to grab anything as a weapon, including the handgun strapped in his drop holster. He fell on top of Jack pounding away with a huge meaty fist. Jack had just a moment to get his arms up in a protective manner around his head. The fists still felt like sledgehammers; he knew he had to do something fast before one of the man's fists got through.

Jack worked to pull his feet into his body, raising his knees up against the man's lower back. He then moved his left leg over trapping the man's right leg. In jiu-jitsui, working from a mount position like this was preferred. Jack wasn't so sure now. The sheer weight of the man was going to make the next part difficult. Jack ignored the blows and reached up to the man's collar and pulled him down as forcibly as he could while rolling him off and to the side. As the huge man began to roll, he drove an elbow into the side of his head, and he felt something give in the man's skull.

What felt like ages had only been seconds. Jack knew the next few seconds would determine his fate. Unlike Jack, the big man didn't know how to fight from his back and immediately started trying to get up. Jack lashed out with open palm strikes to both ears, then threw an elbow into the man's broad nose. Out of the corner of his eye, he began to see the prisoners leaning over their bunks, they appeared to be yelling and cheering, but Jack heard none of it. He was attuned to only one thing—finishing this man.

The soldier had other ideas. He'd finally remembered the pistol, and he went for it. Jack saw and began a countermove, but the man was fast as well as strong. Jack had anticipated the man trying to shoot him. Instead, the other man whipped the gun against the side of Jack's head.

His vision began to darken, he rolled off the soldier and reflexively clutched at his head. *Oh, my God*, he'd never been hit so hard. He couldn't focus, hell, he couldn't manage to open his eyes. He felt the dirt beneath his fingers and realized he had to get up. *Move, fight, run…do something!* He managed to partially open one eye and saw the other man staggering backward. One hand holding the gun, the other holding the side of his head. He was raising the gun to fire. Jack had no time to move. *This is it.*

Then, hands reached down and tore at the guard's face. First one, then more. The farmers began to exact their own revenge. The NSF guard managed to get off one wild shot before being pulled off his feet. The farmers were still chained and restrained by the long iron bar, but they managed to work together to first disable their former tormentor, then deliver their own brand of punishment.

Jack's vision was coming in and going, but he stumbled to what appeared to be a release lever for the iron bar and pulled it down. All of the men in the bunks could now slip their chains off the bar and go after the guard. There was one man in particular, his gaunt, but familiar, face leaned over an upper bunk.

"Hey, Preacher, nice of ya to stop by."

The friendly greeting didn't match the carnage his fellow inmates were enacting on the guard who was obviously long dead. Jack just shook his head.

CHAPTER TWENTY-FIVE

"You have eyes on?"

"Roger that," came the gruff, but familiar, voice. "Movement—hold position."

Scott froze, knowing full well that detection now would ruin all the weeks of recon and planning by Garret, Jack and Skybox. So much had changed, both in the world and for him, within. At some point along this path, just surviving had stopped being enough. The gangs had taught them to work together, the Messengers had forced them to be brutal. What they faced now required them to risk everything.

He'd been engaged now less than two weeks, and he was probably going to die. The call from Jack to get this op going had put everything else on hold. Jack's original feeling about what was happening at the farms had been correct. The farmers had been denigrated to forced labor, and all of their crops were being confiscated for NSF use. The team from the AG had attacked the previous day, wiping out the relatively small number of NSF guards. The farmers were already on a transport going south toward the AG along with every tool, seed and supply they could stow.

"Overwatch, what you got?"

Todd sat in a hide, high above the compound. The scene he was watching through the Nightforce NXS scope made his trigger finger itch. *Bastards.* "Get ready, guys, this is a full assault force. We got three APCs rolling in. First one is the Black Team NSF regulars, the next two could be foreign. Shit, they look Asian, maybe even some of the Red Army regulars."

Man, this was some seriously deep shit. The radio call from Jack had set them on a course no one expected. His message had changed everything. Skybox, Rollins and several of the SEAL team had remained behind, eventually making their way here to meet up with Jack. The commercial farming district was just outside Yokena on the western edge of Mississippi.

"Wait, what…" Bartos' familiar voice came over the comms. "What da hell!"

"Quiet, Cajun, we knew it was a possibility." The man they called Sentinel had been warning for months about how desperate the president was getting. With the increasing failures of the resettlement camps, they had taken to commandeering food crops by force. The use of the NSF for anything other than guard duty had apparently been problematic, so, the rumor was, she had brought in mercenaries—apparently even some from our country's former enemies.

Stopping the NSF, as well as possibly gaining supplies, convinced Scott and the group from the coast to now become guerilla fighters.

"We train for war and fight to win." One of the SEAL's said. "Sending the message in three, two, one."

The 'whoosh' of the RPG was accompanied by precise fire at all of the exposed troops. Each man on the small unit sounded off as their targets were cleared. Scott cleanly took out one of the National Security Force and one of the mercenaries as the RPG took out the tailing personnel carrier. They had all been survivors; now they had been forced to become warriors. Taking America back one cornfield at a time was how Bartos had put it.

"Holy shit, boys, more on the way." The trail of dust showed a line of trucks heading in their direction. The distinct sound of a fifty-caliber opening up left no doubt—they were thoroughly fucked. Voices on Scott's radio began to shout commands, "Exfil, Exfil…MOVE, GODDAMNIT!"

Bartos, Scott and the other four members of their team leaped from their hiding spots and sprinted toward the ditch leading down to their vehicles a mile away. Acting as overwatch, Todd began the arduous climb from the attic window in the old house. He knew it would take too long to get down. He was too old, too out of shape and too fucked. The first of the tan Humvees was rolling up the two-track toward the barn now. The machine gun had gone silent, but probably only because they were reloading.

Todd got to the downstairs kitchen and stopped. The yard outside was filling with soldiers in black fatigues. All armed to the teeth and ready to avenge their fallen comrades.

"You, in di house, we have you on IR. Come out and we will not harm you." The Asian accent was strong, and the thought of that person riding in a US Army Humvee made Todd want to vomit. If they were watching him on IR, then they should really pay attention to this. He set the huge Barrett .50 caliber on the dining table, sighted in on the lone gunner manning the fifty and calmly squeezed the trigger taking the man's head off. Working the action, he readied another shot, but a sudden sound from behind stopped him.

"It's ass puckering time, Todd, get low, real low."

"What the fuck are you doing?"

Skybox just grinned as he calmly left his gun on the floor and walked out the door with his arms up. "You come here now. On the ground." The clipped English was filled with hatred, but Skybox just kept grinning. He crossed the wooden porch and carefully stepped on the bottom step. He glanced toward the NSF commander, winked at the man then dove behind an armored vehicle just as the nearby barn exploded. The force of the explosion was enormous, taking out all the troops on the blast-side at once. The house where Todd was crouched simply disintegrated. The six improvised bombs they had placed in fifty-five-gallon drums were filled with the deadly mix of diesel and fertilizer. They effectively leveled the compound and annihilated most of the troops, rendering many of the others nearby unconscious.

Scott's team had been waiting for Todd when they saw Skybox and knew it was about to get hot. The concussive blast had flipped vehicles and toppled trees far into the trees near where they were hiding, but they ran charging into the blast zone to help their friends before the dust had even cleared. Skybox was fine, he was already moving and firing.

The foreign mercenaries fought well. They reacted swiftly, finding cover and assessing the situation. The lightly trained NSF regulars were cut down in minutes.

"Cajun, can you come get Solo?" someone called over the radio.

"We have several bandits making a run for…"

Radio discipline was all but lost. Adrenaline was pumping through every fighter. The sounds of screaming, smaller secondary explosions and gunfire were joined by the vicious growling sounds of Solo tearing into flesh.

Garret's men were surrounding the transports up near the ridge. The transports had been one of the main goals for the AG crew. The line of trucks would have plenty of food stocks that would help with the group's planned getaway cruise. The NSF had been raiding farms, stores, restaurant warehouses and even some well-hidden religious groups' warehouses for months. While no one had much anymore, collectively, it had added up to a potentially enormous haul.

Scott went to rise just as a line of bullet impacts stitched across the dirt in his direction.

"Who is that firing? We still have live fire coming downrange." He heard the words coming through the tiny earbud.

"We have bandits making for a single vehicle moving east. Anyone that can take them?"

"Bartos, you need to get Solo. Well, shit. Cancel that, he just took off after that Humvee."

Scott got his shit together and caught a glimpse of what Solo was running after. The black-uniformed pair were dragging a bald-headed man into the Humvee. Scott ran for the closest vehicle. "Bartos, Bartos! Skybox, I think they got the Cajun!" His radio mic, broken sometime during the battle, prevented anyone from hearing.

CHAPTER TWENTY-SIX

"Ok, no more of these for a while, alright?" Bartos said as he came to. He knew he was in a vehicle moving somewhere fast. He'd been running up the hill to get Solo when...what? Something, no, someone hit him in the face with the buttstock of a rifle. *Goddamnit,* he was getting tired of that happening. As the thought resolved in his head, the full pain of the blow to the head announced itself. "Oh, fuck."

He tried to grab his head but realized his hands were bound with a white plastic ty-wrap. He heard voices, they sounded scared, like someone arguing. Not in English, though. Well, hell, he didn't know anymore what in his head he could even trust.

This was bad...really bad. Wherever these goons were taking him, it wouldn't be for Sunday tea. Another thought stayed in the back of his mind. *If they question me, it's all over. Not just for me, but for my friends, too.* Better for him to be dead than alive and interrogated. Maybe if he could piss them off enough, they would just shoot him.

"Hey, how you guys liking America so far? Enjoying taking orders from a woman?" No reaction. *Hell, they may not even speak any English.* "I guess you know your asses are in deep shit. You lost everything back there. You know, caca, crap, do-do, chickenshit...nothing? So, what happened when your country lost electricity, huh? Oh, yeah, nothing. What's electricity? Am I right?

"Hey, y'all can just let me out anywhere. I appreciate da lift, honest. Gonna give you fucks five stars." The butt of the rifle hit him again in the forehead. As blackness took him once again he downgraded the review a full star.

~

Todd looked confused and yelled, "Huh?" One of the Navy medics was still removing splinters of wood and shards of glass from the man. His hearing probably wouldn't be back to normal for days.

Skybox drank a warm beer he had found in the confiscated food trucks. "I told him to get down," he said grinning.

"Sky, do you think we are safe here? I mean, won't they send more backup to see what happened to this squad?" Jack asked walking up.

Although not mentioning it to his friends, Skybox had just been relieved to see none of his fellow Praetor commandos were in the enemy group. "I don't think so, Rollins has birds up on orbit overhead to keep an eye out. This is so far from Jackson or any other AO for the NSF that this group would likely have been on their own. With that much firepower, they should have been able to handle anyone they met. This mission should have been a cakewalk for 'em."

Jack shook his head, "Cept for a crazy fucker with a death wish and a knack for making big fucking bombs."

Rollins gave a grin, looking up from his video screens momentarily, "That was a big fucking explosion, man."

"Yeah," Skybox answered. "Think I may have missed a decimal or something in those calculations. I really didn't mean to drop an entire house on Captain Todd."

They all looked at Todd.

"What?" he said loudly.

"Where are Scott and Bartos?" Skybox asked.

"And Solo," Jack said looking around.

~

Solo was in hot pursuit of the tan Humvee but was beginning to be outpaced. He heard the approaching sound of another vehicle.

Scott saw the bloody white dog in the road ahead and pulled ahead of him, opening the door. Solo hopped into the passenger seat, and Scott floored it. "Help me out, Solo. Let's find Bartos." The winding country highway had few side roads to take, and the dog's head stayed pointing straight ahead. Scott was pushing the truck as hard as it would go but hadn't seen any sign of the other vehicle. "Shit, shit, shit."

Twenty minutes later, they rounded a sharp bend in the road, and Scott hit the brakes, locking the truck into a sideways skid. Two enormous trees were blocking the road. Solo bolted through the open window, leaped the trees and vanished quickly out of sight up the road.

Scott had been calling for help since he got behind the wheel. Now, he saw why no one was answering. The exposed and broken wires and crushed plastic housing left the radio useless. He shut off the engine, stepped out and listened. *Nothing,* not a damn thing. "Come on, Bartos," he offered to no one.

He searched the truck tools, but there was no wench, cable or anything else to use on the felled trees. "Goddamnit!" he yelled. He checked his position on the map but failed to find any side roads that would bypass this section of road. *Solo, it's up to you.* He slammed his fist into the metal fender in frustration. Reluctantly, he turned the truck around and went back toward the team in Yokena to get help.

~

Bartos had roused himself to near consciousness when he noticed the

Humvee was no longer moving. The sound of doors slamming followed by two nearby explosions preceded a rushed acceleration. He was on the back floorboard mentally assessing his situation. His hands and feet were bound. Pack and water were gone. What else could he feel? His boots were still on. They hadn't searched him as he could feel both a knife and a multitool in his pockets. That meant he still had a couple of things on him that could be useful. Useful if he could get free, that is.

His head ached, the pounding was hard to ignore. How many of these assholes were there? He thought three, but he needed to be sure. Rolling to his side, he realized he wasn't blindfolded, instead, his eyes had nearly swollen shut. He could just barely see a slit of light through each. *Well, shit!*

He moved his head side to side until he could make out the head of the driver. He had heard two doors slam, so he knew another would be somewhere, up ahead in the passenger's seat. The light didn't dim, no matter how he moved his head. So, beside him, behind him or… Rolling nearly onto his back, he saw what appeared to be a circle of daylight just above. The other soldier was manning the machine gun turret in the roof. If there was another somewhere in the back, well, then he was truly fucked.

What were his options? Mentally, he went through a checklist of contingencies, moves and countermoves. The fact he was being held prisoner never crossed his mind. His enemy had already made one fatal mistake. *They should have killed me!*

CHAPTER TWENTY-SEVEN

Scott had been frantic upon his return to the compound. "We have to go now, they have Bartos." Garret lay a reassuring hand on his shoulder, but he threw it off. "Goddamnit, listen to me. We have to go now. Who's with me?"

Jack walked up, bruised and bloodied. "I'm in, Scott. Let's go get him."

"Wait, wait just a minute. We will go, but we need to get what we need first," Garret said. We need to be able to move that tree, and since they have a head start, we need some eyes in the sky. Let me grab Rollins." The lieutenant walked off hurriedly.

"He'll be okay, Scott. You know Bartos."

Scott nodded absently, not reassured. Every minute standing here could mean another mile farther away his friend was.

"Todd got a bit banged up, too," Jack said pointing to the big man sitting on the back of one of the Humvees. I guess you saw the stunt Skybox pulled."

Scott's vision had narrowed to a small point, frustration and anger beginning to boil over, and he was beginning to question the wisdom of coming back for help, but Jack's words about Todd brought his rage back under control. He saw his other friend and had to quickly go check on him.

~

"Come on, Rollins—get 'em ready." The Navy man was hurriedly prepping the last of the mini-drones to follow the course Scott had given. He inserted new power cells into each, and, once again airborne, they could give them advanced warning of anyone approaching and hopefully, allow them to get a glimpse of the enemy vehicle direction. "They have a good head start on us, but we will need to verify where they are heading," Skybox said.

"We know where they are going, these people were based out of the damn prison camp in Jax."

"I hope not."

"What do you mean, Skybox, what's going on?"

Skybox motioned at the lieutenant, "Garret heard from his dad, something is going down. Seems like they are planning to liberate that internment camp in the next few days."

"Shit, why now?"

"I don't know, but they are hauling Bartos right into what will be ground-zero of the Navy's first attack on the US mainland." Skybox looked at his friend, "We can't let them…"

"I know, Sky," Scott said cutting him off. "Just trust Bartos, ok, he can be…formidable."

"Believe me, I know that, Scott, but if they question him, he could lead them straight back to the AG."

"He won't."

"We need to be sure," Skybox said.

"Sky," Scott said wearily. "Just trust the insanity. Bartos will be ok. We have to go get him, though."

"How, Scott? Not like we have Blackhawks or planes at our disposal. Sorry, man—they're gone."

Scott couldn't contain himself, "We don't do that, Sky, we don't give up. We battle on—you of all people should know that. If nothing else....I need to go get Solo, he's in pursuit."

~

Garret and his men had been sweeping the compound for anything useful. Vehicles, ammo, weapons and, of course, the trucks hauling fuel and food. Those were all heading back to the AG with armed escorts. A smaller group of the former SEAL team plus Jack, Scott and Skybox were about to be heading off in the direction Bartos had been taken.

"Todd, go with Lt. Garret," Jack said loudly. Unsure if he actually heard him, he was relieved to see Todd get up and shuffle over to the truck heading back to the coast. His friend was suffering, not just the hearing but battered and bruised, while his other longtime friend was now apparently a prisoner of the NSF.

Jack had been happy hearing Scott's engagement news earlier in the day. It was just sinking in how foolhardy and dangerous this little plan had been for all of them. They had wanted revenge on the NSF for the brutality on their friends here at the farms, and truthfully, the AG was getting desperate for supplies. Supplies like what these captured trucks and trailers held. The cost had already been too high in his opinion.

"Scott?"

The man was busy refilling clips from an ammo box and strapping everything he could to his tactical vest. "Yeah, Jack?"

Jack looked at the man already knowing the answer to the question he was about to ask. "Why don't you let us go after him? You could head back with Garret and Todd."

Scott stopped what he was doing, momentarily confused, then seeing his friend's expression, he got it. He had stopped thinking about the engagement, the baby, the plans to get the ship out of harm's way. He'd stopped thinking of everything except getting his friend back. He shook his head. "Can't do that, Jack. Bartos wouldn't take the easy way out. He needs us."

"Scott, Bartos is certifiably insane, and if they can get anything other than silly putty out of that bald head, I'd be surprised. Now, I'm not all that interested in your well-being, truth be told. I ask only for personal reasons. Gia will skin us all if we let anything happen to your sorry ass."

"Load up, Preacher, if you're coming with us," Scott said with a hint of a grin. "How's the captain?" He nodded his head in Todd's direction.

Jack's face became more relaxed. "Banged up, temporarily deaf, but…I think he's better than he has been in a long time. Today gave him something to fight back against, something tangible. You know…he told me about what you asked him."

"About leaving?

Jack nodded.

Scott started to respond, then thought better of it. Todd still had some demons to bury and some memories to let go of. The AG needed him at the helm, but it would be his decision to make. He walked over and patted the man on the shoulder and gave a single bob of the head before loading up.

Skybox waved his hands in a circle then yelled over to Garret, "We're heading out. We get the Cajun, and then we'll circle back to the AG. Be safe, guys."

"Take care of my men, Commander," Garret replied.

CHAPTER TWENTY-EIGHT

His vision was getting worse, the swelling would leave him blind if he waited much longer. That would not do. He couldn't risk being taken in, interrogated, possibly revealing the truth of where he was from. Bartos had no delusions about being able to withstand 'enhanced interrogation,' more commonly referred to as torture. While the intel you got under duress might not be reliable, everyone broke, everyone. No, he had to make his move now.

The rear seat was bolted to the floorboard in several places. The head of the bolt was sharp enough to use on the strap binding his hands. He found the edge by feel and began rubbing it fast. He was very familiar with the nylon tie strap and all the ways the little restraints could fail. While it seemed solid, it was nothing more than plastic. Thankfully, these were not the better quality type that law enforcement often used. This was the kind you might get at your local hardware store. It took longer than he expected to get the strap to fray and eventually break. Once free, he didn't move. The man above should have a decent view of their prisoner. Right now, he had the element of surprise.

A line of sweat was dripping down his slitted eyes rendering what little vision he had nearly worthless. The watery lines of light and shadow came with a salty sting that forced him to keep them closed tightly and concentrate on his sense of touch. He slowly eased the knife from its hidden pocket. The razor-sharp blade clicked into position with an audible 'snick.'

The moves on each target had been set in mind for several minutes. Slowly, he lifted an arm free and ran the sharp blade over the back of the driver seat. He cut through the cloth and vinyl seat covering to expose the springs and foam. He gauged where the driver was sitting then plunged the blade between the springs and deep into the driver's back and chest. Quickly, he swung up and slashed at where he imagined the gunner's thighs would be. He made contact instead with metal.

Shit. He couldn't see anything. He plunged the blade again and this time it met flesh. The howl of pain that erupted was cut off by a wild swerve of the out of control Humvee. He heard a sound from behind him realizing there had been a third man. The top gunner was no doubt going for a sidearm as was whoever was behind. His free hand found the door handle and he kicked himself off of the floor and through the now open door.

It occurred to Bartos that he sailed through the air for an absurdly long time. This was, of course, just his opinion. The impact into hard packed ground ripping through clothes and flesh. Somewhere ahead, he heard and felt the sound of a hard impact. The heavy military vehicle had hit something solid. He felt his shoulder give way as a shriek of pain shot through that side of his body. He bounded and rolled and eventually came to rest in a heap at the bottom of a ditch. His eyes fully closed now, his unconscious form unable to fight back even if any of the enemies were still alive.

CHAPTER TWENTY-NINE

Bartos didn't see the man approaching, but his eyes had swollen tight at that point. Even had he been conscious, he was in no condition to escape. The man's round features were punctuated by a broken nose and a bloody cut creasing his forehead. He had been thrown from the rear of the Humvee into the front windshield when it crashed into the trees. Dazed and confused, he somehow had the presence of mind to take a gun and look for the bald man, the one who had killed his comrades. The thought of them dying here so far from home made him furious.

He had staggered back down the road fifty yards before he saw the single boot lying in the weeds. The blood kept dripping into his eyes which were already wavering. He knew he had a concussion, maybe more serious injuries, but this American bastard had to die. How had they beaten them? These guys were supposed to be simple farmers.

There...there he is.

The lump at the bottom of the ditch looked more like a pile of discarded clothes than a man. He raised the M16, tried to aim his unsteady hands, then just gave up and squeezed the trigger intending to spray bullets in the direction of Bartos. The gun did nothing. It was jammed or damaged in the wreck. *Fuck!*

The useless gun clattered to the pavement. Ho Whu Chin flipped open the Kizer Gemini knife and stepped toward the unmoving form. Fifteen feet, he stopped and called to him, "Hey you, bald man. What your name? Why you do this?"

Bartos heard parts of what sounded like someone speaking but could not push through to consciousness. He was sure all of the men in the vehicle were surely dead anyway…had to be more of the voices in his own head he was hearing. The sound…the voice came again. It sounded like someone speaking to him underwater. It faded again.

Whu gripped the blade as he had been taught by his uncle, a renowned warrior with the Chinese Night Tigers. The special forces had a well-earned and fierce reputation. He moved closer and saw the chest movement indicating life. "You battled hard, bald one. Now I end your pain."

The flash of white darting from the opposite side of the road was the last image the mercenary saw. His pain was just beginning.

Scott and two of the SEAL team members cleared the road and sped through. "Anything?"

Rollins shook his head, "Too much cover, can just barely make out the road." He was looking at the video screens from multiple drone feeds. The man rubbed his eyes; concentrating on the small bouncing videos on the screen was making his head hurt.

"Shit, shit, shit." Scott hated the thought of what Bartos was going through. The man was a champion, always out there on the pointy end of the stick. He had seen the Cajun and Solo do some amazing things, but this was war, not some skirmish with thugs or religious fanatics. He needed Bartos as much as he needed anyone. In fact, he had a very important question to ask the man. If— he was still alive.

Skybox was in the passenger's seat up front. "Scott, they undoubtedly called this in. The guys back at the farm never had a chance, but these fucks…" he checked his watch, "…have had almost an hour. We have to assume they are sending backup from the camp in Jackson."

Scott nodded, he knew that by 'backup' Sky was implying that it would likely be an overwhelming force. "How much time does that give us?"

"Assuming they don't have aircraft or drones, we probably have less than an hour. We have to catch that Humvee, get Bartos and clear the area by then, or we will be fucked."

Jack patted his leg, "Trust Bartos, man, he is unkillable."

How in the hell can we catch them? Scott wondered. They had a good thirty-minute head start. The military truck screamed down the two-lane road, Scott and the others scanning for any sign of the NSF's Humvees, Bartos or the dog. Fifteen minutes later, Rollins looked up, "Got something!"

The Jeep pulled up short of the wreckage, and everyone but Rollins jumped out and took cover.

"Holy shit," Jack muttered.

Within seconds, each of the soldiers said, "Clear."

Skybox took the lead and headed cautiously toward what was left of the Humvee. He motioned the others to spread wide and sweep the area. They could see a body, or at least part of a body, hanging from the top turret. Debris and weapons littered the immediate area. Jack and Scott were at the rear, each assigned the relatively safer areas of the ditch and wood line.

"Driver's dead," came from one of the others.

"Shit, they hit hard, there's nothing left of the guy."

"Quiet," Skybox ordered. "Stay alert, we have no idea how many there were."

Scott was sweeping the black barrel of the M16 in a wide arc as he scanned. Then, Jack's voice from the far side of the road froze him in mid-step. "Scott, I got something."

Scott forced his legs to move and quickly joined his friend. The something was the ruins of what might have been a human body—possibly. Now, it just resembled meat with some shreds of cloth. The face was gone, the neck had a gaping wound, it was held to the body by virtually nothing.

"It's not him," Scott said. "About the right size, but this guy had hair." A few tufts of coarse black hair could still be seen on the scalp. "Looks like he was wearing black, too." Bartos had been in olive drab cam like them.

Skybox walked up, "All of 'em are dead." He pulled up short when he saw the body. "Jesus Christ, what the fuck happened to this guy?"

Scott looked at Jack and almost in unison they said, "Solo."

Rollins yelled from the Jeep, "Hey, guys, we got incoming."

Scott started calling for Bartos, then Solo.

Skybox ran to the car yelling instructions, "How far out are they?"

"Maybe twenty minutes, twenty-five max."

"Ok, scan the area for heat signatures, then use visual to look for a big white dog."

Scott and one soldier went north of the crash while Jack accompanied a group south. Each was calling for Bartos and the dog. Scott knew he was alive, but in what shape? If he was in that wreck, it couldn't be good. Time was running out, his legs shook, they had to find his friend.

"I have paw prints heading south," one of the men with Jack radioed.

All of them went in that direction. They searched until the very last minute, but no other sign was found. No footprints, no blood, nothing on the IR scanner. Reluctantly, Skybox made the call; they had to leave. "Now!"

CHAPTER THIRTY

Bartos had come to with a hot, wet tongue licking his face. It smelled metallic, coppery, like…*blood*. "Solo. How did you get here?" He feebly reached out to blindly feel the dog. Solo's large head pushed into him. Bartos knew what that meant, he wanted him to move. "I'm trying, Solo."

Truthfully, everything hurt, he felt sure he was broken all over. He knew how to land to avoid injury, but with his eyes swollen shut and his feet still bound, the leap from the car had been reckless. *I may need to cut my eyes just to be able to see.* The swelling was so intense, no light was getting to his eyes.

He took a mental inventory of his body, happy to see everything still seemed to work. Unfortunately, it all hurt like hell. He held the dog's jaw and asked one command, "Safe?"

Solo dipped his head toward the ground. "Okay, good." Safe—for now. Somewhere in his barely conscious state, he remembered something from earlier. He was sure the men had talked to someone on the radio. *They called in the attack, must have asked for help.* "Solo, we have to move—this place is going to get busy real soon. I need your help, okay?"

The dog had a limited understanding of commands, but today was not about training, it was about friendship. Solo led Bartos back up onto the road, stopping where the fallen soldier was. Bartos used his feet and then got down on his hands and knees. Here, too, he smelled blood, he knew it was a body. His fingers felt over the crumpled form. "You do this, boy? Looks like your style…nice work."

It took a few more minutes, but he found the man's knife and pocketed it. His had been lost in the fight with the gunner. He next found the rifle several yards away. A quick inspection by touch revealed too much damage, so he removed the ammo clip and left the gun. Solo then led him to the wreckage. Bartos was straining to hear anything, but the forest stayed silent. Unable to see, his other senses were becoming more attuned to the things around him.

"We only have a few minutes, Solo. Show me what is here." The dog bumped his leg on the right side. He reached into the car through the missing door, eventually finding the straps of a small molle pack. Possibly a first aid kit. He and the dog spent several more precious minutes looking for anything of use before vacating the area. He rested a hand on the dog's shoulders as Solo led his friend deep into the woods to safety. Limbs and rocks kept hindering the escape, but Bartos trusted the dog completely. *How in the hell had he caught up to them?* he wondered.

By the time Scott and the others reached the crash, Solo and Bartos were many miles away. Solo briefly stopped and turned his head listening for a sound, but in the end, dropped his head down and kept leading his friend farther away from the road, from the others, from danger.

Bartos could tell it was nearly night. The heat of the day was beginning to wane, and he could no longer feel the sun on his face when it made it through the canopy overhead. He could feel frustrated with his temporary blindness, but he didn't. It was simply an additional challenge. He was just thankful to still be alive. Solo had been his lifesaver, of that he was sure, but now it would be up to them both to get through this. He sat under a rocky overhang, Solo had left him, probably to go hunt for food and scout for dangers. Bartos took the time to inventory his meager supplies.

He had the folding knife from the soldier. It was sharp and seemed to be good quality. The first aid pack had been a disappointment. Just by feel, he could tell it was nearly empty. He'd recovered one assault rifle and four clips of ammo. He could tell the clips were nearly full just by their weight. The one other backpack he'd managed to retrieve from the wreckage was a mystery until now. He went through feeling everything, trying to assess the contents. Some were obvious, some much less so. A poncho or possibly an emergency blanket. A thermos or metal drinking bottle that seemed to be half full. A handful of what he guessed were protein bars. Obviously, this squad had not expected to be out for long or anywhere they couldn't get food and water.

The backpack had several other items he couldn't identify. One seemed to be a lighter and another probably a compass, but he couldn't determine how to open it simply by touch. He repacked all the items. He took a tentative swallow from the container, and, determining it was water, he drank it all. There would be streams in the forest, he knew he could get more. What else did he have? He felt up and down the legs and pockets of his clothes coming out with a small set of lock-picks. Not so useful. A PSK, or pocket survival kit, with fishhooks, line, razor-blade, matches and a piece of mirror. He repacked everything but the razor—that he might need if his swollen eyes didn't decrease soon. His bootlaces were paracord, so he could also use those in a pinch. All in all, it wasn't much, but…he'd had less and survived.

Movement sounded off to his left. He cocked his head to hear better. Four feet moving in unison, not two. The dog trotted up softly and licked his face and arms. "Damn, buddy, glad to see you, too." The dog had never been affectionate to him. Bartos thought briefly that he might just be seeing if the meat needs seasoning. He took the rare opportunity and hugged the dog who accepted the touch but only for a moment. "I hope you got yourself some food and water, Solo, cause we ain't got shit."

CHAPTER THIRTY-ONE

THUNDER RIDGE PROTECTORATE

Archangel studied the maps looking for flaws in the plan. The Praetor commander had underestimated the new president. She was even more reckless…more dangerous than he had expected. Levy was right in the urgent need to rein in the woman. That was not Archangel's job, though, not this time. Someone else would be called on for that.

His job was even more challenging. How to keep the former military forces away from the aid camps. The protectorate strongholds like this one were dangerously close to failing. Vincent had done a good job assembling all the intel. Archangel was shocked to see how little supplies were left. The camps had been going for nearly two years but should have been self-sufficient by now. Instead, they were using the makeshift 'aid' camp occupants as forced labor to supply food and manpower.

What went wrong? He had seen the Catalyst plans, they were well thought out. The facilities, even the selection process for who got in, was all very meticulous. The teachers, CEOs, doctors, engineers. The near absence of most politicians, military types and the overly wealthy. It had been the core plan of what should have been a near-Utopian society. The foul odors assaulting his nose indicated it had not fulfilled its goals.

While the occupants of the small city were all brilliantly talented, that did not mean they all had skills that were immediately useful in the new throwback society where they found themselves. He watched as a man and woman struggled with a wheelbarrow loaded with hay. The man, he'd been told, was a runner-up for the Nobel prize for physics several years back. Now, he was mucking stalls for the horses. That man probably resented the fall from grace even more than the average Joe Schmo did. Not only that, he sucked at this new role. All his Ph.D.s did little to help food grow or chickens lay more eggs. In his gut, Archangel knew that was the issue. That was the real reason these camps were falling apart. They didn't get workers, they got thinkers. They needed more doers and fewer talkers. In time, the brainpower might be helpful, but for now, they were just extra mouths to feed. He watched as the hay spilled out into the road, the couple arguing over the overturned wheelbarrow.

Vincent dropped a set of photos on the table and followed Archangels' eyes to the scene. He shook his head, "Getting these people to work together is like herding cats."

"Worse," Archangel said. "At least cats would have a common understanding when it comes to survival. These people are clueless. They've held top positions and led comfortable lives, many had scores of people under them doing the real work. Now it's up to them."

Vincent shrugged, "The original plan included a fair share of workers, farmers and such. Sadly, they were some of the last to be picked up—so only about half of the ones on the list were ever brought in. Once they were here, it went downhill fast. The others looked down on them, maybe not intentionally, but the work itself was obviously manual labor. Most saw the farmers as worker bees, just a drone needed to keep the hive alive. That attitude more than anything else drove most of those people away. Of course, the farmers and ranchers were independent types anyway and didn't take kindly to being told what to do."

"So, they all left?" Archangel said.

"No, not all, at least not here, some camps they did. All the farmers, carpenters, mechanics, even many of the nurses and teachers. The losses were too much. The NSF boys started trying to keep everyone in the protectorate zones by force, and it started getting ugly."

Archangel pointed to a small device on one of the shelves. "Those are the new hive drones?"

Vincent nodded, "They are damn good, they basically provide an umbrella of coverage for security and can even project an image that conceals what is below to fool satellite imagery." The body of the unit was small, the vaguely double-helix wings looked almost like gossamer versions of DNA strands. "This one is solar powered. The ones for nighttime are a bit larger."

Shaking his head, Archangel went back to the map. "Yokena? Is that where it happened?"

"Yep, report earlier today indicates we lost a whole squad there and most of the vehicles and weps. They were one of the multi-national groups doing food pickups for this camp."

"This can't be the first time it's happened. Why is this one important?"

Vincent frowned, the wrinkles in his dark face resembled the topographic map they were studying. "I mean, we have had other casualties and lost supply trucks before, but not like this. The guerillas were well armed, well trained and had good intel. One report suggests they may have had drone coverage of the firezone."

"So, Vincent, you think they had help?"

"We know they did. Army, maybe Navy. Some of the stuff was improvised, but since the pres clamped down on food and fuel to the military bases, it's been heating up. Just a matter of time before it all blew."

"I don't like the idea of fighting our fellow soldiers."

Vincent nodded, "I know, man, sucks ass, but don't let anyone else hear you say that. Who's in charge of P-group now?"

Archangel shrugged and started going through the satellite photos from the area. "After Midnight disappeared and the ranch failed...I lost track."

"What about all our embeds?"

Archangel knew what Vincent was asking. The Guard had embedded mostly invisible Praetor-5 and a few Praetor-9 soldiers in every branch of the military. They were there to provide immediate intel from every camp and battlefront in the world. They could also take command if the need arose.

"Communication is the problem—we can't get to most of them with the president's comms blackout."

"Her people won't even be aware of them," Vincent said.

"True." That was one of the more closely held secrets of the Guard.

"Quis custodiet ipsos custodes?" Archangel mumbled. *Who will guard the guards?* The unofficial motto of Praetor. "Okay, so we pay a little visit to Yokena to see who was crashing our party. Let's bring all the toys, who knows what we might need?"

CHAPTER THIRTY-TWO

NEAR YOKENA, MISSISSIPPI

Rollins was recalling the drones. Scott had begged them to leave them up to look for his friend. The Navy man explained that they were nearly out of power, and in a few more miles he would have been too far to control them or receive the sensor data and video.

Skybox gently placed a hand on Scott. "We will pull back far enough to wait. Bartos will be fine for now."

"You don't know that, Sky. He was almost certainly injured in that crash. The NSF is going to go ballistic when they see what we did. If they know a prisoner escaped, they will stop at nothing to find him."

Skybox couldn't argue that it was frustrating to leave a man behind, but he'd had to do it more often than he cared to remember. His friend would not be able to let it go, he knew that. Bartos was a good man and damn tough. Unfortunately, he might need more than that to avoid capture. The NSF had shored up its fighters with foreign troops, mercenaries. Some of these would be formidable opponents.

Scott looked to Jack whose head was resting against the window, eyes closed. He knew the man was tired but couldn't imagine sleeping when Bartos was missing, probably injured—maybe worse.

"You need rest," Skybox said nodding over to Jack. "He's got the right idea."

Scott loosened the tactical vest and removed the earbud. "Maybe later. How far do we need to go?"

"Nearly to the coast. May as well go back to base and regroup. The supplies and farmers from Yokena are about an hour ahead of us. If those guys have drones, they could spot either of our convoys at distance."

Scott knew they had packed up everything they could in the community including seeds, tools and even some commercial tractors. This, along with the salvaged military equipment and supplies liberated from the NSF, made the mission a success. To everyone there, the mission was only half complete. The plan had been to also hit the internment camp and free everyone there. They lacked the manpower to make that happen, and instead, it seemed that camp had been the one to send more of the black-clad troops toward the farms in Yokena. Somewhere in the middle, they had found the wreckage of the Humvee, and probably not too far away, would be Bartos. They were heading in the opposite direction, away from his friend. If the roles were reversed, he felt sure Bartos would be doing the opposite—going directly into the teeth of the enemy to save his friend. He thought about Gia, about the engagement. Had that made him weak, was he now second guessing doing anything she might view as reckless?

He motioned to the driver. "Pull over."

CHAPTER THIRTY-THREE

INTERNMENT CAMP, JACKSON, MISSISSIPPI

Archangel pulled his neck wrap to cover his nose and mouth. The smell from the so-called 'aid camp' was horrendous. Vincent had told him to expect it, but the reality was even worse than he had feared. "Goddamn!"

Vincent looked over and shrugged, "This is your first one, some are a bit worse."

The fetid odor of decay and rot was in such stark contrast to the protectorate he'd departed from earlier in the day. "This is some Third World kinda shit, Vince. God Almighty, I can see why the Army is pissed that these things exist."

"Well, it is Mississippi," Vincent said with a grin before motioning to several of the guards outside the command building. "Get those cases from the rear of our Humvee and store them in the base commander's office. He'll know what they are." The guards saluted and quickly disappeared into the parking area.

The command center was separated from the 'housing' area by fifty yards and several runs of high fencing. The well-manicured lawn of the former Arkansas National Guard base went right up to the high fence. On the other side were mud, trash, huts and hundreds of gaunt, silent faces looking out. Beyond them were more fences and miles of farmland with various crops, none of which these people were allowed to eat. *This was a mistake, we should have gone straight to Yokena,* Archangel thought.

Vincent touched his arm, "You okay, man?"

"Yeah, sure." Archangel forced his muscles to relax. This was not his fight, he was here on a mission. *Focus.*

They walked on farther, the destination, a large warehouse ahead. Once inside, the smell diminished, and he began to realize one of the black-suited soldiers was speaking to him, one of the people responsible for this place. "What did you just say?"

The man in front of him was in his mid-forties, slightly plump with a jolly expression that seemed wholly out of place. When he spoke, the waddle of fat under his chin jiggled slightly. "I said," the man began with a note of irritation, "I'm Captain William Bailey, my friends call me Will. I am in charge here."

Archangel wondered briefly how this fat, pitiful excuse of a man had even survived until now. What had he been before the blackout, some mid-level department head? A politician? The tactical belt around the man's waist appeared to be losing its battle to retain the belly spilling over it. This man was overweight while thousands were starving under his watch. Prisoners or not, no one deserved to be treated like the people being held here. Archangel ignored the man's outstretched hand. "I'm not your friend and get the fuck out of my way."

Vincent guided him past the shocked base commander to speak with the men directing the resupply missions. They wanted specifics, what they were hauling, normal routes and timetables and anything else that might clue them into who had attacked. How large of a force would they possibly be facing? An Asian man also in an NSF uniform was waiting, his posture told them he hated this place as much as they did.

~

The two Praetor commanders were back on the road ninety minutes later. Accompanying them were additional vehicles with two-dozen heavily armed NSF troops. "You believe, Chiang? I mean about his men capturing one of 'em?"

Archangel didn't much care one way or the other. This was not part of his official mission. His job, as unpleasant as it was, was to protect aid camps like the one he just left from being attacked by the Army. "They should have made it back to that camp or reported in by now."

Vincent nodded, "Probably just highwaymen. Still, that's pretty ballsy to go after a military force directly like that. Be nice to interrogate the man, find out where they were from."

"Military force," Archangel said dismissively with a laugh.

"Look, man, I know. I've been dealing with the asshats for months. They are a shitty excuse for soldiers, but since Chambers started bringing in some of the outside talent….well, they can be pretty effective. Most of that supply detail was made up of coalition troops."

Archangel had worked with foreign fighters all over the world. The SSG, or Black Storks, in Pakistan, Spain's UOE Green Berets, French GIGN and Israel's elite Sayeret Matkal. He knew and respected the talent, dedication and training of men in these services. Just because an elite soldier wasn't American, didn't diminish the potential lethality.

Since 9/11, the Department of State had gotten much closer to the military to help push political goals backed up by military strength. With the fall of most countries and regimes around the world, the president had her pick of Spec Op soldiers to fill out her security forces. Not just from former allies of the US either. The man at the aid camp, Chiang, had the characteristic look and weapons of a former Chinese Night Tiger. Rumor was, even some Alpha Groups' top people had been brought in from Russia. He was not yet sure how comfortable he was with all this. These men would fight for money and survival, not for America.

"Vincent, when you got that alert that day, did you envision all this?"

The black man laughed, "Are you fucking serious? Shit, man, I remember thinking, 'Why the hell is command messaging me about a fucking blackout?' I was on leave that week getting in some fishing up in Minnesota. So far off the grid, I had no idea how bad it all was." He glanced out the side window at the vacant fields as they passed. "Nobody could have expected all this."

I'm not so sure about that, Archangel thought.

CHAPTER THIRTY-FOUR

The familiar feel of the handlebars and shift levers granted him a calm he rarely felt. Skybox was pissed, and Jack woke up just long enough to tell him he was crazy, but even he agreed, it was at least something to do. Scott always carried his bike and kit when he left the community. Seeing it strapped to the back of the Jeep was so normal no one ever thought about it anymore. While a convoy might be spotted by a drone operator, a lone cyclist…maybe not. Certainly, he wouldn't be worth coming after, even if someone with the NSF took notice.

Once again, he sped down the back-country roads of Mississippi, shoes clipped into pedals and rifle across his back. He had mapped out a search grid with Skybox before they parted ways. Bartos was traveling south, he would have to clear the immense forest area before coming to any roads. Scott would traverse a line about fifty-miles long for the next several days, then drop back to an even longer arc. The chances of actually seeing Bartos were remote, but he was counting on Solo possibly catching his scent and then making contact.

He had a few water bottles and a small LifeStraw brand water filter to make more. He carried a small pack of provisions, and Skybox was going to leave some additional supplies farther out. The locations had already been input into the Garmin GPS on the bike. When he found Bartos, they would simply call the AG for a pickup and take shelter till they showed up. It was the perfect plan—*it was a ridiculous plan*, and Scott knew it. The chance of finding his friend was infinitesimally small. The one thing it could do, though, was let them know when the NSF had cleared the area. As soon as he was sure none of the NSF were around, no drones in the sky, he could call in Skybox, Garret and his team for a more proper search and rescue.

There was one other possibility. If Bartos still had his radio, Scott might be close enough to hear a call from his friend. Bartos had a habit of checking in on a very specific schedule when he was away from the base. Would he stick to that out here? *Maybe.*

He pedaled until dark and then kept going. Scott was beyond exhaustion. The adrenaline from today's action had receded, leaving his body an empty shell. Even so, he had made the fifty-mile pass twice already. He pulled up next to an old farmhouse he'd spotted earlier and removed his pack. He ignored the house and instead climbed into the loft of the nearby haybarn. Part of the roof had collapsed. The smell of rotting hay combined with the musty tang from countless rats' nests.

He dropped onto the floor and looked northward at the darkening sky. Stars were just beginning to emerge for their nightly display, but Scott ignored them and instead, focused on several that were unlike the others. First one, then another of the flickering lights were moving in the sky. *Drones*, he realized. That was good and bad. It meant the NSF was going all out to find who had done this. They wanted the people who attacked that squad. Did it also mean they knew about the escaped prisoner?

He had no way to know. He checked his GPS map, orienting it to give him a bearing on Yokena off to the northeast. Yes, there were a few drones there, but many, many more over what must be the crash area. They had to know Bartos was still out there. He would have the answers to who had attacked them, he would know where the supplies were.

Bartos was good, and Solo was incredible, but this was an army looking for them. Scott had no idea what condition either of them was in, but even at 100%, they would be no match against the NSF firepower and men. Scott watched as one of the lights that he thought was a stationary star now seemed to be moving and getting brighter. It was headed in his direction. Quickly he moved back under the barn roof that was still intact and unfolded a reflective mylar blanket and crawled beneath. He wasn't sure if this would mask his heat signature, but it was something Skybox and Rollins had suggested.

Several times, he thought he heard the whine of the little drone engine, but in the darkness of the barn, he couldn't be sure. His mind interpreted every noise as a danger. Eventually, the stress and fatigue of the day won out, and his body surrendered to sleep. The almost silent drones continued their dance across the sky.

CHAPTER THIRTY-FIVE

YOKENA, MISSISSIPPI

The Praetor commander had surveyed the battle scene at the farm, quickly realizing this was more than farmers fighting back. This had been a well-planned and executed assault by a small guerilla fighting force. It appeared the few NSF guarding the farmers had been overpowered. He assumed the captive workforce was liberated and may have even joined in the fighting. What came next, though, was surprising. There was clear evidence the liberators had then stayed on scene to ambush the supply crew coming to make the routine pick-up. *Why would they have done that?*

While the tactics were very solid and, in his mind, smelled of military planning and personnel, it wasn't the Army. In fact, any of the branches would have moved in here in force, killed the NSF and taken what they wanted. Chances are, they would have then moved on to the closest of the aid camps, most likely the one a hundred miles back toward Jackson. So, it wasn't the military....who then?

"Sir," one of the NSF men approached cautiously. They all seemed to focus on the scorpion patch on his sleeve before looking at his face. "No way we can get a bearing on where they went. Too many tracks to follow. These farmers had trucks and tractors all over the place."

He'd expected as much and dismissed the man without commenting. What was he doing out here going after what amounted to petty theft in his mind? It wasn't the military, he should focus on other targets where the threat was more obvious. Something about this, though, something had his attention. Years in the service followed by years sharpening his spy craft gave him an intuition that he relied on. *What am I missing?*

Lifting the radio, he called, "Vincent, any signs from the escapee?"

A brief pause before, "Nothing, Archangel, no signs of anyone north or south of the wreck. We'll expand it out farther tomorrow."

He signed off and pocketed the two-way. He had tons of equipment and hundreds of men just looking for a target. *Where are you hiding?*

The barn had been destroyed by a nitrogen bomb. A simple mix of diesel fuel and fertilizer, both apparently available here by the tons. He surveyed the remainder of the scene. The house was taken out, too, apparently in the same blast since it had no signs of explosion other than the collapse. He walked up to the collapsed structure. Nothing recognizable remained other than part of the staircase and the front steps. He and his men had already been over everything here.

He walked up the steps to where the front door would have been, then turned and came back down. He stopped and went back up a step. Something…something didn't feel right. He checked each of the steps again. There, one had a small bit more movement than the rest. He got down on the ground and used his tactical light to shine into the back of the wooden steps. Reaching in he pulled out a small device.

"Gotcha."

The little metal unit was familiar to him. Not just the purpose, but this specific type. It was a clicker, a remote detonator. This version was exclusively used by only one military unit in the world. A clandestine branch known as Praetor. The device confirmed Archangel's greatest fear, he was up against a fellow member of the Guard.

CHAPTER THIRTY-SIX

Solo put his nose close to Bartos' face. It bothered him that the man hadn't moved much during the night, but air was being exhaled from his lungs. He lived. To Solo's way of sensing—if he could breathe, he could fight. The simple logic would not have been too different from the man's, had he been part of the internal conversation. Twice during the night, the dog had heard voices and seen lights in the distance. He'd wanted to go to investigate, but whatever bound him to this man was too strong. He somehow knew Bartos wouldn't make it on his own, not in the condition he was in. Solo lay there throughout the day, and as the night fell, the man began to shiver. The air wasn't cool, he sensed it was a bad sign and moved up against the man to share his warmth.

In the pre-dawn hours of the following morning, a noise overhead roused the dog awake. It was a buzzing similar to the big fat bees he sometimes chased, but much louder. It was a sound he had heard from far away several times already. He cocked his head to get a bearing, then saw the little machine hovering just over the treetops. He had seen Bartos and his friends using machines like this. He was unsure of its purpose but sensed it might be watching him. He lay at the edge of a rocky overhang. Bartos was far back under the ledge. He wanted to lead the thing away from Bartos. He leisurely rose up on all fours and stretched, then began wandering down toward the spring he'd found previously. The buzzing machine followed for several minutes before flying off to look at something else.

Bartos' *body* decided at some point during the previous night not to die. He woke up mostly wishing it had. "Holy fuck," he said...or, more accurately, attempted to say. His lips were glued shut from dried saliva and vomit. His tongue refused to move and felt like a dry hammer sitting in his mouth. His eyes remained closed despite all efforts to open them. He could tell the swelling in his face had decreased some, but at best, he could only see a tiny sliver of light creeping past his eyelids. He wanted to call for Solo, but again, his mouth refused to make any sound that might be considered a voice.

His body ached all over, both arms were numb where he had lain on them too long. One knee was screaming in pain and had a limited range of movement. He winced at the pain also coming from his shoulder which reminded him that he also apparently had broken something, probably a collarbone, leaping from the car. *Jesus,* he thought. *You are in bad shape, friend.*

He snapped a finger and patted a leg. No sound, Solo wasn't here. He'd be back, though, of that he was sure. The thought was erased when he heard a familiar distant hum. They were using drones to find him. Would that be Rollins or the enemy, though? Moving his head to follow the sound brought a wave of pain and nausea. He'd had a concussion, that much was obvious. He lay back. *Man, I am thirsty...I need some water. How long was I unconscious?* His mouth was achingly dry, but he couldn't do anything on his own.

He thought again about the drones. How could he know if they were friend or foe? Simple, really, treat them as an enemy until you know otherwise. Stay out of sight. Here, hidden under this rock, they shouldn't be able to get anything on IR. That was good, keep it that way. Where was Solo? How had the dog found him? He drifted back to sleep.

~

"Damnit, dog, I'm awake, what?" the sounds more garbled whispers than words.

Solo had persistently been bumping Bartos until he had finally awoken. He petted his friend, his savior. The dog was anxious, he could tell that. Surprisingly, he also found one eye now was partially open. He had a blurry squint of the world again. His head still ached, and other signs of dehydration were starting to show.

Solo's muzzle was dripping water. In fact, it looked like the dog had dipped his whole head under water. He leaned into Bartos, the wet fur dripping with spring water. Bartos was surprised, but understood, and gratefully licked the moisture from the dog's hair. It wasn't much, but it helped greatly. "Thank you, Solo," the words clearer now. "I need more."

Solo bumped him again arching his back into a rigid stance. Bartos knew what that meant, danger, close. "Move or fight." The dog was already heading away as if to say, *Move, you idiot.* Bartos quickly gathered his pack and the rifle and headed after the dog on wobbly legs.

Solo led him to a small clear running stream where he drank his fill and refilled the water bottle. It appeared to be mid-day. The IR cameras on the drones would be nearly useless right now because of the heat. His assumptions on the drones being NSF seemed likely. If Solo was moving away from them, they damn sure weren't friendlies. The dog kept outpacing him, but he did his best to follow.

The relationship with Solo had been the strongest of his life. While it might seem strange to many that they were so close, he didn't care. His had been a lifestyle that didn't include romance or family; it was one of threats and the elimination of those threats. Family would have meant weakness. He thought about Scott as he walked. To Scott, family meant completeness. Bobby, Kaylie and now, Gia. Scott needed that, and they meant more to him than his own life. Bartos could appreciate that, but only in an abstract way. Family didn't mean the same to him. Of course, his family consisted of a dad that was an assassin, so there was that...

Fuzzy recollections and questions kept drumming around inside his battered brain. *Did Todd, Jack and Scott get away? Were they successful in beating the NSF troops at the farm?* So many questions and no real answers. The biggest one was, *How in the hell had Skybox made that bomb? That was like the coolest thing ever.* He tried to smile, but his swollen face wouldn't manage it. Solo suddenly looked back and dropped to his belly. Bartos did the same and rolled silently into thicker brush. His eyes had opened a fraction wider now, but he couldn't see anything behind them. Solo suddenly darted to one side and quickly was out of sight. Ten minutes later, Bartos heard sounds of movement, then he saw three soldiers in black uniforms topping a small rise about fifty yards back. He crawled under cover and quietly raked dead leaves over his camos and readied his weapon, hoping not to have to fire.

Pass on by, guys. If he or Solo killed this group, it would let all of these people know exactly where to look. His best estimate was that he was about twelve miles from the crash site. Too far for weapons fire to be heard, but there would likely be others out here as well. He caught a glimpse of Solo easing stealthily up behind the men. They were dead already and just didn't know it.

Solo got into position as the men got within twenty-five yards, then fifteen. One would pass within five yards of Bartos's left shoulder, another about ten yards to the right. The one in the center, though, was heading straight at his hiding spot.

The men had no military discipline. They were talking and looking to each other more than paying attention to the surroundings. They were close enough now, he could begin to hear what they were saying.

"So, they got nothing on IR, and yet we are still supposed to keep wandering around out here?"

"Yeah, they got a few deer, dogs, even a bear on the drone feed, but only human they saw was on a bicycle thirty miles farther south. Definitely not the escapee."

"Ok, you two knock it off." The third man was looking at a folded map. "Fifteen more minutes and we circle back a half mile farther west."

The trio passed by the concealed form of Bartos. The man passing just feet away had been focused on the map. Solo was ready to pounce, but Bartos covertly held up an open palm, the signal to stand down. The men would get to live another day.

CHAPTER THIRTY-SEVEN

Scott rode the shorter loop of highway for four days, stopping only briefly every four hours to power the two-way radio on and listen for several minutes. The long distance was taking a toll on his bike and his body. Twice he had to fix tire punctures and was now using the filter straw to refill water bottles. It was all very time consuming; the musty tasting water was leaving him a bit nauseated as well. Each night he still saw drones in the air but fewer last night than previous nights. "Go for Biker Boi." He also checked in with the AG several pre-planned times each day but left the radio off the remainder of the time to save the batteries.

His brother's voice came through, "How are you holding up, man, any sign of Gopher?"

Gopher was the radio handle Bartos had picked, one of the characters from the old "Love Boat" TV series. "Nothing yet. Thought I might have heard Solo during the night, so stayed close to that twenty but no sign of either. Fewer birdies in the area. They have to give up eventually."

Bobby paused on replying, and Scott felt like Bobby was talking with someone else, "Hey, Bro, don't assume that means anything, they may have just switched tactics. You are advised to move out to the backup position. Do you copy?"

Scott knew that was coming, he just hoped it wouldn't be today. He felt like Bartos was close. Moving back to the next highway would add another fifteen miles of straight-line distance that Bartos and the dog would have to cross. It also lengthened his fifty-mile bike loop to one closer to ninety. Each way on the longer route would take five or six hours. He would be lucky to pass a single spot once a day. He'd been eating little and babying the bike but still wondered how long they both could keep it up.

"BikerBoi, did you copy?"

Reluctantly, Scott said yes. He thought his brother would sign off, but he didn't.

"Something else is going on, Bro. Our buddy has been talking to people, and they've been making plans."

What buddy? What plans? Scott wondered. He could tell Bobby was trying to determine how to say something over the open airways without actually saying it.

"A little distraction, like letting the cows out while the rancher's out hunting."

*Oh, shit…*Scott knew instantly what that meant. *Hot damn!* He controlled his enthusiasm with a more measured response. "Roger that. Dropping to backup route now."

Back aboard the AG, Bobby Montgomery began to sweat despite the cool air blowing from the overhead vents. He marveled at his younger brother's willpower and stamina. While no one doubted Bartos' ability to survive this, Scott had made it his personal mission to make sure he did. Skybox watched him closely and nodded, relieved that Scott understood. Despite the Navy's reluctance to take direct action, Fleet

Commander Garret had agreed to a coordinated joint strike force in an attempt to liberate the camp near Jackson.

The strike teams were a hodgepodge of Army, Marine, Navy and even some National Guard. The Army presence in Mississippi had decreased significantly after the training base up north near Grenada had gone silent a few weeks earlier. Sentinel had said that base had been overrun by NSF after the president declared the commander a rogue enemy of the state. Everyone now knew what that meant. He wasn't following her orders.

Bobby pointed a shaky finger at the huge wall map. He highlighted a stretch of road from Port Gibson to Utica. This would be the new route his brother was patrolling. The spot where Bartos had escaped was marked, as well as the old National Guard camp that they now knew was the location of the NSF Internment camp.

"Skybox, any chance your greyshirt associates could go in there and help my brother find Bartos?"

Skybox didn't answer right away, but he'd had this same conversation multiple times with others. "No, well yes, if I could reach them, but we aren't set up that way. I only talk to command. Have no idea how to even reach another member of the Guard. It's been a long time since I heard from anyone. Last I heard, our command structure was compromised, so I, presumably like most of us, have gone dark."

"So, you have no idea where any of your people might be?" Bobby asked confused.

Skybox was a bit unsure how to answer the man. "They are everywhere. Every base, nearly every battalion will have an embedded member. Every SOF unit will likely have multiple Praetor team members, but no way to reach them."

Another softer voice sounded from the hall. "Can someone tell me where my future husband is?"

Doctor Gia Colton stood in the doorway to the room looking pale and angry.

~

"Whose bright idea was it to go after those guys?"

Gia was ready to explode. Bobby and Skybox had offered a condensed version of recent events. She was not in the mood for logic. She wanted Scott back here now. "Go get him, bring him back."

"We can't do that," Skybox offered. "No one else can do what he's doing."

She looked at the map, noting the highlighted route. "Give me a car, give me Scott's Jeep—I'll go."

Both men shook their heads, "Gia, if we knew you were coming back we would have…" Bobby didn't finish the sentence as the woman was bent over retching into a trashcan.

Oh shit, something clicked in Bobby's brain. The pieces all dropped into place, and he knew why she was desperate to get Scott back safely. He looked at Skybox who looked alarmed. After all, the woman worked with dangerous viruses all the time. Bobby knew what the soldier was thinking. He smiled and shook his head. "Sky, we really do have to get Scott." He handed Gia a damp rag and a bottle of water. "How far along?"

CHAPTER THIRTY-EIGHT

He was comfortable in the wilderness but felt most at home in the rivers and swamps. Wetlands provided a unique environment for someone like him. The woodlands he found himself in now felt oppressive, hot and devoid of easy food. Bartos was losing strength, he'd not regained enough of his vision to hunt. The few roots and plants he ate offered little in the way of calories.

Solo seemed to sense his condition and had brought a dead rabbit for him the night before. Bartos had never eaten summer rabbits. He'd learned the hard way the diseases and parasites they carried, including tularemia. He thanked the dog but shook his head. Getting sick out here would be the end. The big dog seemed reluctant to consume it, but eventually did. Bartos knew Solo probably was as desperate for food as he was.

Sometime the previous night, he had heard a dog bark. It could have been Solo, but he wasn't sure if he was out patrolling or lying beside him. An ever-present headache and dizziness combined with the damaged knee made sleep nearly impossible. He found himself questioning what was real, what was simply ghost. Awaking each morning and putting on the pack was also an agonizing chore. The straps tugged at the shoulder where a huge knot had formed over his broken collar-bone. That arm was utterly useless as well. He had fashioned a sling for it but wondered how he would be able to fight or shoot if it came down to that.

"This day five, or six?"

Solo just looked at him. "Yep, it is definitely the day before who gives a fuck."

His hand searched the pack for anything to eat. All that remained was half of a dry protein bar. "This is it friend, all we have left." The whole bar would offer only a fraction of the calories he needed for the day. The fact he was at a deficit already didn't escape him. While in theory, you could survive weeks without eating, that didn't mean you could do much else. He wasn't lying in a hospital bed; he was running for his life. Okay, he was gimpily hobbling for his life, but it still took energy. He knew his body had shifted gears, literally beginning to eat itself to make fuel. First would go the fat, of which he had little. Then, the muscles themselves would be used to keep his body alive. Long before that, he would lose the energy to continue. He had to get away, get clear of the woods and the patrols.

"Solo, you're looking pretty thin, too, that tiny rabbit wasn't much, was it?" The beautiful dog thumped its tail several times. Bartos broke the granola bar into several pieces and lay them in front of the dog. "Eat, my friend."

The dog's head pulled back, and he looked at the meager food, then at Bartos. He nosed the food back toward the man and lay his head down facing away.

"I love you, too, you stubborn bastard. Look, one of us has to live."

Bartos gave in eventually and ate the crumbled food, it mattered little to his stomach. He was still starving, but Solo seemed pleased. Painfully, he slipped the pack and rifle over his good shoulder and the duo began their southward trek.

∾

"Someone is out there. Solo, you hear 'em?"

Bartos kept walking, stumbling, fleeing from something unseen. Night had fallen, but he hadn't stopped. He hadn't even noticed, it seemed. Solo kept bumping his leg to no avail. No one was there, the dog would have known. As much noise as he was making, had anyone been there, they could have homed in on him and killed him easily.

Solo could tell his friend was not himself, he was still nearly blind and starving. Instincts were taking over. The dog's senses told him to stop the foolish dash through the dark woods. He posted his body in front of the short man who tripped over him. Bartos crashed to the ground with an agonizing thud. Solo licked his face, but his friend wasn't responding. Air still passed out of his nose though. He lived.

Solo needed water and food, too, and used the time to go hunt. He marked the area well to warn others away and to help him find it again. The man had thought someone else was out there. He might as well check and see. He found water in the hollowed trunk of a fallen tree. It was black and full of insects, but it filled his needs. Lifting his muzzle higher, he took in small gulps of air. He tasted the scents on the evening breeze, his ancient brain processing the information. A faint smell like burnt fuel was evident. That meant a road somewhere ahead and... something else. Something not familiar.

Two hours later Solo crouched in the tall grass. The wood line behind him had given way to open pasture. Somewhere ahead was the source of the smells. The road, he had already identified. The other was a man, not a friend, but a threat. He wanted to go back to check on Bartos, but they would be heading in this direction tomorrow. Someone had stopped pursuing them and had laid a trap that they were about to walk right into. Bartos had been right after all.

CHAPTER THIRTY-NINE

Archangel studied the animal in the night scope. Up in the old deer stand, the dog didn't concern him, but its behavior seemed oddly preternatural. It had emerged from the woods as if it already sensed danger ahead. Now, it had lain there for twenty minutes unmoving. He knew he was running out of time to capture his prey. The teams searching the forest were not looking for the man. Their job was to flush him out right here. He clicked a mil-stop on the scope to adjust for the light wind.

What if the man was a Praetor commander? The thought had pestered him for days. Why would a member of the Guard be working with terrorist fighters? The guerilla warfare tactics were a standard, but all he could determine was someone had chosen allies poorly. He scoped the tree line once more, but no other heat signatures were present. He switched the unique optics to night vision. This amplified the visible light to an incredible sharpness. These were the top of the line battle gear before the CME hit. He could see that it was a large, light-colored dog. It seemed to be looking directly at him.

He felt something crawling up his arm, and when he went to brush it away, it bit into his skin. *Fuck. Goddamn fire ants.* They were probably all over him now. He slowly brushed them away and resisted the temptation to give voice to the pain or move anything but his hand. His training, like all Spec Op soldiers, had included pain resistance conditioning. The weeks they had spent in sniper training down in Fort Benning had been some of the worst. Lying under a hot ghillie suit in the extreme Georgia heat waiting for a target to appear. It wasn't unusual for the trainers to dump canisters of ants, roaches or even bees over them as they were forced to remain hidden and silent.

Mentally, he put a barrier up against the pain and any other distractions and returned his eye to the scope. The dog was gone. He swept it in all direction but saw nothing. Flipping the switch, he went through various levels of IR but still, nothing. He settled himself and went back to watching the tree line. *It was just a dog anyway,* but covertly surveilling it had been good practice for the real enemy. For some reason, though, it unnerved him; maybe it was the way the dog seemed to know he was there, but no…the fact that he lost it. That was what bugged him. He was Archangel, best of the best. Eighty-nine missions, eighty-eight kills. He would have had a perfect record, but the man had a heart attack and died before he even arrived on-site.

Vincent hated this part of the job. His days of being a foot soldier were too many years in the rear-view mirror. As a P-9 on permanent reassignment to Ms. Levy and the Memphis camp, he got out into the field rarely. Why had she made him accompany Archangel to this shitty little patch of nothing? Keeping an eye on the man was the likely reason. Levy was as distrustful of her allies as her enemies and with good reason. More than once he had stopped an attack on the woman. Still, he couldn't understand why a lost shipment and a potentially missing prisoner were so important to her.

He had one squad deployed to the north, but Archangel seemed convinced the target was moving south. If the poor bastard did go that way, he would regret it. Multiple fire teams were stationed on the southern front. Pursuit teams had now been brought in, and they and their tracking dogs would have the forest swept clear in twenty-four hours. The GPS map he was holding was updated in real time. The teams had already cleared the most eastern and western sectors. These guys were good, not like the NSF idiots.

"All teams, listen up. Target is to be taken alive at all costs. This bastard is useless to us dead. Shoot to wound only." Vincent wasn't sure if they would listen, but then again, he wasn't convinced the man was even out there. He sat the GPS unit down and motioned for another man to come over. Even in the darkened command tent, he could see the soldier's pale features. This man was one of the two remaining drone operators still on station. "Harris, any other sign of the man on the bike today?"

"Negative, sir, whatever the person was doing, he or she has moved on or could be holed up somewhere."

The glimpses of the biker had been a curiosity. No one alive exercised for fun anymore, yet this person had ridden hundreds of miles in the past week all along the same stretch of road. It was a loose end, something that didn't fit. Even if it wasn't connected to the escapee, it bothered him. Particularly so, now as that road was the southern front where Archangel and the other fireteams were located. How had the cyclist known to stop, or had he?

"Harris, tomorrow morning orbit several of the birds farther south."

"Yes, sir," came the instant reply. "How far?"

Vincent looked back at the screen with the map. "This road just past the river here will do. The Bayou Pierre"

"That would be Highway Eighteen, sir. Very good, sir, looking for the primary."

"No, I don't think the primary will get past Archangel. Instead, look for the cyclist."

CHAPTER FORTY

Solo watched his friend sleeping. Maybe it was more...the man was weak, sick with hunger, and his body was broken. It pained the dog, as they were brothers, sworn to protect each other. He hadn't moved on the man in the tree, he was a killer. Someone not to be toyed with. Hopefully, Bartos would agree with his choice not to attack. There were others out there, he'd seen them, too. Those others looked the same as the killer, but they weren't. They could be dealt with.

The sun was climbing toward mid-day when Bartos woke up. He did so in fits and starts; parts of his body seemed less willing than others to face consciousness. The hunger was consuming him, and he felt like lying back down as soon as he sat up. "Hey, Solo...still not dead." The dog chuffed an unenthusiastic acknowledgment. "Hey, I can see...mostly." The swelling around his eyes had gone down considerably. He took a long drink from the water flask and pulled on his pack. The sound sleep had helped, now it was time to go.

He used a sapling pine for support as he shakily climbed to his feet. The knee was still a problem, but he could manage. The lack of energy would continue to slow them until he got food or stopped moving. He was to the point of running his hand through rotten logs for insects or termites. He got several small morsels this way but not a meal. The Mississippi woodlands during the summer had an abundance of food. Seemingly, not as easy here. His starvation had been more because of his blindness and need for stealth than anything. Now he could see, so now he needed to change his situation.

He saw squirrels, did he have time to make a snare? No. Shoot them? Couldn't risk it. Snakes would be here, now he might spot them. Instead, he began noticing edible mushrooms, chanterelles and oyster mushrooms. He cut these and put most in the pack but began nibbling as well. Then, a strand of elderberries. He filled his belly with these and dropped extras into the pack. The foraging helped, his stomach was filling, and the vitamin-rich plants were satisfying but offered few calories and no protein.

Solo beat him down to a wide stream and was hungrily lapping at the water. Bartos filled his bottle and began looking up and down the sandy bank. This was closer to what he was familiar with. Low lying wetlands. "Look there, Solo." The dog ignored him. Scrapes and tracks on the shore, and a small depression in the reddish-brown sand. He all but ran to the spot and began digging. Small, white ping-pong ball-shaped eggs came out with the sand.

"Turtle eggs, Solo." The dog now showed some interest. Bartos took his knife and sliced into the leathery egg and brought it to his mouth squeezing out the contents. He cared not for how it tasted, although, in truth, it wasn't unpleasant, just slightly musky. He opened a few for Solo who was familiar with the little morsels. The dog lapped up the small treats and anxiously awaited more. The nest had only a dozen eggs, and they were soon gone. What they had done for the two weary travelers, though, was nothing short of miraculous.

Back on the trail, several minutes later, Bartos recognized the level of fatigue was fading. His body was still in great pain, but it was bearable, and his senses were sharp again. Sharp enough to know someone was behind them. He took cover behind a large elm as Solo ducked away in the opposite direction. He now heard the dogs, not Solo, but others - hounds, tracking dogs. He gave a small whistle, and Solo froze and looked back. Bartos gave him the hand signal that the dog absolutely loved to see. Kill everything.

Bartos was tired of being the pursued. It wasn't in his nature, and frankly—it pissed him off. The trackers on his tail had to go. Fuck it if it gave away his location. He was going to fight his way out of this. Besides, something from the other day had finally registered. One of the guys on the previous patrol had mentioned a guy on a bike. He was pretty sure he knew who that would be, and he was damn sure going to reach him.

He crouched and watched as the tracking party came into view. Two men holding at least five dogs. They would be spotters, should be a couple more behind them with guns. The dogs had the scent already— Solo would deal with them later. He preferred stealth, but that might not be an option here until...he saw a silenced M16 across the back of one of the trackers. They were within about thirty yards when the sounds of Solo attacking the trailing soldier caused all to turn in that direction. The tracking dogs hearing the other dog turned on their handlers and began straining back to the northeast. Bartos eased up behind the first man and stabbed him in the throat. As he eased him to the ground, the man released the dogs. He cut the strap on the M16, brought it up and over the dying man's shoulder and shot the other man who was still focused on what was happening behind them. Now all the dogs were free.

Bartos followed the dog pack back toward the others and saw Solo dragging a man down by the knees. Another man was trying to fire, but Solo kept his fellow soldier between them. Bartos eased to a tree and placed two suppressed rounds into the man with the gun. Solo took care of the other, then faced off against the pack of dogs surrounding him. Bartos thought about intervening, but realized his friend had this. Solo was apparently tired and not in a sporting mood. The first hound that lunged at him he bit in the neck dropping the brown hairy dog to the ground. He then straddled the suffering animal and pissed a hot stream over it. Solo looked like a special effect from a horror movie. Blood and gore dripped from his mouth. Streaks of blood painted wild lines down his white coat. Another dog foolishly took a tentative step forward as two more moved behind. Solo shook his head as if to say, *That was the wrong move.*

Solo faked an attack toward one, then turned on the lunging pair meeting them mid-air. The fight was unexpectedly brutal, even for Solo, and over in seconds. Two of the dogs were dead, the others injured or cowards. They quickly headed for cover. Solo seemed to be undamaged from what Bartos could quickly see. "Psychotic bastard, you love that shit, don't you?" Solo wagged his tail and began rolling on the ground. "Aight, hurry the fuck up with your celebrating, we gotta move."

He stripped the bodies of packs and anything useful, dropped the rifle he'd been carrying for the silenced version and took as many clips as he could find. He now also had two Sig Sauer XM17 9mm handguns. He strapped one holster to each leg. The prize find was the radios, though. He could now listen in on the NSF command channel and use the other one to try and reach the guy on the bike. He took a watch off a dead man's wrist and mentally calculated how long before Scott would likely be listening in. *Come in, BikerBoi,* he thought.

CHAPTER FORTY-ONE

The road had become monotonous to Scott. He had passed the same points multiple times now. The Trek Domane racing bike clicked along rhythmically accompanying the whisper of sound as his skinny tires rolled over the asphalt. The thought of Bartos and Solo being close kept pushing him. The idea of the pending attack on the camp scared him. Every time he turned around at that end of his loop he thought about continuing. He could have been in the area in a couple of hours, maybe he could see what was going on. *What if Tremaine Simpson is still alive?* It was a foolish thought, he had no idea what the man even looked like, and even if he did, how would he locate him among tens of thousands being held there? As he approached the town of Utica, he turned and headed back just as he had done the previous three times.

He focused on the land passing by instead of the effort the ride required. What still shocked him was the emptiness. The complete absence of people. Houses were empty, doors left open revealing dark interiors, fields empty of livestock or crops. No sounds of any type other than the bike, the road and an occasional bird call in the distance. People were becoming scarce all over but definitely more plentiful closer to his home. Here it was desolate emptiness. He felt like other survivors had to be around, but if so, they had learned to stay hidden. *Not ride around on a freaking bicycle.*

The CME had done its job, then the Messengers came through destroying everything in their path. Now, the government was doing the rest. He'd decided that if anyone survived all that, he guessed, the Chimera disease likely would finish them. Off in the distance, he caught a glimpse of color and the briefest of sounds. As he approached, he realized it was a person. Someone standing deep in the woods watching him. *Bartos?* He could only see a partial silhouette but saw now it was two pairs of legs, one much smaller than the other.

He needed to make a choice, pedal faster or slow down and investigate. He reached the decision quickly pulling to a stop on the side of the road. His gun was within reach, but he left it in place and slowly raised his hands. His eyes swept the open meadow on the left side of the highway thinking of possible ambushes. Satisfied, he focused again on the pair, "Hello, there. Don't mean any harm, just searching for my friend."

The woman slowly eased out of the woods, the girl trailing just behind her, nearly out of sight. It had taken Scott ten minutes to get them this close. He'd had to lay his guns down in the grass and move away before she took a single step toward him. She still hadn't said anything and was eyeing him cautiously.

"Hi, I'm Scott, and I'm not a threat. Of course, if I were a threat...I'd probably say the same thing."

As the woman moved out of the shadow and into the sun, he saw she was a little older than he'd imagined, maybe late twenties or early thirties. Pretty, with a very natural but somewhat muscular appearance, everything about her seemed to say 'uncomplicated.' The girl couldn't have looked more different, she was probably at least twelve but on the small side. Hers was a more exotic look, dark hair, striking features. She would grow into a beautiful woman, assuming she got the chance.

Neither of them spoke; Scott saw a glint of moisture on the woman's face. *Tears*, he thought. The closer they got, the more surprised he became. Strapped to the woman's waist was a pistol. *Why is it not in her hands?* he wondered. They stopped about ten feet away and silently stared at him still straddling the bike.

He tried once again, "Hello."

The woman, who he assumed was the girl's mother, walked out to the road and looked in both directions. "Saw you go by a few times already. No one has been on the road in months. Are you with them?"

Somehow, he knew who 'them' was. "No. I'm just a guy looking for his friend." He was unsure where to take the conversation. Anyone still alive in the world had survival skills and likely had already seen their share of cruelty. He looked at the young girl, and for some reason, his mind flashed back a couple of years to just after the blackout where another girl had stood in a yard outside a mobile home. That little girl was gone now, and her face still haunted his sleep.

He'd dropped his pack by the side of the road. He nodded to it, "If you're hungry, I have some food." The girl's eyes drifted hungrily to the pack, but her mother gave a sharp head shake.

"No one just gives away food, Scott."

"True. I would like to think that some humanity remains." He was glad the woman was talking, but he was getting precious little out of them, and it could still be a set-up. "Look, I'm not bad, but I am also not naive. You came out here, so you want something, maybe it's just information. I will happily share my food, my water and my story."

"Nobody knows anything, rumors, and lies. Crap the government wants us to know."

He really could not get a read on the woman, was she a threat, was she desperate? In his own desperation, he reached for his gear. "I'm just going to head on then. I'll be back a few more times until I find my friend."

The woman didn't speak, nor did she reach for her weapon. He realized she was going to let him ride off. The first person they had seen in months. It was then that the girl spoke. An anguished, soul-crushing plea. *"Mom, please…"*

Scott removed his foot from the pedal and looked first at the girl and then to the mom. The woman's face glistened with fresh tears. He saw the strength and the melting resolve there. Reaching into his pack he removed the two MREs he had packed, as well as the bottle of honey. He was using the honey as an energy boost, but he thought they could use it. He set the contents on the road beside him. He nodded to the pair and headed off.

The following day, when Scott first passed the same area, the food was gone. That somewhat confirmed a suspicion that he'd had. Both of them had seemed malnourished, but the woman's behavior puzzled him. She was fearless, but not threatening…hurting, but unwilling to talk to a stranger. The encounter was one among hundreds he'd had, but in the last two years, they never went like this. The previous night he'd raided the supplies that Skybox had left for him. He couldn't do that many more times, but he set the plastic bag of dried meat and fruit on the road in about the same spot. He felt eyes on him as he pedaled away.

On the return pass, the bag was gone. Four hours later, he came through again and noticed a small white arrow on the road drawn in chalk. Beside it was written the name Scott in small neat letters. He turned away intending to pedal on. This was not his mission. *Focus on Bartos.* He managed to pedal several hundred yards before returning to the spot and staring at the white arrow. *Shit, this is stupid,* he thought.

CHAPTER FORTY-TWO

Again, caution and instinct made him check his surroundings, then he walked the bike in the direction of the arrow. Scott fully realized this could be a trap, everything these days seemed that way, but he had changed in the years since the CME. No longer was he the loner, hiding away brooding over a friend's betrayal and his failed marriage. Finally, he felt he knew his place, and much of it came from helping others.

He found the woman and the girl near a small stream. A tattered tent was pitched nearby. They watched him as he approached but didn't get up. The girl was chewing on a piece of the jerky he'd left.

"Thank you, Scott," the woman said softly. "I apologize, but..." she trailed off. "Wasn't expecting any kindness from you. Nor anyone else really."

He noticed the dark circles under her eyes, the thin face even more pronounced than he realized. "Ma'am, what's your name?"

She just shrugged, "Names don't matter anymore." Her obvious sadness felt like a hollow echo.

"I guess you didn't find your friend?" She pointed to the bike, "Still riding."

He shook his head, "Need to do a radio check soon, see if he might finally check in." He eyed the campsite. If this was all they had, he wasn't sure how they were surviving. "Ma'am are you guys ok? Do you need help?" He reached into his small pack to see what was left. "Did you eat anything?" He was looking at the woman but saw the girl give the briefest shake of her head.

He held out the last of his rations for the day to the woman. "Please, eat this—you need the calories." She hungrily eyed the MRE in his outstretched hand but turned away. These two were starving to death, he could see that now, but the woman seemed to refuse to take any help from him—for herself at least.

"Are you her daughter?"

The young girl nodded, "Yes." She paused before adding, "Sir."

"Ma'am, your daughter has eaten, she will be ok for a while. Now it's your turn." She shook her head.

He unwrapped the meal and set it in front of her. "Don't be stubborn, I have more for myself, and I've been eating pretty well."

She stared at it, seemingly unsure of what to make of it. She dipped a finger into what was supposed to be marinara and then sucked the red sauce from her finger. Her eyes closed in a look of pained delight.

"I can help you?"

The woman took another tentative bite then looked at him questioningly. "Not sure we are willing to pay the price for anyone's help."

He had no idea the story of these two, but over the next several hours he pulled it out of them. One sad fact after another. Surprisingly, he learned the woman had been a deputy sheriff over in Port Gibson when the blackout happened. Her husband worked security at the airport in Jackson.

"When the power went off, neither of our cars would start. Radios wouldn't work. We waited for days for help to come. I assumed my department would send someone out when we didn't show, but they never did." With some of her strength regained, the woman had been much more forthcoming.

"So, you didn't know the blackout was everywhere?"

She shook her head, "We like it way out here, you know, away from everyone. Both of us grew up on farms, wanted to raise our daughter the same way. Problem is, you don't always know what is going on. Two weeks later, a van showed up at our front door. Bunch of guys in black uniforms telling my husband he had failed to check in. They took him, and we were on our own."

"What kind of security work did he do?"

"He was with the TSA."

Scott knew what that meant. If he was still alive, he was now part of the NSF. "So, you never heard from him?"

She shook her head no. "We made do for a while, then things got bad. Really bad. Some people took over our house one day when we were out looking for food. Others came, some on motorcycles. They killed the first people that took our house, but then they just burned it down. We were mostly out of food anyway. We'd been living mostly on eggs from the chickens at that point, but then, those were gone, too. That's when we started living out here, hiding, watching the road."

Scott knew there was more to the story, much more. "Yesterday, when we met, you'd been crying."

She looked down, her toughness all but gone. "We were just so hungry. I couldn't..." she sobbed. "I couldn't just keep watching her waste away."

"You were going to..." He knew the rest. Sadly, it did not shock or even surprise him. Nor would it be the first 'merciful killing' he'd come across. There was a limit to what people could endure, and it was even harder watching a child suffer so much. She'd still not told him either of their names. That was ok with him, he didn't pry. Names did mean something, though, sometimes they were all you had left to call your own.

"Listen to me, please. I can help you both. We have a growing community down at the coast. I can get you and your daughter there."

"On that?" she said with a tiny smile.

"No, not on the bike, we have a few cars and fuel."

"No." She shook her head again. "No, we…"

He knew she had no real reasons, it was simply fear. Anyone still alive had to be brutal. Out here she could at least somewhat protect her daughter. She had no idea the dangers out in the world, she still had no idea what had even happened. "Ma'am, it isn't going to be safe out here for too much longer. My group is made up of good people, friends. We work together. We have food and we trade with other communities. No one there will hurt you or your child." He looked over and saw the girl was sleeping soundly.

"Scott, why do you care? Why would you want to save us?"

He thought of many answers; as they rattled through his head, most seemed trite or placating. "Because every life matters now."

CHAPTER FORTY-THREE

There was a crispness to the pre-dawn air. The magenta sky was painted with streaks of pinks and purple. Scott Montgomery stopped pedaling and coasted, just enjoying the moment, the beauty, the near perfect stillness. As he coasted, the ticking of the rear wheel of the almost silent racing bike was the only sound in the stillness of the morning. He adored Gia, appreciated his friends and had finally accepted his fate as a leader, but this…this was where he was home. Speeding through near darkness at crazy speeds just to turn around in a few hours and do it all in reverse. It wasn't something that most people got, not something easily explained. To him, though, it was simply…just perfection.

The momentary glimpse of beauty passed as the sun began to rise, and the painted sky began to fade to blues and yellows. The series of faint blinking lights in the sky were back and closer this time. The drones were moving farther south, toward him. The fatigue and sickness he'd been enduring the past few weeks were gone—in fact, he felt great. According to his Garmin cyclometer, he'd ridden over 1100 miles in the last eight days. He guessed his body had finally acclimated to the new routine. How much longer could he keep it up, though? He'd left more food for the woman and her daughter, promising he would check on them again. Their story tore at his heart, but he had to handle one thing at a time.

If only the damn NSF would leave, he could radio Skybox to come up with a crew, and they could go search for Bartos and transport the woman to safety. Of course, the enemy would likely only pull out when they had captured or killed Bartos—how would he even know? He wouldn't, but as long as they were still looking, he had to believe that he lived. Scott would stay on patrol until his body quit. He owed that to his friend.

Just as the sun peeked over the trees, he heard a sound that defied logic. It was as out of place now as seeing a dragon or a spaceship in the middle of the road might be. The hair on his arms was standing up, and tiny goosebumps were beginning to show. The excitement continued as he pulled the bike to a stop and gazed up in disbelief as two fighter jets streaked silently past just over the treetops, 'US Navy' painted on the sides. "Hot damn!" Commander Garret had finally gotten over his issues with the use of military force on American soil. The actual sound of the jets arrived several seconds later chasing to catch the sleek war machines now almost out of sight in the distance. Scott knew where they were heading.

He jumped back on the pedals with a renewed vigor. Maybe this would give the NSF bastards something else to focus on. In the far distance, he saw more jets and what appeared to be a heavy lift prop plane also heading to the northeast. The president's force stationed at the internment camp was about to have a wake-up call to remember.

Todd looked at Tahir in amazement. "So, you are telling me it works?" The Navy engineers and mechanics in the room were all smiles.

Tahir nodded, "Mostly, yes, ship's navigation is back online. I rewired the weather radar back into the ship's systems. Helm control still has a few issues to work out, but yes, the system is functional. Finally having external electricity allowed us to work on everything."

"Hot damn!" he hugged the man and danced awkwardly.

"There is still much for us to do, Captain Todd," Tahir offered in vain, but they both knew that they had cleared a major hurdle. The Aquatic Goddess still had life in her.

DeVonte poked his head into the engineering section. "Hey, guys, it's begun. Skybox and the lieutenant are in the comms room if you want to come see what's happening." "Hey, kid," Todd yelled over with a grin. "She's working, she's a ship again."

"That true? Man, that's awesome." The boy was all smiles.

Tahir dampened the enthusiasm but only slightly. He talked as they climbed the stairs. Still seemed like a lot more things to get fixed, but at least the ship could move...theoretically. As they neared the next landing, Todd asked, "Could you work on the elevators next? Yeah...that'd be great...really great."

The communications room was a beehive of activity. Bobby was manning one set of earphones while Garret and Skybox hovered over a map with handheld radios in hand. They occasionally marked areas, presumably where the attacks were happening. Skybox moved a push-pin, "That would be Scott," Todd said. Above Scott was a question mark in pink marker. The presumed location of Bartos.

"Okay, BikerBoi, find a place to shelter. No idea what this will do to those guys hunting Gopher."

Lt. Garret was motioning for DeVonte. "Hey, man, can you go find Rollins? He should still be on-board here. Tell him to get up here to the conference room on the double and bring his drone link."

DeVonte had no idea what all that meant but went to find the man. Kaylie was in the corridor holding onto a very unsteady Gia. "What's happening, DeVonte?"

"Can't talk, girl, the attack is what's happening. They are freeing dem peeps up near Jackson."

"Dr. Colton, maybe I should get you back to bed, you don't look too good."

"No, I need to talk to Scott, honey. Sky said I could talk to him next time he checked in. What did that boy mean by the attack?"

"The internment camp, according to DeVonte, I think the Navy is attempting to free the people being held there."

"Idiots."

"Who's an idiot?" Kaylie was worried about Gia. She'd been talking crazy all morning. She'd even called DJ over to see if he could come take a look at her. Unfortunately, all non-essential traffic from the Bataan was canceled while they were in active mission status.

Gia sighed, "Attacking an aid camp with fighter jets." She sucked in a breath. "That proves the term 'military intelligence' is an oxymoron. They just better not let Scott get caught in the crossfire."

Kaylie led her into the conference room just across the hall from comms. Several minutes later, Rollins and DeVonte showed up. The Navy man began setting up his viewing screens. Tahir came in with a laptop. It had an active link into the Bataan air wing command channel. Rollins nodded and hooked his system into a port on the computer. The screens flickered and came to life as data and then video signals began feeding across.

Lieutenant Garret and Skybox came in. Skybox gave the handheld to Gia who smiled gratefully.

Garret stood in front of the drone monitors now showing live feeds from the battlefront relayed through the Navy tactical ops center. "Yes, watching it now. Correct, we are estimating up to 30,000 friendlies being held there."

He paused and looked around the room. "I'm sorry, can you repeat that?" He motioned to Rollins. "Pull up this one on the main screen." An IR image replaced the aerial camera view. They could make out guards as bright, whitish green figures around the perimeter. By their posture, some were obviously fighting with ground troops. Occasionally, one would fall backward, and the heat signature would begin to fade.

Kaylie glanced at Gia, but the woman was smiling, happy to be able to speak with her fiancé. She was ignoring the other activity entirely. *That's good*, Kaylie thought. *Just focus on him and the baby.* Todd had let her in on the news a few days earlier and asked her to keep a check on Gia while Scott was gone.

"Yes, there, that was where we saw the prisoners last time," Garret said. The drone began a slow orbit of the compound. "What do you mean no sign of the prisoners? They were there a week ago."

"Shit," Bobby said, "we're too late."

"Wait," Rollins said. He adjusted something on the drone link system. "Forgot these are not my drones," he said to Garret. "Ask the Flight Ops operator on that bird to decrease sensitivity so colder objects will show up."

Garret passed the message along, and in a few minutes, new images began to show, the faint blobs of light that resembled herds of cows they had seen earlier. "Whew," Bobby said, "I was getting worried."

The look on Garret's and Skybox's faces said he should have been worried. "They're dead or dying. All of 'em." Rollins said. "Those bodies are reading just over the ambient temperature. We were too late."

"Hold on—some of those are moving, shit, all of 'em are!"

The voice of Gia Colton cut through the chaos, "Get your troops out of there and into quarantine. That camp has been poisoned with the pathogen. I suggest a fuel-air or MOAB drop on that base before they get out. Those people in there are lost." She leaned heavily on the table before looking up. "Sky, please go get Scott, now!"

He looked at the pale woman bewildered at how in the hell she knew anything about the biggest conventional weapon in the US arsenal. He nodded his head; it was time to get Scott, with or without Bartos.

CHAPTER FORTY-FOUR

INTERNMENT CAMP, JACKSON, MISSISSIPPI

The smell of night jasmine and honeysuckle drifted through the slight breeze of the evening. This was one of those times that even the old world couldn't compete with. No need for phones, TV or Facebook. The night would have, in fact, been nearly perfect if he could have just wrapped it up in the palm of his hand and held onto it for a moment longer. Tremaine Simpson looked down at his empty hands. He thought about his brother, Wilson, dead and buried, and what of his Aunt Mahalia? He guessed he would never know if she survived or not.

His face rested against the fence post holding up the plastic tarp. Tre had no idea exactly where he was but assumed it was somewhere near Jackson. He was unconscious when they had dragged his bleeding body out from under the old shack. He was unaware of the kicking, cursing and spitting from the men who had discovered the scene inside. When several of them began to piss on him, he had roused briefly, then was out again. He'd ignored the pain and the humiliation. His brief thoughts had been of his family, and he wanted his old Bible, neither of which he would likely ever see again.

That had been months ago, he wasn't sure how long. When he didn't die from the gunshot wound, they had brought him here. They hadn't treated him, but instead, questioned him for hours on where his family was, what other weapons did they have and other things he hadn't even comprehended. Eventually, the questioning turned to torture. At some point, after several weeks of the agonizing treatment, he realized they weren't after information. They knew he'd lived a simple life off the grid and had no real value. It was simply punishment for him fighting back. They wanted to keep him alive, just so they could keep punishing him.

Every so often one of them would treat his wounds with some type of ointment and give him just enough of the pasty cornmeal mush to eat so he didn't starve. They might even lay off the beatings for a day, then it would start up again. He had started dreading that day, the one they didn't come for him. That was the day his body seemed to forget some of the pain. His mind began to spark a little hope, and then, the following day it started over again. He breathed in the heavenly scent once more and began to pray. He began the way he always did now, *Please, Lord, just let me die.*

The night smells faded as a new day broke over the prison camp. Cooking fires and the smell of feces lost out to the stronger odors of death and rot. Tre awoke expecting to be dragged away to the dark place where he was tortured, since yesterday had been his day off. He tried to grin through broken teeth and swollen lips. *A day off.* What a strange way of thinking. Now, they were giving him another day of relative peace? He felt sure he would pay for the privilege later.

He forced himself to his knees and then to his feet. He shuffled out from under the tarp. A light rain was falling, he held his mouth open to catch water, then used the blue tarp itself to funnel a few more drops down his parched throat. He had not been restrained since being brought here. They didn't bother as they could always find him. He had no idea how many people were in this camp but guessed several thousand in the compound he was in. You could see other compounds stretching to the distance. He assumed the people were divided up according to the jobs they did. Those who farmed corn were grouped near those fields, those who helped with other crops, probably the same.

In the few times he had tried to walk the compound where he was confined, he couldn't see what job this one was for. In his condition, he hadn't been forced to work, but no work meant no food. He only ate what his torturers gave him. His shuffling walk stuttered to a stop as he saw the guards, the ones who normally came for him. They were questioning a young Hispanic girl. She could only be in her teens but was holding an infant to one of her tiny breasts. The baby was naked and lighter skinned than the mother. Tre knew little about babies but thought this one could only be a few days old.

He watched as the guards yelled something, and one of them took off at a trot. The girl was crying; he could see her body shaking, racked with the sobs. The baby leaned back and also began to cry. Tremaine wanted to go to the girl, comfort her, but did not. The other guard came back slowly carrying a five-gallon bucket. He could see water sloshing out as the man walked up and set it down heavily in front of the girl.

The guards began to laugh, but Tre was too far away to hear any of the words. They motioned at the baby and then to the bucket. He thought briefly of all the babies he had baptized over the years. Ducking their tiny heads beneath the waters of the Pearl River, so they could be born again unto the Lord. How many of those babies had survived, how many of them might be here in this very camp?

Whatever they wanted the girl to do, she refused. One guard slapped her while another kept her from falling. Another hit seemed to nearly knock her out. The girl was sobbing in agony. Other prisoners were watching from their tiny shelters and tents. This is what the guards wanted, he knew that. This was them delivering a lesson. They were in control, they could do what they wanted. Our lives don't matter.

The guards grabbed the girl's arms, her hands still cradling the baby and forced them toward the bucket. *Oh, Lord, no.* They forced her to submerge the infant under the water. His tiny head disappeared beneath the edge of the bucket. The guards laughed and waited. They knew someone would react, and sure enough, someone did. It wasn't Tre, even if he wanted, he was too weak to move that far or do any good. An older man off to his right stood and began to run at the men in the black uniforms. He was yelling at them to stop. The shot from the guard tower split the man's head open. Tre could see the man's one eye go dim before his head hit the mud.

The girl kept looking up, shaking and sobbing. Tre offered what seemed to be a pointless prayer for the mother and child. The guards were still holding her, making her drown her own child. She was so young, so pitiful. He couldn't watch any longer. It was all so appalling. How could people do this to one another? He passed by tents and heard the coughing from inside. The hollow faces and distant expressions of eyes that could no longer register the pain of what they saw.

Earlier, he'd seen men suspended for days on fenceposts, their bodies twisted into agonizing positions. They were taken down days later, once they were dead. A horn blew in the distance, and all those who could began to silently march toward the east, to the fields or animal pens, wherever their work assignments were, he guessed. All had the look of the condemned, the damned. Many would no doubt be jealous of the old man and the baby, at least they would be free from more of this.

The misting rain had stopped, and the rising sun was attempting to shine through. Off to the south, he caught a tiny bit of movement in the sky. A bird, but no…it didn't move like a bird. Its movement was too precise; it looked almost like a tiny plane. He soon realized he wasn't the only one who saw it. He heard the guards yelling something about drones, a few gunshots rang out, but the drone simply stayed on position hovering.

Then, one of the guard towers exploded in a massive fireball. The next fifteen minutes were a surreal mix of confusion. The guards seemed to be fleeing, the prisoners gathered together for some sense of safety. No one seemed to notice the guards who were dragging the large plastic cases out of the commander's building.

As more explosions rocked the air, Tre could feel the concussive heat; some were so close. Then, the sound of jets flying low echoed across the fields and forest. He had the briefest glimmer of hope before the canisters landed nearby spraying a white fog. Within minutes, the man who had been Tremaine Simpson was no more. While his body still lay there crumpled in the mud, little else of the man remained. His final thought, *Thank you, Lord.*

CHAPTER FORTY-FIVE

Bartos could see the trees thinning and an open area up ahead. Finally, he'd made it through the forest. The sounds of jets passing overhead earlier had buoyed his spirits, although he had no idea whose they were, nor where they were headed. What he could now see was an open pasture surrounding a stand of hardwoods. Solo suddenly blocked his path.

"What the fuck, dude. Why not?" he whispered to Solo.

The dog arched his back again, then brushed a paw against its muzzle, it was his unmistakable sign of hidden danger. *Trackers behind herding us...into a fucking ambush.* He ducked, reaching out to scratch the dog behind the ears. "Thanks, buddy. You already scoped this out, didn't you?"

It took nearly an hour longer following the dog before they reached a place the dog indicated was safer. Here, too, Solo gave the danger signal but then locked onto a spot in the far tree line. "Just one over there?" Bartos asked. "Ok, Solo, go play," he gave the signal of two fingers hitting his palm. "Let me know if you need help." The dog disappeared into the high grass.

Bartos started belly crawling through the grass in the same direction as Solo. It was easily 200 yards to the trees, which is where he assumed a sniper was likely waiting. Why this one was less dangerous than the other, he didn't know, but he trusted the dog's threat assessment. He kept bumping his knee, and with a mostly non-functioning arm, the crawling looked more like a short man throwing a temper tantrum. Halfway across, he heard a single bark. That would be a call for help.

Bartos stood, rifle at the ready and began his hobbling run. He saw Solo darting out of cover and a man in black backing away drawing a hand-gun. The sound of Bartos' suppressed rifle spat two, then two more shots, and the man went down. Solo did an immediate turn and headed higher up into the small rise of trees. Bartos dropped again just as a bullet whizzed past mere inches overhead. He heard Solo on the attack again. He stood to run, then he heard a strangled gurgle. He knew the sound well, Solo had gotten his man. *So, they had stationed multiple snipers—smart.*

He quickly searched both bodies, taking the packs and briefly grabbing one of the M40 sniper rifles and ammo. Carrying two rifles proved too difficult in his condition and impractical, so reluctantly, he dropped the heavier M40.

The sniper's shot had to have been heard, so they wasted no time moving on past the ambush and soon came up to a paved road. *Shit, no vehicles.* "Looks like we're still hoofing it, friend." The bloody dog wagged his tail. "More playtime?" Bartos asked somewhat rhetorically. "Yeah…most likely." The watch began to buzz as the alarm he'd set earlier went off. He crouched low, raised the radio, set the frequency and pushed the talk switch. "Gopher to BikerBoi, you home?" He had to make this fast. *Pick up, Goddamnit.*

"About time, Cajun," was the near-instant response.

Archangel had clearly heard the shot and immediately broke cover and radio silence. "Vincent, I am on the move, reroute birds to cover sector

5. Get that fire team on the radio to find out what they were shooting at." He was already removing the camo netting and limbs covering the LSV tactical utility vehicle. The Light Strike Force Mark II was an off-road beast designed for the Singapore Army. It was part off-road jeep, part recreational all-terrain vehicle and completely bad-ass. While designed for stealth, the thing bristled with offensive weaponry including a grenade launcher and multiple mounting points for high caliber automatics. Today, it was simply transportation, though…for now.

Vincent's subdued reply came back in moments. "Angel, no comms reply on fire team Echo. Drone coverage in four." Vincent paused before continuing, "Something else, Angel, we have been recalled back to the aid camp. It's under attack. Guess you saw the birds earlier."

Archangel hit the steering wheel as he started the engine. "Fuck!" The bastard had slipped right by him. "Screw the recall, we are getting this guy."

"No-can-do, Angel. The NSF guys already got orders to redeploy. They are being picked up now and heading back toward Jackson. Just you and me and Alpha and Charlie fire teams down by you."

Archangel drove like a man possessed. Tree limbs swatted at him, but he didn't slow. He knew where the escapee would need to cross, and he wanted to beat him there.

"Birds on station. Two friendlies down, one appears to have been … holy shit, mauled maybe. No sign of target."

Fuck, who is this guy? Archangel knew he was being out-played. That was just something that didn't happen.

"Vincent, take the birds high and south of the road, see if you can get anything on IR."

"Birds have been orbiting that sector for hours. We were watching the guy on the bike, but he went dark a few hours ago. Ground temp is too high to get much of anything on FLIR right now."

Something tickled the back of his brain. *The guy on the bike, he'd moved farther out?* The guy they were hunting was heading in a direction that seemed to be going straight for him. Couldn't be a coincidence. "Do you have a last known position for the cyclist?"

"Yes, twelve miles south of your current location. By road, though, you are looking at closer to forty. Sending you the coordinates now."

"Copy that," Archangel replied.

Ten minutes later, he stood over the remnants of Echo team. One was shot, the other was nearly in pieces. That man's throat was gone, and a huge patch of skin was torn from his face. Angel knew this wasn't just from a human predator. While his mission was now two-hours back up the road at the attack on the camp, he just couldn't let this go. He needed this man, he wanted to know what other member of the Guard was involved and…*I really want to kill that dog.*

It took Archangel over two and a half hours to get to the location. He'd stopped to pick up one of the members of Charlie team to ride shotgun. Vincent would be picking up Alpha and the lone member of the other fire team when he came through. He slowed and checked the GPS. Four miles ahead looked to be a small school, maybe a daycare center. He flipped a switch, and the heavily modified vehicle's engine shut off. The propulsion immediately switched to four silent electric motors, each independently driving the wheels of the machine.

They silently approached to within a half mile of the building before pulling far up into the woods and covering the LSV. Both men unloaded gear and packs and began trotting through the woods to a likely spot. "You sure he will come through here?" the other man asked.

Archangel's withering look silenced the man. "Vincent, on location, any activity?"

From the interference, he could tell Vincent was mobile now, no doubt heading in this direction. "Negative, Angel, we lost coverage for a few minutes when one of the birds went down, but no changes noticed. Cyclist should still be holed up, and the target hasn't shown."

"Roger that." He didn't like the break in coverage, but it happened. Doing the math, he knew the escapee could have made it the twelve miles by now, but he didn't think this guy would have been in that good of condition. Unless…unless… Nah. He admittedly was mentally hoping the target wouldn't be a fellow Praetor. The one thing he wouldn't do was kill or capture one of his brothers.

He positioned the other man seventy-five yards to the east, so they could have as wide a field of fire as possible. He inserted the magazine into the Remington M40 and worked the bolt action to load the single 7.62mm NATO round. While this was no longer a typical sniper mission, you used the tools you had. Vincent would have additional tactical rifles in the Humvee. Fitting the small earbud in, he did a quick radio check, "Charlie-2, this is Bravo-1, do you copy?"

The crisp reply was instant, "Copy, Bravo-1. Mark DTT at 200 meters." Distance to target is something a spotter would normally relay along with wind speed and other factors. Today, at this short distance, none of that should matter. He began sweeping the scope over the building's windows looking for the cyclist. *Come on, you bastard, show yourself.*

CHAPTER FORTY-SIX

Archangel was struggling with why this had become so personal for him. The escapee had been good, maybe not Praetor level good. He had been spookily accurate so far, and what about the cyclist down there? At the core, he knew there was another Praetor soldier somehow involved. The trigger switch back at the farmers compound had all but confirmed it.

He settled his thoughts, forced his breathing to slow. This was what he did. He became a weapon just as much as the rifle. He'd sat in trees, on mountains, knee deep in muddy swamps for days watching targets. Waiting for the moment to be right. His mind silently did all the calculations for distance, windage, obstacles. The man he was after might be good, but he was the best.

Forty minutes later, Charlie-2 radioed in a whispered voice, "Contact, single male 200 yards south."

Archangel watched as a man in bike shorts and a t-shirt crossed in front of one of the windows in the brick building. "There's our cyclist, now who is he waiting for?" The answer came soon enough.

"Angel, we are in position."

"Roger that." *Good, Vince has finally arrived.* He would be deploying the other men now.

A radio squawk and one word, "Movement," preceded a gunshot.

The target in the building disappeared. "Who shot?"

He heard Vincent doing a comms check. One member of his team was not responding.

"Angel, be aware…"

Another voice cut in, "Multiple targets converging your twenty." That was the drone operator. Was he talking to him? Fuck, these NSF guys were fucking amateurs. What the hell, he saw nothing. The man in the window was still out of sight.

"Charlie-2, you got anything?" An animalistic snarl echoed from off to his left. It sent an involuntary ripple of fear through his body. Nothing scared him, and the fact that this did, made him want to kill that fucking beast even more.

"Charlie-2, respond."

He heard sounds of confusion and chaos both over the radio and echoing through the forest. A sniper's best advantage was always concealment. That was totally fucking gone, he realized. Movement caught his eye. He saw a bald-headed man in green camos limping across the road below heading toward the brick building. He leveled the MOAR reticle just ahead and slightly above the man's head. He had wanted to take him alive, but he was out of time and patience. He waited for a clear shot. He didn't want a twig deflecting the massive round.

Out of the corner of his eye, he felt more than saw a red and white blur coming from the direction of Charlie-2. *Shit, the dog. Ignore it, go for the kill.* He wanted that dog dead, though. His breathing was erratic. He could clearly hear the dog's approach. His training and conditioning took over as he again focused on the mission and slowly began to squeeze the trigger.

The forest sounds suddenly stopped. The sudden silence jolted him to risk a quick look. The bloody dog was there to his left, seemingly frozen in place ten feet away. Waiting for....*what*? The menacing voice to his right froze him the same way.

"Angel, you really don't want to do that." The shadow fell across his face. The voice continued, "Please don't make us kill you."

Archangel pulled his finger out of the trigger guard, rolled over and looked up into the steely eyes of Skybox.

CHAPTER FORTY-SEVEN

Scott saw Bartos coming out of the woods and rushed out to meet him. "Damn, Cajun, you look like shit."

"Nice to see you, too, brother," he said wearily. "Can you help me inside? I have to sit."

Scott got him inside the brick building. "Where's Solo?"

"Playing," was the man's only response.

Scott got food, water and some pain pills for his friend. "Sky's out there somewhere. He radioed that he'd found a military vehicle stashed nearby on his way up."

Bartos' bald head nodded. "Yeah, he caught me before I blundered out of the woods. Solo is giving him a hand now. I managed to get one, but I know there were more out there. I expect the threat has been eliminated, since I'm still alive."

The two men had exchanged two brief radio calls earlier in the day. Right on schedule, Bartos had finally checked in. Scott gave him the location, although Solo apparently had already picked up Scott's scent by then.

Scott helped the man out of his pack and guns, noticing the purple bruise and swelling. "Shit, man, shoulder broken, knee and face all swollen up—what else did you screw up?"

"Eh—life is a contact sport my friend, you should play sometime. May also have a concussion…again." He took a long drink from the water bottle. "By the way, Scott, thanks!"

Scott looked confused, "For…?"

"Giving Solo a strong scent to follow. It smells like you haven't bathed in weeks. He had no trouble leading me straight to you." He shook his head. "That dog…damn, I owe him big. I was completely blind after the wreck. Still, don't know how that dog caught up to that Humvee, but damn glad he did."

Scott proceeded to tell him about what happened in Yokena and driving Solo as far as he could. "We would have come in after you, but…well, shit. They began to bring in the big guns. We had to pull back."

Bartos laid a hand on his friend's knee. "It's okay, man, you did the right thing. You took a chance, though, riding that thing out here," he pointed at the bike.

"Guy on a bike is not a threat, remember?"

They both stopped talking as a military Humvee pulled up outside and three guys exited, guns at the ready. Two of them in black uniforms, the last was an enormous black man in a gray camo t-shirt.

"Oh, fuck," they said collectively.

"I guess you took out one of my drones. What about my other man?" Archangel asked hopefully as the two descended the hill toward the road.

Skybox looked at Solo who was guardedly walking off to the side. The fresh blood stains on his white fur left little doubt. He shook his head no. "Sorry."

Archangel seemed unconcerned, "I think he and I met last night. He is an impressive animal," the man said in a tone of obvious respect.

Skybox no longer held a weapon on the man but walked side-by-side with the other Praetor commander. Angel had already radioed Vincent telling him to stand down, collect what remained of his team and meet at the building. "What are you doing with those guys, Archangel?"

He shrugged, "Could ask you the same thing, Sky. We're following orders."

"From whom? Surely not the president. That woman is nuts."

"Of course not, she runs these pretend soldiers, not us. Our orders still come from our civilian command. The Council."

"Any other members of the Guard with you besides Vince?"

"Negative, but that's all you get until I know what's going on."

Skybox nodded, "Agreed, we all need to have a chat." While Archangel technically outranked Skybox by several levels, there was obvious respect between the two. Each had fought alongside the other multiple times.

"I heard about Pakistan, man. Sorry," Archangel offered.

Skybox shrugged, "That was a shit-sandwich from the get-go. No way to salvage it." He'd lost a lot of good soldiers over there. All of his people in that mission had died; everyone except him. "I thought you had been arrested, something about forced rendition."

"Simple misunderstanding, some feelings got hurt when I shot a politician's dog."

Skybox looked at Solo who again seemed ready to pounce. "Not very nice of you, but hardly worth imprisonment."

"Oh, they weren't upset over the fact I shot the dog, they were pissed I hadn't killed the politician."

Skybox smiled, knowing it was so far-fetched it was likely true. After an awkward reunion with Vincent, one of the NSF members was told to attend to Bartos' injuries. The man was pissed and did so reluctantly as Scott and the other NSF guy stared at each other in an uneasy truce.

The three Praetor commanders took their discussion to another room in the darkened building. Skybox had explained he was on assignment with a lab trying to find a treatment for the pathogen. "So, you're a lab rat?" Vince said with a laugh.

Skybox started to correct the man, then shrugged, "Basically."

The black man grinned, "I can't say much, I'm a glorified babysitter. Security for one of the main protectorate camps." Each of them knew what Archangel's specialty was and neither asked for details.

The quick updates out of the way, Skybox redirected the conversation. "I think we need to consider taking direct action."

"Against whom?" Vincent asked.

"Our leaders, whoever is making these horrendous decisions. Surely, you both now realize that Catalyst is not a plan for survival. It's become a plan for mass-murder."

"So, it's time to remove our Caesar?" the older man said.

"It's not unheard-of, Angel, it's part of our mandate, in fact. We serve the republic, not the person."

"I fucking know all that, but we are not the Praetorians of ancient Rome. We are the Guard," Archangel said with a tone of finality.

Skybox looked at the man incredulously, "Who will we guard when everyone is dead?" He began to make his case to the other two. "Look, there are good people out here. People not just trying to survive but trying to help others. People like my two friends in there. They are not the enemy. Whoever is behind this genocide is."

Something in Sky's words caused Archangel to flinch. Skybox noticed,

"You've realized this, too, haven't you? Whoever is running the Catalyst plan has to go. If we don't stop them, we are more than just complicit."

"Quis custodiet ipsos custodes?" Vincent mumbled.

All three men nodded. They all had thought it, *Who will guard the guards?*

"You know about today's attack on the internment camp up the road, don't you?"

"Yes," Archangel said. "It's an aid camp, not internment, and yes, we were ordered back there, but I wanted to catch your little bald-headed friend out there, so I opted to ignore the order."

"Good thing you did," Skybox said. He then proceeded to tell them of the bio-weapon released on the occupants. Archangel's reactions made it obvious that this was news to him. Sky relaxed slightly, regaining another level of trust in his brothers-in-arms.

"That fucking bitch," Archangel said. "She's lost her fucking mind."

"So, where do we go from here?" Vincent asked.

CHAPTER FORTY-EIGHT

The conversation between the three Praetorians had sounded heated and frustrated at times. It was mid-afternoon before they all seemed to be in agreement and made plans to depart. Vincent helped Bartos into a seat in Skybox's vehicle, actually Scott's Jeep. Archangel was kneeling beside Skybox still marveling at the dog. "Solo, no offense, but I hope we never meet again." The dog seemed to agree as he pulled back slightly from the man. The two surviving NSF soldiers were waiting in the Humvee for the Praetor commanders to rejoin them.

"What about them?" Skybox asked motioning to the two men in black. "They look like they want to kill us. They will report this?"

Vince shook his head sadly, "No...no they won't get the chance." They all got the unspoken meaning.

Skybox leaned in, "By the way, I like your new toy back there. Mind if I borrow it?"

"The LSV?" Archangel said grinning. "Sure, help yourself, but you might want to lose the transponders before you take it for a spin."

The Humvee pulled away going in the opposite direction as the Jeep was heading. Scott strapped the Trek into the rack and gave Skybox a lift a short distance down the road. Sky climbed out and disappeared into the foliage. Several minutes later a sleek gray and black vehicle began to emerge with Skybox behind the wheel.

"That is an LSV?"

Skybox nodded, "Pretty cool, right?" He spent a few minutes removing the tracking devices and checking the weapons.

A heavily drugged Bartos was leaning out the rear window marveling at the machine. Solo was stretched out behind the rear seat. "Fuck me, I am really glad to see you guys. I have no idea what the hell happened back there, but…wish it'd happened a week ago."

"Go to sleep, Bartos."

Scott turned to say something to Skybox just as an enormous blast rocked the Jeep from side to side. "What the fuck was that?"

In the driver's seat of the LSV, Skybox was looking at an enormous billowing mushroom cloud rising into the sky. "Damn. Never seen one actually used. That was a MOAB, largest non-nuclear bomb in the US arsenal." The Massive Ordinance Air Blast was more commonly referred to as the Mother of All Bombs.

"Who used it and on whom?" Scott asked.

Skybox told him about what had been done at the camp and Gia recommending the bombing. Scott's face looked ashen. "All those people."

"Let's go home, Scott."

He nodded and headed back toward the Jeep. "I have to make one stop first."

∾

In the vehicle heading north toward the blast, the two men in the front shielded their eyes. Vincent gave a morbid chuckle, "Guess that's the end of Captain Bailey."

Archangel had no love for the fat little bastard who ran that camp but definitely took no joy in the destruction of the whole camp. He again thought back to the black Pelican cases Vince had delivered to the man. What was in them? He thought he knew, and if so, it probably meant he could no longer trust the man sitting beside him.

The men in the back looked at the expanding cloud in shock, realization of where it must be slowly sinking in. The two talked quietly, possibly of finally getting away from the NSF. While they had survived where many others had not, they weren't feeling all that lucky. Something had gone on in the schoolhouse; something they weren't allowed to hear. All they knew was that one of the men there turned out to be a friend, not an enemy, of the two men up front.

"You think Skybox is right?" Vince asked.

Archangel didn't answer.

"What's your plan to stop the military? This shit is getting close to home now." Angel cut his eyes to the backseat with a clear look of irritation. "We don't discuss this in front of the children." Even though he knew the 'children' in this case, the two remaining security force soldiers, would not be surviving the day.

The Jeep slowed to a stop, and Skybox pulled the LSV close behind. Getting out, Scott said, "You mind leading the rest of the way? Seeing that beast in my rear-view is giving me the willies."

"Chickenshit," Skybox called as Scott disappeared into the woods.

A few minutes later, Scott re-emerged with the mother and daughter. The older woman was leaning heavily against him. She stopped short when she saw the vehicles and Skybox leaning against the tactical LSV. "It's ok, they are my friends. The one we were looking for is injured, he's in the back seat."

She still looked nervous but allowed herself to be led to the open passenger door. Bartos scooted awkwardly to make room for the girl. Skybox motioned Scott over. "I assume there is a story here?"

He nodded, "They are at death's door. I don't even know their names, but I think we can help them."

"Can we trust 'em?"

Scott looked back at the woman staring straight ahead. "Yes."

He gathered up the rest of the food in the Jeep and split it up between the woman and the girl before following Skybox back toward the coast.

The woman was nibbling on a bit of homemade granola that Angelique had made. A sound from the backseat surprised him.

"Mister, how long has it been…you know, since the world ended?"

"It's Scott, hon, and it's been just over two years."

He saw in the mirror a nod of acceptance.

"Sylvia," the woman said, looking back to her daughter. "I'm Trish."

She took another bite, "I'm sorry I'm not better at this, but…thank you, Scott. Can you tell me more about where you are taking us?"

CHAPTER FORTY-NINE

NORTHERN ALABAMA

The colonel studied the map plying across the hood of the truck. His second in command held a corner to keep it from blowing away in the stiff wind.

"Confirmation, sir, they dropped it." The radioman spoke from inside the truck.

"Good, very damn good! Now we are getting somewhere. We are going to root these bastards out and take this country back."

Major Kitma was less confident. Using the backchannels of the Patriot Network, he'd learned from his old friend, Mr. Porter, about the joint strike mission in Mississippi. Dropping the bomb on enemy troops would have felt more like a victory, but he knew it had been to kill infected civilians and to limit the spread of the pandemic.

We should have started sooner, he thought. *Before it all got out of hand. We could have been a force for good, saved this country. Instead, we helped that woman build those damn internment camps.* As one of her first acts, the new president had ordered the base commander to assist in clearing roads and construction of the 'Relocation Assistance Centers,' as they were called in the early days. Within weeks, the commander ordered the process stopped as the newly ordained 'NSF' troops began rounding up more citizens at gunpoint and herding them into the labor camps.

It wasn't like they went after every American at once. They targeted those deemed to be the most problematic. Citizens who were on a list in each state to carry a concealed weapon. Then, those with a federal firearms license. From there, they quickly moved on to anyone with a licensed firearm or a hunting license. Eventually, if you were licensed to drive a motorcycle or could legally operate a HAM radio, you were likely to be rounded up. By the time they got to imprisoning former vets, national guard members and then ordinary citizens, no one was left to protect the rest. Of course, many had gone into hiding at the first signs of government action. Many of these were now part of the ad-hoc Patriot Network.

That had been almost two years ago, and it had only gotten worse. *So many deaths, so much suffering.* How someone could do this to a fellow human was beyond his understanding. He was a soldier, trained to kill, and he had seen and done more than his share of it but only enemy combatants. Never innocent civilians.

This was the president's agenda. She had all but lost military control from the very beginning. Then, she began an attempt to push the world's largest remaining military force into obscurity. She cut the command channels for communication. Cut off food, supplies, fuel and, of course, funding. Many of the enlisted troops had eventually gone AWOL realizing there would be no punishment and that it may be the only way to see their families ever again.

Marginalizing what remained of the once powerful military had been a strategic victory for Chambers. But you don't put baby in the corner forever. Not one that big, at least. Faced with its seemingly inevitable demise, the US Army had been the first to fight back against the forces loyal to her. At first, it was in minor skirmishes such as retaking Maxwell Air Force base in Alabama. Then later, freeing the first of many of the labor camps. That was when the president had declared them enemy combatants and renegade warlords.

Later, in the battle for Atlanta, the NSF began using a new tactic. A devastating campaign of using advanced aerial drones to fire on the Army. Several months ago, when pushing deep into North Carolina, they began seeing the plague victims. The image of that first camp outside Fuquay-Varina, where the bio-weapon had first been released, was horrific.

Kitma struggled to contain that memory. He'd lost good people in that fight, some of the survivors had to even be considered casualties. What they had seen, what they had done to save themselves was just too much. For the remainder, that event had solidified the resistance. While the force out of Fort Benning were not the only ones fighting back – not all US military bases had resisted. The president still controlled a majority, but not by much. The Marine base at Camp Lejeune had joined, eventually, so had Fort Bragg, then more. Still, they knew, at some point, they would be going up against regular Army—brothers-in-arms—no one was sure they were ready for that.

Currently, they were leading a convoy from Georgia toward a National Guard base in northern Alabama. With most bases in a communications blackout, they never knew if the next base would be abandoned, manned by NSF troops or converted into another of the damnable internment camps.

There was a coalition of sorts being formed. The Navy was most active, followed by Army units, some Marines and a scattering of Air Force bases not under the president's control. It was quickly becoming an all-out civil war. Kitma scratched a mosquito bite just under the Latin phrase tattooed on his dark bicep, 'Non-Ducor Duco.' While he told everyone he was from Johannesburg, no one in that country would ever claim him. His lineage was instead from a small country on the West African Coast. An area well-known for its fierce warriors.

"Major, any word from Maxwell?" Colonel Willett asked.

"Yes, sir, they only have enough avgas for a couple of sorties but are standing by," Kitma responded. The large Air Force base a hundred and fifty miles south was part of the coalition. All their forces were stretched thin, low on fuel, manpower and supplies, but were ready to help.

The convoy eased to a stop several miles short of the base. From here, they would launch mini-drones to recon the area before moving in. These were the canary in the mines. If they saw NSF troops or worse, it could change their plans drastically. The small pager Kitma kept hidden in a pocket went off, surprising him. The fact that it still worked was amazing. The message itself was long overdue in his opinion.

'P-Command - Tasking Instructions to follow.' He read the message. "Colonel Willett, sir, we need to talk."

CHAPTER FIFTY

HARRIS SPRINGS, MISSISSIPPI

Solo climbed out of the Jeep first. Skybox helped Bartos get to medical. Scott had radioed ahead, and Angelique was there to give him a hug and ready to help the two newcomers. Scott saw Gia glaring at him from an upper deck. This was one of those impossible situations he just wasn't good at. He'd all but lived on his bike the last week, been sick, lost even more of his body weight and been nearly shot multiple times. Now, he was about to hear how selfish and stupid he had been from the woman he loved.

Instead, Todd and DeVonte came down the gangway to greet him.

"I just saw him," Todd said grinning. "He looks like shit." He said it like it was a good thing. Scott supposed it was better than the alternative—*looking dead.*

"Glad you're back, Boss. Got you a surprise." DeVonte pulled a hand from around his back and produced a glass of ice tea. Honest-to-God ice. Little opaque cubes of frozen water. How ordinary and yet…Scott took it from his outstretched hand almost reverently and raised it to his lips for a tentative drink. Oh, man, it was so cold, so good. So ordinary, yet so wonderful. "Oh, my God, this is good. Thanks!"

"You can thank Angel, she has been full of surprises lately," DeVonte said.

Gia had made her way down, he saw her through the gathering crowd. She was still trying hard to stay pissed, but her resolve was weakening. The look Scott gave her melted what was left of her anger, and she ran to him. The embrace and kiss were pretty epic. He wasn't sure where it ranked for all of mankind, but for Scott Montgomery, it was definitely in the top two. "Hey, G, miss me?"

"Gonna kill you, just not here in front of your friends," she said through her clenched teeth and forced smile.

"Love you, too."

They kissed again. She held him at arm's length, giving him a visual once-over. "You don't look good, hon, you've lost a lot of weight."

"I'm fine," he said wearily. "Just tired, put in a lot of miles."

"Finish being a hero then meet me down in medical. I want to draw some blood. And who was the attractive woman you brought back? Is this some habit with you that I should be aware of?"

He shook his head and laughed, "They just needed...." he stopped realizing she got it. She was just jerking his chain. "So, tell me, woman—how do you know about the bomb?"

She shrugged, "I have lived and breathed military for the last two years, you pick up some things. Besides, we have had to look at all contingency plans for controlling the spread."

He kissed her again, "Ok, I want to check in with the others, see how the attack went. I'll see you in a few."

Todd and DeVonte accompanied him first to the radio room where Bobby updated them on the attack on the camp. "So, no signs of survivors?"

Bobby shook his head, "That thing was a monster. Biggest conventional bomb in the world. There is literally no sign of the camp."

Scott nodded, "That's good, I guess. I mean, I hate it for those people, but that would have sped up the infection reaching us by months. Did you tell the Simpsons?" He was looking at Bobby.

"They know," he said sadly. "They are devastated, not just about Tre—they all had friends or family that had been taken to that camp."

The bile rose in his throat as the hatred Scott had for the president and her troops kept growing. He hated everything about these camps. So many lives lost, so many families ripped apart. There was nothing more he could do for now, but increasingly, all he wanted was vengeance. "Guys, where do we stand on repairs?"

They all began to grin. "So, you haven't talked to Tahir yet," Todd said. "That little guy is amazing. The ship is well on her way back to fully functional. Wastewater recycling is down, along with a handful of other systems, but most of the major stuff—done! It works, Scott. In fact, in just a couple of weeks, we could take it out for a shake-down cruise…except…"

"Except you need fuel. Right?"

"Yeah. We really need Bartos for that," DeVonte said.

"He's going to need some time. The Cajun is pretty banged up right now. Crazy bastard is lucky to even be alive. I'm heading down to the clinic and get checked out, but thank you, guys, for everything. I'm serious—you guys rock."

"Hey, Bro," Bobby said. "That was a nice thing you did, staying out there. Not giving up on him."

Scott shrugged, "I didn't do anything, hell, he all but saved himself….as usual."

Bobby nodded and smiled, "Still…"

Scott gave a nod, he got it. *We don't abandon family*, was the unspoken message. Bartos was family.

～

"Hey, Uncle Scott," Kaylie gave him a quick hug as he entered the clinic. She was starting an IV on Bartos who was sleeping away on the cot.

"Jeeze, what did you give him to knock him out?"

She was inserting the needle into a vein in his arm. "Him? Nothing, he just laid down and went to sleep. Not sure he'd gotten much rest out there. Multiple injuries, dehydration, cuts and hundreds of bug-bites." She gave a tiny laugh. "Most men would be dead, but knowing him, he'll probably be back to 100% by tomorrow."

"Kaylie, I brought back a mother and daughter, too. I'd appreciate it if you could check them as well. Severe malnutrition but could be more. They don't talk much."

Gia walked in, lab coat and mask on. She was back in business mode. "God, I should have made you shower first. You really smell." She removed Scott's shirt and checked him out. She pulled a syringe from her lab coat and drew a few vials of blood and then had Kaylie take blood pressure and temps. "Scott, how far away from the labor camp were you? The one the Navy attacked."

The question sent chills through him. *Am I infected? Have I just brought the damn disease here and contaminated the AG?* At the same time, another voice whispered inside his head, *Don't be a pussy, stop acting afraid.* "Um…I guess the closest I got would have been forty miles or so, but that was before the attack. I was sixty…or maybe seventy away when it all went down. Why?"

She ignored the question. Damn, his future wife had no bedside manner. Probably best she didn't work with humans. She looked over the chart adding a few things.

"Any nausea?"

"Yes, some."

"Bowel movements?"

"Really…no, I mean, yes. I think."

"Headaches?"

It went on until she asked, "Favorite color?"

He smiled, "Blue—no, yellow."

"Off you go," she said smiling.

"To the bridge of death," he replied, quoting from the scene in an old Monty Python movie.

Kaylie just looked perplexed.

Scott questioned, "Is anything wrong, Gia? I mean, I know I was out there a while, and I lost a little weight, but I feel fine."

"I'm sure you are, love," she said, now, fully back as the love of his life. "I just want to make sure. Have to keep you alive until the wedding at least."

She gave him a quick peck. "Some of your stats are a bit off, and you have some bruising around your back and stomach. Probably nothing, but I'll want to check you out again. For now, though, just go get a shower."

Kaylie echoed the instructions, holding her nose as she did so.

"Gladly, and love you both, but y'all are horrible doctors. Try not to kill Bartos, it would upset Solo."

CHAPTER FIFTY-ONE

Despite Bartos' resilience, Scott beat him by several days recovering and resuming his normal duties. Bartos ambled around the ship for days with an arm in a sling and a crutch. Todd mocked him for being a baby. Jack was somewhat more sympathetic. "Jesus, man, I thought you were tougher than this—you going soft? Getting captured by NSF mercs….what's next?"

"Screw you."

"What about those farmers, a couple were down in the infirmary with me, not talking much. All the rest get here ok?"

Jack nodded, "Yeah, I am sticking around a few more days just to keep an eye on 'em. They were treated bad….really bad. Honestly, I think they all want to go kill as many of the black-clad bastards as they can. We have most of 'em housed out at the old Harrison place. Figured they would prefer to be on a farm for now. Plus, all the stuff we brought down is there. Except for the supplies, of course, they are already in the ship's hold. Angelique and Ms. Mahalia are having some canning and freezing parties trying to put up as much of the fresh stuff as they can."

"Good…good," Bartos said. "Farmers are a tough lot, I'm sure it bugs the shit out of 'em – what happened. Do you think they'll leave with us? I mean, when the AG sets sail?"

"If it gets as bad as Scott and Skybox say….shit, yeah. Hell, everyone is going to want on this boat. Before then, though, you gotta get back into the diesel making business."

Bartos knew that. He'd already been out to the refinery site twice in the time he'd been back. "I know, I know. I have Scoots and a few of the Navy people picking up waste oil now. If I can get this arm working again, we'll be back in business."

"What can I do to help?" Jack asked. "I'll be heading out again in a few days. What should I be looking for?"

Skybox was with Ghost and Solo when Scott found them. Seeing Tommy up close like this was still unnerving. The man could stand like a statue and then move with such fluid animation as to seem inhuman.

"What's up, Scott?"

"I talked to Bartos, he agreed to keep the meeting you had with those other guys quiet for now."

"Thanks."

"I haven't mentioned it either, but I don't like keeping secrets from my friends, my fiancée. Especially when it involves our future. Can you give me some idea of what's going on?"

Skybox sat down on the grass, idly throwing a ball for Solo to catch and occasionally bring back. "I'm sorry, Scott, but no. Not really, just please understand that we are a country at war, and the line between friend and foe isn't that clear yet."

"But those guys were your friends?"

"They are my fellow soldiers. We are all Praetorian Guards. That is not the same as friends. We have orders that seem to be in opposition at the moment."

"So, you didn't tell them about us?"

"No," he looked at Scott with a look that was hard to read. "Honestly, they didn't even bother asking, they knew I wouldn't reveal it."

Scott understood Skybox's reluctance to discuss it, but the whole situation was so unusual he couldn't let it go. "So, they didn't tell you anything? Nothing about their orders or who was giving them?"

The other man threw the ball again, Solo turned and sprinted off after it. "We talked, Scott, that's about all I can say. They may not be our allies, not yet, but I don't think they are the enemy…not the real enemy at least."

Scott wasn't ready to give up, he knew his friend wasn't telling him something. He glanced up at Tommy stoically facing out across the grassland. Skybox felt a deep loyalty to the Guard, he knew that. It likely ran much deeper than the friendship they had developed, but Skybox had put himself in danger when he squared off against those men. "Sky, I get it…I think. Never been in the military, but my dad was, Todd was. I know there is a brotherhood there, a bond that you won't break. Someone is imprisoning Americans without cause and using them as forced labor. When they are threatened, they are using a bio-weapon on these same innocent civilians. Do you know who this is, and do you have a plan to stop it?"

Skybox looked at Tommy, Scott realized they were making eye contact. Tommy was staring back at Sky; he wasn't sure what was passing between them, but they were communicating on some level. Skybox nodded and stood, giving Solo a quick scratch behind the ears. "Working on it, Scott."

~

Scott stared blankly at the tablet trying again to makes something appear that wasn't there. The food supplies had dramatically improved, but there was still a problem. The figures in the table he had gotten from Angel left no doubt the AG would need more supplies to be able to leave for any significant length of time.

"We gots a problem, Boss." DeVonte walked into the ship's cabin Scott used as an office and flopped down into one of the floral covered chairs opposite the desk.

"I don't have time for problems."

"This one is serious, Scott, a girl done gone missin."

Scott slowly lowered the tablet he was holding to the desk and gave the boy his full attention. "Who is it, and what do we know?"

"It's one of Kaylie's friends, Diana. You know, kinda short, blonde hair."

Scott nodded, he knew her. She was the daughter of one of Todd's friends. Her parents didn't make it through the collapse, but she had proven to be a lot stronger than them. "I know her," he said grimly. "What happened?"

DeVonte gave a small shrug, "Well, you see, that's just it. No one seems real sure. She just wasn't where she was supposed to be. She's been working most days over at the Harrison place with the farmers. Didn't show up yesterday, and she wasn't in her cabin. Angel said she hasn't been in for any meals in a couple of days.

The Harrison's was one of many old farms that had been supported by the community in exchange for food. No one with any lineage to the original owners remained, but it would forever be known as the Harrison's. Jack had set it up as a kind of hub for the rescued farmers. They bitched and complained about the sandy soil and how much worse it was than Yokena, but damn if they weren't plowing and planting before that first week was done.

"Well, shit," Scott said. The community lacked any sort of police force other than Bartos and Skybox when he was around. After the Messengers' battle, they had spent a month or two using deputized search parties going after the few survivors who had escaped the storm. One small group turned out to be Marauders. The ruthless bastards who had been second only to the Judges in the levels of cruelty they dispensed. The Messengers' 'Army of God' were all a murderous bunch, but they had been rounded up and dealt with. After that, things had calmed down around Harris Springs. Yeah, they had the occasional fights and disagreements, but those rarely needed any law enforcement. "So, who was the last to see her?"

"Scott…we got this. Bartos just wanted me to make sure you were aware. They are working it as a missing person. Nothing sinister here… at least not yet. One of the Navy guys here is an MA, and he's helping out."

Scott nodded, MAs in the Navy were Masters-at-arms; basically, they were the law enforcement guys in the service. "That's helpful, please let Garret know I appreciate that. Keep me posted on it, ok?"

"Course I will. BTW, Scott, I was wrong."

Scott's eyebrow raised slightly.

"You remember when I said you getting laid would help you be less grumpy? Yeah…I was totally wrong on that."

"DeVonte."

"Yes, sir?"

"Get the fuck out."

The kid got up grinning and put his hand up, "Sorry, man, sorry. Just call it like I sees it."

Scott buried his face in the palms of his hands. "This job really sucks."

CHAPTER FIFTY-TWO

DJ looked at his mentor confused. "But...but all of this work on the Archaea, are you saying that it was all for nothing?"

"DJ," Dr. Gia Colton said, watching for Tahir's reaction as well. "You can't study life, especially microbial life without studying death as well. Our planet has had at least five major extinctions so far. It is a self-correcting eco-system. We hear about the one that killed the dinosaurs, a massive asteroid impact, but there are lots of others, some many times bigger. The largest to ever occur on Earth, the end-Permian mass extinction, or 'The Great Dying,' is described as the most severe biodiversity crisis in Earth history. It alone wiped out 95% of marine life and 70% of life on land about 252 million years ago.

"Keep in mind the simple fact that 99.9% of all life before us, all life that ever was on this planet, is now gone...extinct. There is a cycle to life itself, it begins, evolves, adapts and then dies. Even humans. You've both heard of LUCA?"

Tahir spoke softly, almost reverently, "Life's Universal Common Ancestor."

"Yes. Where did we come from, what genesis separated itself from chemistry to become life? This primitive cell was something more, something amazing."

"This would predate the Archaea then," DJ said questioningly.

Instead of a direct answer, she said, "If you could send your DNA off to be traced back to the very beginning, not just human evolution, that would only be a few hundred thousand years, but back to the very beginning, you would discover LUCA. Yes, Archaea would show up in our past, but that would not be at the beginning. It is one of the six kingdoms, one of only two without a nuclei. It's not a plant or an animal, so what is it?"

"Life," said Tahir.

She sat on the edge of her desk looking very much the part of the beautiful college professor. "Why are we here? How long do we have? Can we survive?

Gentlemen, you see, life is way more complex than we know. For billions of years, it has been an endless series of adaptations, test and fail, success and mutate. The process is constantly building a better life-form. We argue whether a virus is a lifeform like that is really a question. We can't look at complex biochemistry and separate out what is life and what is not. From LUCA to now, the process has been one of constant adaptation.

"Humans are the sum of all that has come before, but…we are not the end. We will also face an end. Perhaps we are already facing it. There is a rather controversial field of study called dysgenics which reveals that humans may have peaked already on the evolutionary chart. We may even be devolving, getting increasingly less intelligent, not more. Our comfortable existence, man's ability to adapt his environment to supply, not just his needs, but his wants, has made us not just soft but dumb. If true, the simple fact that less intelligent people tend to reproduce in greater numbers than more intelligent people will inevitably cause the decline to increase."

"So, how does all that fit into this…into the Chimera?" Tahir asked.

She moved to the board and began to draw. "Hidden inside all of us is inactive genetic material that, if we knew how to activate it, could radically alter us as humans. We know, in fact, that all humans carry a secondary DNA called an i-motif. It looks nothing like the typical double-helix, behaves completely different and is nearly impossible to study—so what does it do? Why is it there?"

"A relic, just a vestigial artifact, like wisdom teeth," DJ offered.

Gia tapped the marker against her teeth making a clicking noise. "So, something that was essential to humans at some point but is no longer needed?"

"Yes," DJ said triumphantly.

"No," she said flatly, deflating her brightest researcher.

"Tahir, are you familiar with the MAOA gene?"

The young man thought briefly but shook his head.

DJ spoke up, "The Psycho gene."

Gia frowned. "That…is one name for it—the 'Warrior' gene is another. It was discovered years ago and suspected long before its existence was proved. It is one factor in contributing to the aggressiveness in humans. What makes some people great fighters, or, if you take it to the extreme, even callous murderers. Perhaps it is biology as much as anything. Originally, we thought it was a mutation, an aberration and quite rare. After all, most people don't go around beating other people to death. Imagine our surprise when we found that all of us, 100% of humans, carry the MAOA mutation. What is different is how that gene is expressed, at what levels and also the interplay with other genetic factors."

Tahir automatically thought of Skybox, the gene certainly seemed active in him. "If we could manipulate that gene, crank it up, you could create super soldiers."

"Precisely, and that is what I think is happening. You put us on the right path, Tahir, focusing on the Archaea instead of the virus."

DJ was finally catching up, "So, someone wasn't working on a bio-weapon so much as a tool to force genetic manipulation into a wide-spread population."

"Forced evolution," she said.

"But for what end?" Tahir asked. "The mutations are not helpful, they aren't making people stronger, better, faster. They are mostly making people dead."

"I'm not so sure about that, I think we are focusing on the dead and infected because, well, they scare the shit out of us. How would we spot someone with more beneficial mutations?"

"Like Skybox," DJ said.

She nodded, "Yes. Just like Sky."

CHAPTER FIFTY-THREE

"We have to announce it soon?" he said feeling her belly. The little pooch of her abdomen was just barely noticeable but definitely getting larger. They'd been discussing wedding plans for weeks balancing them with everything else going on. Angel and Kaylie had taken a more active role in planning the event. Lots of people were still out searching for the missing girl, but momentum seemed to be building for the wedding date to be set.

"Bobby already knows," she blurted.

"Seriously?"

"Yeah, Skybox, too. I was sick, well, you made me sick. You know, when you went off to be stupid. Anyway…"

He smiled, *neither had mentioned it.* "Well then, maybe we should just tell everyone."

She grinned and clapped, "Oh, thank God. I am about to bust to tell people."

He gathered she was far enough along not to be worried anymore. He was clueless on all this, but he was over the moon excited. He was going to be a dad. *How could something I didn't even know I wanted suddenly mean so much?*

"Should we try and reach any of your family?" he asked tentatively. "Maybe Commander Garret or Skybox could get a message to them."

A shadow crossed her face briefly before the smile returned. He'd asked her once before, and she admitted not knowing whether her family had made it. He'd met her family once at Gia's first wedding. Her father struck Scott as a brooder with little personality. He was aware of some of the phone calls between Gia and her parents leading up to that day. The relationship had been strained prior to the nuptials, but they had made an appearance. He recalled her father trying to force her to accept a check, and she refused. The man had later given it to Scott to pass along to his daughter. When he reluctantly did, she just tore it up without even looking at it.

"No, Scott. It's time to move on."

He cocked his head studying her. What pain was his future wife carrying? Surely, they were proud of her. She was brilliant, and how could they not be proud of who she had become? Finally, it hit him. They were within one of the infection zones. Even if they were still alive, they likely couldn't get out, nor would she want them to travel here— possibly bringing the virus with them. If she was close to a cure, though, that might change things. He was about to make another comment when he saw the tears.

Damn, I have to get better at this...

Bartos and Chief Petty Officer Warburgh were getting nowhere fast. The GTO that Bartos used for most trips sat on the side of the road with the hood up. The Navy man watched as Bartos removed clamps and hoses to reveal a small white plastic cylinder.

"Bad fuel?" Warburgh said.

"Yep, just like we thought. That shit's starting to disintegrate in the tanks. This filter is all gummed up. I can make it work by bypassing it. We have another one in-line. We've equipped all the cars with extras, but that's not going to help for long. We need fresh gas soon, or we'll be back to horse and buggies."

"Yeah, Navy is facing the same issues. No fuel, except the nuclear boats, but they're running out of food and sailors. I hear you been working on a possible fix?" the man said questioningly.

"For diesel, yeah. Some of your guys and mine are doing final assembly now. With my bad knee, I'm not a lot of help right now. Thought I might be more useful helping you today."

"Glad you did," Warburgh said. "Otherwise, I would probably be stranded out here."

He and Bartos got back on the road in a few minutes. Despite Bartos' lingering issues from the concussion and injuries, his mechanic skills were still on-point. Still, he was a bit uncomfortable around the Navy man. Perhaps it was the sidearm he kept strapped to his waist, more likely just the man's demeanor. Even sitting beside him in the old car, Warburgh was ramrod straight. An unmoving and inflexible officer.

The Navy investigator was already reviewing notes from the earlier days of the investigation. "So, the girl was last seen leaving the AG to go to the farm. That was around six AM last Friday. We have heard that she never arrived. What else do we know about her?"

Bartos watched the road pass by as he thought about the girl. "She's cute, in sort of a tom-boyish way. Seems popular, lots of friends. Angel says she is the one who organizes the birthday party each month for all of the kids with birthdays that month."

"Sounds like a sweet girl," Warburgh said with what sounded like genuine empathy. "Bartos, what are you thinking, she got lost, accident, foul-play or did she just give up?"

He knew what he meant, in the years since the CME, life had gotten so tough. So much of the old world, the easy world, was gone—some people just couldn't handle it. Eventually, the sadness and emptiness caught up and consumed them. He shook his head, "Diana seemed to have it together. She lost her parents, yeah. Her mom got sick and passed away during that first winter. The father, well, he mostly drank himself to death afterward. The girl, though…she seems tough. I don't know her all that well, but she has a good reputation. Now, with electricity on at the AG, decent food…" He sighed, "I got a bad feeling."

The two men exited the car to go and speak with the current caretaker of the old farm. Two goats came up nipping at Bartos' pockets looking for a treat. Smiling, he pulled several fingerling carrots out, giving two to each. Despite his disdain for people, Bartos had a love for all animals, even the ones he would one day likely kill and eat.

They spent several hours talking to everyone who worked with Diana. The farmers from Yokena all came by to shake Bartos' hand reverently. The acknowledgment of what he'd done for them was simple and sincere. Both men examined the workspace Diana used. They went over every conversation anyone might have had with her. Who was she seeing? Had she been upset lately? Had her work been slacking? Warburgh kept taking notes, but Bartos didn't hear anything particularly noteworthy. This was something else, something new, something dangerous. He felt it down deep. Diana was gone, she wouldn't be coming back.

CHAPTER FIFTY-FOUR

Kaylie and Gia had set up an unusual exam room for an unusual patient. Tommy, aka the Ghost, sat on the bank of the small bay. Skybox and Roosevelt were there as well. Few people managed to get this close to the former Spec Op soldier with the ugly head wound. Scott and Kaylie had been the first ones to see him when he arrived in town just after the CME. Tommy couldn't talk, but Skybox seemed to be able to read something in his long-time friend's eye movements and expressions.

Today seemed to be a good day, Tommy was calm. Not every day was like this. In the clinics where he lived after the IED blast, he was in a mostly vegetative state, no one gave him any chance of even partial recovery. But here in Harris Springs, Skybox found his friend walking, surviving, fighting even. Something had definitely changed, and Skybox had asked Gia and Kaylie to see if they could determine what. Unfortunately, Tommy had an adverse reaction to enclosed places, so the exam room was here, outside.

Roosevelt was patting Tommy's arm and talking soothingly to him while Gia checked his pupil dilation. One eye was fixed while the other was dilated. Kaylie was checking reflexes which alternated between non-responsive to off the charts speed. They even managed to hook him briefly into a portable EKG to read brain wave patterns. The exam took most of an hour and included drawing several vials of blood which the man seemed not to even notice. Toward the end, though, he was growing visibly frustrated and wanted to leave. Gia patted him on the back and suggested they let him go for today.

Skybox watched his friend quietly walk away and slip out of sight. He smiled as that had been a trick Tommy had been perfecting all his life. "So, Doc, any ideas what is going on with my friend?"

Gia didn't respond immediately. Skybox knew that Tommy had apparently also been a passenger in the helicopter crash that killed Gia's husband and child. She started slowly, "Sky, I'm so out of my field here, anything I say will be very likely wrong. Most of his medical history is based on what you told us. There are some things which I believe are clues, though." Her face darkened with concern. "Your friend is a walking contradiction."

"How do you mean?" Skybox said.

"Well, for one thing, he shouldn't be alive—not with that much brain matter missing. That shrapnel basically lobotomized Tommy. In some cases, we know the brain can essentially rewire itself after trauma. So, other parts take over the job for missing or damaged areas. This is in the very basic areas—higher function areas have not been repaired. You see how clumsily he walks, how his body trembles when it is at rest?"

Roosevelt spoke up, "But he can move like a shadow, and when he fights, it's like watching a ballet or something, sho nuff is."

Gia nodded, "That is a very good point, I would imagine that certain things for him that formerly were in the technical or analytical parts of his mind are now governed by the creative regions that were less damaged. His fighting ability could be one of these things. Some head trauma patients have been known to develop brand new skills such as being able to paint or play music for the first time in their lives. Several have become *savants* in fact. The quality of their new talent rising far above even the most gifted."

"Why is he improving now? Will he continue to get better?"

"I can't answer that, Sky. I need to go over our tests more, but my best guess is no. He physically has a limit as to how much he can recover. Too much has been removed for him to ever be whole. So much of the left hemisphere of his cerebrum is gone, I don't know how he functions even." She finished packing away her equipment in the leather bag.

Snapping the metal latches, she stopped and locked eyes with the warrior. "Skybox, let me give it to you straight. They kept Tommy heavily medicated in those facilities…to the point his brain was unable to do much in the way of recovery. That is what changed, he is no longer on any medication."

"He was medicated for the pain. I mean, that is what they told me. Was that a lie?"

"No, no…I don't think so. My guess is that would be pretty standard for someone in that condition. The amount of swelling in the brain, the horrible burns, other injuries. It had to be excruciating. Pain levels to the point that would overwhelm a person's nervous system. Untreated, he probably would have died."

Skybox turned and began walking back to the ship with the three others. "But he is past that, doesn't seem to need the pain meds anymore, right?"

"Sky, listen. When you hold onto that man you feel your friend. You want…maybe even need him to still be in there. Maybe a small part of him is, but when I held his hand, I felt a body trembling in pain and fear. Tommy is in agony all of the time. He has simply learned to control or channel the pain somehow. Who knows how long he can do this or what happens when the pain gets to be too much."

Skybox went silent, his hopes for his friend fading fast. "So, that's it? We need to medicate him again?"

"I'm not saying that, although it may be the most humane choice. The human body is an amazing machine. We are capable of so much that we don't fully understand that anything could happen. I don't think he will make any significant improvements, but I would guess his former doctors would be impressed with how far he has come. My guess is that he doesn't sleep, not well at least. He looked exhausted, and Roosevelt has said he lives like an animal most of the time. Perhaps if we gave him just a mild sedative, something that would at least allow him to sleep well several times a week. That might be enough relief for him to maintain some balance."

Skybox nodded reluctantly.

Roosevelt mumbled under his breath, "Not an animal, I said he was a predator."

CHAPTER FIFTY-FIVE

UNKNOWN LOCATION

The young woman's hair was matted, caked with blood and hung in front of her face. Eyes kept watching, kept darting back and forth like a caged animal. The smell of piss and shit tainted the already fetid air, but even that did not cover up the other smell. Something darker, something hidden, something dead. She was afraid, yes, but beyond that, she was certain. She fully knew this would be her last night on Earth. Her last time in this body. So, as foul as the air was, she breathed it in gratefully because it was life, and each breath could be her last.

The footsteps came again. She had known they would; again, her eyes peered into the shadows of her prison. She tried to force them to see into the darkness. A shape, a figure…something. Someone. The terror she felt could no longer be contained. The breath she savored now burned inside her lungs, it needed to be released. Slowly, silently, she exhaled. The need to hide from her captors trumped all other thoughts, but that was just crazy. They knew where she would be, they had chained her to the wall. They were watching her now, a cat eyeing the mouse just before it pounced. If she listened close, she would be able to hear them, a breath, a heartbeat…maybe just a tiny sound as they parted their lips or swallowed. Her ears were no more helpful than the eyes. Why were they doing this? What did they want?

The pounding in her head was back. Why wouldn't it stop? Something, something in her mind was pulling at her. How long had she been here? She no longer had any idea. The days and nights all ran together in her rapidly fracturing mind. *This is not me, this is not how I end*. Her determination could not keep her alive any more than it could keep her sane. *Fight back, fight!*

She needed water, her mouth was dry. Maybe that would help the headaches. What was happening to her? Where were they? She looked at her wrist; she felt the irritation where the shackles had rubbed the skin away. In the dark, her fingers rubbed across the rough, chaffed skin and then the smooth bloody grooves. They did not touch the shackles though, those seemed to be missing this time.

There! It was a breath, perhaps half a breath. It could have been just the scrape of a shoe. Someone, though, someone was there, watching her. Waiting for her to die. She made up her mind, the steely determination that had caused so many problems in her life rose up again. If they came again, she would kill them. *How?* She was chained to a wall. She had no weapons, nothing to fight back with. If she had any chance, she should have done this when she first got here. She'd been strong then, she could have taken them. Had she only realized what they were going to do to her, she would have fought. Only…she hadn't realized she was strong. Instead, she was suffering, she felt like a victim. She wanted pity.

CHAPTER FIFTY-SIX

HARRIS SPRINGS, MISSISSIPPI

Scott watched as Skybox and Ghost sparred with the wooden staffs. Jack was back and going through some of the stick fighting techniques he'd picked up over the years. His fighting discipline was called Keyshi, a somewhat offbeat and brutal form of martial arts. Scott smiled remembering it was Jack's training that he had used on Skybox when they fought on the oil platform. So much had changed, enemies became allies.

The fact that the other man was engaged was even more amazing. Tommy, or Ghost, as most still called him, still couldn't talk, moved little, never sat as far as anyone knew, but he was training, fighting. interacting with purpose, anticipating moves, feinting blows and picking up the new instructions with ease. Roosevelt was right, the man moved like fluid. He didn't step as much as flowed to a new position. It was artistry, a dance, and it came from inside an empty shell of a man. As soon as the sparring stopped, he returned to an upright position, eyes unfocused on the horizon. *What is going on inside that man?* Scott thought.

The buzzing of a drone in the distance reminded him of what he was doing out here. Rollins was repositioning them over another part of the canal and parts of the old town looking for any sign of Diana. The girl had been missing for nearly two weeks now. Most assumed she had just left, but Bartos had convinced Scott to keep the search going.

Bobby and Kaylie came up, Jacob not far behind. "Are we ready?"

They had volunteered to search a section of the search grid. Everyone in the community had been out searching at some point. Scott didn't think anyone would find her, he still felt that she had just left, but she'd been Kaylie's friend. The relatively good mood unfolded itself and disappeared as the report from Rollins came over the radio. Kaylie muttered, "Oh, shit," and began to run.

Warburgh beat everyone else to the location spotted on the drones. Kaylie's hand covered her mouth as she saw the pale human arm extending from the pile of trees and debris along the Intracoastal Waterway. Her dad wrapped an arm around her shoulder as they watched from a distance. "Honey, it may not be her. Don't think the worst."

Scott went closer to help. The hurricane and flood earlier in the year had created massive debris piles at several points along the canal. This area was one of the worst. Others assisted as well; Warburgh was tossed a rope someone had tied off to a thick tree. He saw Todd in the growing crowd, "You think it's her, Cap?"

"God, I hope not. If it is, though, no wonder we haven't found her."

Scott climbed the pile using the same rope and on top watched as the Navy investigator worked his way down to where the body was lodged. He could see the arm was stiff and pale, almost bluish. Warburgh moved some of the debris, and more of the body came into view. He looked up at Scott and shook his head. Finally working his way to the spot, he reached down and slowly detached the arm and held it up. People with a vantage spot back up the bank gasped in unison.

"It's plastic," he said. "Probably a store mannequin blown out here in the storm."

Scott didn't know how to feel, disappointment at it not being Diana didn't feel right, but it would have been resolution. He could see Bobby holding Kaylie tightly to his chest, her sobs evident over the mostly silent crowd. The emotional toll was too much for them. No matter the outcome, he decided right then to scale back the search to official personnel only. He couldn't put his niece and others with a connection to the girl through any more of this.

Bartos was leaning against the scaffolding looking at the jury-rigged filtering system. In the weeks since the ordeal, his collarbone had mended, but the knee was still hurting. The ligaments, he was told, needed longer to knit back together.

"Scoots, this shit is nasty. You sure it's still good—not contaminated?"

The other man nodded and grunted something unintelligible.

Bartos shook his head, "If any of that flood water got it, we're going to have problems when we fire this puppy up."

"How much are you starting with?" Scott asked from the floor below. The pumps were sucking the waste oil out of the dilapidated tanker truck and into what Bartos had said was a holding tank. The hoses carrying the thick fluid were thumping and moving across the floor in tune with the pumps' rhythmic heartbeat. The whole contraption looked like something the coyote would have built to catch the road-runner in those old cartoons.

"Five hundred gallons. Any less and we'd probably just wind up with tar. The pressure vessel can hold about three times that much, but we want to start small."

Scott nodded, he understood the process in principle. Heat up the oil to a certain point, run it through a series of filters and you should have useable diesel. "So, how far away do we need to be when that thing starts up?"

"Stop being a pussy, Scott. Just because I am heating oil up to incredibly hot temperatures inside a container that certainly wasn't intended for this kind of pressure or heat, what's the worst that could happen?"

"We could all die, Bartos."

The bald man snorted, "Well, yeah, there is that, I s'pose." He climbed down the rickety framework. "I'd say about half a mile then." The whole contraption made an ominous sound. "Maybe a little bit more."

CHAPTER FIFTY-SEVEN

"So, am I going to turn into a zombie?"

"Hush, my husband-to-be…and they were never zombies."

"According to Sky, they acted a lot like zombies."

"Well, even if they were, you would be immune. I hear they only eat brains."

Gia stuck the needle deep into his butt cheek. "Ow! That hurt…on multiple levels." He rolled off the exam table and pulled up the somewhat ratty shorts he was wearing.

She pulled him close and kissed him. "My poor baby. Your test was all good. Just wanted to give it enough time to be sure."

"So, what was that you gave me?"

"The latest antiviral," she said with a grin.

"Wait…what? You have the treatment—a cure?"

She shrugged, grinned and began replacing items into their respective drawers.

"Holy shit, does anyone else know?" he asked excitedly.

"My team knows we are close."

He knew they had been keeping Skybox over at the bio lab on the Navy ship the last few weeks. "So, was this something you developed from Sky's blood?"

"Yes and no," she said still grinning. "The version of the pathogen he carried was too far removed from the current one to be of much help. What his bloodwork did tell us was how to isolate the gene mutation. Once we were able to get samples of the current virus, coming up with a way to treat it effectively was much easier because of what we learned with him."

Several thoughts occurred to Scott simultaneously; he asked the most pressing one first. "You say treat it…not cure it. So, we, and I mean me, will not be…you know, immune?"

Some of the joy left her face, "Maybe, honestly, I don't know. I think you are safe from the version out there now, but if it keeps mutating, who knows? A small percentage of people have a natural immunity. Sky's appears to be unnatural, but honestly, at some point, a variant of the disease could prove lethal to them as well."

"Have you taken it?" he asked.

His head was resting on her stomach, the pregnancy now far enough along that you couldn't miss the bulge poking out of her loose-fitting lab coat. "I can't take the risk, Scott."

"What risk?"

"This is a new transgenic treatment. It will alter your body to fight the Chimera disease. Who knows what effect that might have on a fetus?"

"What about the effect the disease could have on you, G? We know it is on the way, hell, you work with it every day."

She shrugged, he knew he wouldn't win this battle, but he had to try.

"Just promise me something, if we know we can't help being exposed, please take it. The baby won't make it if you don't."

She nodded reluctantly and embraced him as tightly as she could; he placed his hand on the baby. This was a terrible time to have a child, yet he couldn't imagine life without one now. He knew Gia would do anything to protect it, including sacrificing her own health. He just hoped it wouldn't come to that.

The group acting as the town council were grouped in a circle of chairs. The slight chill in the air was held at bay by the small bonfire in the middle. The talk so far had centered around the failing search for the missing girl, better news on Bartos making workable fuel and progress reports from Tahir and Todd on the improving condition of the AG.

"By the way, Scott, congrats again," Bobby whispered during a lull in the conversation. "Can't believe I am finally going to be an uncle." Scott just laughed, "You guys are awful."

Making the second announcement several days earlier had been the epitome of anti-climactic. Everyone was in on the secret except Scott and Gia. Apparently, Bobby and Sky didn't keep secrets as well as they thought.

They had assembled the entire community after the late meal several days earlier. Scott and Gia stood up and made the big announcement. He had gone on and on about family and community and this being the first new baby in the community; the audience had just looked at them. No one clapped, no one smiled, no one even stopped eating. A few shrugged their shoulders and went back to chatting with friends. Scott was humiliated, Gia looked dumbstruck. It was then that Todd could contain himself no longer and busted out laughing. The whole crowd erupted at that point, lining up to give hugs and congrats.

"Total assholes."

"Yep!" Bobby agreed. Scott was pretty sure it had been his idea.

"Why are we meeting out here, Scott?" Bobby said.

"It's nice out, and we never do this anymore." Scott brushed the hair out of Jacob's eyes. He was amazed the boy had even let him hold him. Bobby and Kaylie were watching him, he knew that. He'd never been around children much, and being a parent scared the bejesus out of him, but he wouldn't openly admit that. "Also, Gia is coming, she has some news."

"Oh shit, twins?" Jack said.

"No, not…just wait for her," Scott said flustered.

The firelight flickered across the faces gathered there. Scott studied them all, one by one. The group was quiet, all seemingly caught up in the moment of relative calm. Jack was back for the moment, Todd sat with Angelique who was holding DeVonte's hand. Tahir was on the other side of Kaylie sitting next to Bartos. Solo was curled up next to the fire. Roosevelt was leaning back appearing to be asleep.

Scott hadn't planned to say anything tonight as it was Gia's show, but these were his friends. There were others, of course, Skybox, DJ, even Garret and Scoots, but this group right here was his family unit. The reason he was still here, still alive.

"You know, since that night two years ago, Todd, Liz, Bartos, and Solo befriended me. We sat on the porch of my cottage and watched the lights of the aurora dance across the sky. Jack, I'd met the day before. He introduced me to the others. I don't think any of us had any idea then just how serious it really was, certainly not how bad it would become. You guys saved me, gave me a purpose and a mission. This community means everything, guys. When I was on the bike, hell, whenever we go anywhere, the people are missing. So many have fled or are gone, so little of what was remains. I am not sure we take enough time to realize how special what we have really is. We face one problem after another, each one more insurmountable than the last, but we keep fighting, keep believing, keep loving. Now, this chapter of our lives is coming to a close. Where will we go, what will we find out there—when can we come back?"

Angel let out a tiny sob as Jacob silently crawled off Scott's lap and went over to sit closer to the water. The somber moment cracked when Roosevelt snored loudly. Everyone chuckled. Scott felt soft, familiar arms around his neck and looked up to see Gia's gorgeous face, her red hair shone like flame in the firelight. She leaned over and kissed him mouthing, "Love you."

She sat in the empty chair beside him. Everyone waited for her to speak, but she just looked around the fire at the group smiling, seemingly soaking in the love radiating out like warmth from the fire. "I have no idea how to follow that," she said with a shaky laugh. The others smiled and nodded. "I haven't known most of you that long, but you have become family to me as well. In all the chaos in the world, you guys… this place is my safe harbor.

"Now, I know my work is not that helpful to the community—not directly at least. I can't run a kitchen nor a whole ship like Angel. Can't fix things like Bartos or Tahir. Can't find supplies or make friends like Jack. Can't lead or protect you like Scott or Skybox, but I do finally have something to contribute."

Scott reached for her hand.

"You does plenty already, Ms. Gia," DeVonte said. "You keep Mr. Grumpy here from bothering da rest of us."

She laughed before continuing. *Okay, out with it already*, she thought. She drew in a deep breath and began, "We believe we have a working treatment for the pandemic." The look from all gathered around the fire was of shock and excitement. Gia registered the emotions and anticipated many of the questions. "It seems to be safe and effective. Scott and a few others have already received an earlier version of it. We're making more as quickly as we can, that's what DJ is doing now over on the Bataan. The treatment isn't perfect, though, and it needs time to make certain changes to your body's defense system to be fully effective."

Angel spoke a question on all their minds, "Does that mean we can stay here? Not have to leave?"

Gia shook her head, "Sorry no, I don't know that we can make enough to treat everyone by then. Also, once this news gets out, the Navy people will likely control distribution. Perhaps the biggest reason to keep making plans to evacuate is the infected themselves—this vaccine won't do anything to keep them from attacking."

"So, how long?" Todd asked. "I mean, before the rest of us can get it."

"Probably a week, maybe a little longer. The bio-vats at the lab are pretty small, but as long as they are monitored closely, we should have enough by then."

Everyone began clapping, and Gia looked embarrassed. Kaylie and Bobby came over to give her a hug, then the rest of the group joined in. After all the drama and chaos, this night was just what was needed. Scott was unbelievably proud of his fiancée and all her dedication and hard work. He sat there silently wishing their wedding day could get here a little quicker.

Todd got the little meeting back on track. "Assuming we are still leaving, we need to determine a destination. Scott asked me to try and head that up, and I have a few ideas I'd like to run by you. First, understand we have some limiting factors, the biggest being fuel. No matter how much the Cajun can make, the ship can only carry a limited amount, and that's likely all we have from then on. If we keep enough fuel in reserve to return, then that cuts our maximum range in half. Kind of the same with food, except, we must pick a destination that can sustain us. So, it must be a temperate, long growing season and some natural occurring sources of sustenance to keep us going until we can grow our own."

"So, we are heading to Hawaii?" DeVonte asked with a laugh.

Tahir spoke up, "That would actually be ideal, great climate, year-round growing season and far enough from infected areas that, likely, we would never see the pandemic reach there. The problem is fuel. We couldn't make it even halfway."

"The kid is on the right track, though," Todd said. "An island would be ideal or someplace with low existing population and natural barriers to help keep us isolated. What we have come up with is this," he held up a printout with three locations circled, all close to each other. He began passing it around.

"Costa Rica?" Bobby said, looking down at the paper.

"It's the best for us. Not that far, we can likely reach it on less than half of our diesel. Which gives us the chance to move on, if need be, or come back here eventually. There is a mid-size island about twenty miles off the coast which is where we think we should go initially. It had a large sugar-cane plantation on it, but twenty years ago part of that was cleared for a luxury resort. It has a deep-water dock on a natural harbor, so we can pull the Goddess right up to the resort."

Tahir jumped back in, "The resort had been closed for renovations when the CME hit, so our expectation is that few people are there. It is also close enough to the mainland that we could go there to fish, hunt, and trade with the surviving locals. While the pandemic might burn itself out before it reaches there, we have to assume at some point it will reach it. The good thing is that until then, it may be one of the safest places on Earth."

"Any chance they have electricity?" Angel asked. "I have really gotten used to having it again, dread going back now."

Everyone nodded heads in agreement. Tahir smiled and shrugged, "We don't know, they have a line to the mainland and emergency generators for hurricanes, but we have to assume no. I do have some ideas on that, though. I need to talk to Commander Garret, but long-term, I think we can get power."

CHAPTER FIFTY-EIGHT

UNKNOWN LOCATION

She lay in silence, her body racked with pain but absent of moisture to any longer form tears. No longer was she restrained by chains, now leather bindings around her arms and legs held her to the bed. The thin mattress beneath was more of an illusion of comfort than actual padding. Her fingers could just stretch down to feel the metal tray beneath the padding.

A hospital bed, a gurney maybe. She knew she was no longer in the dark, wet space; the sounds were different. It smelled antiseptic with a less pronounced odor of human activity. A blindfold of some type covered her eyes, but she got the feeling the room was bright. *What are they planning? Who are they? Please, God, just make all this stop!*

It didn't stop. It didn't stop for a very long time, and when it did, she would no longer be the same. She wasn't so sure now that she would be dead, but she knew she wouldn't be the same. Someone, a man, she thought, stood over her, watching. *What does he want?* she wondered. She was naked, of that she was certain, but long past caring. Modesty was the least of her worries. What if he raped her? She couldn't be sure that hadn't happened already. The thought seemed detached as if it had broken off and somehow was no longer a part of her.

The pounding in her head was growing worse, she felt the fever returning. "Hello," she tried to say. Nothing came out, she was unable to speak. Something was in her mouth, it was round and hard but it was not the man, of that she was sure. This was a gag of some type. What if she vomited, would she choke? Choking would mean death, death meant release from this torture. Oh, what a welcome release it would be. She should vomit just to piss off whoever was out there, the watcher.

Despite her mentally forcing herself to be sick, she could not. It would not come—nothing. It felt like her stomach was devoid of actual content. She was empty, wasted, a discarded husk of the girl she had been. The pounding in her head kept her from working on it further. She was so weak, she couldn't even die. *Please, please, please stop,* the voice in her head begged.

* * *.

The pain didn't stop, it ebbed and flowed but stayed her tormentor. New pains joined it, cuts, scrapes and pinpricks. At one point, she was sure her entire body was covered in ice. She might be freezing to death, she wasn't sure. *What is happening to me?* Every nerve in her body seemed to be on fire. She knew now her ears were plugged as well, or maybe they had destroyed her hearing. Taken a sharp object and punctured her ear drum, that wouldn't have surprised her. She only realized she was deaf when she failed to hear herself moaning anymore.

Her back had sores where she had been strapped to the bed, unmoving for too long. She could feel herself using the bathroom at times. *How?* She wasn't eating or drinking. In fact, *how am I alive without water at least?*

Time had long since become unimportant. She was here, this was now.

Yesterday's pain was irrelevant, she refused to consider what tomorrow might bring. To lay in agony and torment hour after hour with no relief and no hope had numbed her. She no longer thought about rescue, she only wished for death.

Unbeknownst to the girl, a lone face watched through a small window. It was a face devoid of compassion but not a cruel face...not exactly. Tears made wet trails down the face. *Soon,* the face said before disappearing. "Suffering is surviving in this world," he whispered.

CHAPTER FIFTY-NINE

HARRIS SPRINGS, MISSISSIPPI

His boots fell heavily against the metal steps, one side still landing harder than the other. It had been weeks, but the knee was still more painful than he wanted to admit. He refused to use the crutch except here in the refinery building. It was a vulnerability, a weakness, some insecurity that he refused to even acknowledge. The truth was, that ordeal had been a wake-up call to him. It was a much closer brush with death than he cared to admit.

"One more batch done, Chief."

"Thanks, Scoots, I guess that's it until we get more." They had processed all the waste oil they could find. The stuff worked great, no difference that they could tell, from any other diesel. The Navy guys had all been impressed, but…it wasn't enough. Not even by half. Still, the tanks on the AG now had enough to probably get to Costa Rica, but it would be close. No coming back, though, not unless they found more. "Go ahead and shut it down, and I'll get the last of it pumped into the ship."

He hated to tell Scott and Todd they were coming up short, but the refining process was not as efficient as he and Tahir had estimated. That, and a lot of the old, used oil they'd found had been contaminated with seawater from the flooding. The AG needed more, the Navy was nearly out. Some tough decisions were about to be needed. Bartos was glad he wasn't the one making them.

～

"Commander Garret," Scott said, shaking the man's hand. "Welcome aboard."

The career Navy man had not been on the AG since his crew had helped tow it here two years earlier. "It's looking good, guys, y'all have done admirable work. I hear congratulations are in order, Scott. Wonderful news!"

The conference room was half full. The meeting was meant to be small with only the essential people involved. Skybox, Scott, Todd and Bartos. Both of the Garret's were present as well as one of the naval engineers, Rollins, and a new man, someone they'd never met. He was in fatigues and introduced himself as Major General Daly of the Marine Corp.

Commander Garret jumped into the conversation full speed as was his habit. "Let me get to it. The Bataan is going to have to pull out. We simply don't have the fuel to stay on station. We are nearly out of avgas and Jet-A for the birds, and our diesel tanks will be sucking air within the month."

This wasn't news as much as it was a known inevitability. Scarce resources had been a fact of life since the blackout. Scott broke in, "We could offer you some of our diesel, but your man already stated it wouldn't make much difference."

The commander nodded, "Thanks Scott, we appreciate the gesture but know you have plans for that. Plans we would love to be a part of, but it's not looking too good." He sighed deeply. "We potentially could take from other vessels, but the whole fleet is running extremely low."

Skybox spoke up, "What about the SOR, sir?"

The older Garret leaned back and scratched at the two-day beard around his jawline. "It's an intriguing consideration, Commander, I'll give you that. One of our other ships has done recon on some of the fields in Texas and Louisiana. They all seem intact. That is crude, though, and even if we could access it, we'd still need to refine it. Your man's setup won't work for that."

Bartos shook his head, "No, that's right, needs more of a full refinery for that."

The Strategic Oil Reserves were the nation's emergency supply. The 727 million gallons were mainly stored in large salt dome caverns around the Gulf Coast, primarily in Texas and Louisiana. Garret passed around a few aerial shots, "Our beloved president seems to believe these are hers, not the nation's. She has positioned troops at every location. I'm afraid that damn woman may have finally found a way to cripple us. If we attack, they might even blow the fields just to keep us from getting them."

"So, we can't easily get to the supplies, and even if we could, we have no real way of processing it," Scott said, realizing he had basically just restated the obvious. "If we don't get fuel, you and the Bataan have to pull out of here, and…we may not have enough to leave. Well, shit…"

Garret laughed, "Come on, Montgomery. This is where you whip something brilliant out. An idea none of us have even considered."

Scott grinned uncomfortably now that everyone was looking at him, "I got nothing."

He could feel the clock ticking, He had to come up with something to get more fuel. He and Bartos had discussed going farther out to find waste oil, but the few attempts to do so had been failures. The tanks they found were already dry or so badly contaminated as to be worthless. Biodiesel was already a big thing when the world went dark, Bartos had told him. They had just gotten lucky that most of the oil dumps around Harris Springs didn't get picked up as often.

Skybox sat across the table from him. "Scott, this is bigger than just us. You know if the military runs out of fuel they are finished—the country will be, too. It's not just the Navy. The Army, Air Force and all the rest will fall like dominos. She can starve them all into submission."

"So, what can we do, man? I mean, where are they getting fuel from? Could you check with your associates?" Scott was desperate for ideas.

"No idea, but I imagine they have vast reserve tanks at the protectorates. Those would likely be some of the most heavily guarded places in the country though."

Since getting to know the Praetor commander, Scott had learned some of his ways. He was pretty sure he knew this look. Skybox was holding something back. "But, you have an idea—right?"

Skybox fanned the Navy's aerial photos across the table and nodded, "I do, but…you aren't going to like it."

CHAPTER SIXTY

Skybox was right.

"You're insane. Not just a little. I mean a lot."

Skybox laughed, "But other than that, you're ok with it?"

"Hell, no, I'm not ok. Give all our fuel to the Navy and Army to plan a sneak attack on the one location you feel is the least protected?"

In truth, the plan was more complicated than that, and the frontal attack was only one part of the man's plan. Scott looked at the photos again. "You're sure these are the ones?"

"Yep, I confirmed it with Rollins, and he confirmed with the higher-ups at Naval Intelligence, the guys who study aerial surveillance for a living. I also had Tahir see if he could get us some real-time satellite recon in the area."

"The smaller tanks contain diesel…refined diesel?"

Skybox nodded.

"And these are not part of the SOR, but you still want to attack the garrison guarding the nearby oil reserves?"

"You got it."

Scott leaned back, mouth agape, staring up at the ceiling. "Sky, it's crazy, our people here will have me shot if I give away the only potential way of escape for...for this." He picked up the photo and dropped it again. "Fuck." The bad thing was, he knew Commander Garret would be all for it. The Navy was just as desperate as they were.

Skybox leaned over, "Scott, its survival, maybe not just of the country either." He straightened up and stretched. "Sometimes, Brother, you just gotta play the long game."

∼

"Well, it wasn't easy convincing them, but the Army is in. A colonel from Fort Benning is sending a small armored battalion as well as some of their Rangers to help us on the ground. They did say this will likely use all the fuel they have left, so this will be an all or nothing gambit for all of us."

The younger Garret's briefing was on behalf of his dad who was effectively the fleet commander now. Everyone was a bit more comfortable with the lieutenant, so the meeting was informal and relaxed. And then, it wasn't. "Ok, from this point forward, the mission details don't leave this room. Deal?" They all nodded.

It had been decided that Scott would not be going on this mission, nor would Bartos, despite his expertise possibly being needed. Instead, Skybox had tapped DeVonte, Todd, Scoots and several others for the mission. The contingent from the AG was necessary for several reasons. One was to have enough 'skin in the game' to justify getting a share of the captured diesel, but the other was harder for Scott to deal with. Jack and Todd knew the area. They both were raised not far from there, and Jack had traded with a nearby survivor camp for much of the past two years.

The mission plans had been refined, but it was essentially what Skybox had drawn up at the table a week earlier. The Army was sending their armored units by sea on a large cargo hauler made just for that purpose.

They would do a night insertion at two locations. Most of the Army Rangers as well as Navy SEAL teams would be airdropped, something the lieutenant had called an MFF from far out to sea. Presumably, they would free-fall down and glide nearly fifteen miles to the target coordinates. A smaller group made up of both teams was going to get in close for recon and hopefully disarm any booby-traps or explosives around the oil tanks. Skybox was leading this last group.

"Any troop strength estimates?" Scott asked.

"From what we can tell, probably around 400 men guarding the facility. That may not be the real problem, though. We have reason to believe they have deployed a lot of tech around these holding tanks. They have to know we will make a run for them."

"But they are all centered around the crude storage here," Todd pointed at the large, squat, white tanks on the photo." He then moved his finger a short distance below, "But our real target is these?"

"Yep, those are commercial tanks, one of the commercial refineries is nearby and stores fuel there for local distribution. It just happens to be relatively close to the SOR field. While the main attack is there, we are going to try and tap this baby and drain it dry."

"Why not just sneak in and do that without all the rest?" DeVonte asked, clearly nervous about playing soldier.

The younger Garret looked at him, "That, my friend…is an excellent question. First, draining it will not be fast, it will probably take eight hours or more, and the tanker we will be using is not going to be easy to hide. Secondly, we couldn't get the Army's buy-in unless we went for the SOR. They want those reserves, and to be honest— they want just as badly to make sure the president doesn't have them. For that reason…" he paused, seemingly hesitant to say the rest.

He took a swallow of water from the icy pitcher. "For that reason, we are also going to be launching Tomahawk cruise missiles at several of the other facilities."

Scott was the first to object, "That's crazy, LT—I mean, Republican

Guard in Kuwait kind of crazy. Other than just losing the oil, it will be an ecological disaster. What's the point?"

The Navy man shook his head, "Doesn't matter, we don't get a vote. It is going to happen."

Tahir was leaned back with his eyes closed, "If the point is to keep the oil away from the president, why not just launch the cruise missiles at her location?"

Silence filled the small room; it too was a good question. *A damn good question.* "We…don't know where she is," Lt. Garret said. "No one has reliable information on her."

Tahir tapped a finger on the table. "I can find her. In fact, I am pretty sure I can. In fact…" he paused. "Do you have bunker-busters in your ordinance?"

Garret seemed a bit stunned, "Yes, we have the AGM-65Es."

"Probably going to need several," Tahir said. "Let me get to work and see what I can do."

"Tahir, I will need proof. Concrete evidence to take to the C.O. for that —you understand."

"Oh, yes, sure…sure."

~

The part of the plan that Scott hated most stood before him now. "Why you guys?"

Jack just laughed, "We've been through this, Scott. I know the area, I know the locals. We've traded with 'em."

The SOR target location in West Hackberry, Louisiana, was indeed familiar to them. The small group of survivors near there had been through a lot, and the assistance from the AG had kept them going over the last winter. Jack's was the face they knew and trusted.

"It'll be fine," he continued. "Me and Todd and the kid are taking the Marco Polo and a few supplies just like a normal trading mission. Just going to do some poking around while I'm there."

Scott shook his head, "You remember the last time you did that, don't you? We ended up in a war."

"Well, shit, Brother…much simpler this time because we know we are going to have one. Look, man, my job is to make sure we can win it."

"Damnit, I don't like it. You are going in there with no backup. No weapons even," Scott said, his frustration growing.

"Well, weapons are outlawed now; if we get stopped by the boys-in-black, that might be a death sentence," Todd added.

Scott shook his head again, "Travel is also illegal, you hard-headed bastard. Why did y'all volunteer for this?"

Jack placed a meaty hand on his friend's shoulder, "You know why, Scott."

Scott looked at Jack, "You've done enough, man. Let someone else carry the load this time. I don't know what you think you are making amends for, but enough self-sacrificing."

"Brother, we need that fuel. I'll be careful, but face it, this is the end of days." Jack sighed and looked at the other two. "We really have no choice. I love you guys and this community, we've been through a lot… lost a lot, but we can have a future if this crazy ass plan works."

CHAPTER SIXTY-ONE

She pulled him close and kissed him deeply. "Something is coming between us, love," he said. They both looked down at the still small, but growing, baby-bump.

"Thank you for not going."

"Not going on what?" Scott asked innocently.

"The thing…the whatever stupid thing you guys have cooked up this time. Just…thanks."

He nodded at his fiancée. "Well, we do have a wedding to plan. Priorities, you know—save the world or keep my girlfriend happy."

Something flashed across Gia's face, and then she softened and smiled, "You chose wisely. So…about this wedding. Have you asked him yet?"

"No, just hasn't seemed like the right time, but I will."

"Hurry it up, Mr. Montgomery. We have lots to do before then. Invitations to mail out, have to get gift registries done, and oh yeah, honeymoon plans. Clock's ticking….tick-tock."

He laughed, thinking of the expense and spectacle her first wedding was, his had been as well. None of that really mattered, and despite this being a real event for the AG, it was still going to be a simple affair. They just wanted to be man and wife. They had spent most of the morning together planning the nuptials. It was a rare luxury for the two of them as she'd had to be at the labs more than ever now. The treatments were trickling in, and about half those aboard had already received the vaccine. Gia had been right when she said the Navy would want to take care of its own first. He knew she had been battling the fleet medical officer on their behalf. *Wars within wars*, he thought.

"Are you even listening?"

"Um, yeah, hon. I am," he lied.

She knew she had him, "Okay, then which one?"

Fuck... "The second one," he guessed.

She shook her head, "What's wrong?"

Scott shrugged, "As my mom used to say...it's a little bit of a whole lot. I am putting people at risk, maybe all of us. If this mission fails, we may all be screwed, and worst of all, Jack is going to be out there on the pointy end of the stick again."

"And you think you should be out there with them...right?"

"Gia, I just gave all our fuel away as our part in all this."

"Still not going to tell me what it's about?" she asked coyly.

"Can't, sorry. Not even to you."

She sighed, "Fine, ok, music is done. You picked number two, 'It's the End of the World as We Know It.' Good choice, I always liked REM."

"Ugh," he dropped his head into the palms of his hands.

Several hours later, Scott finally admitted he had no idea what he liked, had zero taste in food, flowers, music and most of the other 'apparently' important things in life. All according to his lovely bride-to-be. He ultimately relinquished all control to her for the ceremony, vows and anything else she might possibly ever want. She grinned happily at him for being 'so reasonable.'

Tahir yelled from three rooms away, "I found something! Woot-woot! I got you now!"

"Did he just say woot-woot?" Gia asked.

"He likes to appear reserved."

Tahir came through the office door, "She's at..."

"She who?" Gia asked, looking at Scott accusingly.

"Oh." Tahir looked embarrassed. "Sorry, thought you were alone."

Scott shrugged, "It's fine, what did you find?"

The young man nodded as he turned the laptop for Scott to see.

"What am I looking at?" The scene was an animation, something more like a NASA animation than anything else he could think of. "What is this, it looks like…."

"Orbital trajectories, yes, yes." Tahir grinned.

"What does that have to do with the president's location?" Scott glanced at Gia who looked even more confused.

"This satellite is not on any official roster, but is obviously one of our birds, and it is still active. I've been trying to get in, but none of my codes from DHS, DARPA or any of the other old alphabet agencies are working. What I can tell, though, is where it is getting positioning instructions from."

"So, it is a communications satellite?" Scott asked.

His friend shook his head. His olive skin taking on a greenish cast in the harsh fluorescent lighting. "No, much too large. I believe it is military, it would have to have been launched in secret."

"Could it be a weapon?"

Tahir shrugged.

"But you have the location of the comms?" Scott asked.

"Yes, yes, just as I expected, she is here," he pulled up a topo map on the laptop.

"Mount Weather, Virginia? Why does that sound familiar?"

"It is a well-known presidential bunker. Supposedly, it is large enough to house most of the legislature and their families as well."

"But it is in an infected zone. Why?"

"I don't know, maybe they have the treatment, or more likely, they are so isolated, so self-contained that they can simply wait for the epidemic to burn itself out."

"Thanks, man, good work. See if you can figure out what that satellite does and let Garret know the bunker location."

The team from the AG departed for the Bataan early the next morning. They would have a few days of mission prep before heading off to the respective staging areas. Jack had reported in that he'd made contact with the locals a few days earlier, no issues. He was slowly working his way over to get eyes on the storage facility. Todd had seemed distracted but wrapped Scott and Bartos in a bear hug while DeVonte and Angel kissed like it would be the last time ever.

Later, Bartos sat with Scott inside the top deck lounge enjoying the seascape vista. "Something felt different about this one, didn't it?"

Scott nodded. "It used to be just about us. Our little group here, it's grown so much bigger, and the stakes for failure just keep growing right along with it."

"I know...what if the Preacher is right, and this is the end times for us…for the country. The people we get on this ship may be all that's left of America when it's all over. Would that be enough…you know, to keep the species alive?"

Scott shrugged, "I don't know, dude. Maybe. We have good people, but it would be nice to have some more skills and stuff. If the numbers Tahir found are accurate, even at ten percent survival, there should still be about 300,000 people alive just in this country."

"But we're a country at war, trying our best to thin that number even more. Add to that the pandemic sweeping south and west…."

Scott knew what Bartos meant and acknowledged that, most likely, in a few more months, very few survivors would be left. He reached over and patted the leg Bartos had propped up in an adjacent chair. "Knee's still bothering you, isn't it?"

The little Cajun gave a reluctant nod.

"Got a question for you. Think it might be strong enough to stand beside me at the wedding?"

Bartos looked surprised, "What are you asking, man?"

"He wants you to be his best man, you goofy bastard," Bobby said entering the room.

"Really?" Bartos looked positively giddy. "Why me? I never been no best man before. Why not your brother?"

"Oh, I already did it once – that one didn't take. He's looking for someone else to blame for this one," Bobby said sitting down.

"Shit, yeah, man. I mean, yeah, it'd…uh, be an honor."

"Shit, yeah is what I wanted to hear. Thanks, Bartos…oh, and Solo, too, if you are ok sharing the stage."

"Yeah, sure, sure. He'll be on his best behavior."

"He's not the one we're worried about."

"Why me, though?"

"You're one of my best friends, man, and…all the others already had plans," Scott said with a smile.

Bobby leaned forward, "He's not kidding, Todd is doing the ceremony, and Gia has asked Jack to walk her down the aisle."

Bartos' smile lost none of its brilliance, "Hey, still fucking works for me! Can't wait!"

CHAPTER SIXTY-TWO

The exuberance of the girl's voice startled him so much he nearly dropped the cup in his hands.

"Mister Scott!" Tiny arms reached out and latched around his neck.

"Sylvia?" He barely recognized the girl he had helped pull from the woods a few weeks earlier. She had been in the medical bay the last time he checked on her. "You are looking much better."

She glanced down a bit embarrassed. "Thank you, for everything."

He noticed her eyes glistening and pulled her closer into a quick hug. "It's ok, glad I was there." He realized he had barely heard the girl talk when they first met and wondered again how close they had been to the end.

She nodded, then buried her face in his shoulder and sobbed. He stroked the back of her head and allowed her the time she needed. The healing would not be quick for her or her mother, but she seemed to be making good progress. "Where's your mom?" he asked several minutes later.

Instead of answering, she took him by the hand and led him to one of the small alcoves around the ship. A lone figure was sitting, looking east at the rising sun. "Hi, Trish." Her daughter was still clinging to Scott as if she was never going to let go.

"Hi…" She was clenching the arms of the chair, but she visibly relaxed as recognition dawned. "Mr. Montgomery…sorry, my mind was elsewhere." She stood and hugged him just as tightly as her daughter had.

"Mind if I join you?" he asked. Trish motioned to one of the chairs beside her as she, too, sat back down. "I apologize," he began. She looked confused until he smiled. "I'm sorry I haven't had a lot of time to check in on you guys. My niece was keeping me posted while you were recovering."

"Kaylie was wonderful, Scott. Everyone has been, in fact. I can't believe a place like this still exists. You even have electricity."

Her expression was hard for him to read, but there was definitely gratitude. He grinned, "That was a recent development and a very positive one." Sylvia saw Jacob nearby and took off after him. The boy smiled as she approached, and they both ran off to play.

"She is making friends fast," Trish said, smiling.

"Kids are resilient, she will be fine. It's you I'm worried about."

She made eye contact with him before responding, "Why's that?"

He looked out the ship's windows and breathed deeply. "Trish, everyone here has been through hell. Some, like you… much more so than others. We didn't get to this point without going through all that. What you went through becomes a part of you, in some cases, it takes over. The pain, the anger, the hurt….the scars."

She nodded silently.

"Sylvia needs her mom again, you are all she has now."

"I just keep thinking…." she sucked in a deep breath. "What I was so close to doing, you know, to her…to us."

He nodded, "It probably wasn't the first time you considered it, was it? Just ending the pain, the suffering."

"No…not at all." She lowered her head and in a small voice struggled to admit the truth. "Many other times in fact."

"But you never did. You chose life, as hard as it was to keep going…you always chose life. Suffering meant surviving. Remember that, Trish." The kids came back into view chasing one another in a game of tag. "You gave her life."

Trish placed a hand on his arm and they sat like that for a long moment wordlessly. Her expression brightened, and she nodded.

"I have something to tell you now and a few things to ask. How much have you learned this past month about what all is going on out in the world?" Scott asked.

"I've heard a lot of things, most seem outlandish, though."

Scott shook his head, "Probably not outlandish enough." He proceeded to catch Trish up on almost two years' worth of news.

The woman had gone pale, and it was several minutes before she spoke. "I wondered what all the activity was about."

"We do have a lot going on," he admitted.

"So, the ship is leaving for South America, and you are asking if we want to come along?"

He nodded, "That is the big question, yes. Some of that depends on us getting enough fuel, but either way, we will have to leave, probably in just the next couple of months."

She didn't hesitate, "Yes…! Yes, of course. There is nothing for us out there."

He hesitantly mentioned the obvious, "Your husband, Sylvia's dad?"

"He's gone, been gone. To be honest, the marriage was not ideal, we had talked of separating before…you know, the blackout. I'm sure he didn't make it. He was not a fighter, not a survivor. My daughter stopped even mentioning him about a year ago. I know it hurts her, but I think it feels better to think of him as dead instead of him abandoning us…or worse, working with the president's security people. What did you call them?"

"NSF"

"Yeah, what a horrible group that must be. No, we will go with you, if you let us, that is."

"Good," he responded. "Now, I need a favor."

Her face instantly began to frown as if she knew there would be a price to pay for all this generosity.

"Calm down," he said with a smile, his hands in a placating gesture. "The one thing about the AG is that everyone works. You said you were in law enforcement?"

She nodded, relieved. "Yes, I was a lead investigator."

"Great, I would like to ask you to resume that role. You see, we have a bit of a mystery on our hands."

CHAPTER SIXTY-THREE

HACKBERRY, LOUISIANA

Jack approached the edge of the clearing cautiously. From the small pack, he removed a pair of optics Skybox had provided. Unlike the night vision optics they had used previously, these also added an overlay for IR, something Sky had called shortwave infrared. The ability to magnify ambient light as well as see heat signatures effectively canceled out any advantage the darkness might offer an enemy. The picture was so clear, he could easily read signs and even see expressions on the faces of the enemy troops. Sky had also coached him, at length, about using it too often or getting too close to the enemy with it. If he was captured with this kind of gear, no one would believe he was just a simple merchant.

This was the fourth night he had ventured out to look at the massive compound. He looked over the framework of pipes and scaffolding going up to various tanks above ground and down into underground storage caverns as well. He'd already reported in the troop strengths, fixed gun emplacements and what looked to be a command outpost. Something he'd seen earlier wasn't adding up, though. He came out tonight determined to satisfy his curiosity.

The night was quiet, right up until DeVonte bumped into him. "Oh, sorry, Preacher. Didn't see ya there."

Jack wasn't sure what part of covert the kid failed to understand, but he felt better about him here than on the front line of the coming assault. Todd was somewhere behind him as well. His friend since childhood was still a bit deaf from the battle up at the farm, but this time, they all planned to stay away from the action. Their job on this op was to make contact with the locals, do a bit of trading and then provide surveillance on the facility. They checked in with the other parts of the team regularly.

Something was wrong, though, very wrong. "Hey, how far back is Todd?" Jack whispered. Todd eased up beside him a few minutes later. Jack cupped a hand over the man's ear and whispered as loudly as he dared. Todd shook his head up and down in acknowledgment. He then looked through his own similarly equipped enhanced SWIR binoculars, sweeping them back and forth until he locked onto the spot Jack had mentioned.

Earlier, aerial reconnaissance had indicated numerous weapons emplacements in and around the facility, including some flat panels that Skybox said were bad news. While there seemed to be troops around the weapon emplacements, using the SWIR failed to pick up any heat signatures. They could clearly see soldiers standing nearby, but they weren't moving. "They're fakes. Mannequins or something," Todd whispered a bit too loudly, his hearing not registering the increased volume. Most of the fixed guns themselves didn't seem to actually be what they seemed either. Too low to the ground and too solid.

"Take a look at the tents in the compound," Jack whispered.

Todd shifted his hands to surveil the presumed NSF encampment. Several human shapes came into view. Some walking a perimeter patrol, others sitting, talking, possibly eating. It took him a moment to figure out what was troubling the preacher. The whole scene looked fake…no, not fake—staged. "Not enough people," he said.

Jack nodded, "Take a look at the tents. Use IR."

Todd thumbed to the setting for active infrared. In most of the tents there were multiple heat signatures, but on closer inspection…it was somehow off. The heat that every human radiates naturally will vary from one to another. Many factors, including layers of clothes, the angle they are turned, even a person's size or shape will affect it. At this range, they should also be able to see some movement within the tents. Soldiers in sleeping bags or on cots tended to move a lot trying to get comfortable. What Todd saw was a very nearly identical IR image from each of the tents. They were consistent and unmoving. *Some sort of heat pack in them to fool the thermals,* he thought.

Jack patted him, and they backtracked down the embankment and back into the deep foliage where DeVonte was. "It's a ruse, Jack," Todd said. "They are trying to fool us. They don't have as many troops or weapons here as they want us to believe. It's a Ghost Army."

DeVonte looked confused, so Todd filled him in. "To fool the Germans in World War Two, Great Britain went to elaborate lengths to stage fake troops and even entire Army units, including inflatable tanks, as if staging for battle. They even dropped dummies with parachutes over enemy territory to confuse them."

"What good would that do?" DeVonte asked. "Fake soldiers can't fight."

Jack answered, "It was to get them to look one place instead of where they should have been looking." He ran a hand through his sweaty hair and looked out into the night. "It's a trap; I feel it."

Todd nodded, "We have to call it into Sky. Hopefully, he can advise."

Skybox relayed the report from Jack to mission command, from there the Navy, Army and Spec Ops teams were notified. As expected, the reaction was about what he predicted, "Gather more intel." No one seemed to care if it was a trap, as long as the target was still sitting out there for the taking. So far, he'd had little respect for anything the NSF had done; they were amateurs. Even with the addition of foreign soldiers, their effectiveness was laughable. That didn't mean they weren't dangerous, though, especially with civilians out here like his friends.

"Lieutenant, what is our window on this?"

Skybox and the younger Garret were leading one of the advance teams currently positioned on the western edge of the storage facility. The oily water of the port lapped against the derelict freighter they were using at the moment. The lieutenant looked up from the papers and shook his head, "Not our call, Commander. Army is running the show. Everyone is ordered to hurry up and sit on their thumbs until go-time. Military expediency and all that."

"I want to go in now, ahead of the attack. I need to see for myself what we are up against."

"Sir?" he said looking up at Skybox.

"I think our friends are onto something. This was my plan, and even from the start, it all seemed a bit too convenient. It being a trap is a very real possibility. If we lose here, we may be out of options."

The Navy man didn't disagree. "Do you think your people are involved?"

Skybox knew he meant Praetor soldiers like himself, *and Archangel,* he thought. "To counter superior force strength, use misdirection and unconventional tactics—it is right out of our playbook."

"So, what are you going to do, Sky, go down and talk nice to them? Just ask them to let us have the fuel?"

Garret walked around the dull gray chart table to look directly into the Praetor commander's eyes. "You volunteered to help with the planning and execution of this mission. I vouched for you to everyone, and now you're bailing on us? Your part of this plan may be the most critical."

"I can meet my team when they jump in, and sorry...but your command is just as out of touch as most others." Skybox put a hand lightly on the lieutenant's shoulder. "We need to save this op, we need to protect those guys out there on the sharp end of the stick, Garret. And…" he paused briefly, then grinned, "I'm not asking."

CHAPTER SIXTY-FOUR

Willet had read through the sealed emergency orders and eventually agreed to transfer command authority to the Praetor commander on site. He'd been vaguely aware of the protocol but always assumed it would be an external transfer. Never had he guessed that his trusted major was one of the elite commandos. Colonel Willett had been initially incredulous, and in fact, he could have refused to turn over command to the man. Truthfully, he was glad to have a functioning command channel back in place. No longer required to act covertly, Kitma rightly assumed other members of the Guard were also now stepping into command roles within their active units.

"Why didn't your people act sooner?" Willet asked.

The African shook his head. "I dunno, I'm not senior leadership. Dey make da call." He thought about it and added, "Sir, we also serve our leaders unless that leadership is unjust or harmful to da republic. It would seem Guard command finally reached dat rather obvious conclusion."

Willett was a man of high energy and found himself pacing the floor. He hadn't expected to lose his command today nor to be called on to go into all-out war against the government forces. Kitma motioned for him to sit, "Please, sir." The Army colonel sat.

Kitma looked at the man until they made eye contact before speaking. "I have great respect for you, Colonel. You stepped up and led when it was needed. You've made tough choices and excellent decisions. I would have veery happily continued following your leadership as long as needed. Like you, doh, I have mah orders, too. I do not want you to step aside, in fact, we want you to command an even larger force." Willett's frown began to soften, and he leaned forward, now genuinely interested in what the man had to say.

Several weeks later, Colonel Shane Willet found himself leading a contingent of the 194th out of Fort Benning. They had quietly come ashore on the eastern side of New Orleans at the aptly named Port America. Joining up with the 1st Armored division coming in from Fort Bliss, they now were driving hard directly toward the SOR storage facility. The colonel's new C.O., Commander Kitma, was busy assembling a larger force for other action farther north. The fuel reserves were essential to all branches, though. There would be no future missions without it. The timetable thus far had been somewhat fluid awaiting the arrival of his tanks and artillery as well as intel from a recon team on the ground.

Colonel Willet had been in combat in both Gulf Wars as well as skirmishes in shithole countries around the world. Now, he was on his own Gulf Coast and about to go to war with his own president. Nothing about this would ever feel right or just. Like most battles, he knew it was going to suck. He ran a hand through his sweat soaked hair before donning his cap again. A junior officer sitting in front put down a radio handset and turned to him.

"Sir, M88 insertion teams are on standby for 0400 tomorrow."

The colonel nodded. Mission-88 was the joint team of Army Rangers,

Navy SEALs and several members of the less well-known Air Force Special Tactics squad. The mission was planned so that the heavy artillery would already be in place just prior to the Spec Ops jumping in. Looking down at his watch, a frown crept across his forehead. *It is going to be damn close.*

CHAPTER SIXTY-FIVE

HARRIS SPRINGS, MISSISSIPPI

"I still don't see why you need to go."

"Scott, sweetheart, stop worrying, I'll be fine." Gia sat down heavily on the bed. "We've been through this."

It was true, they had, but Scott still didn't like it. He knew she was going to keep visiting the other labs until they all had the treatment perfected. While he still was unsure where the labs were, few places remained safe.

"G, listen. It's not just the infected anymore. The country is falling apart —it's all-out-war in many places."

"Like the one you aren't telling me about? The one that Jack and Todd are dealing with?" She knew it was bothering Scott to keep anything from her just as much as it killed him not to be there with his friends.

His eyes dropped to the floor. "That…" he sighed and looked out to sea. "That's a supply run, that's all. They will be fine, and I promised you I wouldn't do anything stupid before the wedding."

She raised an eyebrow, then tilted her head slightly as if that was not entirely right.

He caught the look, then stammered, "I mean, until the baby comes."

"Only partially true, Scott Montgomery. You are done being reckless, your hero days are over. Our baby and his mother need you to stay safe." She reached out a hand and pulled him toward her. He bent down and kissed her sweetly.

"I'm trying, honey."

She smiled, "I know you are, but it's killing you. What I don't know is if it is because of your sense of duty or…" She lay back on the bed. "Maybe you just need the thrill of the fight now. Maybe your warrior gene has been turned on, too. No going back if that's true."

Scott gently climbed up on the bed and then atop his fiancée. "I'll tell you what has gotten turned on."

She reached a hand down from his chest toward his waist, then lower. "Ah…I think I understand why you want me to stay now."

He kissed her, then with a show of willpower that surprised them both, he slid off her and lay next to her cradling her softly in his arms. They lay like that for several minutes, neither speaking. Finally, he broke the silence.

"Gia, I have loved you forever, you are the reason I exist now. You and our baby are my life. Despite everything going on, all the struggles the world keeps throwing at us, I've never been happier." He ran a hand over her body, lifting her shirt up to expose the very noticeable baby bump. His fingers smoothly rubbed her tummy as he looked deep into her eyes. "I can't believe this is even real."

Her fingers intertwined with his as their lips met. She softly whispered, "I know." She reached for him again, but differently now. She wanted him, inside her, needed him to physically be a part of her once more. They made love, slowly, gently. Neither in any rush for it to be over. Silence permeated the ship's cabin as the two bodies moved as one.

Scott's face nuzzled her neck, his soft kisses pushing her closer to the very edge.

Their passion was a fire that both energized and consumed them. They had made love many times, but this was something more. Each touch felt electric, like they were experiencing one another for the first time. But, they were so comfortable and so familiar that each knew intrinsically how to move, where to touch. When to be soft and when to be more. The couple had become masters of each other's body. Gia arched her back as waves of orgasm hit, her ecstasy raced through his body as well and he released into her. His soul pulsing as she pushed back. Exhausted, they stayed that way, neither wanting to break the spell.

The moment was so perfect that he wished for a way to capture it just so he could play it back later to feel it all again. He knew he had never been in love before. This was where he was supposed to be, right now, this exact spot in the cosmos. Her love was exquisite, she was beauty, she was love.

He opened his eyes a short time later to see her looking at him through tear-filled eyes. They were still in the same position, facing each other on the bed. Her fingers traced the outline of his face. A slight smile was her only expression. He knew this was one of those times; he knew not to speak. He kissed her softly. They lay that way for a long time before she spoke.

"Thank you, Scott. I don't deserve you."

He shook his head and began to speak, but she shushed him.

"I treated you so badly back in college. I knew you were in love with me, but instead of returning it, I just used you. I thought I knew what I wanted, and...I think maybe I just assumed you would always be there for me. For so long, I refused to even think about you. The men in my life other than you were..." she stopped and turned away for several long seconds. "You are just different, you are my heart, and I should have followed it from the very beginning. Now..." she stopped again.

"What, hon?" he whispered.

"It scares me, Scott. It can't be real."

He pulled her closer and ran his fingers gently through her long red hair.

"I'm not going anywhere," he said. "I'll do my best to stay out of trouble as long as I know you are mine."

She was sobbing now, almost inconsolably. Her shoulders shook with the tears that seemed to be tearing her soul from her body. She muttered something he couldn't quite make out, then rolled to the side. He'd reached the end of his understanding of women, much less pregnant women. He lay a hand on her back and soon heard the soft, familiar sounds of her sleep.

He lay on the bed wide awake watching her sleep. She was an amazing woman, not just to him, but to the entire world. Trying to keep her here, all for himself, was selfish, but *damn,* he wanted to be. Her chest rose and fell, and he placed his hand on her swollen belly once more. He had no idea of how it was supposed to feel. Would it be too soon to feel the baby moving or kicking? *No clue.* This woman would be his wife, and this baby would make them a family. He thought briefly of his friends on the mission but gave up the pretense of leadership. It just felt good to be him right now.

CHAPTER SIXTY-SIX

HACKBERRY, LOUISIANA

"Okay," Jack said coming back out of the 35-foot Hike riverboat into their makeshift base camp. "I just talked with Garret and Bobby letting them know this whole fucking thing looks like a setup, we need to get the hell out."

DeVonte looked sick. "But the military's still planning to attack?"

"Looks that way, yeah. Once the military machine gets going, it's hard to shut down," Todd said. "They would rather just go ahead and hit this place and hope they get lucky."

"They keep asking us to go in to get an even closer look. They don't believe us since the place isn't rigged to blow." DeVonte had gone in during the night to check and found no evidence of explosives anywhere. "No matter what we say, though, they are coming in tomorrow morning—we all know that."

"Fuck that, Preach," the kid said grinning.

The radio in Jack's hand beeped with an incoming message. "Sit tight, headed your way – Sky."

"What in the fuck does that mean?" Jack wondered aloud. A slight noise came from behind.

"Hands-up!"

They all turned at the shouted command. Half a dozen black uniformed troops emerged out of the dense foliage all aiming short barrel automatic rifles.

"Oh, shit," Todd muttered raising his hands.

"Fuck, what we do now?" DeVonte said.

"Raise your fucking arms," Jack whispered loudly. Obviously, not all the NSF troops were fake.

∾

Tahir raced frantically through the ship's corridor. "Where's Scott?" he yelled. No one seemed to know.

Angelique was coming out of her office on the mid-deck when she heard his voice. "He's down in the galley with Bartos." The young man nodded thanks as he sped by and toward the hatch at the end of the corridor. She called out, "What's wrong?" but he had already disappeared down the steps.

Tahir found Scott seconds later, pulling him urgently aside. "You have to get them out of there now."

"Who...out of where?"

"Everybody. Anyone near the SOR. Move them out, or they are dead."

Chills crawled up Scott's back, every nerve on edge. They began moving quickly toward the communications room. "Tell me what is happening," Scott said as they navigated the people heading to eat in the small dining area.

"Trust me on this; make the call," Tahir said, now winded and struggling to keep up.

Scott reached the radio room first; his brother was on duty alone. "Bobby, can you get Jack's group on the radio? It's urgent."

His brother nodded and began spinning the dial on the huge radio as Scott turned back to Tahir. "So, what's the problem?"

"It is a trap, the entire SOR storage facility is a trap for the military."

Scott shook his head. No, this couldn't be true. Skybox checked this out, early reports said lightly defended and no signs of the enemy rigging the compound with explosives. He trusted his friend, but he was baffled.

"Jack's no longer responding. Should I try Skybox?" Bobby asked, the stress level in his voice creeping up noticeably.

"Yes," Scott and Tahir answered nearly in unison.

"How can it be a trap, Tahir?"

In response, the man logged into one of his laptops nearby and began typing a series of IP addresses. "I finally got into the satellite. You know, the one I said the president's compound seemed to be communicating with?"

"Yes, yes, of course, but what does that have to do with…" Scott left the question unfinished as he watched what must be a real-time feed from the satellite. The image was unmoving and showed a small section of the Gulf of Mexico. The exact location was well known to them. Dead center of the image was Cameron Parish, Louisiana, and the tiny community of West Hackberry. The sense of dread in the room was quickly becoming a tangible entity.

Tahir clicked to a schematic view of the satellite. Only it was obviously not a satellite. "Guys, this is an orbital bombardment platform for something called a Kinetic Energy Weapon."

"Oh, holy shit, 'Rods from God.' Someone actually built it?" Scott asked leaning in for a closer look. "We are so totally fucked."

Bobby's voice rose in tempo, "Hold Sky, AlphaCat just threw us a curve. I am patching him and BikerBoi in."

Tahir filled in everyone over the next several minutes. The Kinetic Energy Platform was located in high orbit and had a payload of solid metal ballistic spears the size of telephone poles. "Skybox, you are familiar with Rail Guns and the depleted uranium projectiles. Ramp that up in size and power to this, but instead of needing high-energy magnets to fire on a target, with a KEP you just let gravity do the work. It is very similar to dropping a small asteroid on a target."

To his credit, Skybox remained calm. "Accuracy and yield, Cat. I need specifics."

Tahir checked the schematics gathering weight and altitude, entering it into a sidebar program. "Guys, if I am reading this correctly, they have accuracy down to fifty yards, regardless of atmospheric conditions. Projectiles traveling at the maximum speed of Mach-9.5" He tapped more keys. "Oh, holy mother…output is somewhere between the MOAB and a small nuclear device. By far, the most powerful conventional weapon ever created."

Skybox stayed silent for much longer than was comfortable. "Everybody is already en route to the party. Even with Preacher's earlier warning, none of them wanted a hold. AlphaCat, how many projectiles do they have, and how long from launch to impact?

"This station has sixteen, but it is almost certainly not the only platform up there. They could never maintain target lock with a single satellite. I haven't found any others but would expect a minimum of four, possibly as many as twelve. From de-orbit to reach terminal velocity to impact would only be a few minutes at most."

Tahir looked around the room nervously, "I can't stop this from happening, guys, I am logged in via a very low-priority maintenance port. Nothing I can do to alter a launch command."

"That's ok," Skybox said. "We just have to avoid the area. Get in touch with Garret, either of them. I'll cancel my insertion teams, but who knows about the Army. Scott, I need something from the AG."

Scott looked around the control room confused, *What can I do?*

Skybox filled him in, "I was about to call you guys. One of our Rangers just arrived at the Preacher's base camp, and there is no sign of any of 'em. All their gear and the *Marco Polo* are still there. I have to assume they have been taken. I'm going in to get them. I am going to need you to bring me a few things."

CHAPTER SIXTY-SEVEN

Scott cautiously looked over at the man sitting beside him in the LSV Spider. Tommy stared straight ahead, completely still, face expressionless, but somehow, Scott got a vibe of building excitement or anticipation. Skybox had told him to get the tactical buggy and the man most knew better as Ghost. Finding him had proven almost as tough as getting him into the vehicle. Bartos and Kaylie had helped, but it was something akin to trying to herd a tiger. They had managed it and gotten on the road heading west in record time. Solo had hopped in the back as if to say, *You aren't having this party without me.* They were both killers, but Scott felt strangely comfortable with his teammates.

He felt way less so heading into a potential combat zone—something he had promised his fiancée he wouldn't do. Also, knowing the KEP hanging over them like Thor's hammer was a hard thing to get comfortable with. He just couldn't stop thinking about Jack, Todd and DeVonte, though. Just as when Bartos was taken, he would do anything to get them back. Thankfully, the rendezvous spot where Skybox was meeting them was only a few hours away, and they had a near empty highway between them.

Near empty was not the same as completely empty. They had bypassed

Baton Rouge and, a few hours later, New Orleans by a wide margin, but just outside Lafayette, Louisiana, they rounded a bend in the road to see a roadblock manned by black-uniformed soldiers. "Oh, shit," Scott said slowing. There was a travel ban in effect which he was violating and a weapons ban. The dual mounted .50 caliber machine guns were also a likely violation of that law. He gave a quick glance at Ghost and noticed the beginning of a small grin on the man's misshapen face. As he brought the LSV to a stop fifty yards away, Solo lightly jumped out and went to pee in the grass along the road.

The NSF troops all had weapons leveled at them, and several were approaching in a very business-like manner. Weapons locked on target, fingers on the trigger, fanning out to give clear fire lanes. Scott felt amazingly calm considering the dire position he was in. Perhaps Gia was right, he was getting addicted to this stuff.

"Tommy, enemy," he whispered. The man sat stoically, but his stone face still hid a grin.

"You, out of the car, hand's up!" came the shouted orders. "Lay your weapons on the ground first."

Scott looked quizzically at the men, then over at the unloaded machine gun in the mounts and shook his head. Raising his arms, he said, "I'll need a wrench, you sure we can't just leave them? They are really a pain in the ass to take off."

Four of the guards were approaching, and at least two more were behind the Humvees blocking the highway. "Sir, are you aware of the travel ban? It is illegal to be on the roads without authorization. It is also a felony to be in possession of weapons of any kind." Two of the soldiers were looking at the light tactical vehicle in awe. It seemed to bristle with every weapon imaginable.

One of the men grabbed Scott, threw him roughly to the ground and proceeded to search him for weapons. Ghost hadn't moved from the car, but the soldiers were more respectful of him. His injuries were so obvious and so severe they didn't seem entirely sure how to handle him.

"I don't guess you guys are just going to let us go, huh?"

"Shut the fuck up. Where did you get this vehicle?"

"So…shut-up or answer…" The boot stomped down in the small of his back driving the air from his lungs.

They made an attempt to pull his arms back behind him, one of them producing a flex-cuff restraint. Scott saw them pulling Tommy out the other side and realized it was time. He snapped two fingers into his palm. Somewhere out there he knew Solo was watching. "This one has a kni…" The man on the other side didn't finish his sentence as he was grasping his throat trying to slow the torrent of blood rushing between his fingers.

The sound of Solo making his attack on the rear guards distracted the one standing over Scott. He rolled and swept the legs from the man, retrieving the Glock-17 from the man's waist and firing one 9mm shot through the man's head. The sound of tearing flesh made Scott glance up, and right then, he saw Ghost moving into action. Two of the four men by the LSV were already down, the other two were trying to get a shot at Tommy who was moving with incredible grace and preternatural speed. The man who had always seemed more like a statue to Scott was now jumping, running and fighting with a fluidity that seemed almost artistic.

Tommy likes knives, was what Skybox had told him. He had brought plenty, strapped to him in every place imaginable. Now, those blades were slicing through the air, then skin and organs, before being withdrawn from falling bodies to be used again. Scott watched in morbid fascination as Tommy effortlessly flayed away the right side of one man's face before throwing the same blade and catching the other in the throat. All with deadly efficiency.

Tommy retrieved the weapons, cleaned them on the dead guards' clothing and quickly sat back down in the passenger's seat. Scott shook himself from the mesmerizing carnage and looked up to see Solo walking between the two Humvees. He paused to piss on one of the tires before trotting back to the LSV where he hopped gently in behind Ghost.

"Are we done here?" Scott asked his non-responsive passengers. He switched the vehicle back on and rolled up and around the roadblock, taking note of three additional bodies. One more than he'd been aware of.

Nearing the rendezvous spot a short time later, a few miles outside Hackberry, Scott pulled to a stop. He checked the time and his GPS and looked over the water covered wetlands. Tommy climbed out silently, his clothes covered in blood, as was Solo's fur. They all turned at a sound back down the bayou. A sleek black Barracuda Interceptor slipped around the far bend and cut its engines coasting smoothly up to the bank. Skybox gave a nod from the pilot's cabin.

Skybox jumped out along with another soldier, then greeted his friends, taking notice of the blood stains without comment. It was just going to be one of those kinds of days. "Scott, you can wait here or take the Barracuda back out to sea. I'll call you once we have the Padre."

Scott shook his head no. "They are my friends out there, as long as I don't compromise the mission, I'd like to go along."

Skybox grinned, "Hoped you might say that—your girlfriend's gonna be pissed, though."

"She's out of town, let's just keep this our little secret for now, ok?"

"Alright, guys times a wasting." Skybox loaded ammo and ordinance into the LSV weaponry, then switched the engines to electric for stealth. He sent the other man, a Ranger named Owens back in the Barracuda to wait near the Marco Polo. "Listen, Owens, stay chill when the shooting starts. We may need to exfil by sea. If so, I need you hot on the throttle—got me?" The man nodded and sped off back down the small canal.

They pulled off the highway long before the petroleum complex, weaving their way back toward the enemy camp. They exited the LSV and made their way through the thick brush to a vantage point. Skybox pointed and whispered something to Tommy who immediately disappeared from sight.

"Scott, we have no time for a real plan, you take Solo and try and get close to that trailer. Tahir believes that is the command post. I am going to take the Spider, pick-up a couple of my guys and go apeshit on these bastards."

Scott had a growing sense of dread but nodded. "What if…you know…" he cut his eyes upward.

Skybox understood completely, "Let's just hope they don't." The thought of a thirty-foot long telephone pole made of solid metal dropping on them from hundreds of miles up would make this a very bad day. "It'll work, Scott, Tommy is going to clear a path, use Solo to help do the same. We're going to take out the main threats as quietly as possible. We'll keep everyone off you, but whoever is in the command post will likely be up to you. Once the alarms go off, we have to be somewhere else. We have to go now. You good?"

"Yes, Sky, good hunting!"

"You too, man. Let's go get our friends."

CHAPTER SIXTY-EIGHT

Skybox picked up two of the SEAL team to use as gunners and eased the LSV to the top of a small berm giving him good sightlines to the NSF controlled compound. Although not 400 troops like they had first been told, the squad stationed here was not insignificant. He wondered if they knew how quickly they would all be sacrificed if the weapon orbiting high above was deployed?

While Skybox had scrubbed the official mission for most of his insertion teams, a handful of the special operators were recruited to assist him in recovering his friends from the AG. Three Army Rangers, including the one on the Barracuda, and four other SEAL team members. Those not in the LSV were easing into strategic positions. The NSF had the numbers and had the battle tech. Sky kept eyeing the large, olive-green microwave panels, he knew how terrible those could be if triggered. He'd seen the test and even had a small prototype used on him in a demonstration. It literally made you feel like you were on fire. The microwaves caused the water in your cells to vibrate fast enough to cause friction and heat. It could cause death at the highest settings but was best used as a physically agonizing deterrent.

The SEAL riding shotgun in the LSV, a man named Krychek, scoped the area making entries in the weapons targeting system for primary and secondary objectives. A single mic click from each of the other men let him know they were all in position. Ideally, they would hide and watch for as long as it took in order to go in at the optimal time. Today, they didn't have the luxury of time. Skybox had worked out a down and dirty plan for engagement and extraction. Some plans are elegant, and then some are just ugly and brutal. This was much more the latter. More of a complicated method of suicide than actual military strategy, but... *Well, fuck it,* he thought.

His first sound-suppressed round was a clean headshot from 100 yards. The second got the man firing what appeared to be a fixed mount .50 caliber center-mass. Each of the remaining gun emplacements on this side would be getting similar treatments. No matter the skill level of the operator, a fully operational machine gun could level the playing field real damn fast. Those had to go, and, one-by-one, they did.

Scott felt a bit exposed without Bartos there to instruct Solo, but he'd trained often with the dog and knew most of the basic commands. When they got within sight of the white-sided trailer, he gave the signal that it was the objective. Then, he made a sweeping gesture and gave the hand signals for 'quiet-kill-all.' Solo dropped his head low and disappeared into the compound. The closest of the massive oil storage tanks towered overhead. On the far edge, he saw a blur of movement as one of the NSF troops disappeared from sight. Several seconds later, another went down. He knew this was Ghost working his way toward him, but he still could not spot the man.

Turning in the opposite direction, he saw Solo launch from cover at a man's neck. The soldier never even managed to grab the gun hanging from his shoulder. He now understood Skybox's plan. The enemy had too much ground to cover and had deployed the actual soldiers too far apart. So far that they might not have a direct line of sight of each other. Solo and Ghost were working their way toward him, it was about to be his time to move. That was when the first unsuppressed shot rang out. He stayed crouched and ran for a building near the command trailer. The shit was about to get real. All he could think of was that steel arrow being decoupled up in orbit.

Scott's hands were sweating and his heart pounding as he knelt beside the block building. Marshaling his remaining courage, he ran and dove for the backside of the trailer. He heard agitated voices from inside. Then, all he heard was the LSV speeding through the compound both guns spitting out a deadly hail of rounds down range. The occasional bass woof of the grenade launcher added the perfect exclamation point to the effective firepower being unleashed. Concussive blasts from the explosions drowned out everything else. He didn't even notice the bullet hole that appeared in the wall just above his head.

Jack was still trying to explain to the NSF officer that they were on a trading mission when the firing outside began. The commander began to draw his weapon as Jack ducked low and thrust a vicious leg kick into the man's testicles. He went down with a noiseless expression of agony that made all of the men in the small room cringe in sympathy. There were two other armed guards in the small construction trailer that the NSF had converted to a command post.

Todd acted almost as quickly as Jack, but his man managed to get his weapon up before Todd reached him. He fired wildly hitting nothing but the far wall as Todd smashed a meaty fist into the man's face. Jack threw an elbow into the nose of the man in front of him and watched proudly as DeVonte clubbed the third man with one of the metal chairs they had all been sitting in.

"Get the guns," Todd yelled. He had a grip on one, but the man Jack was fighting with was not ready to give in. DeVonte's target just glared at him as he raised his handgun to fire. A blast went off and all turned to the now open front door. Scott Montgomery stood in the door, gun in hand looking for the next target. He moved in just ahead of Solo and both quickly cleared the room. The one guard lay dead, the other two were suddenly cooperative.

"Todd, Jack…" He stepped toward the young black man, helping him up, "DeVonte," he said with a voice of calm that belied his actual state of being. "How goes it, guys, anything exciting happening?" As if choreographed, an enormous explosion rocked the trailer back and forth. "Oh, yeah…um, we need to get the fuck out of here."

"Damn glad to see you, Scott," Jack said as he picked up a gun and headed for the door.

"Same here," echoed Todd and DeVonte.

"Solo out, guard," Scott yelled as the four men exited the trailer on a dead run. Ghost appeared on their left side just as the LSV came into view on the right. Scott saw Skybox touching his ear then pointing straight up. He knew what that meant. Tahir had obviously radioed that the orbital weapon had been fired.

"Move your asses!"

They all grabbed onto the black LSV as it slowed and turned back toward the boat landing. Shots rang out and they heard DeVonte scream as he was hit by a round. Todd looped an arm around the boy holding him tight against the roll cage as they all sped out of sight.

CHAPTER SIXTY-NINE

High overhead, the solid rod began its one-way trip to the planet's surface. It would reach ballistic speeds within a minute. One hundred and fifty miles below, only a handful of those involved knew what was coming. Colonel Shane Willett and his contingent from the combined 194th and those from the 1st were proceeding at full speed. "Looks like they are trying to start the party without us, boys," the colonel yelled to his men when they heard the gunfight. They tossed the battle plan and headed straight for the storage fields.

Willett had been briefed on the 'Ghost Army' as well as the 'Rods from God' weapon but chose to ignore it. He was out for blood, and a smaller force defending the SOR just made his job easier to his way of thinking. As the facility in Hackberry came into view, neither he nor his 280 men knew they had less than three minutes to live.

The Naval officer shook his head but kept trying to reach the Army detachment. "Roundhouse to BigDog, come in."

Commander Garret shook his head in frustration. While they had everything riding on this mission, too, he wasn't going to be stupid. He'd ignored the guys in Harris Springs before and regretted it. When they explained the dangers involved today, he canceled all mission activities connected with the SOR raid.

"Sir," a petty officer leaning over a console nearby said. "We have the bogey acquired on radar. Damn, that thing is moving…" Then he added, "Sorry, sir. Impact in 90 seconds."

Garret dropped his head, *Those damn fools.* Yelling at his radioman, "Get me fleet command. Launch authorization alpha. Take that fucking mountain out. Do it now before that impact screws up comms. *Goodbye, Madam President.*

The LSV slid to a stop moments later beside the Marco Polo. They were just under two miles from the storage facility. Scott hit the ground helping Todd lower DeVonte down. The Navy Barracuda boat was just rounding the bend and pulling in beside the other boat. Skybox looked at the boy. The wound was nasty but not life-threatening. "Krychek, throw me your blow-out kit." The Ranger checked his ruck and tossed the large wound trauma kit over. Sky applied the field dressing as Todd and Scott were carrying DeVonte onto the Navy boat.

"We have to go now, people. Impact is eminent."

Scott looked back at the Marco Polo and then to the bad-ass looking tactical vehicle. He hated leaving them both to the disaster ahead. That was when he saw Jack slumping off the back of the LSV. "Oh fuck, Jack!"

Surprisingly, it was Tommy who came into view and grabbed Jack dragging him quickly up and into the boat. The pilot was already backing away from shore and buried the throttle fully once clear.

"Jack, Jack! Preacher!" Scott was checking him for wounds. His chest was moving raggedly, and his eyes were open. One of the SEALs, seeing what was going on, jumped down and helped Scott roll him on his side.

That was when they saw the raw, gaping wound spread across his back. Scott looked up and locked eyes with Todd who was attending to DeVonte. He gave a small shake of his head and saw all the color drain from Todd's face.

"Big round, no exit," the man said. He was cleaning the wound and stuffing it with the clotting agent. He tore open a battle dressing. "Going to need some help, have to get this wrapped around him tightly." Todd had crawled over and was cradling his friend's head. Scott helped lift Jack's body and felt him writhe in pain. The bandage went under and around. The medic pulled it tight to seal off as much of the wound as possible. He made eye-contact with Scott, then broke it and looked for the full trauma kit. "Need to start fluids on both of them."

Skybox was up front in the pilot's cabin. "Faster, faster!" he kept yelling. "Get us out of this bayou, or we're all dead." They could just see the channel opening up to the sea ahead.

"Command says 90 seconds to impact," one of the sailors yelled. Sky looked at his watch, then caught part of what was going on in back. He twisted around more to make sure Tommy was there and saw him in the shadows against the enclosed cabin wall. He was grinning maniacally. Curled up at his feet, a bloody-furred Solo appeared to be sleeping.

Powered by a pair of 575 hp diesel engines, the high-speed Barracuda was clearing the outer buoy markers in seconds. They were five miles from the site, *But will that be enough?*

"Thirty-seconds."

The first use of a space weapon, and it happened to be targeting him. Skybox caught just a flash of light high overhead before seeing the entire coastline behind them erupt in a massive fireball. The solid rod of depleted uranium punched neatly through the middle storage tank and continued below into the salt dome cavern filled with crude oil. The kinetic impact ignited everything around it, including the air. The concussive wave stretched out for almost ten miles clearing everything in its path. The combined armored divisions under Colonel Willet, less than a mile away, literally ceased to exist as anything but disassociated molecules. Then came multiple sonic booms which shattered most of the windows in the boat and sent it careening well out of the water.

"Holy Shit!" someone said from the rear of the boat.

"Everyone take cover, we may get secondary impacts," Skybox shouted.

The ballooning cloud of fire looked every bit the monster it was. None of those aboard had ever witnessed an atomic explosion, and while this was non-nuclear, it was damned close to what that would look like.

"Uh, sir," the pilot said looking at a rear facing monitor.

Skybox realized the source of the man's concern as he, too, saw the wave approaching from behind. The boat was fast, nearing fifty knots. The wave was traveling at nearly four times that speed. It was already nearly fifty-feet tall and growing. Sky punched the nav system. Quickly going through menus to find what he wanted. *There,* the deepest channel around. Most of the Gulf in these parts was relatively shallow. A wave grows as it travels through shallow water but, theoretically, should decrease in deeper water. He pointed to the location. "That heading, now!" The man expertly angled the boat in that direction. It was going to be close.

Jack had gotten fluids and morphine and was drifting in and out of consciousness. He had been awake to see the brilliant flash and whispered, "Oh, God," as the boat had been lifted from the water and slammed back down. Scott grabbed Todd's hand which was shaking uncontrollably.

Todd looked up, "I don't know what to do, Scott. I can't lose him."

"I know, Brother. Be his friend. Tell him what he means to you...to all of us."

DeVonte was awake now and watching in awe at the growing wave behind them. He too had gotten morphine. "Now that's some shit you don't see every day. Hey, Boss...what's wrong wid Jack?"

Scott took the boy in his arms and leaned him up, so he could see better, "He's hurt bad. He took one in the back. Messed him up inside."

"No, ugh, uh…no, that's not right." Tears started streaming down the boy's dark face. "Hang in there, Jack," he said feebly.

The wave behind them was all they could see now. It looked more like a solid wall than water.

"It's going to be close. Hang onto the wounded and brace for impact," Sky yelled from the front.

They felt the little boat rising quickly—out the side windows they could see the color shifting from the light green to a deeper blue. Scott had no idea how far up the wave they would rise before being flipped and tossed under, but he held onto DeVonte and wrapped his legs around Jack. Then, it was over. The wave subsided without cresting and they gently rode it back down to normal sea level, although they were traveling at an incredible speed which took several more minutes to bleed off. "Deep water, guys. We should be ok now." He turned to the pilot and indicated the Navy ship fifteen miles out. "Radio ahead that we have one, possibly two, trauma cases coming in." He went back to check on his friends.

CHAPTER SEVENTY

GULF OF MEXICO

Skybox helped carry DeVonte from the barely intact Interceptor boat. The bullet had passed through the kid's thigh but seemed to have missed the major artery. The ship's medical team was waiting with a gurney for him and Jack. DeVonte stopped them while he reached out and grabbed Jack's hand as Todd, Scott and Krychek were lifting him onto his gurney. "Hang in there, Preacher." Jack partially opened one eye and offered a feeble smile to the boy.

They whisked both of the injured away into the darkened bowels of the ship. Skybox watched the receding figures, "He will get the best care anywhere." Todd was unable to speak, Scott just nodded.

Scott knelt absently scratching behind Solo's ears. The dog was not a fan of affection but allowed the man's gentle touch. "All this for nothing."

The comment stung Skybox. It had been his plan; these injuries were on him, and it showed. "Not totally for nothing, Montgomery."

Scott made eye contact with a questioning expression. Skybox turned to nod his head indicating he should follow. The two men walked back to an open hatch and stepped out to get a view back toward the coast. The dark smudge of smoke hanging in the air clearly indicated the impact site. All Scott could think about was all the poor souls in that little town. All gone now.

"You see?" Skybox was pointing farther to the west. Just coming into view over the horizon was a ship. After several minutes, they could tell it wasn't just a ship, it was a tanker.

"Is that…"

Skybox nodded, "The kid in there had a good idea in that meeting. Why not just sneak into the commercial tank and steal what we needed? We discovered the tanker a few days ago moored at an offshore pumping station. Your man, Scoots, and a few of our guys managed to reverse the flow from the diesel storage tanks. While we were waiting for you and Tommy to come over from Harris Springs, I had them begin pumping. They topped her off and slipped away about an hour before you arrived. The Volestaad there is full of 100% commercially refined diesel. They are en route to the Bataan and from there to top-off your Aquatic Goddess. The rest will be split between the Army and Navy."

"Well, damn." *It had worked,* Scott thought. They would have enough food and fuel to leave. Looking down at the blood covering his hands and clothes, though, it still didn't feel like a fair trade. He looked back inside to where Todd was still standing. "Thanks, Sky…I need to go check on him. You know…"

Skybox nodded understanding fully. He watched as Scott took Todd by the arm and led him in the direction they had taken Jack and DeVonte. Solo eased up off his haunches and padded behind them softly.

～

The surgical nurse came out first, her scrubs covered in sweat, bloody stains running far up her arms. She had a grave look as she stripped off the latex gloves. "You guys, come with me," she pointed at Todd and Scott. They rose and followed her back through the hatch and into an area portioned off by thick plastic curtains. She stopped short and turned, "You know the damage…"

Todd stopped her, "We understand, he…he's not going to make it," he stuttered. "Is he conscious?"

She nodded, "Coming out of it now, but he's very weak. Probably only has minutes, no idea how he is still hanging on." Any lingering hope the men might have been holding onto began to dissipate.

"Because he is a fighter. He's our Jack."

Scott held onto Todd tightly. The man was clearly coming apart at the seams. As they entered the tiny cubicle, Jack lay rigidly on the pristine white sheets. He was hooked to IVs and monitors, some showing alarms, but mercifully, all had been muted. His eyes fluttered open, and he slowly focused on Todd.

"Hey, Brother," he said weakly as he clumsily felt for, then grasped Todd's outstretched hand. Todd leaned over and put his head on Jack's shoulder hugging him gently with the other arm.

"Hey," was all he could muster through the flood of tears.

"How's the kid doing?"

"Not sure yet, but they said he would be fine, he's still being worked on," Scott said.

Jack nodded weakly and struggled to focus on Scott. "Tell Gia I'm sorry, I don't think I…" He grimaced as some pain shot through his body. "I, oh, damn." He sighed and waited for it to pass. "I don't think I'm going to be able to give her away like I planned."

Scott took the man's other hand and fought back the tears. He had no idea what to say. Jack's breathing got a bit more erratic, and his eyes became unfocused. "Thank you," he managed to say. "Thanks for coming to get us."

Scott smiled, "It was a nice day for a ride."

Jack nodded with a feeble smile. "Take care of Cap here, okay? He needs you. Bartos too, tell him I'm sorry and that…that I love him."

Scott stopped fighting back the well of tears and they began to flow. "Jack, thank you. Thanks for saving me that day. We all owe you so much more than you would ever admit," the words barely coming out between the sobs.

Jack let go of Scott's hand and reached up to him. Scott leaned down into the man's weak embrace. "I'm ready, Brother, don't be sad; it's not the end. Sometimes sacrifice is worth it if it offers life to loved ones." He struggled to take in a breath, and Scott and Todd both ached for their friend.

Jack gasped with the tiny amount of air he could take in and motioned to his green rucksack hanging on the wall. Scott took it down and handed it to Todd who opened it to find a worn leather Bible. While outwardly, Jack hadn't felt deserving of God's love since the battle with the Prophet, inwardly, he couldn't deny a lifetime of faith and service to his Savior. A page was marked with a paper clip. Todd read it aloud for his lifelong friend. John 15:13 was highlighted. "For the greatest love of all is a love that sacrifices all. And this great love is demonstrated when a person sacrifices his life for his friends."

Todd read several more of the marked Bible passages, and Jack lay still for a very long time. His eyes continued to move from Todd to Scott. His struggle almost over, tears began to well up in his eyes and slip silently down his weathered cheeks. He final words were a mere whisper, "Love you guys. I will miss you!"

CHAPTER SEVENTY-ONE

MOUNT WEATHER ANNEX, VIRGINIA

Two days earlier, President Chambers had been in full-blown panic mode. The call from Levy could not have been clearer. She had signed her death warrant in firing the KEP device, the one code named Thor's Hammer, at the oil field. The weapon's operational capacity was the one bright spot in months of darkness for her. "Ed!" she called out in frustration. *Where is he?*

Her presidency was over, she had no illusions about that. Levy had said as much on the call. Now, she was scrambling to put an escape plan into play. Something to cover her immediate departure from Mount Weather. Sadly, she only had one card left to play. Her chief of staff walked through the metal door with a look of resignation. "Yes, ma'am?"

Ma'am, she thought, not even Madam President any longer. "Ed, have my chopper ready. We're leaving. Please have my bags loaded." The man shrugged, he was the chief of staff, not her personal valet, but he would handle it for her.

"Yes, ma'am," he said with great effort.

"Any casualty reports from the Gulf? Did we get the bastards?"

He knew 'the bastards' she meant were the military presence, not the hundreds of her own people she had killed in the attack or the nearby town full of civilians. "Navy was mostly unaffected, the Army presence in the area was all eliminated."

She flashed her once famous smile and nodded in appreciation. Levy was an idiot, never around when it was important. The rebels had to go. It was time to play her trump card, her ace in the hole. She picked up the phone and clicked one of the pre-programmed numbers. Ed watched as she spoke to someone on the other end. "Release the variant, then let them go." She paused briefly, listening to the reply. "Yes, all of them, that is an order. Do it now."

She clicked off and turned to see her chief of staff was now holding a gun, and it was pointing at her. Her immaculate red lips smiled as she saw. "Edward, are we having a moment?" The man took a step closer.

"What did you just do? Call them back and cancel it, whatever it was."

She smiled again and tossed him the phone. "You figure it out." She looked at the unassuming man. "I was wondering who she had on my staff. Should have known it would be the top man. I take it you weren't some hot-shot Wall Street whiz then, eh?"

He grabbed the phone out of the air and thumbed to find the last number dialed. No name, and judging by the 881 prefix, it was an iridium-based number—not one of their government phones. Probably one of her independent contractors. *Mercenaries,* he thought. He clicked the safety off. "Lady, the country is going to be much better off to be rid of you."

The Tomahawk cruise missile had been fired from the Ticonderoga class warship far off the Atlantic Coast forty minutes earlier. It impacted the Mount Weather facility at over 550 miles per hour. The shock wave of the first warhead reached deep into the compound, knocking the chief of staff from his feet. He scrambled to level the gun at the retreating woman, but she was already gone. The ceiling started to rain down, along with tons of concrete and dirt. Within minutes, three more of the cruise missiles wreaked destruction throughout the facility.

As the dust began to clear, Madelyn Chambers exited from an escape tunnel deep underground. She could hear secondary explosions going off above. She brushed a bit of dirt from the charcoal gray Hermes power suit and walked briskly to the Beast, the heavily armored presidential limo she had kept stashed here in the underground garage. Her driver was always on call, although they had not driven anywhere since her swearing in. She saw him looking out a side window at the rain of debris from the mountain above. "Driver…now! Get us out of here!"

"Ma'am," he said nervously, also noticing she had no security detail. "You, um, you want to go out there?"

"No, you fucking moron, I want to stay here and be buried under this goddamn mountain. Get the car started or give me the keys." She may have failed at being president, but a lifetime in Washington had taught her one thing – how to survive.

The man rushed over, clicking a remote as he ran, to start the engine of the massive Cadillac CT6 limo. "I got that," he said as he took her two bags and dropped them in the trunk before opening her door. "Madam President, uh…you do know what's outside, right? I mean, you know, infected?"

Well, shit, she thought. She had actually forgotten that, but it wasn't like she had many options. "Just get us away from here. Head to the coast of North Carolina." Before things got bad, she'd quietly moved her presidential yacht out of the Potomac down the coast to the seaport in Wilmington, North Carolina. It was stocked with provisions to last years with the small crew she kept on board.

They watched as the heavy, steel doors rolled up and away; the dusty sunlight shown through a rubble-strewn field outside. Beyond that, were multiple rows of high fence lined with row upon row of people scrambling and clawing to get inside. Not people she knew, *infected*. Fuck it, they could have this place and anyone inside who survived. She had the antidote, she knew she couldn't catch the disease, but that didn't mean she was safe. The infected were like wild animals; if they could get the car stopped, they would tear both her and the driver apart.

As the driver sped out the cavernous opening, he eyed her in the rear-view mirror. "Madam President," he said tentatively, "if I open the gate, no way it will close after us. Those….things will be inside the compound."

She nodded. "What's your name?"

"Biggs, ma'am, Ted Biggs."

"Ted, everyone inside that mountain is already dead. If we don't get out of this horde in the next few minutes, we are going to be as well. Fuck the gates, just get us out of here."

If he had any remaining doubts, they disappeared as another missile came screaming directly over the car, detonating deep inside the lower levels of the mountain. The detonation shook the heavy limo violently, but they kept heading for the double gates which were slowly beginning to swing open.

CHAPTER SEVENTY-TWO

HARRIS SPRINGS, MISSISSIPPI

A light rain fell as Scott and Todd disembarked the small transport boat and escorted an honor guard carrying Jack's body back home to Harris Springs. Ghost leapt quickly from the boat and disappeared into the nearby woods, he was followed by Solo seconds later. Skybox helped DeVonte to a waiting wheelchair and began rolling him toward the AG. Scott was tired of thinking of the losses and gains. It was all becoming too much. Right now, he just wanted to honor his friend's memory. They looked up to see every deck and many of the balconies on the enormous cruise ship lined with people from the community.

Scott wasn't sure how everyone knew, but was grateful for the show of love for the man. Both Bartos and Angelique stood stoically by the gangway. As they neared, the expression of pain was evident on their faces. Angel ran to DeVonte, Bartos hobbled over and looked at them. He put an arm around Todd, and after several minutes, pulled Scott in as well. Nothing was said, words were both unnecessary and wholly inadequate for this homecoming.

Scott left Todd with Bartos and walked up the ramp alone. He was fighting a range of emotions and wanted nothing more than to have a drink and curl up beside Gia. He knew she would be furious with him for going, but he felt confident she would keep that to herself for now. As he passed through the ship's corridors, people nodded respectfully. Many touched him on the arm or back in a reassuring manner, but nothing could ease the pain of losing his friend.

He entered his stateroom cabin to find it empty. The bed was still made-up, and Gia's go-pack was not in its familiar place. *Is she still not back?* They'd been away on the Navy ships for several days. Surely, she wasn't still at the other lab. *Maybe she came back to find I was off doing something stupid and just had enough.* He fell across the empty bed, the stress, fatigue and misery finally catching up with him.

~

Gia still wasn't back for the service for Jack two days later. It was a simple, bittersweet affair, both spiritual and, at times, irreverent. Todd led the memorial, and it seemed almost cathartic for him to relive some of the memories from happier days. "Jack always said I saved him. Liz and me…he was in a tough spot back then, but the truth was—he saved us. Truthfully, I've never known a man with so much love."

Other stories were along the same lines. Everyone seemed to have their favorite Jack saying, and half-way through the service, the audience was in tears, not just from pain, but from laughing so hard. Scott looked to the empty seat beside him, concern growing over Gia's delay in returning. Commander Garret hadn't heard from her, the other lab normally radioed well ahead of time for a pick-up. The lab had also not responded to any of the Bataan's calls. *It isn't like her.*

Kaylie sat to his left and gave a little nudge when it was his turn. Glumly, he walked up to the podium, hugging the woman who'd just spoken—one of Jack's long-time church members. He took a sip of water and looked up at the crowd; it appeared that every member of the AG community was here.

"How do you describe a man like Preacher Jack? A man so at odds with what he was, yet also completely comfortable with his place in the universe. He made no pretenses that he was just a man, but he was a man of faith. Inside him burned a passion that few of us could ever match. Jack told me once that he really wasn't afraid to die, he just didn't want to be there when it happened." The audience let out a polite chuckle and heads nodded to one another.

Scott looked around the room and then tucked his notes back in his pocket. "Let me give you the truth. Truth is…my heart is breaking. Not just for me, but for Todd and Bartos and all of you that knew this wonderful man. Many of you are aware of what happened in the battle with the Messengers. Jack won that battle for us, won it by battling the leader alongside Roosevelt and Tommy." He gave a nod of acknowledgment to the older black man sitting in the front row.

"Later, Jack felt like he had traded a piece of his soul for that victory. He told me he felt broken after the ordeal. He wasn't alone in that ugly truth, but I'm not sure any of us bore the heavy burden that he did. Jack never spoke of that day being held hostage by the man calling himself the Prophet. Not long ago, Mister Roosevelt relayed to me some of what was said, though. In the end, he'd tried to teach that evil bastard a lesson of love and forgiveness. He said, 'What love you leave behind is the true measure of a man. What you are holding onto is measured by who you are willing to die for.'"

He paused, tears streaming down his face, as was the case with most of those looking back. "Let's face it, surviving out there now is damned hard. Jack gave his life to save us. He knew the cost and paid it without complaint. In the end, he knew his actions had given us a chance, given us another day, given us hope. When we fight…and be damned sure we will have to, I fight for him, 'cause he fought for you." He looked skyward, "Take a break, Preacher, you've done enough. I will miss you, you goofy bastard, with all my heart. God bless you, friend, and thank you for being a part of all our lives." Scott walked away from the podium to absolute silence.

Jack was laid to rest in a plot on the hill, not very far from the grave of Todd's wife. Bobby, Skybox, Tahir, Garret, Todd and Scott carried him to his resting place. As the hole was backfilled, Scott embraced all of his friends wordlessly, ending with Todd. After several minutes, Todd pulled back and looked at the mound of fresh dirt, then over to his wife's grave. "What do we do now?"

Scott thought to an earlier response to that same question. His answer hadn't changed. "We do what we must. We rise-up, battle on, we live... we love. Todd, we do what we must to survive. We honor Jack's sacrifice."

CHAPTER SEVENTY-THREE

Tahir sat with Skybox looking over his shoulder at the laptop. They now had confirmation that the Navy had fired at the Mount Weather facility, but had they been successful? With everything that was going on, this seemed somehow less important, but both men needed to know. "Okay, we have a bird moving into position now. It will be an oblique angle but should verify if the attack was successful," Tahir stated flatly.

Sky had no idea how the man could tap into top-secret channels like this but was glad he could. The laptop screen began to show the rural area of northern Virginia. All he could see were trees and a few roads until Tahir began adjusting the settings. Suddenly, the image resolved down to a scar across the expanse of green trees, then to the remains of the mountain. "Jesus," Tahir said.

Skybox shared his friend's reaction. The aerial bombardment had been quite thorough. Where the mountainside had slid away, huge slabs of broken concrete were visible. In places, dark cavernous openings appeared to go deep inside the hill. "Look there," Skybox said. "It's an open hangar door into the parking area."

Tahir zoomed closer, "Losing the image in seconds, the bird is moving out of range. Looks to me that the security gates are open as well."

"That means someone got out," Skybox sighed. "Damn, what are those things that look like ants going in and out of those openings in the hill?" The satellite image faded as the drone flew out of range.

Tahir pulled up a still shot of the base and magnified and enhanced it. The 'ants' resolved themselves to be human. "They are the infected."

He was talking to Bobby about Scott; the man had barely been seen since the funeral. Skybox knew he was taking the loss hard. As a soldier, he had gotten used to saying goodbye. He'd lost way too many people over the years.

"It's been tough on him, man, I'm not gonna lie," Bobby said. "Losing Jack was awful, but now he has no idea where Gia is. She should have been back days ago. The boy is worrying himself sick."

Sky nodded, "I have to go over to the Bataan shortly to go over some things that Tahir and I found. I'll check in with the guys there to see what they know."

"Thanks, man, we need him and Todd back up to speed. The Navy is bringing the fuel for us tomorrow. After that, we have to finalize our departure and wrap up some of the smaller tasks."

The image of those ants on the anthill flashed through Skybox's mind. He did not want to be in Harris Springs when those things started showing up. Briefly, he wondered if he was even a part of this migration—and what about Tommy? He filed that way for later.

Skybox looked at the message. The small digital pager had stayed silent for so long he rarely even checked it. All members of Praetor were required to keep it on or near them always. He'd not always been in a position to obey that order, but today he had. These were not tasking instructions but instead, an acknowledgment. It was notification of a change in his command structure. He read it twice before deciding he needed to make a call.

Three hours later, he sat in the communications room aboard the USS Bataan. It was the only operational facility with a working encrypted video messaging system. Lt. Garret had arranged it and now stood outside the door barring anyone else from entering. Memories of being aboard a ship and talking to P-command reminded him of the early days of this crisis. As he watched the white scorpion Praetor logo on the stark black screen, he wondered how far they'd actually come since then. *Not far enough.*

"Hello, Sky." The bloodied and battered face of Archangel was barely recognizable. If not for the voice, he would have had trouble identifying him as the man he'd seen just a six weeks ago.

"Angel, what the hell happened? Are you in command?"

"Please, let me talk," Archangel said. "We have a lot to discuss and very little time to do so."

Twenty minutes later, Skybox left the conference room, his face ashen, his confidence shaken.

The younger Garret knew something was up. "Heading back to the AG, sir…Sir? Skybox?"

Skybox ignored the man and walked down the long corridor. Down several flights of stairs, and through the sealed doors to the bio-containment labs. He was more than familiar with the area, spending a great deal of time here with the science team the last several months. Several lab technicians were in the laboratory.

He tapped on the window to get DJ's attention. He motioned for him to pick up the old-school telephone handset they sometimes used to talk to visitors outside.

"Hey, Sky," the young man said cheerfully. "We don't have you scheduled for…"

Skybox cut him off, "Do you have any idea where Dr. Colton is? I need her immediately."

DJ stammered, unused to the commanding tone of his long-time patient and friend. "She, um she's gone to one of the other labs."

"I realize that, but can you reach her? Do you know where the lab is?"

DJ shook his head, which was barely noticeable with the bio-suit he was wearing. "Sorry, no, classified and all that. I believe it's one of your guys' locations."

He meant a Catalyst facility, one of the Praetor controlled labs.

The younger Garret appeared in the door behind them asking if everything was ok. *Everything is definitely not ok.*

Skybox wasn't sure Archangel meant to show him as much of the facility as he did, but something stood out, one other person there he'd recognized, even though it was for only a fraction of a second. A lone female in the background accompanied by two guards in black uniforms. Gia Colton isn't at any lab, he realized. *She's been captured.*

CHAPTER SEVENTY-FOUR

Scott Montgomery felt the floor tilt and the world went sideways. Skybox reached over to support the man. "I'm sorry, Scott, did she say anything about the facility she was heading to?"

Scott's mouth was filling with cotton, he couldn't form the sounds to make the words come out. *Captured*, he was fixated on that word. "Lab-4," he finally said. "Seems to be the one she's had to go to most often… at least recently."

"No idea where that is?"

Scott thought, "Um, no. I assume the Navy does. Why in the hell would anyone take her?"

Skybox ignored the sobs of grief now coming from the man, "Not a Navy lab, its supposedly one of my people's but not sure I can trust that either. Garret says they chopper her into a neutral location and leave, she then travels to the actual site on a Praetor bird. They've never been able to track them, no matter which lab she is heading to."

The uneasy truce negotiated between Praetor and the Navy had been mostly negotiated by Skybox. For almost eight months it had held up, but now…he wasn't so sure. The why was easy though, she had the cure.

Scott went berserk, "We're getting married in a few weeks, the baby. The baby...I have to find her. Can the other man help, Archangel...he's the one we met, right? Him or Vincent?"

"I don't know where they are, and he wouldn't tell me. Vincent, well..." Skybox frowned, "Vince's loyalties apparently were elsewhere. He and Archangel had a disagreement."

That was an understatement, Vince had tried to kill Angel. Somehow, he'd already had the command channels' authentication codes, and with it, he could have taken over P-Command. That would give him command authority over every Praetor commander worldwide. The irony that Archangel had now done the same thing wasn't lost on Skybox; it was one more twist to this unbelievably strange day.

Scott was going through a manic range of emotions. Skybox had no way to comfort his friend. He sat alone with him in his cabin for an hour. "I have to go, Scott, I'll send someone to check on you later. We will get her back."

He walked out of the ship's cabin and down the long corridor. The bright, tropical carpet seemingly a mockery of the seriousness of the moment. What he decided not to tell Scott might have been the biggest problem of all. With Archangel in charge of Praetor, that meant he now knew exactly where Skybox was. All pretense of safety here on the AG vanished when he'd made that call. P-command could track him whenever they wanted. *On what side does Archangel fall? Where are his loyalties?*

Tahir sat there with a blank face absorbing what Skybox was saying. "Yes, yes...I think I understand. You aren't giving me much to go on, but for Scott, of course."

"You already know some locations for possible bases, don't you?"

"Well...maybe. We know some possibilities, a few we would likely have to rule out due to the spread of the pandemic."

"Like where?"

"I know there are government bunkers like Greenbriar in West Virginia, but that's out, too close to Baltimore. Raven Rock Mountain in Pennsylvania, Cheyenne Mountain or underneath the Denver Airport. North Bay, Ontario. Selfridge base in Michigan. Oak Ridge, Tennessee." He continued to name off locations, both the obscure and the well-known. "Mount Weather would have been on the list, but well, it's gone."

Skybox shook his head, "No, no...most of those are too far away anyway. She got there in just a few hours. Also, it's not DIA, I know what the facility below the Denver Airport looks like, and that isn't what I saw. By chopper, she would realistically need to be within 900 miles of us."

"Could be she was transferred to a jet."

"Shit, that's true; but the runway at that airport wouldn't work well for that. For now, let's assume she got there by helicopter."

Tahir began to tap the pencil against his lips. "What places would you suspect? A place that housed your people, Praetors and NSF guards?"

"Military bases, although many of those are abandoned or not friendly to the president's Security Forces," Skybox said. "Can't really rule them out, though." His brow furrowed as he thought. "Internment camps? Must be hundreds of those. Every major city and hell...nearly every major highway has several."

Tahir shook his head, "No, they would not have the infrastructure. And they are too vulnerable."

"Agreed. Existing bio-research labs?" Skybox said hopefully.

"Let's hope not," Tahir responded. "Way more of them than you would believe. Besides the government based, lots of commercial labs, hospitals and even a lot of universities maintain very well-equipped research labs."

"Ok, let's skip that for now."

"Protectorates," Tahir said. "We know those are well defended and well equipped. Although some have apparently fallen…most of them must still exist."

"Which ones do we know of?"

Tahir took a printout of North America and began making marks on various locations. After ten minutes, he handed it over.

"And how do you know this?"

"I just do. The data was not so secure when the 'shit hit the fan,' as you like to say. And…I remember stuff," Tahir said modestly.

"Northern Texas, outside West Memphis, Ashville, North Carolina. These are the only ones I think would be in range. This…" Skybox looked hopeful, "…this feels right to me. What can we do to help narrow it down?"

Tahir shrugged, "If it is one of these, I can find it. Someone logged something on a computer. A flight, a message, supply requisition…something."

Skybox patted him on the arm as he rose to leave, "Good man."

He was reaching for the door when Tahir asked the one question he'd been asking himself, "So, what will you do when we find her?"

"Honestly…I don't know."

～

A short while later, Bobby and Todd sat across the table listening to Skybox explain what he'd found. Somewhat reluctantly, he let them know that he had to assume his location was no longer a secret to the enemy. "By extension, if they know where I am—they know where you are."

"Time to relocate the rebel base then, commander?" Todd asked trying unsuccessfully to lighten the mood.

"This ship needs to be ready to move at any time," Sky said. "I don't think they would waste one of those orbital rods on us...hopefully. The Navy attack probably destroyed any apparatus to use that awful thing, but they could do just fine with conventional weapons. Your saving grace is that carrier sitting out there. The Bataan is the best weapon and best deterrent you have. As long as it is close, you are probably safe."

"How long will they stick around with their main scientist gone?" Bobby asked looking over at Todd.

"Exactly," Skybox agreed.

"I like Garret...shit, both of 'em, but you can't expect them to stay here and stationary without Gia. They lost their best asset. Now they also know how vulnerable they are from the KEP."

Todd looked at the other two men. "I'll talk to Commander Garret. Bobby and I can have the ship packed and ready to depart within two days, three, tops. What do we do about Gia though?"

Bobby shook his head, "And my brother. No way he will leave her behind, not with her being held prisoner especially."

"I'm working on that. Not sure of our options, but once we have a location, I am going to press my people hard for answers...and action."

Trish stuck her head in the door and beamed when she saw Bobby. "When you have a second, I need to talk to you. Have some news on the missing girl, and I can't find Scott."

Skybox pulled the pager from his pocket, the buzzing loud enough for the others to hear. He looked confused as he read the message. "Go ahead," he said absently as he scrolled the text again. "I have to go."

CHAPTER SEVENTY-FIVE

Angel left Scott's cabin in tears. She hugged Kaylie out in the corridor. "No better?" his niece asked.

"No, in fact, he is in there packing a tactical bag. He's determined to go find her."

Kaylie knew that was coming, "He has no idea where to even look. Tahir said even the Navy pilots have no idea, and they are the ones who dropped her off. Apparently, they went back to the airport, and the place was abandoned, no clues…nothing."

"Shh," Angel whispered as she maneuvered Kaylie down the hall. "He's breaking my heart, girl. I've never seen anyone so desperate."

"Do you blame him, Angelique? His fiancée, his child. Shit, just when things were starting to look a little better." Kaylie walked to the small sitting area off the main corridor and flopped into the deep cushions of a pale blue armchair.

They heard a muffled crash from down the hall, something breaking and a cry of anguish. Kaylie rose quickly to go check on him, but she was blocked by Angel's arm. "Leave him be for now, hon. He has to work through this pain." Kaylie responded, "You really care for him, don't you?"

Angel looked at her somewhat embarrassed. "I do, yes, but not how you think.

It might could have been romantic if things had been different, and if not for DeVonte, but Scott is, I don't know…he's just a good guy. He's like an older brother to me but…more. He was just one of the best of us…and now…"

"And now he's broken," Kaylie said sadly.

Angel nodded.

Skybox came through the hatch to the stairs. "Ladies," he said in greeting. "He still in there?"

"Yes," they both replied as he walked past. "But I don't think…" Kaylie began to say, but Sky was already in.

"Follow me."

Scott just looked at the man, Scott's red swollen eyes echoing the hopelessness he felt. "To where?"

"Just get your ass up, we have a lot of work to do if we are going to find her. Lying here wallowing in it isn't helping."

"Does Tahir have a location?"

"Not yet, but we don't need it."

Scott got up, completely bewildered.

"Bring your gear, you won't be coming back to this cabin anytime soon. There's been a few developments."

Kaylie and Angel were outside the room again, both going into protective mode against Skybox. Angel got up into the big soldier's face and was about to tell Sky to back the fuck off and leave Scott alone. She didn't get the chance. "Stow it for now. Ladies, can you join us? This is going to need to be a group thing."

～

Everyone crowded into the conference room aboard the AG. Scott was not at the table but instead, slumped onto a padded bench along the back wall. This was Skybox's show.

"Thanks, DeVonte," who was still hobbling around with a cane. He'd been asked to round everyone up for this impromptu meeting.

Bartos was just entering, reeking of diesel and burnt motor oil. "What's happening?"

Skybox motioned for him to have a seat. "Couple of things, all important, so listen up. First, I am leaving. I've been reassigned, to be more accurate."

A collective gasp went around the room. No one had even considered that this could happen. They all knew he was active duty, but…well, he just seemed a part of the community now.

He went on, "I knew it was a possibility when I spoke to command earlier. There is a lot going on out there, and none of it good. Todd will fill you in on things going on here but understand, our timetable for staying safe just shrunk considerably. We may now be on the NSF's radar and…" *Shit*, he really didn't want to give voice to the other, but, "When the president's compound was fired on, she gave the order to use the bioweapon, the Chimera variant on all of the prison camps and a lot of other remaining population centers of any size on the East Coast. The infected are now driving south by the tens of thousands. Not sure why they are heading toward us, but they are. They will likely be here in weeks, not months."

There was a collective gasp from the group.

He decided to continue, "Second thing," he paused briefly to take in the room, "Scott is going with me."

The noise level in the room increased significantly. Questions came from every direction.

"Tahir, can you put it up?" He nodded and used the remote to power on the flat screen TV.

On it was a grainy image of a very pregnant Gia being escorted at gunpoint by two NSF soldiers. Scott leaned up, then stood and silently began to approach the screen.

"Tahir retrieved this from the Bataan's comms computers. I have no idea how. Ok, expand the view out." Archangel's battered face filled the remainder of the screen. "My new assignment is to report to this man. He is where Gia is. I don't know if I can trust him, in fact, I probably can't, but that is where we are going. A protectorate camp outside of Memphis."

"Memphis?" Bobby said. "That was where the Messengers had a big battle and lost."

Skybox nodded, "Tahir has done some digging, it appears to be a significant operation. The base is called Thunder Ridge. No guarantee that Gia will still be there, but that is where the answers are."

"How will you get close enough to find out?" Bobby asked. "I mean, you're supposed to be there, but Scott isn't."

"Not just Scott, I'm taking Tommy as well. But…well, I'm still working on that part."

"I'll go," Bartos said eagerly. "I'm in," echoed Todd, then Bobby.

DeVonte started to add his name, but Angel cut him off, "Uh-uh, oh, hell no. Don't even think about it, Cowboy."

"Sorry, guys, this is going to be a lean, fast strike team. I have requested a couple of the Navy Spec Ops guys. Two Rangers from the lost battalion are still with us as well to help plant a locator beacon, but that's it. Bartos, I'd love to have your level of crazy, but you are too banged up." He thought for a moment before adding, "I wouldn't say no to Solo, though."

Bartos shrugged then winced at the pain in his shoulder. "Up to him. You and Scott both know most of the commands, and he loved the last time, so…yeah, sounds smart to me."

CHAPTER SEVENTY-SIX

NEAR SPARTANBURG, SOUTH CAROLINA

Commander Kitma looked at the valley ahead in disbelief. Losing his long-time friend and ally the previous week in the oil facility attack in Louisiana had been devastating. Now this, though. Infected were pouring southward out of the crowded northern states and all of the internment camps. The Appalachian Mountains were a natural obstacle causing many of them to head south in search of food and more hosts to infect. Here in South Carolina, the natural terrain was funneling all of them more eastward toward the coast. His assignment was to prevent them from going farther. Sadly, he already knew he would fail on this assignment, and it would likely be his last. Once they got as far south as Atlanta, the mountains faded, and the way westward would open up. Then, the remainder of the country would get to see the full horror of this disease.

He looked at his second, "Major, go ahead, blow the bridges." The man nodded and began barking orders into his radio. Minutes later, in the far distance, he could hear detonations as bridges all over the region were demolished. Other units would be doing the same thing. A squadron of fighter-bombers from MCAS Beaufort was assisting with those too remote or in areas already overrun by infected. While not much of a deterrent like the mountains, it had been noticed that the infected preferred not crossing rivers. Taking out the bridges helped funnel them toward Kitma's awaiting battalions.

This could well be the republic's last stand. He knew America would survive or fall based on what happened here in the next few hours. No one knew why the infected tended to herd together, some primal instinct or something. Safety in numbers perhaps, but in either case, it was freakish to see up close. His briefing from P-command had told him to expect something akin to a B-movie classic zombie. This wasn't at all what he was seeing.

The leading edge was less than a mile away. He and his people would all likely be infected by now as well, but if they could thin the numbers of the horde, it could still help. Through the Steiner binoculars, he watched them with morbid fascination. These had been people, teachers, neighbors, preachers maybe. Now they were like a pack of wild dogs chasing after prey. They were angry and wild. Most were naked or nearly so, it looked like the clothes had been torn from their bodies. Most were covered in cuts and blood and gore from past fights or feedings. What was most unnerving was how fast they moved, and the fact they were obviously communicating with one another. No, this wasn't zombies, the infected were much, much worse.

A few seconds later, the sound reached his ears. A perpetual moaning combined with thousands and thousands of feet pounding the ground toward them. Then the stench, a wet-dog smell with something more that faintly reeked of rotting fish. He heard some of his men begin to gag. He just prayed they would maintain fire discipline. The US Army hadn't fought a battle like this in a very long time. Firing on a charging force called for old-school tactics. The truth was, no one he knew had fought an enemy like this. "Pick a target, gentlemen, and fire at will." The major passed along the order calmly, and up and down the line, weapons began to fire. The last remnants of the US Army began the laborious process of killing much of what remained of the country's citizens.

The first wave of the horde fell, but that was barely a dent in total numbers. The infected saw the soldiers as hosts to be taken, an enemy to be consumed, and nothing would stand in the way of their insatiable bloodlust. Chambers clicked empty, and new clips were slammed home, but the horde used those few seconds to gain ground. They were now forced to crawl over the growing pile of dead bodies, but some were getting through and getting closer and closer to the soldiers. Kitma could do the math, they had more bodies to throw at them than his men had ammo to throw back. It was a losing proposition. "Blow the trenches!"

The major yelled, "Cover!"

The valley floor detonated with row after row of quarry explosives. They had spent much of the prior days drilling holes for the explosive mix and laying the Det Cord across the landscape. Each row was hundreds of explosions going back nearly a half of a mile. The blast radius of one had been mapped out to just overlap the edge of the blast in the next row. The infected went up in pieces, many nothing more than clouds of blood. Clouds that were now drifting back over his frontline troops.

"Major, give the order. Fall back."

The line of troops, tanks, and equipment made a swift retreat, but not all, he noticed. Hundreds of his soldiers were now on their knees, vomiting or holding their heads. The order had been given in advance to fire on any of their fellow soldiers who became infected. Commander Kitma now waited to see how many would actually follow those instructions. Once they were established a few hundred yards farther back, a handful of shots rang out targeting their fallen brothers-in-arms. Then a few more, and soon after, the hundred or so infected troops left behind lay unmoving on the ground. *Good,* he thought sadly. *That will be the hardest thing these men ever have to do.*

He looked out over the valley at the tens of thousands of dead, but as he feared, just as many were coming out of the rapidly clearing smoke. "Artillery rounds, Major. M377 Flechettes."

The 90mm airburst artillery shell was specifically an anti-personnel round. Each shell detonated above ground dispersing hundreds of smaller razor-sharp darts of metal in a fourteen-degree forward arc. The deadly "metal rain" had been outlawed as inhumane and hadn't been used anywhere in recent times, but thankfully, a stockpile of the brutal ammo had been located. As the orders were given, firing lanes for the M1-A1 tanks opened up. The shelling was unleashed with deadly efficiency. As each round detonated, he could see bodies fall for twenty yards, many literally sliced in half by the flechettes.

Still, they came. The day became a scene of fire, retreat and fire. They were bending, but so far hadn't broken. His aide had moved them behind the front line. The infected were enraged, and between breaks in the firing, some broke through. Ripping, tearing, biting, sometimes kicking and punching his soldiers into submission. The virus turned them into a sadistic, rabid version of a human. Those who fought back died, the ones who didn't, were often maimed and left to become new host for the disease.

He shook his head at the waste of life. Seemingly, uncaring about his own. Then came the message he'd been dreading.

"Contact rear."

They had been encircled. Infected were now on all sides, they were the cheese in the middle of the trap. Guns began clicking empty as ammo shortages became critical. He didn't bother telling his men to affix bayonets, those who remained were already doing so in preparation for hand-to-hand. All tanks that were out of ammo were instructed to simply drive through the still advancing horde of the infected. The crunching sound of bone and bodies beneath the treads was something beyond horrific. Kitma finally found himself locked into the cabin of the tank he'd been riding in all day. Out of ammo and short on fuel, they pointed the beast at the thickest part of the infected. His drivers would handle this, no more of his orders were needed.

There was one other thing he could do, though. Maybe he could help someone else.

CHAPTER SEVENTY-SEVEN

HARRIS SPRINGS, MISSISSIPPI

Scott found his brother in the comms room. The massive radio system now featured several laptops and computer monitors as well. A large map on the wall showed the US with much of the eastern half of the country filled in with snake-like tendrils of highlighted pink. He knew there were reports of the infected moving deeper south and west.

Bobby slipped the headphones down around his neck. "Hey, man." He stood up and embraced Scott. "What's up?"

"You know I have to go after her."

Bobby nodded, "I uh…well, shit, yeah, I know, I hope you find her, man."

Scott nodded absently. He knew he was mentally unfit for this mission, nor was he being much of a leader, but *Fuck it.* "Listen, Bobby, the ship is nearly ready. Todd's handling the final set-up, help him out. He needs you for this. Losing Jack…" he trailed off. "Just help him, ok? He looked closer at the pink markings on the map. "Tahir says you may have a few weeks before you have to leave."

Bobby nodded, "Yeah, heard that already. We'll be ready."

Scott leaned against the door, his vision blurring and coming into focus. He shook his head, "No, not that."

Bobby put out a hand to support his brother, "You okay, man? You're looking a bit shaky."

Scott ignored the question. "My point, Bobby, is that we have room for thousands on this ship, and we are taking just a fraction." He rubbed a hand across his forehead, fighting off a headache, willing his eyes to focus. "America needs to be saved. It may be up to us."

His older brother nodded but looked confused. Scott continued wearily, "I want you to put out the word. Tell anyone on the Patriot Network that they are welcome to join us. Bring supplies, bring weapons, do what they can to get here. Once the US is safe, we'll come back, and they can go home and start rebuilding. It's their only real chance."

Bobby followed Scott's gaze to the map, "Many…hell, probably most are already gone."

"I know…I should have thought of it sooner, but I didn't know if the old girl would actually ever move again. There will be survivors, even in the red states. Find them, Bobby."

Scott's older brother wrapped him in a bear hug. "I never knew you were such a great humanitarian. Thanks, man, this is awesome."

"Don't thank me yet, you have to keep 'em in line. We know that they are an independent bunch."

Bobby nodded, not letting go of his little brother. "Go get her…and get back here."

Scott nodded and left the small room, tears beginning to well at the corners of his eyes.

～

He found Todd sitting in the dark in the cabin that had been Jack's. "Hey, man." He saw Todd's head nod in acknowledgment. "You ok?"

"No."

Scott sniffed back a runny nose and rubbed at his eyes. "Yeah…"

The two friends sat there in silence for a long time. Neither actually saying much, but words were not what was really important. Scott told him what Bobby was going to do. There could be a lot of new faces around in the next few weeks. The years of trying to keep the AG secret were over.

"Sounds good," was all Todd said.

Eventually, Scott rose to leave. Todd reached out a hand to stop him. "I should be going with you, Scott, we're…we are a team."

Scott agreed they were, he had been at his best when supported by the man in front of him and Bartos, Solo and Jack. Things had changed, though. "This is my mission, Cap. Yours is to be ready to lead our people to a new home. My pregnant wife will want a nice bungalow on the beach…I promised her that."

Todd nodded.

Angel was surprised to see Scott, she hugged him and gave a quick peck on the cheek. She then pulled him over to the dining table where Kaylie, Jacob and Roosevelt were already sitting. As he sat down, Jacob surprised him by climbing from Kaylie's lap into his. Feeling the boy's head resting against his chest was the most comforting thing he had experienced in weeks.

"When you heading out, Uncle Scott?"

"Later today, Sky is getting the gear packed now." He glanced from his niece to Angelique. Her eyes were watching him closely. "Angel, you may have some additional mouths to feed in the coming days."

She nodded, "Bobby already filled me in. We're going to get cabins ready just in case, and the guys are doubling our fresh water storage." Her tone shifted abruptly from ship's business to personal. "Scott, you sure you're ready for this? Why not let Skybox and the soldiers go?"

He gave a small chuckle and shook his head, "No…I am very much not ready, but I have to. She and our baby…" his voice trailed off. He had no more tears to shed. It was time for action now. What had been building for days was a simmering rage. "We'll be fine, Angel."

Scott looked at Roosevelt who had remained oddly quiet. "Nothing from you, friend?" Scott said with a smile.

Roosevelt shook his head. "Nah…you don't need no ramblins from an old man. You gonna do whas right, yes suh, you will. Mister Scott, you just one dem folks dat gotta make a difference in da world. You don't even realize it, you thinks you doin stuff just for you or for these people here, but you ain't. You got big things ahead 'o you, big decisions. But I do have one favor to ask…I mean, if'n you was wantin and all. If you happen to see an of dem lemony candies while you out there…" The old man winked, and everyone laughed.

He felt Jacob squirm and climb higher up on his chest. He embraced the sweet boy whose tiny head now leaned nearer to his and was amazed at what came next from the child who no one here had ever heard speak.

"Please don't go."

CHAPTER SEVENTY-EIGHT

CENTRAL GEORGIA

Kitma's voice was strained, the connection full of interference. "Sentinel, alert de odders. De infected have regrouped, we have been overrun. Dey are heading...south."

"Please repeat that."

"Steven...dey are coming your way, take da boi and leave, you aren't safe anymo, this is it, my freend. Load up yo damn truck and go. May God look after you."

Steven could hear the sounds of gunfire and what sounded like distant screams coming over the radio. In the cabin deep in the woods of central Georgia, Steven Porter said goodbye to his closest friend. A man he'd met in person just weeks after the CME. A man he now knew was more than what he seemed. A man much like his friend, Gerald, who had pushed him to become somehow more as well. So many more things he wanted to ask Kitma, but the signal faded and then was gone.

He wiped his eyes dry with his good hand and scanned the large basement. JD was watching him from the leather sofa. "You heard?" The boy nodded.

Steve rose up from the chair and walked over leaning heavily on the racks of food. "You know the plan, two thirty-day load-outs for each of us, food, weapons, and tools. We can use the Rhino to get supplies down to the truck. We will take the computers and the library." JD looked at him surprised, his eyes full of questions.

"This looks like it, dude, the fall of America." He walked over to Gerald's wall-size map of North America. Push pins and sticky notes covered much of the US region. He pointed to a spot, "Kitma was somewhere up here, near Spartanburg, South Carolina. We are here," he pointed a finger at an area just below Warner Robbins, Georgia, the two fingers all that was left on the mangled hand.

"That's less than...hmmm, let's call it 225 miles. Assuming the infected move at an average pace, that puts them here in..."

"Eleven days," JD said.

Steve nodded, looking closely at JD. The boy was quickly becoming a man. The black tactical vest, pistol and knives now just a normal part of their attire. Neither of them was the same person anymore. Two years ago, when they had stumbled up the steps to this cabin, both were lost, and he, in particular, was a broken man, having struggled to travel home after the blackout only to find his wife gone and his son dead. He'd met JD in the company of another man. A fascinating individual named Gerald Leighton. Gerald didn't survive, but in his passing, managed to give them the means to do so. They had grown since then, finding purpose in survival, then in helping others do the same. Eventually, he became Sentinel, a key player in the growing Patriot Network.

JD was already opening up the large black storm cases. They'd practiced this, just like the original Sentinel had instructed them to in his guides. Steven knew from the drills that they could be on the road within two-hours. The truck, an old Land Rover Defender, was hidden a mile away. The beast of a truck would go through nearly anything, which was good as the nearest paved road was ten miles away. He would take a bit more time, though. This was a real bug-out. Probably, they would never be coming back to this place. This fortress of a cabin, that had been their refuge from all the darkness in the world.

"Where are we going?" JD asked.

Steven looked at the map on the wall once more. "We have to assume the infected zone moves south and west. They seem to be drawn to warmer climates. They'll move faster west once they get into Georgia where the Appalachians level out. We head to Florida, we may be trapped. I think we go west." He was thinking of reports coming out of bayou country of someone with a possible antiviral treatment.

"I think we only have one option."

He called up to the main floor. "Pam, we gotta talk."

The former Lt. Pam Lackey looked down the ladder. "What love?"

CHAPTER SEVENTY-NINE

NORTHERN MISSISSIPPI

Scott had assumed the Navy would be flying them up near Memphis. He learned quickly that was a no-go.

"We don't move that way. Praetor soldiers move by whatever non-military means are available. In this case, we're going to use some of the vehicles we captured up at the farms. Something large enough for us and our gear." Skybox said.

Scott couldn't remember what all they had liberated from the NSF, he'd been too busy heading off after Bartos to notice. Walking down to the staging area, he was shocked to see a pair of almost new dark gray Chevy Suburban 1500s. "Damn, those are nice." "Yeah, armored too, one even has a gun turret up top. Only thing, Scott…no bike rack."

He motioned to the group, "Let's get busy, we need to load these things up and be ready to roll in ninety minutes." The extra seats were removed, and the space used for additional gun cases, ammo and drones. Scott was astounded at the level of firepower Sky was bringing.

"You must think you are walking into a trap."

"I always feel that way, Scott."

"Maybe we'll get lucky. You waltz in and find where Gia is being held, then bring me in to help get her out."

He smiled and shook his head, "Didn't you hear, luck just left town. It's just us now, friend."

The gear was stowed, and the other soldiers did a final weapons check. Scott was already familiar with most of these soldiers. The pair of SEALs, Krychek and Rollins, the Army Rangers, Owens and a new man who towered over the rest, named Nez. All looked serious and deadly capable. He felt minuscule and weak standing beside this ensemble of hulking strength and abilities. They all turned as Solo padded up followed closely by Tommy whose blank expression seemed to be hiding something else today.

Scott had said his goodbyes to most of his friends, but Tahir had been over on the Bataan with Trish, which had seemed odd to him until Bobby said they had found a clue on the missing girl. The other person he hadn't seen until now was Bartos, who came limping up. Scott was amazed to see him without the cane. "Looking good there, Cajun."

"Ah, thanks. I've been working it hard. Hoped I would be good enough to travel with you asshats, but..." he looked down at the knee, "it still no work so good."

"It's ok, friend, this one is on me. Besides, I need you here."

"Oh, yeah, sure...I just, you know...I wanted to look after Solo and all."

Scott nodded and smiled, "Come here." He pulled the little bald man into a fierce hug. "Take care of yourself. I need you to be ready to stand with me and my bride, ok?"

"Okay, enough with the love and kisses," Skybox yelled. "Can we get the fuck on the road?"

Laughing for the first time in what seemed like ages, Scott said goodbye to his friend and loaded up.

~

"Seriously? No shit—that is what they're calling it?" Krychek asked incredulously. "Thunder Ridge. That sounds like it is right out of a Hollywood B-movie or something."

Skybox grinned into the rearview mirror. "Hey, it's Tennessee, that just happened to be the name of the place they chose to put the protectorate."

"Speaking of crazy names," Scott said, "Why Skybox?" It was a question he had asked so often it was almost a running joke.

"Because Big Swinging Dick wouldn't fit on his name patch," Owens said.

"I've told you, Scott, you don't get to pick your call sign. Someone else in your squad does that for you, or, in the case of my group, battlefield call signs were given out before each assignment. My last one just stuck, no biggie."

"Yeah, sure," the group said unbelievingly.

Scott was amazed at how relaxed the soldiers were. He was so tense he felt like throwing up. Somehow, he felt sure he was the only one. He was the pretender, he didn't belong.

Skybox had already explained that he had to go into the camp alone. The rest of the team would hold-up somewhere close and come in when he gave the signal. The Spec Ops guys' main job was to plant a locator beacon over the main part of the facility, then fall back and help with the exfil. How he and Tommy were supposed to get into such a heavily protected facility was something Scott was still waiting to hear. If Sky confirmed that Gia was still there, though, he'd find a way.

"I need to be there, Sky," Scott argued. "I'll let them capture me for...trespassing or something, then you can get me out once inside."

Skybox shook his head in a slow, sad manner that let Scott know it wouldn't work. "They wouldn't, friend....they would just shoot you."

~

They crossed the Mississippi, and as they approached the I-40, the scene of a horrific battle unfolded. Burned out hulks of cars and trucks joined an occasional weaponized vehicle, all of them bombed or shot to hell. Large impact craters lined much of the highway and even the overpasses. As the car passed by, skeletal remains could be made out, many hanging out of open windows. Skulls broken and blackened from what had occurred here. On one of the large buses, the top of which was ripped open like an exploded can of soda, a partial emblem was identifiable. Scott recognized it instantly, the same symbol his brother now had tattooed on his hand. *Messengers,* he realized in disgust. They had taken on Thunder Ridge here and lost.

A half-hour later, they pulled into an abandoned Hampton Inn just past Memphis. The hotel was in mostly good shape, somewhat isolated along a road leading up toward a large state park. "This will work," Skybox said. "Let's unpack the gear from my truck, I'll take it on up tomorrow morning. Best guess is we are about eighteen miles south of the camp."

"You don't know for sure?" one of the soldiers asked.

"Um, no. They won't give me exact coordinates until I'm within a few miles. That's when they will shut down perimeter defenses along a corridor for me to enter."

"And that's when you're going to let us know where to come?" Scott asked.

"Hopefully, I can get the coordinates to you, but don't come until I give the word. It would be suicide otherwise. Besides, man, if she isn't there…"

"She's in there—I feel it, Sky."

Scott tried several of the doors to the rooms finding them all locked. He watched as Krychek just kicked a door and walked in. The giant Native American Nez seemed to lean on one, the frame bowed and he walked in with his gear. Scott stepped back, raised a foot and was about to kick when Rollins tapped him and handed him something. "Key, dude, save your leg."

"Um, thanks," replied Scott realizing the man probably saved his pride even more.

Skybox called out loudly, "Everyone stow your gear, and let's meet in the lobby in ten."

The vehicles were pulled around back out of sight. Everyone was gathered around a black potbellied stove that seemed out of place in the modern hotel lobby. A small fire had been started in it mainly to give the room some light. One of the guys fished a coffee pot out and some water and sat it on the metal grate to warm. "Fucking Navy," came a voice from the shadows. "Do y'all do anything without coffee?"

"Ask your wife, Owens."

"Ok, guys, get serious," Skybox said as he took a device from his pack. It looked like a tablet, but when he tapped a button, the map that was displayed on the screen was projected up onto the blank wall. "Thanks to Scott's friend, he got one of my mission toys working. Here is the area of Thunder Ridge. He circled a large green area on the map. My best guess on the camp is it's somewhere near here. Good access to water, these rocky bluffs to the north would be a natural barrier and overlooking the valley would make it much easier to defend. There are also miles of natural caves under the mountains to use."

They spent the next several hours going over likely weapons emplacements, areas for the team to recon and other mission-critical details. After a long while, the Spec Ops team was growing frustrated. "This place is a fortress, Sky. They could be housing a full brigade of troops… shit—a regiment. We wouldn't know," Owens said.

Rollins asked, "Can I use my birds to get a look?"

Skybox shook his head, "Negative. They will have sensors that can pick them up. If you have to use them, go in passive mode only and assume they will be spotted."

They spent hours going over possible means of assault. It became clear to Scott the group had been involved in a variety of covert ops. "Sky, how far back does Praetor go?" he asked. "I mean, is it linked to the original Praetorian Guards of Rome?"

Sky shrugged, "Maybe. We like to think so, and we follow some of the ideals laid down by them, but who knows? When the CIA stepped out, and I found myself part of Praetor and under civilian command, it never seemed like we were some group of mercenaries. We had the full power of the government, could embed with, train with, deploy with nearly any military we needed. Our equipment was the best, and frankly, my fellow soldiers were some of the smartest and most capable. I'm not sure there has ever been a force as good and as significant as the Guard. Whoever the Caesar is that we are serving, they wanted the best group in the world, and they got it."

Scott spent several hours going over the map and the set of aerial images of the areas. Something finally occurred to him, and he leaned back catching Skybox's eye.

"You see something, Scott?"

CHAPTER EIGHTY

THUNDER RIDGE PROTECTORATE

She clicked off the display, exhausted. The complications unleashed by Madelyn Chambers had to be dealt with as well as the woman herself. She realized now she had been rooting for the Navy to get the job done and save her the trouble. Security cameras had spotted her getting away just before another salvo of missiles finished off the bunker. Ed had failed in his assignment, that was a pity. His family was being punished now for the man's failure.

She leaned back in the leather seat, wondering again how she had arrived here. Why she was the one tasked with saving the world. It had been her father, she knew the evil bastard of a man was preparing her for this. While most kids had some sense of love from their parents, she couldn't recall a single kind word from her father other than an occasional nod or, "That was adequate." She idly wondered if the man was still alive. She knew the estate out on the island still existed. She could tell that by satellite images. It was not from a sense of love, nor even duty. The former Levy was a threat to her and the plans she had. Just like the president, he had to be dealt with as well.

She had pulled Archangel out of prison specifically to handle that task but had hoped he could help with the military problems as well. Now, things had gotten out of hand with him, too. Vincent was supposed to settle him down, but now he was dead. More was going on there, more with the Praetor group. It annoyed her more than anything else, she no longer knew who was running the Guardians. That was going to have to change. She lay back on the hard mattress trying to find a comfortable spot. She didn't like complications, yet she knew she was running out of time to finalize her plans.

Seven hundred miles away Madelyn Chambers watched her driver as he dodged another group of the infected. The front grille of the car had remnants of many that he'd been unable to dodge on the long drive. An amber light began to flash on the driver's console. "What's that?"

The driver, whose name she'd forgotten, looked down, "Low air supply, ma'am."

"Like a flat-tire? I thought the Beast had run-flat tires," she challenged angrily.

"No," he shook his head. "No, Madam President. It is our oxygen supply. I've been running on self-contained air since we left…you know, to avoid the plague. The tanks are refilled by an oxygen generator, but they have a limit. When the warning light turns red, valves will open allowing outside air into the system."

She understood what that meant but was unconcerned for herself. She had received vaccines against the virus just as all of the top people in the bunker had. She looked at the top of the man's head as he drove. He, however, would not have been considered vital enough for the treatment. "How far to the port?"

"Maybe an hour….could be ninety minutes," he said.

She nodded, "Please raise the glass." Silently, the thickly reinforced glass partition rose up separating the driver's seat from the rest of the car.

She watched out the window as the landscape began to change from forest and hills to rolling pastures. Ahead lay her escape. The presidential yacht had sufficient food, supplies and equipment to last for months. Where would they go? What part of the globe would be spared? She was better at the planning and organizing than the execution. She realized that about herself, that was why she surrounded herself with doers. People who could help get stuff done. People like that fucking Ed. Ugh…she would have been on Marine One and down to Wilmington hours ago if not for his betrayal. And what about Levy? *Will she let me live? Do I even have a chance to escape this?*

As if in planned response, she noticed the light on the dash turn from amber to red. She cinched the lap belt around her snuggly. She'd watched Levy deliberately infect people to see how long it took. She also knew what came after. The victims lost their humanity and became angry, killing animals.

Twenty minutes later, she saw the driver's head twist violently, then drop. He snapped it back up again as if he'd mistakenly fallen asleep at the wheel. The Beast was equipped with all manner of safety devices including collision avoidance and lane departure controls, but it couldn't defend against a driver who was completely out of his mind. She watched in detached fascination as the man began to twitch then hunch himself up on the wheel as if to fight off the symptoms by sheer willpower. He stabbed a finger toward the dash.

"Ma'am," came the raspy voice. "I am pulling over." The voice was riddled with pain. "You probably need to…to go."

The Beast slowed as she saw the man arch his back in a totally unnatural manner. She placed her thumb on a lighted panel to reveal several options. One switch activated to kill the engine remotely, then another that shut off all air to the front cabin. Then she sat back and waited.

In a few minutes, she could see the driver convulsing. The massively heavy car rocked back and forth slightly with the movement. His head popped into view through the safety glass and he turned to face her, the hatred and anger evident on his now inhuman looking face. He scratched at the window; even facing death, the desire to kill and spread the virus was paramount. His movements soon became languid and the gestures feebler. After ten minutes, he was still. Only a corner of his head was within view, but she waited until even the smallest of muscle twitches had ended before switching the air supply on in the cabin.

The driver remained still. Not even the infected could live without air, that might be why they seemed somewhat averse to water. It was a hope at least. She struggled to pull the man from the seat. He'd soiled himself in the process of dying, and the smell and thought repulsed her. She roughly pushed him onto the highway, then went over to his body, removed his suit coat and used that to protect her dress from the nastiness of the driver's seat.

Restarting the engine, she pulled the limo back into the lane and headed once again toward Wilmington.

CHAPTER EIGHTY-ONE

HARRIS SPRINGS, MISSISSIPPI

Tahir spoke softly to DJ who still seemed confused at the request. "What has this got to do with us?"

"You remember the Star Trek episode when a second evil version of the captain is beamed aboard?"

"Duh. Every nerd knows that one. 'The Enemy Within' from 1966."

"I'm impressed, so you are not totally ignorant of quality entertainment. Well, that is what our inspector here is thinking. Someone here is not who they seem. Just because the world went to shit didn't mean all the evil bastards went with it."

DJ still seemed confused, "This is about Diana? You think what... someone on board murdered her? Like a serial killer or something?"

Trish walked in overhearing the question. "DJ, we are just following up on a lead."

The young man cocked his head quizzically, "What, a sailor? Someone on the science team?"

She shrugged, "We don't know. A lot of the crew come over to the AG. It's a possibility, that's all. Warburgh is speaking to the captain now about duty rosters and who was on shore leave the day she went missing."

DJ still was unconvinced, "Look, they all go over to Harris Springs. It's the only other place they can go, and to many of 'em, the people over there have almost become a second family this past six months." He slipped off his lab coat and placed it on a hook. "Not sure how I can help you but whatever, sure. I liked the girl and all but, well... you know...in the scheme of things, just seems odd to pursue it this hard, ya know?"

Trish was watching for visible clues, signs to see if someone were nervous or lying. "How do you mean?"

"Just that we are about to be pulling out. Soon as we get the rest of the vaccines ready, I am transferring back to the AG permanently. The Bataan and its crew will be gone, and we will be heading to Costa Rica. Besides, you don't even know if there was a crime, even Kaylie thinks she just ran away."

Trish relaxed a little, the sharp little researcher seemed on the up and up, and...he had a point. "DJ, I'm doing this because it was important to Scott. He asked me to. Besides, some of these Navy guys will undoubtedly be joining us when we leave, right?"

A slightly chastised DJ nodded, "Yeah, I know a lot have already asked to. In time, the rest of the fleet may even wind up there. At least until the pandemic dies out."

"So, do we want a possible murderer on board our little cruise ship? My daughter is over there, your girlfriend, all of our friends and family will be on-board. A killer with the ability to hide in plain sight scares the hell out of me. I need to know for sure before we cast off that that isn't the case."

Warburgh called from the open hatch for her to join him. DJ looked at Tahir, "She's good."

"Yeah, very thorough. You might want to be nice to her. I have a feeling she might wind up being your mother-in-law."

The expression on DJ's face went from confusion to a goofy grin, "Wait…no, her and Mr. Bobby?"

Tahir nodded, "Yep."

~

Warburgh led Trish up the corridor to the small meeting room. "Lt. Garret is rounding them up now." Twenty-three sailors had taken shore leave the day Diana disappeared. They were going to interview each of them to see who might have last seen the girl. "I still think this is a waste of time."

She knew he did, but to his credit, he was just as thorough chasing down her leads as he was his own. Trish looked over the list and called the first man in. This man, a Carson Layfield, happened to be a woman. Her close-cropped hair and stern expression left no doubt she had gone to great lengths to downplay her gender on a ship full of males. She wouldn't fit any of the likely profiles, and Trish would need to toss out about half of her listed questions, but she walked with her back to the interview room anyway.

This was the routine for the next eleven hours. Other than having lunch brought in and a few bathroom breaks, it was monotonous and uninformative. The only thing she really got out of it was how much these people missed their families and how much they enjoyed going over to the AG. She read back through all her notes on the way back to shore. Warburgh was housed on the Bataan and Tahir had gotten bored and came back earlier, so her thoughts were her own. Something a few of the sailors mentioned had triggered a thought. Three of them said they came to shore on a boat with someone from the quartermaster's office. Most likely on their way to trade for food at the farm. The Bataan was the farmers' biggest customer. They had assumed the report was about a sailor on leave, but what about someone who regularly came over as part of their duties? At the farm, the person could have even had contact with Diana, or at least seen her.

She read the eyewitness report once more. "Unknown time shortly after the evening meal. Saw two people heading to marina docks where the Navy transports come and go. Both figures appeared to be smaller, but one seemed to be assisting or possibly forcing the other along. A female voice was heard."

The report was from an older woman sitting on her stateroom balcony that night. It would have easily been fifty yards away and literally everyone these days was thin. No one had put much thought into the report originally. Probably because there was so little to go on. It could have just as easily been nothing. A boyfriend and girlfriend out for a walk. A sailor who had gotten a bit too much drink getting an assist by a shipmate. Still,…she tapped the pencil absently back and forth like a metronome. There was something there. She would have to talk with Warburgh and expand it to other of the ship's personnel. That would be a fun conversation.

CHAPTER EIGHTY-TWO

NEAR MEMPHIS, TENNESSEE

"What?" Skybox asked.

Scott put the encrypted radio back in the pack and had a confused look. "According to Tahir, the designs call for them to use an SMR as a power source." This had been Scott's question as he looked at the meager intel on the Thunder Ridge facility. All those people, all these defense systems. Scott wanted to know where they were getting all the power to run it.

"Okay, Einstein, what's an SMR?"

"Oh," Scott said absently. "Small Modular Reactor."

"Wait...what?" Rollins said coming fully alert. "Those fucks have a nuclear reactor buried down there? Shouldn't this have been in some of the pre-mission briefings or something?"

Skybox was familiar with nuclear power generation but had never heard the term SMR. "So, is this something like a submarine might have?"

The US Navy had extensive use with nuclear-powered vessels going back to the early 1960s. In fact, every sub and supercarrier built since 1975 was nuclear powered. "No, Sky, those wouldn't work here, they are called naval reactors, and while the size would be fine, they are really designed to work at sea, and the power output here would be insufficient." Scott rubbed the bridge of his nose and continued.

"For a long time now, researchers have been trying to make nuclear reactors more efficient and safer. It is absolutely one of the most efficient ways to generate electricity there is. The problems are the inherent dangers involved, the enormous cost and well… a very bad public image. Not to mention the not so little issue of disposing of spent fuel rods. The SMR takes away most of these problems. The smaller size means less cost, less infrastructure, and they could be located in a lot more places. In theory, each city might have one, just like a wastewater treatment plant. Some of the designs I've seen are crazy small, like the size of a station wagon. Most of them are radically safer than traditional plants in the simple fact that they cannot melt down. The rods are only exposed if they are generating power. Shut off the power, and the rods are cooled down. Some do this with salts…well, sodium instead of water. Ingenious designs, really."

"So, why are we just hearing about these?" Rollins asked, his interest growing.

Scott shrugged, "Development has been slow, there are tons of bureaucratic hurdles with any tech involving nuclear energy. A few systems have been in testing out in South Dakota but never heard if they got approval or funding to continue. Apparently, though, some did."

"Ok, they have a small nuclear reactor, how does that help us?" Skybox asked.

"Well, the SMR design still would generate intense heat, employ dangerous materials including a highly reactive sodium coolant and generate some nuclear waste. This means a dedicated team to handle it and, most likely, a place to dispose of the spent fuel nearby."

"In other words, they are going to be terrified of the damn thing."

Scott nodded at Sky, "Exactly, it is still atomic energy, and to most people, that is about the same as saying 'evil magic'. It will be isolated away from the population down there and have its own access to the surface to move spent fuel and to vent in case of emergency."

Skybox smiled, "Now we are talking."

～

"Look Scott, the first few days, who knows where I'll be? They may even keep me in quarantine. They know I have been exposed to the virus, and they won't have Dr. Colton's assurances that I am not a carrier." Skybox saw him wince at his fiancée's name. "Just saying, man, don't expect to hear anything from me for a while, probably a week at the earliest. I will have to earn their trust and gain some privileges to walk around freely. Something went on in there, something between two of my people. I am going to have to sort that out before I can go look for her, understand?"

They had already been through most of this, and Scott nodded, "I still want to go in with you, I need to see for myself."

"You can't, mate – they would kill us both before we got close," Skybox said.

Scott nodded reluctantly, "Yeah, I got it, man, you may be walking into a trap yourself. Just be careful and let me know if you see her."

Skybox pulled on the gray camo shirt and checked his watch, "Okay, I'm going to drive on up as far as they indicated was safe, then go in on foot. I'll radio back the exact location as soon as I know it. You get on the radio with Tahir and work out the details." He nodded back to the group of elite soldiers relaxing in the hotel lobby. "Use them, Scott. They are exceptional at what they do, and we both know this is bigger than just us or even Gia. They need to plant that beacon for the airdrop. We just have to get your girl and any other innocents out of the way first."

Scott looked at his friend. The man was risking so much for him. He was unsure if he would ever even see him again. Losing one more friend, one more person seemed like more than he could bear. He was already walling his emotions off to the possibility. "Skybox…" he searched for the right words and failed. Skybox just stuck out a fist.

"Hooah," the soldier said with a light fist bump. Scott smiled and watched as Sky climbed into the truck, the statue-like silhouette of Ghost sitting on the other side, the only other occupant. "We can do this, Scott—be the warrior!"

As the Suburban drove out of sight, Solo bumped his leg. The dog was as anxious to get some action as any of them. The calm, relaxed attitude of the Spec Ops soldiers had an undercurrent of energy that Scott was unable to identify. Inherently, he knew this was not like fighting beside his friends at the AG. Yes, these men could undoubtedly shoot and fight with the best of 'em, but each had other skills as well. Some of those he was aware of, and others were still a mystery. Still, what chance did he, Solo and the four men really have to get into or bring down something like the Thunder Ridge facility?

Skybox had decided to take his friend, Tommy, along as he was confident in his ability to detect and evade the defensive traps. Scott was still not sure how he communicated with his friend, nor how Tommy could function with so much damage to his brain, but after seeing him in action—he got it. Like Solo, there were just some weapons you didn't want to go into battle without. Sky wouldn't be able to get Tommy into the facility immediately but hoped to have him in close for support when needed.

Tahir's voice came through the radio clear and strong, "So, those guys are the redshirts?" Scott looked around the room at Rollins, Owens, Krychek and Nez.

"No, AlphaCat, pretty sure that would be me." If anyone was likely to get killed on this op, he damn sure wasn't betting on it being any of them. "Do you have access?"

"Partially, but the system has layers upon layers of security. Not just the obvious, you know, because of the SMR, but the base security itself is incredible. I don't know, dude."

"Look you ugly, falafel loving fuck, we have to get this. You don't need access to everything, just the alarms."

His friend's smile was heard through the words. "Just seems like an elite bunch like you guys would want to avoid alarms...not set them off. And when I say elite...I am of course talking about everyone but you, BikerBoi."

"Too bad you can't see my hand right now. Just keep working on it, asshat, ok? We don't have much time."

"Of course," came the reply. "By the way, my friend, nice to hear you again. Thought you had slipped over the edge. Left the rez, you know?"

Scott thought of a response, then decided on honesty. "Hanging on by fingertips, man, just barely keeping my shit together."

CHAPTER EIGHTY-THREE

GULF OF MEXICO, MISSISSIPPI COAST

Fleet Commander Garret looked thoughtfully at his son. He had his mother's eyes …and her stubbornness if he was being honest. The bittersweet thought of the woman neither of them would ever see again flitted through his head. The lieutenant had grown close to the people of Harris Springs. It was easy to see why. They were very endearing. In so many ways, they represented the best of America. Industrious and hard-working, they were constantly rebuilding their community. Not just to recapture some of what was lost but simply to make things better for themselves and others. From reports he'd read from other military leaders around the country, what they had accomplished here was unique. Despite his personal failures, he thought of the AG and its occupants with a sense of pride. He'd helped get them started, and they had, for the most part, thrived here.

"Dad, we have to do this. You know it is the right thing."

The older Garret nodded, "I do know, but that doesn't make it any easier. I'm not sure there is any Army out there anymore to work with.

None of us have any fuel for the jets or choppers. What can we even hope for?"

"We can protect them. They are putting out an evacuation call for America. Anyone on that Patriot Network that can get here is invited to leave with them on the ship."

The Commander nodded, but that just made them a bigger target. "What if they drop another of those space weapons, or worse…a nuclear strike? We would all be gone." The two of them were talking strategy, but at its heart, it was more personal. The commander knew his son was falling for a young woman on the AG. He'd met her once and very much saw the attraction.

"You took out the president. Isn't she the only one who could attack?"

His father shook his head, "We took out the presidential bunker, no way to know if we got her. May just have pissed the bitch off even more. Also…" he paused while he swirled the last bit of scotch in the tumbler and swallowed it in a single gulp, "I believe Mr. Montgomery and the Praetor commander are going after the real problem."

"Memphis?"

"Yes, the protectorate there almost certainly is where the real command authority is. No one is safe until that base is taken out."

The lieutenant voiced a disagreement, "Scott just went to find the doc. What can a handful of guys and a dog do?"

His father smiled, "You might be surprised. If they can pinpoint the C&C, we can take it out. But we will have to get them some help. Son, we need to put out our own Patriot's call. Find as many outposts, garrisons and ground commanders as you can. Let them know we have diesel fuel, ammo and supplies if they will join us. Get General Daly involved as well. We protect access to Harris Springs for the incoming evacuees, and we make one last stand for America here," he jabbed a finger at the map. "Rally point for that is Memphis."

∿

Those who answered the call began the move toward Memphis. From newly minted commanders filling in for fallen leaders to battle-weary veterans. The organized military had effectively ceased to exist over the previous two years, but the warrior spirit still thrived in many who were still valiantly holding the line. The 3rd Marine Battalion from Camp Legume fresh off of battling the infected headed west. The 1st and 3rd Army Stryker Squadrons from Fort Hood joined remnants of the 6th Squadron Calvary out of Colorado. None of the outfits were full strength, in fact, most were a small percentage of their normal combat size, but still, they came.

As promised, the Navy staged refueling tanker trucks at key points along the way. The hodgepodge of military hardware was mind-boggling. From old school buses full of infantry to M1-A1 battle tanks. The soldiers all looked tired and haggard. These were the men who had stayed at their post instead of going AWOL to check on family and friends. They had been underfed and forgotten by the country they served. Still, each had a fire in his eyes for a fight they thought might never come.

Marine Major General Daly had assumed command of all ground forces and was maintaining a small squad of older aircraft for close-in ground support. Commander Garret tracked the responses and troop movements, much of which were coming in via the amateur Patriot's Network. The president may have cut off the bases from direct contact, but she'd not been able to silence them completely. "How is it looking, Lieutenant?"

The younger Garret looked up from the maps covering the chart table and smiled. "They are coming. We have hundreds of units from nearly every branch heading toward Memphis. Troop numbers will still be low. We estimate around 10,000 men in total. Some additional air support would really be welcome, but what they have, they basically dragged out of mothballs." Row upon row of fighter jets and attack copters lined the hangars of the Bataan as well as hundreds of other bases around the country. All useless without modern aviation fuel to fly.

"Let's just hope the enemy is in the same shape on that point."

"Sir?" a petty officer manning a comms station called out. "A couple of the units near Chattanooga are running into large groups of infected. They want to know if they should engage."

The commander looked at the maps, the known regions where infected were present was shaded. Many seemed to be heading straight for the coastal regions. *Something…something…*.he was overlooking something important. "Negative! Do not engage. Give the order and someone bring me our lead science guy, DJ, and get his friend, the little Pakistani fellow. Get him over here from the AG."

"Aye-aye," a junior officer said as he turned to make the call.

DJ looked nervous and out of place in the war room. Gia had always handled the command briefings. This was his first time even seeing the highly secure area. Tahir sat beside him, and they faced several Navy officers including both Garrets.

"Gentlemen," the commander began. "You have some idea of what is going on out there, right?" Both of them nodded.

Tahir had been the more active participant in the mission, but everyone on board was aware of the imminent attack on the Thunder Ridge base. "Yes, sir."

"Good, time is short, and lives are at stake, so let me get right to the point." The older Garret stood and walked over to the huge wall map that had been brought up from the chart room. "Scott and his people are here, we believe the objective is in this area," he drew his finger in a circle. "Now, we put out the call to other military units who are able to converge on that spot in the next several days. Some may be as much as a week out, but the point is, your guys are going to have one hell of a backup force."

He turned from the map and leaned heavily on the back of one of the leather office chairs, crossing his arms in front of him. "The problem is, the infected are literally everywhere. Units are running into large groups of them. If they engage, they lose time, people, ammo…everything. If they don't engage, the damn things follow and wait for them to stop and start attacking like a pack of wolves. The commanders no longer want to fire on them as their blood is highly contagious as you both well know. So, gentlemen, we need another way of dealing with them, and you are going to help us do that."

DJ looked at Tahir confused, but noticed his friend was smiling and nodding.

CHAPTER EIGHTY-FOUR

WILMINGTON, NORTH CAROLINA

The scent of the ocean greeted her as she opened the door, grabbed her bag and headed for the gate. Although she'd never been here, the encrypted nav system in the Beast brought her within feet of the dock. She was relieved, the last few hours had been some of the longest of her life. Dense pockets of infected had roamed the highways making travel a challenge. Eventually, she had given up trying to dodge the brainless dotes, trusting the brawny vehicle to deal with them. The hood and grill of the presidential limo were covered with gore. The wipers had maintained a pair of clear portholes in an otherwise red-filmed windshield.

While officially, the United States hadn't had a yacht for the president since 1977 when the USS Sequoia was sold, unofficially having a floating version of the White House was fairly common. No longer a Navy vessel, the California was a 60-meter German-crafted Lürssen super-yacht and was the epitome of style and performance. Now, thanks to a complete retrofit at a private defense contractor in association with the shipyards in Bath, Maine, it was also one of the safest places in the world for her to be.

She didn't think Ms. Levy was aware of the yacht. Chambers, herself, had actually commissioned most of the work. As secretary of transportation, she had vetted the firms involved, then gotten very active in the redesign. Once she was sworn into the top office, she'd commissioned a Coast Guard crew to covertly relocate it down here to Wilmington. In the months since, she had added several of her private security forces to the ship, stocked it with every manner of food and supplies and kept it as her ace in the hole. It was now time to play that card.

The ensign watched the woman as she got out from behind the wheel of the presidential limo and began to walk up the aluminum gangway, her polished black heels clicking and scraping as she walked up the short incline. "Madam President?" he asked questioningly.

"Don't just stand there, take my bag," Chambers barked.

He took the bag from her outstretched hand, then looked back to the car she had exited. "You…you drove yourself, ma'am? Where is your security…"

"No time, please instruct the captain we will be departing immediately —no excuses. Run along now." She didn't want anyone else questioning her authority. She was in fact still the president, despite what some might think.

The ensign decided cooperation was the smarter course, nodded his head and led the way into the massive craft. He showed her to the richly appointed suite, left her bag and exited to notify the captain. She marveled at the luxury touches everywhere. While the yacht already had world class interiors, she had chosen the award-winning designer Luca Dini to put the finishes together. The last time she had seen any of this it had been renderings and textile samples. "Oh, my!" she exclaimed excitedly. *This will be perfect.*

The video call screen lit up with an incoming call, and she languidly touched the button to activate it. At the same time, she felt the gentle purr from the massive engines start-up. An older and very handsome man's face came into view. Behind him, the control room with all of its hardened and very advanced electronics were all coming to life.

"Madam President, we weren't expecting…"

She cut him off as well, "Yes, yes, the bunker was overrun by the infected. I lost my team getting away. None of this was planned, Captain. We just need to get somewhere safe for the time being…you know? Until things settle down."

The captain nodded and looked at something to one side of the camera. "Infected?" It was less a question than a statement. He quickly recovered, "Do you have a specific destination in mind, Madam President?"

"Hmm, something….tropical. Maybe, St. Kitts, just surprise me."

While she was not on the level of Ms. Levy, Madelyn was not without her own tricks. This ship being one of them. She was a survivor and had all intentions of staying one for a very long time. She had not bothered with clothes, makeup or any of the normal items a traveler might pack. Duplicates of her entire wardrobe would be in the suite's wardrobe room, and new containers of her favorite toiletries and makeup were already waiting for her at the dressing tables. No, the one bag she brought contained only two things. A thumb drive with the firing sequence for Thor's Hammer and the nation's nuclear launch codes.

In the command center at Thunder Ridge, Archangel was waiting for Ms. Levy's decision. "I don't have time to meet him right now. If he is not Vincent's replacement, then you handle him. I trust your judgment. Get him up to speed as soon as possible, though. I need you dealing with your primary issue. You know, the main reason I pulled you out of that prison." She walked briefly out of camera view.

"Also," she went on, "the military, well, what remains of the military, is up to something. They went after the president, now they want power. They know a lot of the legislatures wound up in these protectorate camps despite us trying to prevent that. The one at Raven Rock, in particular, has enough senators in it to start their own nation."

He decided not to mention that camp had been one of the ones to fall the past week. Insurgents had blown a gate, and the entire facility was overrun by infected. The woman didn't seem interested in a dialogue. She only met with him now by video link, so he never actually knew if she was here in the same facility or somewhere else on the planet. Her paranoia seemed to be growing. The apparent betrayal by Vincent seemed to have thrown her over the edge.

Walking back to the adjacent meeting room, he turned a chair around and faced his subordinate. "Skybox, I know you have questions, but they have to wait. I need to get you up to speed here securing this facility."

"Wait...what?" Skybox asked with general confusion.

"You are being promoted and, in time, will be assuming Vincent's role in securing this facility. You have the background and know the tech."

"But.." he started to protest, then noticed Angel cutting his eyes up and to the right where a small video camera was positioned. He choked off his protest, Angel knew of his disdain for whoever was behind all this. "But I just arrived," he amended.

"Yes, yes, I know, but these are difficult times. I am going to get you integrated at once. I know you have been given the antivirals as have all of us." That in itself was telling. The doc's cure had made it here along with her it would seem.

Skybox nodded and smiled, "Yes – thanks to my blood, I believe. By the way, the lead doctor who did that has disappeared. Gia Colton, she was one of ours. Any idea where she might be?"

Archangel shook his head nonchalantly, "The name seems familiar, but don't think we have her. You can check with the science labs we have onsite, they might have some ideas. If not, you would have to bring it up with our civilian boss, Ms. Levy, but she is quite busy at the moment."

He nodded and stood, "Show me my new job, Boss."

CHAPTER EIGHTY-FIVE

HARRIS SPRINGS, MISSISSIPPI

The code streaming across the screen was gibberish to most people, but to Tahir, it was the keys to the kingdom. He fidgeted in his seat like a small child anxious to open a gift on Christmas morning. The backdoor he'd found was a programmer hidden access point. Luckily, whoever had done the system security for the facility at Thunder Ridge had used a snippet of some framework code he had created years earlier when working with the DoD.

So far, it was only giving him access to the most mundane of information, but the beauty of the code was the inclusion of a toolkit buried deep inside of it. While innocuous looking to anyone developing the system, he had buried a small sysadmin access into one of the tools that would covertly tunnel in where root access could then be gained. "I have you now."

DJ looked up from the other system. "Are you gaming again?"

"Huh? Oh, sorry, no, the other thing I am working on," Tahir mumbled. The two of them had been following up on the commander's request since the meeting. While working on two very different and very complicated tasks would be inordinately challenging for most, Tahir simple thrived on it. The man lived for the challenge and being here on the AG had rekindled his hacker spirit in amazing ways. Besides trying to game the security system at Thunder Ridge, he and DJ were trying to develop a type of defense against the infected. Not a defense against the disease, Gia and her team had essentially done that already. However, an effective way of dealing with enormous hordes of raging animals, which the infected became, was something new.

DJ had mentioned that a few of the labs had tried various ways of killing the infected en masse using everything from aerosolized toxins to napalm. Something Gia had told him earlier had stuck with him, though. Apparently, Commander Garret also had been briefed on it. She said the infected were somewhat reactive to certain sounds and smells. To be precise, they reacted toward very low frequency sounds; they also gave off two types of pheromones. The most common one drew them together, another seemed to repel them from one another. Using these two factors, he and DJ were working quickly to develop either a lure or a repellant to help protect the troops encountering the hordes.

Currently, they were running various computer models on the audio waves as that seemed to be the easiest to develop. The only problem was, they needed to get near the infected to test it. Judging by the rate they were advancing, in a couple more weeks, they would be able to simply walk outside and take their pick. That would be too late.

"So, you never kept live specimens?"

"Of the infected, are you crazy? Of course not. Well, other than Skybox —technically, he carried the affected genes, but he never showed any reactions to sounds…we did test that. No, all we kept here were dead bodies in cold storage, so we could get cell cultures from them."

Tahir tapped the pencil against his lips as he watched the compiler working on the security system code. "A cell culture wouldn't react, would it? To the frequency, I mean."

"I doubt it…maybe, but how would we know?" DJ answered. Both men loved the brainstorming part of these types of projects. "Not sure if we could tell if a cell was reacting toward or away from anything. Also, we would have no way of knowing if the results would be the same in a host. We could infect live animals and run test. That was something we did in the Devil's Tower lab, but the Navy has been unwilling to let us do live animal testing on the Bataan."

"Well, we can only do so much with computer modeling, DJ. We can get the specs to the teams in the field and let them experiment to see what works or find us some infected to see for ourselves."

"Wait, what?" DJ looked scared at the very thought of going out there.

Four hundred miles to the north, Scott would have easily been able to test out anything his friends could have supplied. Owens crouched by the window clicking the fire selector on the M16 to the burst position. "Those fuckers are everywhere," he whispered unnecessarily as everyone in the room could see them clearly. Nez was on guard duty when the first had shown up in the middle of the night. None of them had been this close to the infected, and despite their presumed immunity, the creatures still scared the fuck out of them.

Solo just watched them curiously. He hadn't received the antiviral since it was based on a human genome, and the science team felt it was more likely to kill the dog than the actual Chimera would. Something in the way the infected moved seemed to interest the dog. He ran from window to window silently watching them move down the highway or wander through the parking lot of the hotel. They were now a prey animal, that much he could sense, but they were sloppy at it, easily avoided unless they were hunting in packs.

Scott watched Solo intensely, the dog was an ally, a friend, and he knew that on some primal level the dog was trying to determine how significant a threat the infected might be. Would the dog be immune, would he get infected if he bit one of them? How could he warn him? Scott tapped the bench he was on to get his attention. Solo glanced over,

Scott pointed out the window and gave the sign for danger. Solo returned his gaze to the diseased wanderers outside, seemingly more curious than concerned.

Krychek brought up the obvious question, "So, how are we going to get past those things to even get to the base?"

"Maybe there will be less by then. Haven't heard from Sky in days… could be a lot more before we get the call," one of the Rangers replied from the darkness.

Scott shook his head, "No, they will continue to grow in numbers. These are the ones coming from east of us. The big cities and the internment camps that were deliberately infected. We have to assume the numbers will get worse before they get better."

Rollins chimed in, "Yeah, Scott is right, guys, but hey, we got a truck out back. All we gotta do is get to it, we can fight our way that far. Owens, you think they could get us in there?"

"Nah, we should be fine, lot safer than in here."

In response to that, a hard thump hit the glass door of the lobby as one of the infected tried to get in. "They can't turn doorknobs, can they?" Rollins said.

"Dude, you've watched too many movies," Owens answered. "They're human, so hell yeah, they can. Right now, they haven't seen us, and not many are coming off the road toward the hotel, but…they will, and they can break a window or open a door same as us."

Scott found several eyes on him; this part of the op was his to lead, and even he didn't like the plan he came up with.

CHAPTER EIGHTY-SIX

CENTRAL ALABAMA

Steven shifted the rugged Land Rover Defender into third gear and accelerated away from the carnage behind them on the highway. Kitma's call had ignited a bug-out plan he had been working on for years. Elvis sat in the back seat and hung his wet snout on his shoulder looking out the window. Pam watched Steven from the passenger's seat, concern evident on her face. "You okay?"

"Yes, love," he lied. Leaving the cabin had been the hardest decision he'd ever made. The cabin was secure, hidden and still stocked with more supplies than they would use for years. He stretched his uninjured hand across to his wife. She leaned in and kissed him as JD let out a groan from the rear seat. "Hush kid, or I'll put you out."

They knew he wasn't going to do that. Driving the isolated backroads of Alabama had been relatively peaceful until the roadblock outside the town of Opp. The highwaymen had looked tough but found themselves outmatched by the RPG Steve had fired into the barricade. His friend, Major Kitma, had provided some nice additions to the Sentinel's arsenal. He thought back to how that friendship got started, the same time he'd first met Pam as well. He, JD and another friend, the original Sentinel, Gerald Leighton, had been ambushed trying to get home, and Kitma took them in. Pam was his medic. Sadly, Gerald hadn't made it, but he had provided them his bug-out shelter and second home, the cabin.

It had taken Steven months to understand everything Gerald had provided and over six months to locate the Defender buried in an empty septic system vault. Once they had transportation, they began making occasional short trips to Fort Benning where the friendship with Kitma and with the pretty lieutenant began to grow.

"What do you think about the call?" Pam asked.

Steve knew the call she meant. The Patriot's call. "Could be a trap," he admitted.

"They said they had a treatment for the disease, though."

He nodded, continuing to sweep his eyes back and forth across the road ahead. "I recall the president saying the same thing early on. 'Come to the aid camps where we can protect you and treat you from the pandemic.' We saw how that turned out." He glanced down at his mangled left hand remembering some of those earlier issues they dealt with.

"We barely got out of Albany ahead of them, Steve. If we keep going west, we are going to be close to that location anyway. They said they had a ship."

He tended to trust broadcasts over the Patriot Network. Over the years, they had worked out enough codes and techniques that fakes were exposed pretty fast. The group that had made the call was one he would have marked as an ally. They had supplied good intel and advice over the years. He had no reason to distrust them, yet...they gave an actual position. That was something you just did not do. Your exact location was perhaps the most closely guarded secret any of them kept. How else could they tell people where to come, though? In the end, it was the fact that everything they said matched up to the final broadcast of his friend Kitma. He had to take the chance.

"Up there…what is that?" JD said leaning up over the seat.

"Some sort of figure in the road, looks human," Pam responded.

Steve didn't like it. They weren't moving like humans. "Oh, shit, masks on, infected!"

Tahir was as scared as he had ever been. Having seen the infected closer than most, he knew how dangerous they were. Now, he sat in the back of Scott's Jeep with Bartos and Lt. Garret heading out to deliberately catch one. "Oh, fuck now…this is more than just bad." DJ sat opposite him looking just as petrified, nodding his head nervously in full agreement.

The two men up front just turned and smiled at one another. They had gotten radio reports of a pod of infected much farther south than expected. A pod, as they were starting to be called, usually was about three to five individuals traveling and hunting together. This would work fine for their needs. The speaker hooked up to the laptop Tahir carried was hopefully all they needed to come up with a way to steer the infected.

How to actually locate the pods and then safely catch a single one of them was another matter entirely. Garret had wanted to toss a cargo net on them as they sped by in the Jeep. The large net was rolled up in the back and was an option, but DJ had an alternative plan: a vet's tranquilizer gun loaded with Ketamine. The knock-out drug they used on horses. He felt sure it would have the same effect on one of the infected. Bartos watched the lad's face in the rear-view mirror. He didn't seem quite so sure now.

"Why would this group be so much farther south?" Garret's question was directed at the back seat.

DJ fidgeted, then answered, "Hard to say, they aren't so far from the larger groups that they couldn't have made it on their own, but more likely, they were exposed sooner."

"Or," Tahir added, "they were traveling south when they got infected, and it only took them once they got closer to here."

"So, where do you eggheads propose we look for 'em?" Bartos asked with a snarky tone. DJ and Tahir both shrugged.

They drove on closer to the small town north of Mobile where the report had originated. Bartos pulled the Jeep over. "I'm going to see if I can find that person who spotted them." He stepped out to get a better signal and clicked the two-way radio on. Bobby's voice came through immediately. "Go ahead, Truckstop, this is Gopher," Bartos replied.

CHAPTER EIGHTY-SEVEN

SOUTHERN MISSISSIPPI

Bartos watched the man cautiously as he exited the old, green four-wheel drive. His first impression of the man was a bit of a letdown. He appeared ordinary, even underwhelming, in appearance; the presence of a wife and child was even more surprising. Although they had talked on the radio countless times, neither had any idea of what the other might look like. "Sentinel?" Bartos said cautiously.

The man's face broke into a huge smile that was both genuine and grateful. "Gopher? I recognize the voice. Call me Steven." The two shook hands as other introductions were made. "When I called Truck-stop to report the infected, they said you guys were already heading out this way and to please keep an eye on the subjects...but not to harm them?" He said the last part as a question.

Bartos had been watching the infected several hundred yards away. They appeared to be deciding whether to attack or not. "LT, can you try that toy rifle from here?"

Garret took the gun DJ was loading with the tranq dart and headed down into the clearing. "Hey, Navy…don't get eaten, I do not want to have to explain that to your dad." Garret flipped him off.

Pam took note of Bartos' limp, "You ok? Need me to take a look?" Bartos laughed, "No, it's not recent, been a rather active few months. We have full medical facilities, Thanks, though."

She nodded, "Is there a particular reason you guys are trying to capture one of them? Is it zombie season in South Alabama?"

The tiny sound from the rifle in Garret's hand was followed by one of the creatures dropping. The other three were scattering in other directions. Bartos smiled, "Only for the females. Have to wait till winter to nab the bucks."

He turned to the Jeep. "DJ, these people need the antivirals."

"Oh, right," he said hurrying off to get his medical bag.

"Wait," the attractive woman said. "You really do have a cure?"

"Well, a treatment, we aren't positive it is a cure, but so far it's working. Look, we have a lot to tell you, and as soon as we get the infected secured, I can let the two geekazoids get busy with their test, then you can follow me back to the AG."

"The AG," JD said holding onto Elvis who looked ready to go after the downed subject.

Bartos squatted down, "Yeah, it's our ship, the Aquatic Goddess, old cruise ship we call home." He began scratching the ears of the friendly mutt. "What's his name?"

"Elvis."

"I have a dog, too, well, most times I do. Right now, he his…on assignment I guess. Steven, can you give me and the lieutenant a hand? We need to get that one tied up with enough rope so we can test her reactions to various sounds."

"Y'all are the weirdest bunch I have met since all this shit started." Steven walked on down into the clearing. "But sure. The first zombie I meet, I definitely want to tie her to a rope and see what she does."

Tahir was putting the final adjustments on the audio wave generator. He already knew approximately what frequency range was needed, but he wanted to test it at varying levels as well as the opposite spectrum in the ultra-high pitches. His theory was if one signal drove the creature off, the opposite might attract it.

Garret held the female down with a knee to the back. He couldn't bring himself to think of it as a girl, although that clearly was what it was. He couldn't believe the level of strength the tiny thing was beginning to exert. "Ok, it's coming around, make a path for me and take her out if she tries anything." He had to yell as the tether was nearly twenty-five feet, and everyone else was back beyond that. He sprang up and sprinted for the line. The female was up and pursuing him in seconds. Bartos tracked the infected with the rifle but didn't fire. She was almost within reach of Garret. As he reached the perimeter, the infected girl jumped after him only to be pulled up short by the rope.

The creature growled, her stringy matted hair framed a face that was more feral than human. She immediately began attempting to remove the bindings. "Good luck getting that off, honey," Garret said. "Navy teaches us how to tie knots the first week."

"Really?" Bartos said. "I think I learned that in kindergarten. What about you, Steve?"

"Boy Scouts," Porter said with a smile.

"Yeah, Boy Scouts this one, LT." He turned to Steve, "You're going to get along just fine here, man."

Garret was still glaring at them, "You let her get a little close there didn't you, Cajun?"

"Sorry, man, I was sure you could run faster than that....guess I was wrong. Tahir, you ready to go yet?"

Tahir and DJ were set up on the back of the Jeep. Speaker, amp and laptop connected and pointing at the infected girl. "Starting now," DJ said. A low hum just at the very limit of recognizable sound began. It stepped down even lower after a few seconds, then after nearly a minute, it was not even registering to them as a sound. They all felt it, though, as a vibration in their bones, in the fillings of their teeth. Then that, too, had passed.

"Out of the normal human sound spectrum," DJ said. Then, the creature who had just been watching them with unfocused and unblinking eyes made a yelping sound and ran back to the other extent of the tether. They all looked at one another in triumph. It took nearly two more hours to find the specific frequency and record all the specifics. The reaction on the infected girl was the same each time. Unfortunately, the opposite wasn't true. No combinations of other sounds would work as an attractor, but they had what the needed. A way to steer the infected away.

Garret was beaming with pride, "Damn, you guys are good. I'm calling this into the Bataan now. You have no idea how many lives you just saved."

Everyone else began to load themselves and the equipment back into vehicles. JD squatted down to watch the girl. DJ walked over and squatted beside him. "DJ and JD, that's going to confuse a lot of people isn't it?"

JD just kept watching the infected girl, "Nah, they will figure out pretty quick JD is the good looking one."

"Damn, not you, too." Looking over he yelled, "Tahir, it's not the Chimera that's spreading its smartassery."

"You have to put her down, now don't you?" the boy said.

DJ wasn't sure how to handle the truth with someone his age. "Yes, we do," he finally said deciding on the truth. "Bartos will do that, and we can put her in a containment bag to transport to our lab. She is no longer human. That part died long ago." His feeble attempt at softening the truth unnecessary, as JD stood and walked to the Defender.

"Yep." The boy said walking away.

Bartos got Steven, Pam, JD and Elvis settled into the AG as the very first of the Patriot arrivals. Garret accompanied the corpse, DJ and Tahir back to the Bataan. "Are you even trying?" DJ complained to his friend struggling to maneuver the thick vinyl bag into the cold storage room.

"Shut up," Tahir said clearly not liking this level of interaction with the infected or the dead. His breath fogged up as he spoke the words. "What would you guys have done if the fuel had run out, and the refrigeration stopped?" he said with a laugh looking around at the other bodies hanging in the room along with carious containment vessels labeled 'Tissue Samples.'

DJ shrugged, "It would have gotten ripe pretty quickly," he said, locking the door closed again.

"But the virus would have been inert, right?"

"Yeah, it needs a live host to survive. Relax, Tahir, you are fine. Our seven cadavers in there are not going to come out and get you while you sleep."

Tahir cocked his head and looked strangely toward DJ.

"What?" DJ asked getting annoyed.

"Eight,"

"Eight what, Tahir?"

"You have eight bodies hanging in that locker, my friend."

CHAPTER EIGHTY-EIGHT

THUNDER RIDGE PROTECTORATE

The sounds of the monstrous HVAC system overhead gave an oddly mechanical feel to the otherwise barren rock cavern. The natural space had been ideal for the protectorate camp. The civilian population was only allowed this deep into the mountain by special requests. Since arriving three days earlier, Skybox had been shown much of the sprawling complex, but this was something else. The vibe coming off his commander was hard to pin down. He wondered briefly if his subterfuge had been discovered, but if that were the case, he would have simply been shot.

"Angel?"

The man cut him off, motioning for him to keep following. They were heading for an unlit area of the cavern. The sound of the air handler faded behind them to be replaced by the pleasing sound of water dripping into shallow pools. "Watch your head, it's a bit cramped." Archangel rounded a large stalagmite and disappeared into a crack in the rock wall. Skybox stooped as well as his headlamp illuminated a natural fissure running high up the wall. Here at the base, it was just wide enough to wedge his body through if he turned sideways.

On the other side, he rose back to normal height. The alcove was small, maybe a dozen feet across. There was a pool of crystal clear water at the center and what appeared to be a stream running away from the water and into or under the rock on the far side. A natural rock ledge reached partially around the small space. This was where Archangel now sat, and in his hands was a Glock-19 pointing right at Skybox's head.

"Okay," Skybox said nervously.

"Remove your shirt and pants, Sky."

He did so, beginning to hopefully understand the labyrinthian journey and the man's silence.

"Place them into this." From his pack, he unfolded one of the large Praetor anti-static bags and handed it over. The silvery plastic was good at protecting electronics from static electricity, but the ones they used also effectively blocked any devices from transmitting. Archangel wanted this conversation to remain private and had gone to great lengths to ensure it.

Skybox handed him back the bag which Angel sealed, then he put the gun away. "Sit, please."

He sat and waited for the man to say what was on his mind. "You have many questions, this is the only place we can speak with any possibility of confidentiality. So, Skybox, ask your questions."

He did indeed have many but started with the most important, "Why am I here?"

"Ah, very good and to the point. I've always liked you, Michael, you showed so much promise even back in your early days with the CIA."

The use of his actual name was jarring. While it shouldn't have surprised him that the man had access to that, it still did. No one had used it in addressing him in years.

"You are here to help me get rid of her, actually, not just Levy, but the whole goddamn lot of 'em. You were right when we met before, it was time to overthrow our Caesar. Your mistake, my brother...as well as mine, as it turned out, was including Vincent in that discussion."

Skybox nodded but remained quiet. The senior commander continued, "Vince was helping the president with her crazy plan of bio-warfare. Ms. Levy seemed uninterested, content to just let it happen. Upon our return here, I reached out to P-Command for instructions only to find our command was gone. All of them—Levy had taken them out. I knew I had to step in, but Vince was waiting. It got ugly fast, but I got the command codes from him before he died."

Archangel seemed to be waiting for comment. Skybox had a hard time imagining Angel taking out the huge man in a fair fight but assumed it probably hadn't been one. His mind was already piecing together the tactical analysis. Praetor versus Praetor was damned unusual. "So, our civilian boss...this woman, Levy, was ok with you killing her head of security?"

The other man smiled and shook his head, "Not exactly, but she had been aware of his betrayal to the president. Poisoning the camps and getting most of 'em destroyed seemed to have annoyed her. She is not a person who likes to be annoyed. It brought a bit more scrutiny on me. Hence...the reason for this," he waved his hands around the space. "Assume nothing you say or do inside the facility is private. She has eyes and ears everywhere. Trust me when I say her paranoia, much like her ego, has no boundaries."

Skybox considered his next question carefully. If this was a trap, he would be revealing too much. "How do you propose I accomplish this? I haven't even met the woman yet."

Archangel shrugged, "I usually don't even know if she is here in this facility. Mostly, we communicate via video calls. But, my friend, you wouldn't have come here without a plan, now would you? Look, you don't trust me, I know that. I have a reputation for...looking out for myself, shall we say? You will have to decide to trust me...or not."

Sky thought on the man's choice of the word 'friend.' None of the members of the Guard would ever be accurately described by that term, but there was something, a loyalty, a brotherhood of sorts. "Are there any more of us here?"

"No," Angel said with a shake of the head. "I put out a call to all embeds, activating them to leadership hoping some would be close... none here responded. Many still exist out there, hopefully, some picked up the fight, but my feeling is she and her Council have been dismantling the Praetor command and rank and file for years. We are a threat to their power. It was only a matter of time before we all reached the same decision you did."

The two men talked a while longer before Archangel handed his clothes back over and stood. "You know what must be done, Sky. I'll do my best to help, but understand, these people are brilliant, they have been running things for centuries."

CHAPTER EIGHTY-NINE

UNKNOWN LOCATION

The pain was no longer the same. It still hurt just as bad, but it was a familiar thing now. She'd watched through half-closed eyes as the face in the window came and watched. She saw only a silhouette, but her mind applied face after face to the image until one seemed to fit. Now, the question was why? He was evil, yes. That was certain, but even evil ones had reasons behind their actions. The smell of vomit and shit filled her with revulsion. The fact that it was hers made it no less tolerable.

How long had she been chained here? Long enough for the shackles to abrade the skin from her wrist, heal and be worn away again several times over. Weeks definitely, months even more likely. With no way of discerning night from day, it was impossible to guess. Even the occasional food was no way to gauge. Just enough to keep her alive but never anything like regular meals. The torture and experiments continued, no matter what her condition. She longed to die, begged for it, but no escape that easy would be hers.

Since any release for her physical form was impossible, she began to use the hours of agony to escape mentally. First, she worked on school assignments she could recall. She'd always been good in school, academically at least. She went through all of the challenging years of literature, math, history. Then English, science and her favorite, biology. Some, she couldn't recall the answers, no matter how hard she delved into the madness of her brain. Those pushed her to think hard, develop new ideas and, in some cases, ignore the truth for an even better truth. Year by year she worked her way through her curriculum. She escaped into a world of her own creation, unlocking ideas and possibilities that would have eluded her otherwise. She wondered if something like this happened to Stephen Hawking as he found himself locked inside a tormented body.

He'd been a genius, and she was just a girl. What would she do, anyway, assuming she got away? How would she live, how would she survive? That thought became a burning question, a riddle to be solved. The fantasy took over her mind, numbing her to the pain. Day after day, she worked out scenarios and possibilities until, finally, there were no other options to explore. Ultimately, she couldn't solve it...not until she eliminated one thing. She didn't need to survive, she just needed to make sure no one else did. Revenge became the next project to occupy her mind. The how, the who...the when.

It wasn't death...it was silence. No water dripping, no sounds of shackles rattling against chains. *What is this?* Someone was gently rubbing her wrist. The sudden change from torment to tender was too much for her. She sobbed to be released, all of her anger forgotten for the moment. The sound of monitors beeping began to fill the silence. Slowly, incrementally, she began to hear other sounds. A cart with a squeaky wheel traveling down a hall. Someone writing with a pencil, the scratching noises unmistakable.

"She's coming around," a nearby voice said.

She tried to open her eyes and was surprised to realize they already were. *Am I blind?* No, maybe...there was light, very muted light, but nothing else. Nothing differentiated between light and dark. She could move her head a tiny amount, but what she saw stayed the same. A milky opaque shroud of nothingness. She had put a plastic bag over her head once as a child, this was the same, yet she felt no bag, no covering of any kind.

"How long before we know?" another voice asked, a...familiar voice.

If he was answered, she didn't hear it. She was too busy taking in sensations from the world around her. Although she couldn't move and couldn't see, her body seemed more alive than ever. Her hand felt the smooth metal table beneath the pad she lay on. Her fingertip traced part of the stitching on the webbed nylon restraints on her wrist. From the echoes, she knew the approximate size of the room with no idea how she knew. She picked up the scents of four people nearby, three were male, one female. The female was ovulating. Again, she had no idea how she knew, but she filed it away as a certainty. One of the males was scared, the fear wafted off of him like a curtain. *He is scared of me*, she thought wryly.

In the distance, she heard someone dialing a phone. Outside a distant window, she heard a muted songbird. That particular bird mates in spring, it must be spring. What time of year was it when they took her? She couldn't recall. *Analyze everything, take every scrap of information you can. The scene may disappear again. They are toying with you. Make them pay.* Beyond the heightened senses, her mind was firing at blazing speed, too fast, in fact. She felt herself overheating.

"Pulse is rising, body temperature 99.4."

She instructed her body to calm; it did so instantly.

"Back to normal," the male voice said.

She lay there, unmoving, unseeing but knowing more about everything. She had been conscious for thirteen and a half minutes. The air temperature in the room was between 69 and 71 degrees. The person with the pencil was left handed. The scared man had consumed alcohol earlier in the day, she could smell trace amounts emanating from the pores of his skin. *Vodka*, she thought. The man was sick, something inside him was wrong, she couldn't be more specific, but she knew it was true.

All of these facts and a hundred more passed through her mind every second. The most unusual thing was it all felt completely normal. Nothing felt off or unusual, it was simply the way she was. As if she had been asleep most of her life, and now she was awake.

She felt the man leaning over her. She heard his laboring breaths, she knew he was examining her body. She did not need to see the man's face, he was the one with the familiar voice. He neared her face, she could feel the heat from his body. This was the man from the window, this was the man she would focus all of her hatred on. This was her captor and tormentor.

"Hello, Father," her words dripping with hatred.

CHAPTER NINETY

NORTHERN MISSISSIPPI

The Marine general absently caressed one of the Colt 1911 Desert Eagles strapped to his waist. Of all the shit from the last two years, this one turned his stomach the most. The mechanized division he was riding with was made up of vehicles and units from all over. They had spent the greater part of forty-eight hours following the Navy's instructions to integrate audio generators into the vehicles' external speakers. They'd even cobbled together some handheld radios capable of generating the soundwave. Now, he watched amazed as the infected ahead began fleeing from the silent frequencies. "It's working, General," one of his men said.

Yeah, it's working, but it's still grotesque. Using infected American citizens as a weapon made the general sick. It did beat the alternative, though. Growing up on a ranch in west Texas had taught him a lot about rounding up cattle. You had to stay even with the lead and to the side to keep a herd pointed the right way. In this case, that meant pointing them toward Memphis, yet avoiding rougher terrain. The infected struggled with large hills and avoided rivers. "Watch our corners,

Captain. If any of them slip behind us…" The young man nodded, he knew how bad it could be.

"What a shitty way to fight a war," the general stated flatly. His great-grandfather had been a legend to the corp. *How will I be remembered?* he wondered. "In a few more miles begin channeling in the left side. Those idiots are giving the horde too much space." Fuck with the cattle analogy, this was more like herding cats. Really fucking pissed off cats with the ability to tear you to pieces or just breathe on you or bite you to turn you into one of 'em. "Gotta hand it to those Navy boys, though, never would have thought of this," he yelled to the captain. He did inwardly wish they'd also been able to supply more of his soldiers with some of the anti-viral treatment. Like his men, he also knew this mission would likely not end well for any of them.

Several hours later, numerous problems with the plan had become evident. One was that their progress toward Memphis was slowing to a crawl. While the infected horde moved fast for humans, it was slow for a mechanized division. Second, it was exhausting keeping them together and away from the lines. They couldn't stop, just like with cattle, they began to disperse when you stopped moving, so no breaks, no meals, no fucking stopping for any reason. Lastly, any gaps in the line proved to be fatal. They had already lost men when a Humvee broke down and the speaker stopped. The horde overran them in seconds. The next vehicle had to fire indiscriminately into the mass to keep the rest of the infected from swarming to the kill. Having Marines fire on fellow soldiers was going to haunt these guys the rest of their lives. Chances were good, though, that…might only be a few more days.

The rains started the second night; the herding vehicles began getting stuck and breaking ranks. "Shit." The general stared out with disgust as smaller jeeps and UTVs filled in the gaps. The horde he was handling was estimated at over twenty-thousand individuals now. His rag-tag battalion had also grown as other units joined in. Memphis was less than thirty miles away, and somewhere beyond was the cause of much of this nation's misery.

CHAPTER NINETY-ONE

NEAR MEMPHIS, TENNESSEE

He touched her naked back, his fingers gently tracing the perfect lines of her body. Gia, his Gia, lying here, loving him, wanting him. She was saying something, something he only half heard. The Suburban hitting a rut along the rain soaked, unpaved road jolted him awake. The dream again, his subconscious torturing him by reliving their last perfect night together. As the memory faded, something nagged at him, something he needed to remember, but it was gone. A painful cramp gripped his stomach, and he gasped as it spasmed, then relaxed. When had they eaten…he couldn't recall, so he pulled a protein bar from a trouser pocket and began breaking off pieces and popping them in his mouth.

It was crowded in the big Chevy, Nez was beside him asleep as most of the others seemed to be. These guys could sleep on command he'd decided. Krychek was driving. Getting away from the hotel had been less dramatic than they feared. While the number of infected had grown significantly, they had all been in front and on the road. As the Spec Op group exited the back and ran to the car, they'd seen no one. On the highway, it had been a different story passing many who ran after the truck and some who stood directly in its path. As they neared the area where the facility should be, the number had thinned noticeably.

"This is as far as we can go by car," Krychek announced pulling over to an abandoned gas station. "Unload the gear, and I'll hide the car." All of them were wide awake and grabbing gear and weapons as they piled out and swept the area for threats.

Owens tossed out two packs from the rack above his passenger's seat. "Haven't seen any of the beasties in about ten miles but need to stay sharp."

Scott thought of the irony that in a world full of creatures like the infected, they were a mere nuisance compared to the human threats. Nez used a tool to unlock the gas station's side door. They all piled in and stowed gear in the darkened interior. Skybox had given them a relatively good idea as to the site's entrance, but they needed to find the back door. Being this close was risky, no doubt the protectorate facility had sensors everywhere.

"Solo, patrol." He watched as the dog sped off. "I'm heading up top, need to radio the AG."

"Make it fast," Rollins said. "Use the rolling freqs like I showed you."

"Yes, dear." Radio discipline had been drummed into him so much it was now automatic. Broadcasting in the clear, anyone looking for them nearby could triangulate a location within minutes. The military spec radios got around this by skipping channels on a predetermined basis, so a signal should only pick up on a scanner for an instant before disappearing.

His brother was apparently the one on duty in the comms room. His voice echoed the opposing emotions of both relief and concern. "Got a lot for you, Bro. You ready?"

Scott keyed back affirmative. "First, you are about to have a shit load of company, good and bad." Bobby filled him in on the growing military presence heading toward them. "Dude, you have to find her and get the fuck out pronto. You are going to be ground zero for a major fucking battle otherwise."

"That sounds kinda great, though, we can use the help—what's the bad?" Scott asked. Once his brother told him what was coming in front of the troops, his blood ran cold. "They are herding the infected? How in the fuck did Tahir figure that shit out?"

"Kid's a genius, a lot smarter than you, obviously."

"Smartass," Scott retorted.

"I have the information, you can get Rollins to rig something up for your team, should help give you a bit of protection. The damn thing works great, only problem is, the migration west seems to be speeding up all the others moving south as well. We have begun to encounter them out at the farms."

"Does the skipper have everything ready to go?" Scott asked.

"Yeah, we're ready, just waiting on our guests, some are showing up already, but looks like it might be close." Scott had to think a moment before he realized he meant the people on the Patriot Network. So, they had made the call.

"One other thing, BikerBoi," Bobby paused a long moment before continuing. "They found Diana's body." The sound of shuffling came over the headset, "Here the, umm…inspector wants to tell you."

Trish's voice came over the radio, "Hey Sco…Oh, damn, sorry. I mean BikerBoi. Yeah, hey, your friend Ta…shit," she paused, "AlphaCat?" she said questioningly. "Anyway, he actually found her. She was in the cold storage locker on the… fuck, out at the lab. I don't know how you guys talk without actually saying anything. Anyway, the girl looked like she had been, worked on, like maybe tortured. We are holding the lab staff for questioning but, anyway, just thought you should know."

CHAPTER NINETY-TWO

THUNDER RIDGE PROTECTORATE

She pulled back away from the mirror with a start, the anger etched on her face slowly beginning to recede like a beast guarding a great secret. She deserved a normal life; it was all she had ever wanted. Not this. No, not this at all. The opulent décor in the luxury suite wouldn't have been out of place at the Mandarin, or Four Seasons, not even at her favorite, the Park Hyatt-Vendome in Paris. Here, buried deep in a Tennessee hillside, it didn't feel like any of those other places. If she was honest, it didn't feel like anything, really.

Her life had been ordained from the moment of conception. She would grow up to be a Levy, a leader. Instead, she wanted to be something else, someone else. Her father had decided for her. She'd been a child, and to him, incapable of making smart decisions. She'd been nine or ten the first time she'd run away from the family estate. Her father had been furious when security found her and brought her back. He'd sent her off to boarding school then, a snobbish place that pulled the very soul from her body. She was drilled on history, politics, finance, yet she craved the romance languages, science and literature.

Again, she ran away, over and over, the consequences of rebellion growing worse each time, until he'd had enough until...they did the horrible, horrible things to her. When she closed her eyes, those were the memories that flooded the space. No happy thoughts, those were but fleeting sparks among a conflagration of evil. The hospitals, retreats and then the chamber. The evil place where her darkness first took root. What kind of man could do that to his child? If he wanted to raise a tyrant, he couldn't have planned it any better.

She dropped solidly onto the intricately embroidered settee thinking again that she was still imprisoned, while others might see the accouterment and think how lucky she was. All she had to do was think back, and all of the silk, cashmere, leather and lace were swept away to be replaced by dark, water-soaked rock walls where her wrist was chained and the image of a man, her father, looking through the one small window on the cell door.

He made me. She was the one who'd eventually learned to say the things he wanted to hear. It had nearly killed her to do so. The priceless look of relief he gave that he'd finally broken his strong-willed daughter. Over the years, she had perfected the art of being his perfect daughter, being a Levy. She wondered if he ever suspected her plan to destroy his legacy or the fact she never stopped running away. She simply learned to hide it better. Much better.

He ran his hand along the smooth metal. Skybox knew there was a release mechanism built into the frame. He'd seen it being used earlier in the day. No matter how secure you made something, you rarely could overcome human nature. You make a person change their password every month, they get where they can't remember it without writing it down and hiding it somewhere close by. If you lock smart people up in a high-security environment long enough, some joker will figure out how to shunt the security to go out for an illicit smoke break. The human-side of operating systems was always the weak link, but in this case, he was thankful.

The latch popped up with a snick. The wall panel clicked outward revealing the maintenance passage behind. While he was heeding Angel's warnings of eyes everywhere, he knew if the lab tech he'd watched do it could get by with it, so could he. The truth was, he just didn't care, he had to take some risk. It had been nearly a week, and he had yet to spot Gia, get word to Scott or hear anyone even mention the infamous Levy. What he had learned, though, was the infected topside were increasing and driving the security systems nuts. The microwave panel array and other station deterrents were constantly going off and cooking off one of the infected. His friend, Tommy, was somewhere up there as well. Watching, waiting for a way in. He felt comfortable his friend would be fine but, as usual, had no idea why.

The technology and devices these guys were using for security were beyond cutting-edge. Active perimeter systems, sensory light and sound systems that could induce seizures which could incapacitate an intruder. The thermal microwave system, armed mini-drones as well as precise-fire AI controlled defensive weaponry that essentially took the gun out of the guard's hand and let the computer system handle targeting and threat elimination. There was a weakness in all these systems, though, and that was from directly above. Anyone dropping straight into the facility might have an advantage. That was his thought until he watched a supply chopper coming in. The pilots were vectored into a very tight flight space along a narrow valley. The ridge guns tracked the incoming aircraft automatically. One gun was always trained at the pilot's head, the camera feed so sharp you could literally see beads of sweat on his forehead as he navigated the tight flight corridor.

As the supply craft got to the landing station, a platform emerged from the ground, the edges bristling with compact missiles housed in sleek SAM arrays on each corner. The automated turrets worked independently, one always trained on the craft, the other four looking for other targets.

He slipped into the courtyard and looked for the cameras. High over-head, the rock ceiling would block any radio signals. *Shit.* He would have to find another way to contact the team. Much of the camp was exposed, not underground. There were paddocks for livestock, meadows for grazing and even what appeared to be small recreation area about the size of a kid's baseball field, all surrounded by high, angry-looking fencing. The open-air areas were not connected; instead, they were accessed from cavern tunnels below ground. As far as he could tell, there was no exit from these areas to the forest beyond, but…this was where Scott needed to come in. He just needed a way to let him know when.

CHAPTER NINETY-THREE

"Sorry, sir, science personnel only." The black-uniformed guard was eyeing him cautiously. Fear was etched all over his face. The one thing the grey camo shirt and trousers did most effectively was command respect. No one wanted to piss off a Praetor commander.

Sky walked briskly at the man and pulled his lanyard close to inspect the rank and name. "Pittman."

"Sir!" the man said as he executed a sloppy salute.

"Put your fucking hand down, son. Do you not have any combat training? Do you not understand that people may be watching to see who the officers are? Are you aware that saluting me could put a bullseye on my skull? Are you trying to get me killed? Is that it?"

"No…no, sir, I swear, I'm not. No, sir. It's just…"

"Just what man? Come on!"

"It's just that we aren't at combat down here. I'm just guarding a door."

The man had a slight British accent, no doubt another one of Chambers' mercenaries. Skybox relaxed his tone and softened his posture.

"You're doing a damn fine job of it, too. Any idea what goes on in there?"

"No, sir, above my pay-grade."

"Aye, mine, too, I'm sure," Skybox said as if the two had been chums for years. "Look, you know the place well. I just arrived a few days ago."

Pittman nodded, "Yeah, pretty well."

"Awesome," Skybox continued. "Look, my C.O. said I could get some fresh air somewhere down this way. Had a bit of trouble in some caves around Tora Bora—anyway, the damn things give me the willies now. You spend any time in the Stan? Worked alongside some Brits, tough bastards. Good lads."

"Af…Afghanistan, sir? No, sir." The guard lowered his gaze. "No access to the outside down here. You want the G passage for that, but you will have to get clearance unless you go out with the GP."

Skybox had already discovered the GP meant general population, the civilians in the protectorate. He still had no idea how many were down here, but it had to be well into the thousands. "Well, lovely," he said with just a hint of Brit-speak himself. He was about to turn and leave when the door opened, and a man in a lab coat walked out. The research scene behind the man grabbed his full attention. He had seen it before on the video feed from Archangel. He needed to get into that section. "Carry-on, soldier, fine job." Skybox nodded, turned and walked away.

The scene above reminded Scott of scenes out of WW2 and the Ardennes forest. Instead of tanks, gun emplacements and bunkers were everywhere. The idyllic looking national forest was a hive of weaponry and counter-intrusion devices. Sky had provided the complicated location of the entrance corridor, but they had not gone in yet. As anxious as he was to get to his fiancée, the way forward looked like certain death. Ghost was somewhere up this wooded trail, how he would have survived in there was a mystery, but Scott felt sure he had. Solo had yet to return, but they were watching a video feed from a small camera Rollins had attached to the dog's collar.

The facilities' defense systems obviously allowed for wild animals to pass unharmed. That was good as Solo was investigating every man-made object in the park, pissing on most and generally being an ass about anything that looked dangerous. This included peeing on, then using his paws to send a cascade of dirt over, an obvious ground level security camera enclosure.

Scott watched nervously as Rollins monitored the video feed, until something high in the air caught his attention. A spark of sunlight reflecting off metal. Thoughts of the KEP device sent a stab of fear through his body. The origin of this object, though, was not up in orbit but far closer to the earth's surface. The object grew as it descended in a free fall from several hundred feet up to come to an abrupt stop at five feet above the ground. The drone, which he could now see it indeed was, seemed impossibly small with an orbiting rotor that spiraled upward from the tiny body like ornate, entertained wings. The cylindrical wings revolved, but the object didn't move, did not vary from its position in front of Scott.

It was then that Scott noticed faint lights emanating from the spinning cylinder. The lights morphed into letters and the letters into words. Rollins' gaze was broken by the faintest of humming from the tiny drone. "Whoa," the man said. "Who has tech like that?"

Scott said nothing as he finished reading the message: "Be ready 0600h." The drone sped up and out of sight within seconds.

How in the fuck had he done that? "Get base on the radio, tell Tahir to sound the alarms." Rollins nodded as he fumbled for the radio. Scott looked at the video monitor emerging from the foliage where Solo was looking at a face. *Ghost.* Scott looked at the others, "Tomorrow morning, guys—this is it."

Krychek shouldered his M16, "So, what's the play?"

Scott pointed at the screen, "Just like we planned it. I follow Ghost in tonight as he obviously knows how to avoid the sensors. He's been out here nearly a week. At 0600 hours, Tahir sounds the alarm, we slip in with the others and then return underground once the all-clear is given. Once inside, you wait for our signal, then plant the beacon and come in with the Army if you are able. Understand?" Heads nodded in agreement. "Gentlemen—we go, we fight!"

Whatever nerves he might have had were gone. Scott was turned on in a way he'd never been before. Angry, yes, determined…hell, yes. But not vengeful or reckless, he was sharp. Rollins gave him the coordinates to get to Solo and Ghost as he made the call back to base. Tahir's voice was reassuring as they synchronized timing. He would trigger one of the minor safety systems on the NuArc reactors just before 'go-time.'

"BikerBoi," Tahir said, "the others are getting close to you, man. Getting in is going to be easy compared to you getting out."

CHAPTER NINETY-FOUR

The figure on the screen stumbled out of the forest and awkwardly walked closer to the camera. The man's hair and clothes were smoking. He should have been in great pain yet showed no outward signs of discomfort.

"Holy shit," Skybox said staring in horror as parts of the creature literally began to ignite.

"How many of these are you seeing now?" Archangel asked the tech manning the station.

"It's on the increase, sir. None until last week, now we are seeing ten to fifteen of the infected each shift. We had to dial the sensitivity on all the sensors way back. Try to deal with them like other wild animals, but…"

"Those that get too close still get cooked," Archangel said in mock disgust.

The infected was literally walking directly toward a panel generating high-intensity microwaves. It would cook him from the inside out before he got much closer. The panels were concealed all around Thunder Ridge and were one of many different types of intrusion prevention devices. The idea of them dialing down sensitivity gave him a few ideas on how to help Scott and the team.

"Sky, you good with this? It's all tech you've used at some point." Archangel had spent the better part of two days going over the normal security protocols. He had a mission and would be away for a few days. Skybox would be helping to keep an eye on things in his absence. He knew there was more to it than that. He was pretty sure he was being tested but was unsure exactly by whom.

"Yeah, I got it," he confirmed.

"Good, just stay out of their way. These people know what they are doing. Now, let me show you master controls. You won't need them, but just in case."

He followed the older man into one of the more sensitive areas of the security wing. "If Levy calls, you want to take it in here," he motioned to a small office with a video conferencing screen. "She is the one sending me out, so don't think she will be calling."

"Angel," Skybox interrupted, "why is the leader of Praetor taking a mission assignment?"

His eyes seemed to say, *Not here.* "I was…pulled from…well, reassigned for this one purpose. This mission is it. Everything else, I just inherited when Vince went boots up. I don't do this, I'll be the same way. The Council won't just lock me up next time."

They spent several more hours going over every aspect of the base's operations. Recoding Skybox's badge for more access and introducing him to the security teams on rotation. "Where is your detainment center?"

"Don't have one."

Skybox was confused, "How does that work, where do you take prisoners?"

"We don't take prisoners."

"I see."

"Next— don't go into the admin wing unless you are invited. Got it? If she is here, and she wants you, she will call. Let the NSF handle the general population. You handle the base itself."

"Sir, yes, sir!"

"Can it, cadet," the lead commander said with a rare smile on his face.

"Lastly, I need to show you our air cover." Archangel led him down the hall and into a cavernous room lined with what appeared to be gaming computers, large curved monitors and chairs mounted on gimbals. Most were unoccupied, but a few had people sitting in them, hands-on joysticks with virtual reality style headsets covering much of their faces. "Here is our local Air Force. They have a separate Air Boss, you are not in that command chain. Each pilot can handle multiple birds, most of which you've never seen or even heard of."

Skybox was impressed; he guessed there must be sixty or more stations which meant pilots as well. "They don't fly out of here?"

Archangel shook his head, "No, no. We have the mini-drone coverage here, but that is all autonomous. I don't even know where all of these UAVs are based, but they can launch and fly on targets all over the country."

"What about space weapons?"

With a confused look, Archangel responded, "Those don't exist, Skybox."

Skybox noticed the way his eyes cut up and to the right as he said it. One of the classic signs of telling a lie. Praetors were all trained in subterfuge, though, and also, he knew from observations that Archangel was left-handed. The up and to the right being a lie was only somewhat accurate, but even then, it was linked to the dominant hand being the right one. He knew the KEP controls were somewhere nearby, possibly in one of the rooms off the mezzanine above.

Truths within lies, battles within battles. He was growing weary of it all.

The time to end all this was long overdue. He'd watched everything his commander had shown him from two mindsets. One was obvious in that he needed to know how it all worked. The second was to understand how it could be used against him if he went rogue or possibly how to use it to reach Gia, if she was even still here. Angel seemed to want him to take out the Council or at least its head. It was all maddeningly difficult. He needed Scott or Tahir's brainpower to make sense of it all. He spent the rest of his time in the security rooms going over video feeds, trying to see where the doctor might be.

Levy was rarely bothered by any of her decisions, but the mission she was sending Archangel on was significant, even by her standards. A fiery rage coursed through her body before she could subdue it. Revenge was a mighty sword in her hands, almost as powerful as the SA1297 virus. Only she had the full understanding of where everything was heading. No one else could be trusted. The anger she felt toward the other members of her Council had been somewhat sated. Angel would handle the rest and the man behind it all. She had wanted to be there, to see his face, but now, that was impossible. She had cameras there—she could peer through her little window and watch him suffer, just as he had done.

CHAPTER NINETY-FIVE

I can't do this. Solo huffed near his face bringing Scott immediately awake. Once again, he'd been dreaming of Gia. Their last night together, her faint words echoing away in his subconscious mind. His eyes opened to see Solo's ass; the dog was looking away. Tommy, aka Ghost, was there too, nearly invisible in the darkness. It had taken him hours to safely work his way this deep into the woods. He had seen numerous gun emplacements and anti-intrusion devices, but all were automated. Tahir had assured them he could deactivate the ones on the entry corridor for brief periods. So far, it had worked, but each time he approached any of the evil looking things, it took everything he had to keep moving. Upon reaching Solo and Tommy near the fenced clearing, he'd been mentally and physically exhausted. He offered Tommy food and was surprised to see him take it. Then, he'd slept soundly, other than the dream.

One hour to go when they changed, stowed the extra gear and made their way closer to the fenced compound. Tommy moved some debris away from a spot revealing a shallow depression. Scott had been unsure how they would scale the high fence, but now he saw. The heavy-gauge security fencing extended down into the ground several feet, but Tommy had snipped away parts of it down in the depression. From the surface, it looked solid, but below ground, the breach would just be large enough for the two of them to pass. Unfortunately, Solo would have to stay outside for now. No way they could conceal him in with the general population of the camp. Scott touched the beautiful dog's head and gave the sign to wait. The dog slipped back into the shadows.

Scott lay there in the semi-darkness waiting and thinking about all that had brought him to this point. The blackout while he was on his bike that day it all happened. Meeting his new friends for the first time. Rescuing Kaylie and fighting for the town. Seeing Tommy standing outside his cottage the first time. Roosevelt, Angel and then being lost at sea with Skybox. Then, rediscovering Gia, finding his true love in the midst of all this. His life now was so different than before. Harder, yes…much. But…well, damn, he felt alive. In many ways, he felt like he was now living someone else's life; this couldn't be his. This was a suicide mission; his intelligent mind was screaming this fact over and over, yet he didn't care. He would not be deterred, he had to find her.

Ten minutes to go, Scott felt for his compact Glock and the knives discreetly tucked into various pockets. He felt wrong to now be wearing the captured black uniform, but it was the only way to blend in. Far off in the distance, he thought he heard gunfire, maybe even heavy artillery. Just a few more minutes…the military being too close would put the whole base on alert and ramping up the risk factor considerably for him and Tommy. *Tommy…Where the fuck is he?* He'd been lying on the ground close enough to touch, now there was nothing. *Shit!* He was on his own.

The night sky was just beginning to lighten as his watch gave a light buzz. Ten minutes later, he heard something faintly…an alarm, but the direction was impossible to tell until a well-camouflaged hatch opened in the meadow. The alarm was easy to hear now as were panicked voices climbing up and into view. Scott slowly crawled under the fence and into the meadow. As more and more people emerged, he stood, dusted the dirt from his uniform and shouldered the angry looking Kel-Tec RFB compact automatic. Like the uniform, the weapon had been one of many retrieved from dead guards at Yokena.

The people emerging from underground looked bewildered and huddled in small groups. Hundreds of people came out of the hatch. Several other guards, looking just like him, exited the opening and took up positions around the perimeter facing outward. He did the same; the difference was, he was scanning for Ghost, not threats. Several minutes later, the alarm stopped. One of the guards appeared to be speaking into a radio. If they all had that, he might be discovered. Scott moved farther away. "What's going on?" one of the civilians asked. Scott looked to see how the other NSF guards were treating the people and realized they were all ignoring them. He did the same.

Almost an hour later, the guard with the radio gave the all clear, and the masses of grumbling civilians and their NSF protectors began filing back into the complex. Scott waited until the flow of people began to thin before shouldering his rifle and walking toward the entrance. He knew his heart should be racing, pulse pounding, but he felt an odd calm as if he did this every day of the week. He calmly watched how the other guards behaved and mimicked it. No one gave him a second look until he reached the bottom of the stairs. Then a hand reached from the darkness firmly grabbing and swiftly pulling him from the line of advancing people.

"Come with me."

Scott recognized the voice, but that was all he could discern in the dark passageway. "Hey, I…"

Skybox silenced him, "Not here."

The echoes of thousands of feet walking in every direction were all Scott could hear, but he trusted his friend. They walked for fifteen minutes before Skybox opened a door and ushered him inside. The spartan room resembled one of the cabins on the Bataan. It was utilitarian and clean, but those were about the only things you could say about it. Sky turned to Scott and grinned, grabbing him into a quick bro-hug, "How are you doing, man?"

"We can talk here?" Scott asked nervously.

"For now, but assume you are monitored everywhere. I have the bugs in this room blocked. Took me a while to get access to any of the security systems."

"Thanks for the message on the drone, pretty clever."

Sky nodded, "So, what all is happening out there?"

"Well, I think I lost Tommy getting in here," Scott said softly.

"Ah, don't worry about him. I assure you he made it. They didn't call him 'The Magician' for nothing."

Scott took several minutes filling Sky in on the military troops and infected heading their way. "We began encountering them near here a couple of days ago."

Skybox was processing it as quickly as possible, "So, Tahir came up with a way to herd the infected?"

"Yes," Scott said. "A low-frequency sound that they flee from." Scott looked around the small room then asked the only question he had. "Did you find her?"

Skybox didn't answer for several minutes but then nodded. "Yes, I saw her on camera. She is back behind the science wing near the admin section."

"Is that where they keep prisoners? Are they forcing her to continue her research?"

Skybox shrugged, "I don't know, Scott, but…from what I can tell, they don't house any prisoners here. She didn't appear to be guarded."

"What are you saying, she wasn't taken prisoner, she is free to leave?"

"I'm not saying anything, friend, just saying what I saw."

The same alarm started blaring again, "Tahir?" Scott asked. Skybox shook his head no. "Something else."

CHAPTER NINETY-SIX

NEAR MEMPHIS, TENNESSEE

The general watched ahead as the column of armored vehicles began to slow. They were getting close; the terrain and trees were interfering with the ability to maneuver the horde of infected. He pulled the wet stump of the cigar from the corner of his mouth. "Deploy along the roads, keep moving them 'sumbitches' north into that valley."

"Sir, recon teams are not reporting in," the aide said.

"That's fine, captain, we know they are in there." He climbed down from the side of the APC and peered through the Steiner binoculars. "Son, you know how they hunt rabbits in Spain?"

A look of utter confusion passed over the man's face. "Sir?"

"Rabbits, damnit," the general said, once again chewing on the cigar, still scanning ahead. "Damndest thing, saw it when I was in Andalucía. The rabbits burrow down deep, see? Anyway, the hunters find the burrow, then use ferrets. They keep the little buggers caged up and just release one on each of the rabbit holes. The ferrets are mean lil' bastards when it comes to rabbit, so they dig down after them, and the rabbit will go bat-shit crazy getting away, and it'll pop out of an escape tunnel somewhere else. You just have to be ready to shoot 'em when they make a run." He lowered the binoculars. "These guys, these infected, son… they are our ferrets."

The mechanized division moved forward again but slower. They also passed wreckage from the battle with the Messengers. The rusting hulks of shot up vehicles and roadway ratcheted up the tension. They had limited air cover and had to wait to call it in due to fuel shortages. Major General Daly was impressed with the determination, if not the size, of his force. It had grown every day as more and more squads and battalions joined in, but still paled in the face of what was needed. The few infantry divisions were to the rear. Artillery was just behind the armored divisions. They were thirty kilometers from the spot marked on his maps. None of them had ever faced an enemy like this, nor thought they would fight a battle here in the hills of Tennessee. This was it, though, he knew it. His men knew it. If they lose here, the country was lost.

Several hours later, the perimeter to the south of the Thunder Ridge facility was in place. "Sir, we have incoming."

General Daly nodded, "That took longer than I expected. Have artillery brigades get ready. How many targets do we have, Captain?"

The captain looked like he would rather do anything than answer that question. "Hu..hundreds, sir."

"Hundreds? No way this place had that many aircraft."

"No, General, UAVs, all appear to be unmanned drones. Three different types identified so far. Primary ones are identified as modified Pegasus X-47A."

The general's blood ran cold; the Pegasus class of unmanned air combat craft were essentially just smaller versions of regular fighters with massive armaments, reconnaissance and maneuverability. "Shit….those bastards are going to fuck up my rabbit hunt. All stations open fire on preassigned targets." He wanted artillery going down range before any of his assets were targeted. "Captain, call in our birds and have AA buy us some time. Keep those damn drones off of us. Have all techs crank up the audio to the max. Let's drive these fucking zombies right down their throats."

~

Rollins lowered the handset and looked at the remaining members of the team. "Guys, we have to get the fuck out of here. The whole fucking Army is coming straight for us." They had heard occasional weapons fire and artillery for the past couple of days, but it was getting closer and becoming sustained. Each of the men knew they were in the no-man's zone between the enemy and front line.

"Friendly fire hurts just as much as enemy," Krychek stated flatly. "Our mission was to plant that targeting beacon and enter the facility only if needed, otherwise we sit back to help Sky, Scott and the Ghost get somewhere safe once done. We can't do any of that if we are dead."

Solo broke into the circle of men. None of them knew any of the commands the dog responded to but watched as he lowered his head menacingly. They had seen him do that countless times already. It seemed to be a reaction to the infected being close. All four of the men swung guns up and out.

"Rollins, you still pumping out that audio signal?" So far, Tahir's defensive sound had kept the infected well away from the group, but it was still as unnerving as hell hearing, smelling and watching the angry, snarling creatures as they passed.

"Yes, although I will need to change out the battery in the next two hours or so." The sound generator was a modified handheld radio. "You guys notice how many more there are now?" He wasn't sure even the sound would keep them safe if the numbers kept growing.

"Incoming!" Nez yelled as he dove for cover. The whistle of an incoming artillery shell could be heard as it went overhead detonating several hundred yards away. More shells hit nearby. The earthy smell of fresh forest dirt mixed with smoke and burning flesh. The forest erupted into hundreds of explosions. Trees splintered into fragments under the unrelenting barrage. The four men were peppered by splinters and debris. They took shelter behind whatever cover they could quickly find. The infected around them seemed unconcerned. Even in their death-like state, they seemed oblivious to the destruction going on around them.

Rollins was yelling. The deafening explosions caused them to shout afterward to even be heard. They couldn't go farther north without triggering the perimeter defenses, to the south the infected and the shelling. "This is for shit, guys! We're dead if we stay here."

Nez and Owens nodded. Krychek had blood running from both ears and could no longer hear anything. The artillary shelling briefly subsided, and they watched as a large group of wretched-looking infected came stumbling past. Many were missing limbs, some had pieces of trees lodged in their bodies. Rollins checked to make sure the sound generator was still working, then adjusted the intensity down. "We follow them in!" he said loudly.

"What?" Owens asked. The look of disbelief mirrored on Nez's normally impassive face.

"We can get closer to them now, but we need to follow behind and let them trigger all the defenses."

"That's a shit plan, sailor."

"You have a better one?"

No one did. They fell in fifty feet behind the largest group. Solo took point, but all of them could feel the danger coming from every direction. "Fucking danger close, dude," Owens said.

CHAPTER NINETY-SEVEN

HARRIS SPRINGS, MISSISSIPPI

Tahir pulled the headphones off. His coarse, black hair sweaty despite the relative coolness of the comms room. He pulled up the laptop feed, the fake alarm at the protectorate camp had gone off without a hitch. As far as he could tell, his intrusion hadn't been detected. Bobby reached over and placed a hand on his shoulder. Concern was etched on both their faces. "They'll make it."

Tahir nodded unconvinced. "That area is too hot, Bobby. It's like the center of the storm. I don't know what else I can do to help them."

Bobby felt equally helpless. He'd been monitoring military radio traffic and knew they were within range of the facility. "I know my little brother, he isn't going to stop until he finds her. And Skybox…. shit. Face it—he is the man."

Something was still bothering Tahir. He nodded in agreement with the other man's statement, but his mind was already running down hundreds of other paths. He'd missed something, but what? Half thoughts and suggestions of ideas surfaced and were eliminated at lightning speed. He absently grabbed a notepad and began making notes, drawing doodles. This continued for several minutes while Bobby continued to talk, but the words no longer registered. Tahir allowed himself to descend into a place of thoughts. He'd presented a question for his mind to analyze, and now it would focus only on that.

Bobby watched as the young man's eyes went glassy, staring off into the distance. Occasionally, the pencil in his hand would make a mark or write something, but mostly he just sat. He'd seen him do this several times over the previous few months. The first time, he thought he was having a seizure, now he understood it was just part of Tahir's mental processing. He stopped talking and went back to monitoring the radio.

Scott's decision to invite the surviving Patriots had taken some time to take root, but they were beginning to come in steadily now. The Porters from Georgia had been the first, but they were just the start. Now, the trickle of people was becoming a stream. All brought supplies, some brought livestock, and all brought weapons. In inviting anyone to come, he'd had to give out the location of the ship. This had been a hard thing for them to do. So far, they'd only had a few incidents, but in time, he knew the government, NSF or some other group of rejects would learn of them and try to come take the AG for their own. Commander Garret had assured them they would prevent as much of that as possible, but the ship had been on high-alert for days now.

Increasingly, encounters with infected were being reported as well. Everyone on board the AG had received the treatment, and it was standard for anyone wanting to join them. How much protection did it offer, though? What happened if the disease mutated again? So much was unknown, but it was clear to Bobby that time was running out for them to leave. Provisions had been stored, fuel topped off, and everyone in the community was on a four-hour notice. If the bugout signal was given, they had only that much time to get aboard with whatever they were taking with them.

Tahir was still in his zone when DeVonte entered for his shift on the radio. "How long this time?"

Bobby checked his watch, "Little over two hours."

"Damn!" the boy said smiling. "Any idea what he's working on?"

"Not a clue. I simply asked him to open the pod bay doors."

"Huh?" DeVonte said, then getting the reference. "Oh, like Hal9000, he's not a computer man."

"No," Bobby agreed. "He's way better."

It was nearly an hour later when Tahir's eyes fluttered open and began to focus once again. He looked down at the pad in his hands and frowned. "No…no, no. Oh, sheeet, no." He looked up seemingly unsurprised to see DeVonte instead of Bobby. "Must go," he said quickly exiting the small room.

DeVonte lowered the headphones and watched with a look of total confusion as the wizkid left.

Bartos looked down the barrel at the man. "What's your business, friend?"

"We heard the call. Want to go with you guys," the man said. "That it?" pointing a finger up at the white cruise ship.

Bartos leaned against a post, lowering the barrel only slightly. He was missing Solo more and more. The old Toyota was full of people, all filthy with a distant look in their eyes. Like nearly everyone, they'd seen hell up close. All were looking at the AG as if it were a mirage, something too good to be true. "It is," he said impassively.

He eyed the car once more, "It doesn't appear that you brought supplies for the journey. That is one of our requirements. Unless you have an invisible trailer or something behind that beater."

The man dropped his eyes to the ground. "We tried. We left Ohio with enough, barely enough but…"

Bartos eyed them all suspiciously, he'd heard countless stories like he was sure the man was about to offer. Beneath the filth, he tried to gauge the man's age. *Could be forty, could be sixty. Body is lean, he's trying to appear weak and stooped but probably isn't.* His eyes moved over the others as the man continued to speak.

"...couple hundred miles back. They took everything, mister. I swear." The man turned and motioned at the two women and the men. "We haven't eaten in days."

Bartos squeezed the trigger shooting the man in the chest. His years of distrust coupled with the crucible of surviving since the blackout had sharpened all of his senses. "You are not what you seem." he said to the others in the car. Looks of shock and disgust registered on each. One of the women produced a short barrel shotgun and started to point it. "Would not do that, miss," he said leveling the carbine at her head.

"This is how you treat newcomers, this is your offer of salvation?" she said bitterly.

"Lady, if you were robbed, they would have taken your guns." He kept the gun on her as he flipped the dead man's shirt up revealing a small handgun tucked underneath. "Y'all are on your own." He raised a hand signaling. The rear window of the old car shattered as the round entered. The woman dropped the weapon and quickly scooted over into the driver's seat and sped off.

Mostly they had encountered good people, but not all. They did what they could to test the arrivals, but with the true Patriots, it was obvious. While many of the new arrivals looked as decrepit and malnourished as this bunch, you could usually tell the difference quickly. It shown in their eyes, a defiance, pride...some spark that indicated a deeper commitment. They always had supplies, they showed empty hands but indicated their weapons, and they all had weapons. No one survived in this world without them. He keyed the radio, "Thanks, Trish, nice shooting."

"No problem, Cajun, turning it over to the LT for a few. Tahir wants to talk to me and DJ."

CHAPTER NINETY-EIGHT

THUNDER RIDGE PROTECTORATE

Skybox clipped a generic looking ID badge onto Scott's pocket as they ran. He was inside the compound; he could feel her nearby. Scott didn't care about the alarm, he wanted Gia. "Where is she, Sky? Show me." His friend shook his head. "Damnit, Sky!"

Skybox slowed, then pulled him to one side of the wide corridor. "Look, I know you have to get to her, but just trust me, please." A line of NSF troops ran past with automatic rifles, black helmets, visors and body armor. He looked at the muddy, black ill-fitting uniform Scott was wearing. "We have to get you kitted out man. You need to look the part."

They stopped by a supply room where Skybox quickly ordered the man to supply Scott with new gear. "I have to go to the command room. Meet me there when you are changed." He showed Scott a locker room nearby he could use. He turned to leave, then looked back, "Having fun yet?" winked and sped away.

The slightly overweight supply officer handed him the uniform, tactical helmet and weapons. "Throwing you right into the fire, eh? Must be a new arrival."

Scott nodded, "Yes, thanks."

"The commander likes you, that's good. Those guys, well, they normally don't speak to us regular types. Scary bunch, the boys in gray."

"You got that right." He entered the empty locker room, changed into the fresh uniform and clipped the ID badge onto the new shirt. The helmet took some time to figure out. The mirrored orange visor seemed unnecessary, but when he put it on, a small display window powered on in one corner. The display showed a map of the entire protectorate. As he turned his head, the view changed. He was able to locate the general population areas, command center, power and facility engineering. Finally, the science wing. He had to fight the overwhelming desire to go there. He was already several feet in that direction when he forced himself to follow Skybox's instructions.

The command center was overwhelming. The guards manning the door had pointed him to Skybox. "He told us to send you right over," one of them said.

Scott nodded and walked over to his friend who was in a small room surrounded by video feeds from around the facility. Behind him, he could see numerous people using yoke controllers of what looked to be flight simulators. The activity level everywhere was frenetic but controlled. "What's happening, Boss?"

Sky looked up, momentarily confused, then smiled. "Damn, it's Stormtrooper Montgomery." He looked over the screens at the room beyond. Then reached over and clicked a switch on the helmet. "Radio link," he said. "Hard to say anything in here without being overheard." Skybox brought up a video of a drone attacking a column of tanks. "The military is attacking, and they have flooded the valley outside with infected."

"No shit, Commander. Sir."

"Oh, yeah, you've been out there. Well, so far, their artillery is missing us by a kilometer. Not sure they can do any real harm to us anyway, but they are getting their asses kicked and nothing I can do to stop it."

Scott thought for a second before asking, "What do you have clearance to do?"

"Base security, I can control the defense systems in the immediate area and in some parts of the camp itself. Nothing I do goes unmonitored, though."

"How did you manage the message with the mini-drone?" Scott asked.

"It's one of hundreds, I didn't think anyone had noticed it had dropped out and gone into maintenance mode."

"Do you know where the team is?" Skybox shook his head. "Show me a map." It took Scott a few minutes to orient himself to the topo map, but he finally found the access point and field he had come in from. He traced a finger back to where he'd left the team. "Here. Drop a drone down and find them."

Scott watched as Skybox selected one of the mini drones and had it descend. "No camera coverage in that area, we will have to wait for the drone feed." In seconds, they could see foliage as the drone passed the canopy of trees on its way to the forest floor. The pre-programmed descent stopped at five feet and began rotating. "Holy shit." The area was in ruins. The shelling here had been devastating. As the drone turned 180 degrees, they found themselves staring into the vacant eyes of an infected. Both men jumped a little. The expression was unreadable, but the creature radiated anger. It ignored the drone and shuffled past. Sky adjusted the camera to follow it, realizing as it moved away, that an arm was missing and a gash on its thigh was oozing blood with every step.

"Lots of bodies, but looks like infected," Skybox said. He clicked some keys to follow the infected shuffling northward. "They would have moved away from the incoming fire, but that would have placed them right inside the perimeter defenses. They would have gone from bad to worse."

Scott was thinking, he knew the guys wouldn't have acted stupidly. "Do you have IR capabilities? You could look for that. The heat signature of an infected is different than humans, right?"

"It is, but none on the drone, I could look at the defense sensor array, though. Damn things been lighting up like a Christmas tree the last few days with all the infected."

"Look for Solo, he should stand out."

Skybox nodded, "Good idea, what are we going to do when we find them?"

"Plant the beacon," Scott pointed to the cavern ceiling high overhead, "right over us."

"You know what that means, Scott. They target that beacon with a bunker buster, or worse, a MOAB…"

"That's their mission, Sky. This base has to fall."

The timetable was advancing faster than any of them could have imagined. Skybox motioned for a man to come over. "Forget covert, this is it, man," he whispered to Scott.

"Yes, Commander?" the technician asked looking directly at Skybox.

"I need a private encrypted channel with this officer," he nodded toward Scott. "Set that up and relay it to my comms system."

The man nodded, "Right away, sir. I'll have it added on… channel five," he said looking at the display on the tablet he was holding.

As he walked off, Sky said, "It won't actually be private but should buy us some time." He powered the helmet radio back on and showed Scott how to switch channels, then, as the tech waved and gave a thumbs-up, they tested it. "We won't have long once that marker beacon is set. Go find her, Scott. Call me when you make contact."

Skybox watched his friend leave and returned his attention to the screen. The team above was his one chance to end this. All of his years of blind obedience, and now he was betraying his leaders and his oath…or was he? Scott's voice came over his earbud a fifteen minutes later. "Nearing the door for the science section. Single guard on station."

"Do what you have to, Scott. Your badge should give you access. Tell him you are conducting a welfare check on my orders. Own it, Montgomery."

On that point, Scott had no problem. His adrenaline was pumping, but his level of confidence was off the charts. He approached, gun held at low-ready, and gave a small nod of the head to the lone sentry. "Safety check," as he waved the card in front of the door sensor which turned from red to green.

"Think they are all gone," the guard said. "None came back after the evac siren. Probably off grabbing a bite."

"Still have to look, commander's orders." The door closed behind Scott leaving him alone in the unoccupied lab. "I'm inside Sky, no one here."

"Acknowledged, watch your six."

The labs occupied a large space, and each seemed to have separate functions. One was obviously an agronomy lab as plants and vegetables were everywhere. In one environmental chamber, he saw corn growing in what looked to be desert sand. The reading of 105 degrees showed on the display, yet the corn seemed to be thriving. In another, what appeared to be potatoes were growing on a vine not underground. The final shock was seeing soybean plants growing in near artic conditions. Frost covered all the leaves, but the plants here appeared to be thriving as well. *What the fuck are they doing here?*

CHAPTER NINETY-NINE

Scott wasn't sure what he expected to see in the labs, but it sure wasn't this. He reverted back to his previous career: gather data, analyze, process. His priority was finding Gia, so he moved swiftly but took time to study all that he passed. Charts with crop drought tolerances, dryland farming, xeriscaping. The lab went on and on with one thing after another all related one way or another to massive climate change.

He turned a corner and entered a smaller lab. This one was similar but different. Small pressure vessels filled one wall. Other containers were marked flammable, one with a handwritten sticker reading 'Mycodiesel.' He was unfamiliar with the term, but looking at the vats of growing medium, he assumed it was related to fungi, or possibly, a bacterium, one they were using to produce a type of natural fuel. Not a biodiesel like Bartos had made, but something directly from the organic material in the vats. His mind was racing, the purpose of the labs was eluding him.

He stopped and studied the space. There were at least a dozen different labs here. He had to assume they were all working on advanced studies. If each was related to a different discipline, the knowledge contained here was invaluable. "Sky?"

"Yeah, you found her?"

"No, not yet. The place is empty. I need you to do something, though. Find the files from the science labs and put them somewhere Tahir can access. The research going on here is amazing, like saving the earth kinda stuff. I imagine it will be backed up elsewhere, see if you can locate it. Doubt he could download it all before this place goes."

"On it. Stay safe!"

A distant boom echoed into the complex. Scott knew he had to find the bio lab. That would be where Gia worked. He glanced at the map in his visor display. It was no help. Fourteen numbered labs were all that showed along with a grayed-out section which he assumed was the admin wing. That would be where the Council was, he guessed.

He continued checking the labs one by one. Some were obvious, like robotics, electromagnetics and one that appeared to be dedicated to pure physics. This lab had numerous smaller rooms, each focusing on a different aspect from cosmology to quantum engineering if the notes on the tables were accurate. He assumed a complex like this would be focused on the pandemic, maybe restoring the power grid, hell—even weapons research, but so far, it was everything but that. It was as if he had the answer to a question that was yet to be asked.

Several of the labs were labeled with warning stickers, some for radiation, others for chemical or high voltage and more than a couple with the distinctive interconnected triad of circles indicating biohazard. His radio chirped softly. Skybox's voice came in a whisper, "Found the team, they are placing markers in eleven minutes. Rollins is sending word to Tahir to get the files. The clock is ticking, friend—move your ass."

"Acknowledged," was his abrupt reply. As anxious as he was to find Gia, the geek in him was simply overwhelmed by the amount of knowledge and research contained in these rooms. He wouldn't have been surprised to see a downed alien UFO in one of the rooms. The science here was beyond cutting edge, and much of what he saw, he couldn't even guess as to its purpose.

He pushed open the door marked 12 and saw tanks filled with fish and sea creatures, shellfish and several things he felt sure were ancient trilobites. Only these weren't fossils of the ancient sea creature, these were very much alive, scurrying around on the fake seabed of the aquarium like giant nautical cockroaches. As he looked closer, he realized none of the creatures here were normal. While no marine biologist, even he could see the creatures looked more ancient, less evolved. A salamander with huge glowing eyes swam to the glass and watched him pass, its green head turning in a near full rotation to stay focused on him.

Darkened glass tanks held various creatures which he only caught glimpses of in the form of bioluminescent flashes. From archaea domain type cavefish to cryptomonads which were part animal, part plant, and even euglena eukaryotes which, according to the sign, shared neither plant nor animal characteristics.

A tray of vials was sitting out with a red bio label reading 'Neurotoxin' on the side. He picked up one of the small vials that had a covered barb on the top. A long rod like a speargun shaft sat nearby, he assumed it was used to inject and paralyze animals for study. Something brightly illuminated in a lone tank off to his left. He slipped the vial into a pocket and went to take a closer look. The lone creature inside was amazing. He'd never seen anything like this in the natural science museums, but then again, soft-bodied creatures didn't often leave fossils. *How in the hell had they...?*

He was looking at a semi-translucent pale white angel hovering in the water. Not a jellyfish, maybe an ancient relative of a sea snail, but this had to be four-feet high and a couple of feet wide. The thin, tapered body was supported by undulating gossamer wings that flashed brighter, bluish light as they flowed and rippled. What was captivating, though, was the almost primate looking face with lips that could have been human. She, and for some reason, he knew it was a 'she,' watched him and seemed to be beckoning him closer. Parts of the creature's head were translucent, and he could see flickering movement inside. While completely alien, it also seemed totally normal. This was an intelligent creature, he could feel it studying him. Not as a predator, but as a rationalizing animal. The angel went dark as a piercing alarm sounded through the labs.

"Move. Scott, you are about to have company."

He rounded a corner and encountered a sealed door with a bio-warning sticker and a large number 4. "Bio Lab 4," he said out loud. He then looked back at all the labs, all the wonderful science here. No way Gia had been coming here. Bio lab 4 had to be just a coincidence. She would have told him had this been where she was spending so much time.

"Sky, I need access; this door isn't opening." He heard the door at the far end open and voices as men entered. "Going to need it quickly."

"Got my hands full, mate, going to have to do your best," came Sky's strained response.

CHAPTER ONE HUNDRED

PACIFIC NORTHWEST

Half a continent away from Tennessee, the distinctive tang of the nearby ocean hung in the air. The soft sole boots made no discernible sound as the man approached the house. He checked the house number on the ivy-covered fence again to verify he was at the right place. The overcast night provided no ambient light from the moon or stars. That was one of the main reasons he had selected it. Since the blackout, sunset meant darkness. No streetlights, no illuminated landscaping. No glow of interior lights or big screen televisions from the houses. Darkness was his friend, this was his world and always had been.

With conscious effort, he slowed his breathing. Not an easy feat considering the hike he had taken to get here. His pulse steadied, and he lowered the specialty night optics to view the surroundings. The ambient night vision in the device also offered an overlay of infra-red, thus, offering the ability to see a concealed enemy even in total darkness. He scanned the drive and surrounding houses seeing nothing out of the ordinary. In years past, in this neighborhood, he would have needed to watch for sophisticated alarm sensors and proximity alarms as well. Thankfully, those were also a rarity these days.

What he mainly had to watch for was the human and canine sentries. He took a half step and froze as he felt a twig beneath his foot. Slowly moving his foot to one side, he continued silently up the small embankment. Crawling the final few feet, he could now clearly see the house outlined in the green glow of the NVGs. Unlike the other homes in the once exclusive neighborhood, this one showed signs of life. He could see a heat signature on several floors and a bit of light leaking around what were probably thick blackout curtains. These people seemed unaffected and unconcerned by the events outside their estate. That wasn't true, he knew, as they were as responsible as anyone for it all.

The man smiled as he zeroed in on his target. He mentally flagged each of the target's security detail, filing them by threat risk and proximity to the path he planned to take. He knew from earlier surveillance how large the security force was. He had now accounted for all but two. He wouldn't move until he had identified their locations as well. Patience was a requirement for him, rushing led to mistakes, and he had not survived this long by making mistakes.

His mental clock ticked off in his head. Slowly, he moved a small limb slightly down, so he could see the far corner of the large home. It angered him that this estate was not suffering like the rest of the world was. Most had no idea of the importance of the man who lived here, nor that he had survived the catastrophe of the last two years mostly unscathed. One might even think they had known ahead of time the sun was going to belch a million-mile cloud of plasma directly toward Earth. No, the people in this house had not known, but...they had been prepared and, even more so, ready to take advantage of the situation.

There, he spotted a cigarette glow near the edge of his optics range. *Sloppy*, he thought. Dialing the IR filter up, he could make out part of a head where the man was, but nothing else. That meant he was mostly hidden behind something, or...*Shit*. The realization changed his attitude. Some of the security forces were wearing cool suits. An outer layer, probably of Kevlar and carbon fiber composite over an inner liner that had a capillary network of cooling liquid which circulated around the body. This effectively masked the wearer from having any detectable heat signature on infrared.

He went through the moves of all the players once more in his mind. Had he missed anyone? Could they have had additional assets out here, and most of all, how paranoid did you have to be to put bodyguards in military-grade anti-IR suits when the rest of the world was rubbing sticks together to make fire now?

No…he had not missed anyone else. Of that he was sure. Now he was sure of where one of the hidden security people were. He also knew where he would have positioned the other one. He altered his preferred path to avoid the likely line of sight of that one as well. The clock in his head said it was time to go.

Like a shadow, the man worked his way through the security cordon without detection and knelt behind a small out-building. The grounds around the mansion had been cleared of shrubs, small trees, anything that could be used for concealment. The team protecting his target was good, and he had no desire to hurt them. His MO was to get in and get out without detection. He could only stay here a few moments before moving, but he had to wait for the guards to move on first. He knew the paths and the timing perfectly. Even without looking, he knew where they would be. Without warning, he took off at a run, still crouched and reached the house. He felt the bricks to his back and side. He was wedged into a dark corner created by two walls intersecting at right angles.

Barely pausing to take in the scene, he turned and began climbing up the brick wall. Forcing his hands and feet into opposing walls, he climbed using the deep mortar lines for grips. The years of rock climbing paying off as he climbed quickly and disappeared into the deeper shadows under the eaves of the roofline.

He paused again and held his breath as the next security patrol passed right where he had been seconds earlier. He counted off eight seconds, then felt for the roof. His fingers moved over the slate tiles to ensure they were all securely fastened. Satisfied that it would support him, he swung himself silently up and over.

The man lay in his bed, the oxygen tank steadily refilling the air beneath the plastic tent every few minutes. How frail the man appeared, nothing like the robust man he had once been. Getting into the medical wing of the house had been no problem from the roof. Then, all he had needed to do was wait for the night nurse to leave the room. All good, so far. He knew better than assuming that would continue.

Something was always there to cause problems. That was why he was such a good operative, he anticipated worse case scenarios in every instance. He scanned the room, someone would be monitoring the man, he felt sure. Would they have video surveillance or just routine medical transponders? He had the man's dossier; this man was obsessed with privacy. He would never allow cameras on him.

His eyes fell on a picture on the nightstand next to the bed. It was a photo of the old man in younger days with a pretty woman who he assumed was his wife, a young boy and a very pretty girl of about twenty. Now, he understood fully why she had sent him. That would be the daughter, known to him only as Ms. Levy. If anything, she was even more dangerous than her father. He quietly removed the nylon case from his pocket. He cautiously removed the syringe from the kit and slowly approached the bed. He was not surprised to see the man in this condition. Just one more indicator of how good her intelligence had been.

The man appeared helpless, but he was not so naïve as to believe that. Once the needle pumped the dark fluid into the man's bloodstream he would only have three minutes to get the information he required. After that, no one would ever be able to get it. Under the oxygen tent, the man appeared to sleep, but small movements behind the eyelids indicated something else. Perhaps dreams, more likely alertness. He was playing possum. *Good.* He wanted the man to know he was here.

Slowly, he lifted the plastic and reached cautiously toward the target. Just as he was about to touch him, the man's eyes opened wide, and he swung up a compact Beretta pistol from the opposite side of the bed. It was too late; the tiny needle was already piercing through to the vein and the toxic cocktail was taking effect. The pistol dropped to the bed, and the hand followed it limply.

"You know why I'm here, don't you?"

The man nodded once. He tried to speak, the words were slurred and indistinct. "I know you, bastard. You are Archangel."

"Don't waste my time, and I promise I won't waste yours. Where can I find the others?" The drugs were having the desired effect, the man was soon incapable of giving misleading information or avoiding answering. Originally developed, then outlawed in its home country, the serum known to the Archangel's colleagues as 'Old No.7' due to its resemblance to a famous Tennessee whiskey, had a murky history, but no one doubted its effectiveness. "By the way, your daughter sends her love." The man's eyes opened at this news.

Four and a half minutes later he placed the capped, empty syringe back into the case, dabbed away a small dot of blood on the man's neck and took a final look at the monitors. The heart rhythm was beginning to get erratic. He shoved the kit into his pocket and checked the area once more before slipping out of the room as alarms began to wail. He allowed a small smile as he heard footsteps run past on the way to the patient's room. He knew he had just killed one of the most dangerous men in the world. The former Mr. Levi. Even better, he now held the man's most closely held secrets. Three more to go. He only hoped Skybox was taking care of number six. The other Levi.

CHAPTER ONE HUNDRED ONE

THUNDER RIDGE PROTECTORATE

They couldn't survive another attack from above. Some of the larger drones were equipped with tank-buster missiles. The first two attacks by the drones were devastating. General Daly lost half of his armored division in the first forty minutes. As each tank went down, it created a hole in the line. A hole that the infected used to great success. No longer being repelled by the sound generators there, they surged back through going after artillery gunners and then the general infantry. Hundreds of casualties turned into thousands, but still, his men fought valiantly.

The way forward toward Thunder Ridge was all but blocked by the terrain and the forest. Several access roads were being used, but the wreckage of burning APCs and tanks were causing havoc for the ones behind. "We are lined up here like ducks in a shooting gallery. Captain, where are our birds?"

"Still fifteen minutes out, General."

He was fresh out of ideas, guessed his forces were down 30% already, and overall effectiveness was plummeting. Pushing the infected had seemed like a good idea, but the enemy wasn't out in the open, they had burrowed in too deep. They needed to open a door into those bunkers to flush them out. He heard automatic weapons fire and saw tracer rounds coming from the ridgeline above. The bullets tore through soldiers and infected indiscriminately. The fire was precise and measured. "Goddamnit, take cover, you idiots! Charlie-2, target those emplacements!" he yelled into the handset.

To his left, three of the M1-A1 massive barrels swung and began firing. The protectorate camps' computer-guided guns' targeting began to fail, then ceased as the shells found their mark.

Solo crawled forward pulling at the collar of the injured man but got no response. The infected were closing in on him, but he knew this man was needed. He sniffed at the man's missing arm. A bone jutted through the meat. He didn't smell like the others who were filling the forest. They had a sickness the dog could smell but simply did not understand. Large hands reached in, "Come on, Owens," Nez said. Owens just moaned. "Solo, pull back." one of the other soldiers yelled from cover. The mini-drone lay in pieces where it had been shot from the sky. "Those guns are going to start firing again any second."

"Where is it, did he get it placed?" Rollins' voice rose higher as the panic began to take root.

"Negative," Krychek said. He pointed to where Owens had fallen. The bottom portion of the man's arm was lying in a small clearing. The marker beacon he'd been trying to place was just beyond. The men had faced difficulties before, but this mission was going sideways in a hurry. Between the infected continually surrounding them to the gunfire and artillery and other counter-intrusion devices, the situation looked hopeless.

"Space toasters are heating up again," Rollins yelled. The large, green, flat panels began to turn. They had learned that the microwave generators had to recharge or cool down every few minutes. Two of them had already gotten glancing hits from the beam and had severe burns.

Rollins on his back and shoulder, and Owens on his face and arm. The arm burn would no longer be an issue for him, though. All of them scrambled for cover. The need to be covert was long gone. The Army showing up and the horde of infected had rendered any need for stealth rather pointless.

"Did anyone see where the auto-fire system was that got Owens?" Krychek asked.

Nez pointed, "Two of 'em. They got him in the crossfire."

The places he pointed to were at least fifty yards apart, and the entire perimeter was beginning to fill with the infected. They watched as several entered the small clearing and were cut down by the barrage of fire. Others began to squirm as the space toasters, as Krychek called them, began cycling heat rays at them. Soon, those were on the ground, hair and clothes smoking, skin charring and then catching fire.

Rollins, Krychek and Nez all looked at one another. They knew what had to be done, the question was who would venture out there to activate the beacon. "He's gone," Nez said, pulling fingers away from the Ranger's neck.

"Shit," Krychek said.

The guns started firing again, more of the infected moving through. One fell directly on top of the homing beacon. "The guns…" Rollins began, "they only rotate left and right. Appears they are firing at about half a meter off the ground."

Krychek nodded, "So one of us could crawl out there and get the beacon between space toaster pulses."

It was a suicide mission, they all knew it. Rollins looked at the two others, both men were much larger than he was. He doubted either man crawling would be below the line of fire. Wordlessly, he started stripping off his pack and gear. "Y'all try and keep those creatures off of me long enough to activate the beacon—ok?"

They both nodded grimly, and Nez repositioned a few feet to one side for better covering fire.

"It's been an honor gentleman," Rollins said handing over the small sound generator before lowering himself to the ground, waiting for a pause from the heat panels and then low-crawling quickly toward the middle of the clearing.

At the sight of Rollins, the infected became hyper-agitated. The numbers breaking into the clearing tripled in minutes. Even the auto fire guns couldn't keep up with the numerous targets. Krychek and Nez downed any that made it close to the now defenseless soldier. Rollins' back was covered in the blood and gore of the infected. He was only halfway to the beacon when one of the infected who was severely injured crawled close enough to bite deeply into his thigh pulling away with a strip of flesh hanging from its mouth. A bullet sheared off part of the creature's face and jaw. Rollins fought every instinct to jerk upward from the pain. "I will not quit," he said, repeating the mantra drilled into him since SEAL training.

It took him several minutes to compartmentalize the pain and continue on, only to realize his way forward was blocked on all sides by the numerous bodies. To go over them would place his body into the fire line. "Shit," he said grimacing from the pain and beginning to suffer from the blood loss, the bullets ripping just over his head like angry bees. Part of one of the infected landed on him causing him to flinch, a bullet tore into his raised shoulder, shattering the bone. "The only easy day was yesterday," he told himself through gritted teeth. Slowly, he dragged first one, then another of the bodies to the side. Nearly impossible to do without raising up for leverage. He chose the smaller bodies which he could just move with the strength in his uninjured arm.

"Toasters!" yelled his fellow SEAL, Krychek.

He was well and truly fucked, out here in the open. Unlike the guns, the microwave panels reached all the way to the ground. He saw the infected approaching him begin to suffer from the heat rays. The beacon was still more than ten feet ahead. Rollins did the only thing he could think of and pulled more of the infected bodies toward him, shielding himself with their bodies. As the panels swiveled toward him, though, the heat was still unbearable. The bodies he was hiding behind began to boil, some rupturing, disgorging vile gore which quickly congealed and cooked. He felt his injured arm get hot and grow numb, then watched as it reddened and then blackened and began to smoke. His vision in that eye clouded, then went dark, and he felt warm liquid draining from his eye socket down his face.

His mental clock was counting down the power cycle as the panels finally shut down one by one. His body was done, but he forced his one good eye on the body atop the beacon and pulled himself forward with his remaining arm. He heard his friends still shooting and urging him on. With his last bit of strength, he made it to the fallen woman and reached beneath her to retrieve the device. Jamming it into the ground, he stabbed at the power button and missed. He tried again, realizing he forgot to enable the system. His energy was spent, and his body broken. Another memory from his early days floated into his mind. 'In the worst of conditions, the legacy of my SEAL teammates steadies my resolve.' His sacrifice was for them, those that battled before and those that might come after.

Bringing his face close, he pushed in the correct keys and activated the power button. A steady green light shown from the bottom. He heard first Nez, then Krychek yell, "Out." A wave of infected was pushing through the gunfire toward him. He lowered his head, deciding his fate should not be that. Getting torn apart by these creatures was not how he would go. He pushed himself up to his knees, letting the auto-gunfire rip into his chest and head.

"Sir, we have a beacon."

"Send the coordinates to Garret and redirect all fire to that location," General Daly said. *God, I hope those boys are out of there.*

CHAPTER ONE HUNDRED TWO

Scott faced the locked door trying to find a way in. He looked up at the display map again. Some of the labs were interconnected where one discipline might dovetail into another. He'd passed a medical lab. Looking at the map, it had an access corridor into Lab-4. He peered back around the door and saw three guards with flashlights working their way toward him. He ducked low and, hidden by the tables and workstations, made his way through the main room back to the entrance to medical. That door opened soundlessly, and he slipped inside.

The stark white room was sterile and empty. It reminded him of the research labs he and Gia worked in while in college. The moment of nostalgia bit deep into his soul causing him to blink away tears. He found the entrance to the corridor connecting to Lab-4 and froze. Like a macabre exhibition, the walls of the hall were a menagerie of preserved lifeforms. Like the sea creatures, nothing about these were natural either. All were formed from the maniacal nightmares of a maniac or the result of the worst medical experiments imaginable. If most started out as anything natural, discerning the base genome was a near impossibility. Scott's pace slowed to a near crawl as he marveled at each vessel.

An animal similar to a wild tapir with a long snout and pig-like head which was attached to a slender muscular body covered with iridescent scales and tiny winglets with hook-like claws at the middle joints. A small fur covered animal slightly larger than a rabbit with vicious looking teeth and claws and an armored spiked tail. He looked at row upon row of the curious specimens until he came to something that was vaguely reptilian in appearance but with hands and arms that were distinctly human. In the last containers were humans; each appeared to be infected, but all were different. They floated in what he assumed was formalin due to the slightly pinkish tint.

They were experimenting here, but why and on what? Genetic experiments, surely, but this went way beyond the search for a treatment. He went back to the last container; at the bottom a sign read SA-1297. Something about that seemed familiar. The naked female suspended in the tank looked angry and horrific even in death. A door opened behind him, he lightly ran to the entrance to Lab 4 and waved his badge. The light stayed red. He heard footsteps and saw the passing beam of a light back in the medical lab. *Shit, shit, shit. Think, man, think.* On a coat hook near the door, several lab coats hung, probably left there when the alarm sounded. He quickly searched each, and on the third, found what he was looking for. In his rush to evacuate, one of the scientists had left his badge clipped to the coat. He waved it in front of the security panel and the light changing to green was accompanied by a nearly silent click. He pushed the door open and slipped inside.

Unlike the other rooms, Lab-4 had a double door entrance. The lab was negatively pressurized with a self-contained air system. He knew from past conversations with his fiancée, this was standard for biological research labs. The blast of air and disinfectant above was normal, too. Once the system cycled through, the inner door clicked open. He stepped into the room with his weapon raised, ready to engage. At first glance, the lab looked as empty as the others, but at the far end, he saw a lone figure bent over a microscope.

"Scott, we need to talk," Skybox's voice from the tiny speakers almost lost behind the pounding in his ears. The figure was female, in a lab coat. A hint of red hair fell from a surgical cap, the protruding stomach the final clue. She turned and studied him with confusion...then a look of rage.

"Why are you in here?" she shouted. "Get out immediately!" She didn't sound like Gia, but it was unmistakably her.

"Scott, I'm coming to you. If you find Gia, stay away. I just got a message from Tahir." Scott could hear him panting, apparently running. He remembered his helmet. *She thinks I'm one of the NSF guards keeping her here.* Skybox was talking again, "Gia is..." but Scott had already taken the tactical helmet off and let it drop to the floor.

The woman's face seemed to morph through disbelief to utter relief as she finally recognized him. "Scott?"

He ran to her and took her in his arms, the sheer relief of finding her overwhelming him. "What are you doing here?" she asked kissing him.

Still holding her tight, "When I found out they took you, I had to find you. I love you, I'm so glad you're ok." He placed a hand on her stomach. "How is the baby?"

She pulled away from him with a start. "You shouldn't have come."

He wasn't sure until this moment he would actually find her, but this would not have been a greeting he would have ever expected. "Gia, what's going on? We need to get out of here now. The Army..."

"Fuck the Army, Scott, they will be dealt with. No one gets into or out of this place."

He heard the faint noise of the decon chamber cycling behind him. Instead of the NSF guard, a bloodied Skybox burst into the lab, gun at the ready, scanning for threats.

"It's ok, Sky, it's just us," Scott said.

Gia groaned, "I should have known. Hello, Michael. So, you are the P5 Archangel selected?"

"Michael?" Scott asked confused.

Skybox aimed at the woman's head. "Hello, Ms. Levy."

She smiled, "Finally figured it out, did you?" She walked around the edge of the table, her pregnant belly even more obvious than before. "No, you didn't, as impressive as you are. You just aren't that bright. Even my sweet Scott here, who is that smart, failed to see it, but alas...he would have in time. Who then...Tahir?"

Scott looked back and forth between the two, a look of total confusion on his face. "Will one of you please tell me what is going on?"

Gia took his arm gently. "Your friend is trying to tell you I am not who I seem. I am his boss, and I run this place. I am the Levy, my precious Scott."

"Your name isn't Gia Colton?"

"No, that is actually accurate. Levy is more a title than a name."

"She is the one who started all this, Scott," Skybox said clicking the safety off his weapon. "We need to end her now. She killed the president, she released the virus and imprisoned all those Americans."

"Technically, I only engineered the virus, the blackout released it...the first time anyway. I did, however, set up the camps before that idiot Chambers lost her grip and started gassing them with 1297." She leaned heavily on the worktable. "So, technically, yes, I am the evil bitch you have been hunting."

CHAPTER ONE HUNDRED THREE

Scott turned slowly to see four of the armed guards entering from the adjacent lab. "Scott…sweetie. You are going to need to put the gun down." He began to comply as she turned to the guards, "Go ahead and kill the commander," pointing at Skybox.

The Praetor commander leaped sideways as one of the men began to fire. Scott dropped, spun and came up with the Glock faster than even he thought possible. One of the guards went down when Scott fired. He felt more than saw Gia retreating to the rear of the lab. Skybox dove for cover but caught a round in his left shoulder. Time seemed to slow as Scott stood and ran at the remaining three guards. The shock registered just before his bullets tore into two of the three.

The slide locked back on Scott's pistol, he dropped it and unsheathed the knife tossing it to his unarmed friend who slid into the lone guard's legs like he was sliding for third base. He sliced the man's Achilles tendon causing him to lurch forward, then thrust the knife up at his inner thigh. The razor-sharp blade found its mark, slicing open the femoral artery generating a momentary fountain of blood across the bio lab.

The guard dropped his pistol and grasped awkwardly to stop the flow of blood leaving his body. He tumbled to the ground already growing weaker. Scott turned from the carnage to see Skybox going after Gia; the back of his uniform was covered with a dark crimson stain.

"Block the doors, Scott, more will be on the way." He caught a glimpse of red hair as Gia fled from the lab mere feet ahead of Skybox.

Scott's mind raced as he ran forward and pushed a locking bar down for each of the doors. Things began to click, finally. *Gia is Levy?* The soul-crushing truth was not something his mind could fathom. This would mean that she, as much as the CME, was responsible for so much of the misery and death in the world. It just couldn't be. He grabbed the sub-compact H&K from the floor as he raced after the two into the admin section.

The echoing footsteps ahead and a trail of blood from Sky's wounds made following the pair easy. Unlike the other sections of the compound, no people seemed to be in this area. *Why is she this way? Can I save her? Had she ever loved me?* The litany of thoughts thundered through Scott's tortured mind like panicking wild animals heading toward a cliff. The real gut-punch came when he thought about what Skybox would do when he caught her. *He kills her, he kills my child, too.* He wiped away stinging tears as he ran.

He turned through an open gray door into what was a large office. The space was carved into the very rock walls of the cavern. Skybox was approaching Gia with his knife drawn. The color was gone from his face. It was replaced by a mask of pain and determination. Gia watched the approaching man with a detached look of pity.

Scott realized she was pointing a gun, not at Skybox but at him. "Drop it, Michael," she said with bitter vile dripping from each word. The mask of evil she wore made her nearly unrecognizable. This could not be the woman he loved, the mother of his child.

"Sky...no, the baby," Scott yelled.

Skybox faltered briefly with a glance toward Scott before lunging after Gia who lightly stepped away.

The pain of betrayal came crashing into Scott like a train as the bullet entered his thigh. "That's going to really mess up your cycling, Sweetie." The laugh was unnatural. The pistol in her hand was very real, though. The pain in his leg somehow sharpened his mental awareness, and instantly, he knew the only mask this woman ever wore was when she was with him. How much effort and skill it must have required for her to seem happy, normal and loving.

"Why, Gia?" he asked through the pain.

An enormous blast shook the room and dust and pebbles fell from the rock overhead. "Your friends are determined," she said easing farther from Skybox who was now on one knee ten feet away.

"Why?" he yelled again choking back the sobs.

"Let's just say I was born into it, dear. I do have to say, Scott, I am truly sorry you got involved. I did everything I could to keep you away, even marrying that idiot Steve."

"Where is the rest of the Council?" Skybox yelled. "You all have to go."

"Oh, Sky, I've taken care of that already. Well, Archangel did. I believe he just eliminated the last of the six. Except me, of course. Their service to the republic was over. Just as yours is."

The gun in her hand rose to fire. Scott stepped awkwardly toward her. His one functional leg pulling the nearly useless one behind. "Levy!" She turned casually to look at him. This wasn't the face he dreamed of. "I can't do this." Her face showed the words hit home. "That is what you said to me that last day isn't it? You thought I didn't hear but...I did. Was it that you couldn't marry me, have our baby, or you couldn't do all this? Did you ever have second thoughts about all you have done?"

Her face softened, her expression morphed briefly into his Gia, then was gone again. "Do you remember my father? From the wedding? He didn't like you very much, which is one of the reasons I kept you so close. I liked making him mad, sometimes in small ways, sometimes bigger. I was never really what he wanted. You were my escape from him, then and now, honey."

Her words stabbed at him. He needed her dead, but even more, wanted to understand. "What made you this way?"

"You wouldn't know this—few people ever did, Scott. My father was possibly the most powerful man in the world. Last of the old-school Levis. He sat at the head of the Council of Six. The seat should have gone to my brother, but he didn't survive the test, I did. My father was a bastard, I hated him, and that is what made me. I was imprisoned, tortured and even exposed to an early natural form of the Chimera as a teen. It changed me, the epigenetic changes it made to my body were subtle but significant." She absently rubbed a slender hand over her swollen stomach. "Mentally, I learned to escape my torturer by retreating into my own fantasy world. You, my sweet lover, are there. It is where I wished I could stay, but alas, it wouldn't work. When I took over the Council, I learned many, many things. As Levy, I had real work to do…no matter how much I hated it…or him."

CHAPTER ONE HUNDRED FOUR

HARRIS SPRINGS, MISSISSIPPI

Steven Porter leaned over the ship's rail alongside Bartos. The two had developed an easy rapport since meeting just days earlier. "They are out there."

"Si, my friend, yes they are. More every day." They could hear and often smell infected on the far side of the canal. They'd raised the drawbridges connecting Harris Springs to the mainland and were using the AG's PA system to broadcast the audio signal that kept them from coming closer, but the numbers kept growing.

They watched a small reconnaissance drone pass overhead, no doubt from the Bataan. "How long do we wait? On your friends?"

Bartos shrugged, "Todd's call. We still have Patriots making it through; when that stops, he will have to decide."

Steve relaxed a bit. As Sentinel, he'd been responsible for helping Bobby and Bartos get the word out as well. As a result of putting out the Patriot's Call, the AG now had over 1200 passengers, but they had room for several times that number. Tahir had said they really needed about 2500 people to have a real chance at sustainable survival. A community that large would give them adequate genetic diversity to avoid any problems down the road.

"What's the deal on that doctor and the dead girl, the one Tahir was talking about yesterday?"

Bartos' jaw was rigid, the anger inside him at that remark was palpable, but the question deserved an answer. Tahir had dropped the bombshell news to all of them the night before. Gia had to be Levy, and she had kidnapped, then killed the missing girl. The fire blazed through him hot and bitter. "The doctor was convincing, brilliant even. I don't know how the kid figured it out, but none of us ever would have. Scott is about as smart as anyone I ever met, yet he got her pregnant, was about to marry the crazy bitch."

Steven nodded looking back out over the coast and the sun as it dropped toward the ocean. "My friend, Gerald, the original Sentinel, had a theory about a secret cabal that ran everything. He said if you could follow the money far enough, you would find the real power. Would Gia be that person?"

"According to Tahir, yes. She leads what he called the Council of Six. I can't connect that to the woman we all knew, though. She seemed kind, funny…very unassuming. She was a scientist consumed by her work but very much in love with Scott. She gave us the cure. That was who we saw. I'm not sure if I will ever be able to think of her any other way."

"And your friend, Scott? How is he going to handle it?"

Bartos had no idea, he wished he was there to help him when he learned the truth. "It will be the end of his world."

"Ok, listen up," the younger Garret said the following morning. "The outpost radioed to let us know we have a large convoy coming in. They think it is the last of the people answering your call. They have supply trucks, equipment and livestock but need safe passage." He walked to the center of the dining area. All eyes were on him. "You all know the infected are out there, and the numbers keep increasing. We have been observing them from the sky. The military up north lost control of much of a large horde several days ago, and they joined with a number of other packs."

"So, what are we facing, LT?" one of the other Navy men asked.

Garret removed his blue ball cap and rubbed a hand through his close-cropped hair. "We need to clear the road for those people to get through. Estimates are, at least 50,000 infected are within ten miles of this spot."

The collective gasp of the crowd was matched with calls for the ship to leave now before it was too late.

"Ok, stow it, ok," Todd demanded. "We are relatively safe here for the moment, and we still have friends out there. This group coming has traveled thousands of miles, we are not going to abandon them. Lieutenant has a plan, hear him out."

"Thanks, Cap." Garret continued, "Look, your call to evacuate these people, what they are now calling the Patriot's Call, was the right thing to do. Fact is, the Navy probably should have done it first. That is our mission, to protect you guys. Anyway, we are going to help secure a corridor to get this last group through, but it will be tough. We don't have a lot in the way of useful weapons, mostly small arms stuff or heavy artillery. We already know the heavy guns are nearly useless. Every person who can shoot needs to be out there. Take the trucks and cars you have collected, fuel them up, and we will make sure you have all the guns and ammo you need."

There were nods of agreement and voiced dissension from the large crowd. Bobby stood and walked to the center motioning for Garret to sit. He walked silently in a large circle making eye contact with as many of the people as he could. When he began to speak, it was with an authority and conviction he hadn't felt in years.

"You know…I am not sure I would be here if these people hadn't risked everything. Many, hell, most of you wouldn't either. My kid brother is the one who made the call to save you. Now, he is out there somewhere trying to…" he choked up briefly, "…trying to give us a chance to save ourselves. You will not stay on the boat unless you fully understand that to be a Patriot, to be an American, means you have to fucking earn it. You work, you fight, you get up when you get knocked down. This may be our last stand on American soil before we have to just give it to those damn things out there, but by God, let's make sure we make it a good one. This group coming in deserves it just as much as any of us did, so shut the fuck up, grab a gun and find a target to shoot. Playtime is over, class is about to get started."

CHAPTER ONE HUNDRED FIVE

THUNDER RIDGE PROTECTORATE

She walked around a seating arrangement to face him. The look of tenderness and compassion returned with a practiced ease. "That leg looks bad, doll, you probably should put something on it before you bleed out."

He cleared his tears and saw Skybox was struggling to stand again.

"As intelligent as you are, Scott, you really are a bit dim when it comes to women. Look at both of you, though. Do you feel it? You should really thank me."

"Thank you for what, you bitch?" Skybox muttered.

"Michael, Michael, tsk, tsk." Another distant blast, even more powerful, caused the overhead lights to flicker off and on.

"I turned on your warrior gene. Well, Sky, yours was already on, but I gave it a little boost. Scott, yours, though, well, I enhanced you all over. Had you not wondered why you had been so sick? Epigenetic changes, love. I modified your DNA."

"You experimented on us?" Scott yelled.

"I did, well, I had to keep modifying the treatment. The 1297 did really get away from me, but it unlocked the berserkers, the rage within the MAOA gene—the warrior gene. That's why you're here now. Both of you should be unconscious, going into shock, but the anger, the drive— it keeps pushing you."

"And all the other freaks out there in your menagerie of horrors. They are your experiments too?" Scott asked in disbelief.

"So why did you kill the girl—Diana?"

Scott looked at his friend in confusion. "She did what?"

"Yeah, Tahir figured it out. Her body was in cold storage on the Bataan. Gia's door access code was the only one used when she went missing."

"The girl, sadly, was a necessary step. I needed a live subject to test the final treatment on. Now, Scott. Let me ask you a question. When Tahir got you the documents on Catalyst, did you read them all? In particular, did you read the one on global warming?"

He shook his head, "That one didn't seem to be a real issue anymore. With humans all but gone, pollution would cease to be an issue. The planet..." he groaned from the stab of pain, "...the planet would recover."

"See," she said as if she were talking to a small child. "That is beneath you. Surely you haven't bought into the media hype that humans are the only thing responsible for climate change."

"Levy, we don't have time for this," Skybox said. "Scott, end her."

"That document was the only one that really mattered, hon. It was the reason for everything else. Scott, honey, do you realize that 99.92% of all living things that have ever been on this planet are now extinct? The age of dinosaurs was 400 million years. Humans, barely a fraction of that. Why? Why do you think humans might be any luckier? Surely, you don't feel like we deserve it more. The truth is, the only reason we have survived is because we adapted better than other life forms. We were also intelligent enough to adapt plants and animals to serve us better. To continue occupying this filthy rock, we have to adapt even more."

"Woman, you are as bad as Hitler trying to build your perfect race," Skybox said.

Gia just shrugged, "Hitler killed millions, and they call him a monster. I will kill billions and be called a savior."

"So, you are trying to save humanity? Give me a fucking break," Skybox said, hands fumbling awkwardly now, the effects of the blood loss causing his preternatural skills and coordination to finally falter.

"Maybe...not the entire world, Michael. Much of it doesn't need saving. Like the Council, like you, like me. We are relics, but yes, I want the species to survive."

"The research labs, they had nothing to do with the CME, or even the pandemic, did they?"

"Ah, there is my fair-haired golden-boy. Beginning to figure it out, are you? Work the problem, Scott. Put together the clues." She spoke like a middle school teacher urging her prize pupil to discover something on his own.

The pain in his thigh was nearly unbearable, but Scott focused on her words. Then the experiments, thinking of them as data, part of something bigger, rather than individual items. Something else occurred to him. Something in Gia's papers back on the AG. "AMOC?"

Despite the situation, Gia's eyes brightened. "Yes, love."

"What in the fuck is she talking about, Scott?" Sky yelled from across the room. The man had slumped even further to the floor.

"Atlantic Meridional Overturning Circulation? The thermohaline circulation collapse of the Gulf Stream ocean current. Warming temperatures increase glacial melt at the poles changing the salinity of seawater."

"Not just the Gulf Stream, nearly all of the ocean currents are slowing.

The Gulf Stream will likely be the worst. It is already at a 1600 year low, and our projections are it will come to a stop in the next fifteen years."

Scott's mind was considering all the ramifications. He knew that scientists had discovered that climate change could be gradual for long periods, then suddenly change, often with catastrophic circumstances. The ocean currents act like a conveyor system regulating the planet's heat. Moving warm water into colder regions and cold water into warmer areas. The oceanic system is one of Earth's tipping points. Would it be possible for it to suddenly stop? "So, Catalyst literally meant a catalyst for change?" he asked.

Gia nodded, "The planet will become a place of extremes. Northern latitudes will become much colder. The UK, Russia, Canada and much of the US even. Other areas will become hot and arid. Our computer model shows a Sahara-like desert covering most of the deep South, Texas and all of Mexico." She lowered the pistol slightly. "Mankind must adapt to have any chance of survival. SA1297 was our last hope of making those changes. To protect our future, we had to modify our genes so we could better tolerate the heat, need less fluids and generally become more physically capable. Some of our changes actually rolled back the DNA of modern man to something more ancient. Our ancestors lived off the land, often in harsh environments. By flipping the switches on and off, we could see what works best."

"So, Tahir didn't give you the breakthrough you needed to solve all this. You knew it all along."

She smiled, "Well yes...and no. The lab here was working on the DNA modifications. I was working on the epigenetic virus. His ideas just got me to look at the problem in a new way."

"But you had the treatment all along," Scott yelled.

"True, but the earlier versions had...drawbacks, side effects, you might say. Tinkering around with the human genome is risky as you will soon realize when you become a risk to everyone you encounter. The version you received was paired with the new genetic treatment. In time, it may become lethal to anyone around you. Then, you will find all your friends becoming like them because of you," she pointed up and away. "They, too, will survive, of course…in a way. Perhaps a few humans with natural immunities…we could have done more if we'd had more time."

The vitamins and antiviral injections she'd regularly given me, Scott thought.

"This is madness. You are responsible for all of this." Sky said.

Scott saw Skybox's eyes and knew he was marshaling his remaining strength to attack. His own rifle wavered between saving his child or saving the world. Briefly, Scott thought to Roosevelt's warning that he would have to make a terrible choice. Sky eyed him, and he knew what was coming.

Instead, the entire cavern shook as several massive explosions tore through the base. The pressure wave hit them knocking each of them to the floor. Gia recovered faster than either of them and leapt for her pistol which had skidded away. She had blood draining from her ears and nose and a cut on her face. Scott's first instinct was for the baby. Skybox's first instinct was to knock the shit out of the woman.

She rocked back, "You are going to regret that, Michael."

CHAPTER ONE HUNDRED SIX

The A10 Warthog screamed over the battlefield, unleashing a stream of 30mm rounds from its auto-cannon. The nearly forty-year-old ground attack plane was mainly used for close in support. Today, it was clearing a path through the thousands of infected. The horde was so thick nearly every one of the 4200 rounds fired each minute found a target. "God-damn," Major General Daly said to no one in particular. A cloud of red mist rose over the valley like a demonic fog. Neither he, nor any of his troops, had received the treatment, and many had begun to fall to the Chimera virus. Reports of soldiers killing fellow soldiers were now being ignored. They'd all known this was a one-way mission. "They're making us a road, son. Take it before it fills up again."

The Abrams M1A1 revved its engines and began to plow over and through the scores of infected. Its treads made snapping noises as the bones of the dead were ground deep into the blood-soaked mud. The Warthog made more passes farther down and circled high and wide as two more came screaming down the wooded valley to take its place. "Update, Captain."

"Tomahawks inbound, ETA four minutes. Radar contacts, there are more drones on the way. They will be here at the same time."

"How many armored units still operational?"

"Down to 47 M1s, three-dozen Bradleys, a handful of APCs and just over a dozen LAVs."

"Well, fuck!" He had moments to come up with a plan that might make all the sacrifices today not be made in vain. If he used everything he had that was capable of anti-aircraft fire on the drones, that might buy enough time to move the APCs in close. Those cruise missiles had to get the job done, though. He would have given anything to have a few bunker busters right then that he could drop on that beacon. He gave the orders. He and 19 other Abrams tanks moved in support of the armored personnel carriers. Almost everything else would be defending them from the attacking drones. This was an all or nothing gambit.

The nimble drones dodged and weaved between the triple-A like kids playing dodgeball. Several were hit on the first pass, but those that got through unleashed hell on the line of defense the general had assembled. The larger drones were firing tank-busters, depleted uranium rounds designed to penetrate multiple layers of armor. While the MQ-9 Reapers carried over a thousand pounds of ammo, that https://www.facebook.com/groups/JKFranks/ exhausted in minutes. Each of the Reapers turned, lining up on the convoy.

The remote pilots, all safely back underground in the command bunker, clicked the trigger releasing their other weapon from its mounted hardpoints beneath each wing. Each drone carried a dozen of the AGM-114 Hellfire laser-guided air-to-ground missiles. The ground anti-aircraft got more of them this time, but it was a hollow victory. The drones were empty, the payloads were on the way, and the men below had only seconds to live.

Major General Daly looked at his defensive line being consumed in a rain of aerial bombardment just as four Tomahawk BGM-109 cruise missiles cut through the smoke of the battle at subsonic speeds. The latest generation, these were equipped with the Navy's JMEWS warhead system. They flew map of the earth until each bunker-busting warhead impacted the site of the beacon seconds later with a combined force similar to a small MOAB. The drone pilots sitting in their flight chairs beneath almost forty feet of rock and concrete were incinerated immediately along with everything else in the command center. The unpiloted drones began circling in high orbit as their automated backup systems took over.

"Hot damn!" the general shouted. "Get those personnel carriers unloaded, I want a gauntlet around the breach in that bunker. Don't let a single black-shirted bastard get out of there alive." The ferret had found the rabbit.

His captain gave the order, and the APC stormed ahead toward the now defenseless base. The sound of automatic weapons could be heard as the infantry troops began to unload. Some were likely directed at the infected, but most seemed focused on the steady stream of NSF soldiers scrambling from the rock and debris near the smoldering impact site. "Sir, are we taking prisoners?"

"Of course, we are, but they will have to march and survive on their own. We'll see how many make it to safety." *Wherever that is*, he thought.

His captain looked up at him again. "General, I have one of the Spec Ops team on for you. Name is Krychek, says he has civilians that need help. They are coming out an exit about a mile north."

"The people brought here for protection," the general said thinking out loud. He'd been so focused on destroying the base he'd lost sight of the fact it was originally a camp supposedly with the purpose to protect the best and brightest America had to offer. He had no plan to deal with survivors. This was a one-way mission. "Shit…let me talk to him."

CHAPTER ONE HUNDRED SEVEN

Two more impacts hit knocking out power in the room. Scott searched around for his fallen weapon but couldn't feel anything in all the rubble. He felt Skybox pulling him to his feet. "Where is she?"

"I don't know, I lost her in that last blast." As the ringing in their ears subsided, they could hear weapons fire in the distance, and closer, the unmistakable sounds of a cave-in. Sky produced a tactical light and shone it around the remains of the office. "No other exits, she must have gone deeper. Guaranteed—she will have a way out."

Echoing footsteps were heard as they entered the main corridor, but they had no way of knowing which direction. Scott could barely move with the damaged leg, Skybox somehow seemed to be recovering. "She's that way, Scott."

Scott nodded, "Go…go get her, I'll catch up."

Skybox turned to leave, then swiveled back. "Hey, sorry about all this, I had no idea. I am also sorry for what I am about to do to her. Take care, man." With that he was gone, his long-loping strides carrying him deeper into the cave system.

Scott saw the butt of the rifle under a pile of rocks. He crawled over and took several minutes freeing it only to discover the magazine clip was damaged. He might have one round in the chamber, but that was all it would fire. He shouldered the weapon and limped down the hall in the direction Skybox had gone. Red emergency LEDs were flickering on now to provide some illumination to the space.

His life was draining out of his body leaving long trails of blood in his wake. He could feel the energy being sapped away. He stopped long enough to rip the tactical belt from his waist and make a tourniquet. It helped staunch the flow of blood but made using the leg nearly impossible. No way he was going to make it. The sound of a gunshot up ahead eclipsed all other sounds.

He tried to rush but fell, then felt arms beneath him, pulling him to his feet, then supporting the weight of that side.

The pair stood in the engineering room. The farthest point away from the smoking crater that had been the command center. The NuScale reactor was going into shutdown mode. The gun in Gia's hand erupted as Skybox dove for cover. "You sure firing a weapon in a room with a nuclear reactor is a good idea, Doc?"

"It's probably not recommended, but, you know, we improvise."

"Radiation might hurt the baby," he said crawling behind heavier pipes for cover.

She laughed, "Yeah, the baby."

He heard her working with something and knew it probably wasn't going to be good. He needed a weapon, any kind of weapon.

"You know, I like you, Michael, you are charming in a brutish sort of way. Scott was right in seeing the good in you—I'll give him that."

Sky loosened a retaining nut and released a metal arm for a shut-off valve. "What about Scott, did you ever really care for him?"

Whatever she was working on went silent. She had no snappy comeback.

"Come on, Gia, be honest for once in your fucking life."

He saw a shadow at the door to the room, and Scott stumbled through the door, gun raised to fire.

"Answer the question Gia!" he said in a weak voice.

"Warning…Warning. Lethal Venting in Two-Minutes. Evacuate the area. Warning…" The robotic voice alert began coming from the reactor control panel. A series of amber lights began flashing throughout the room.

Scott saw the silhouette of Gia bent over the console. He saw his friend ready to charge her with something in his hand. She casually raised the pistol toward the approaching man. He aligned the sights of the sub-compact H&K at her head and squeezed the trigger. The gunshot echoed loudly in the open space. The shot had not come from his rifle, it only clicked on an empty chamber. He watched horrified as her shot found its mark. Skybox's body hit the floor with a dull thump.

The shadow moved past him in a blur. Gia turned toward the door, but even she wasn't fast enough. Ghost arced an arm upward, his blade slicing deeply through her arm. She dropped the weapon and went to the floor seething at the man. "Tommy!"

He looked confused, surprised that this person in front of him was suddenly an enemy. His blade was poised to continue the slashing attack, but Gia moved nearly as fast as he did. Scott looked in desperation at the limp form of Skybox and now Tommy battling against his former fiancée. She reached Sky's body and came up with the metal bar making contact with Tommy's head with a sickening wet sound. Tommy reached up, grabbing at his already tortured skull and faded into the shadows of the room.

"Drop it, Scott." Gia had regained her weapon and leveled it at his chest.

He tossed the useless rifle away and walked slowly toward her. Unarmed and defenseless, he no longer cared about the end. "It's over, Levy," he said refusing to refer to her as Gia again.

She was pressing her injured arm close to her body, the blood staining the white lab coat and dripping from the bottom edge. "You may be right, dear." She used a toe of her shoe to nudge Skybox. "Definitely over for Michael. Sorry about that. He was just one more failed experiment, though."

"You have to stop," he said weakly. "Hasn't there been enough death already?" He turned slightly at the sounds coming from far down the corridor. He assumed it would be the Army, maybe Krychek and the rest of the team. What he didn't expect to see in the darkened door was the infected.

"Scott," she said in a whisper. "Step toward me," she said menacingly, then again in a much kinder tone. He took a step closer to the woman. His eyes darting from her raised gun to the rabid looking creatures pouring into the room.

"Closer!" she whispered so loud it was nearly a shout. He didn't move. "The baby," she pleaded. "They won't attack you."

Confused, he turned and focused on her. Her beautiful red hair, perfect features and a heart full of poison. "What do you mean they won't attack me?"

She reached a hand out and pulled him forcibly close to her. "You have a newer variant of the 1297 treatment much like them. They don't attack their own kind due to a pheromone they all give off. To them, you are one of them." He felt the baby bump pressing into his back. Looking down, his shoe was pressed up against the unmoving body of his friend. "Will I become a carrier of the disease? Will our child be like me…or like them?" She didn't respond.

The infected moved to within a few feet but got no closer. Their smell, like a wet dog, was overwhelming as were the unholy sounds they made. The vacant eyes stared at nothing, but they were excited and smelled prey nearby. "Tommy?" he called out. Her pistol dug into his back.

"Don't," she said angrily.

"Tommy, get out of here, get somewhere safe if you can."

"Stop trying to be the hero, Scott. I'm the one trying to save the world, not you. Sorry you don't approve of my methods."

"Levy, your fucking methods are trying to eat us. Also, you need to get over your damn daddy issues." His hand brushed against a tiny bulge in his pocket. Carefully he reached in. *I might not be as defenseless as I thought.* "Besides, I wasn't trying to save the world...I just wanted to save you." He used his thumb to uncap the vial of neurotoxin he'd taken from the oceanographic lab. His finger ran along the slender needle. This was the choice. Roosevelt was right. Kill Gia and...kill his baby, but give humanity a chance to survive. His hand holding the vial began to shake. He couldn't do it...wouldn't do it.

Without warning, Tommy appeared between them and the infected. Unlike Scott, they had no problem going after him. His knives slashed out cutting down three in seconds and quickly moving deeper into the ranks. He felt Gia's gun move from his back raising in the direction of the blur that was Ghost. Scott closed his eyes to the carnage in front, pulled his hand from his pocket and drove the needle backward deep into the mother of his unborn child.

"Oh, God! What have you done?" She went rigid, then collapsed to the floor holding her stomach. The small ampule of poison still embedded in her side. The gun fell feebly from her hands which were beginning to shake violently. Her throat made a gurgling sound as she grabbed for him.

Through tear-filled eyes, he stepped to the woman he had loved and cradled her. Her face showed the excruciating pain as the toxins attacked her body. She locked eyes with him; he could see the terror as well as a vulnerability that made him wonder how much of Gia she had been. Her mouth tried to form words, but he had to lean his head in close to make it out.

"I did..."

"I do love you, Scott. Always."

The sounds of automatic weapons came from the corridor. Those infected dying under Tommy's blade began to diminish as well. He looked down into the dimming eyes of one of the most evil people to have ever existed and realized he, too, felt for her. His brother had been right, he didn't know women. "I love you, too," he whispered as the light in her eyes went out for good. His trembling hands closed her eyes then traveled down to her stomach. He rested a hand there for a moment as well.

CHAPTER ONE HUNDRED EIGHT

Scott raised his hands as the soldiers burst into the engineering room. Leading the way was Nez, the big Ranger who helped pull him to his feet. He looked down at the bodies of Gia and Skybox.

"You okay, Montgomery?"

Scott just shook his head and limped from the room. An Army medic met up with him as he exited the compound into the bright afternoon sun. Minutes later, he was sitting on the rear deck of a personnel carrier, an IV attached to a clear bag of something hanging over his head while the gunshot wound in his thigh was bandaged. The sounds of helicopters were everywhere. Through the trees, he could see the massive double rotor chinooks landing and others taking off.

Krychek walked up, giving a nod, and seconds later, a large white dog was also on the platform leaning against him. "Hey, Solo."

"Everyone is pulling out, Scott. This whole valley is going to be overrun." Krychek said.

"To where?"

Krychek looked haggard, "Taking everyone to the coast. All the civilians from here that they can take will be offloaded to the AG. The rest, as well as the guards and scientists, are being handed over to the Navy. The infected are literally everywhere now." He leaned in, placing a hand on his shoulder. "Sorry about Skybox, sir. We'll get you out on the next round of choppers."

Scott started to tell the man not to call him sir but didn't. He'd just murdered his girlfriend and baby and watched the toughest man he'd ever known die. His mind struggled to hold onto many other thoughts. "What about Tommy? You know…Ghost?" he said weakly looking up at the soldier.

"No sign of him, Scott. We weren't sure if he even made it inside." Krychek said.

Ghost had disappeared again. Somehow, he knew this time it would be for good. Scott owed his life to Tommy every much as he did Skybox. He closed his eyes and offered a silent thanks to both.

The last load of civilians heading to the AG lifted off two hours later for the 90-minute ride to the coast. Krychek and Nez sat stoically on the long bench seat of the helicopter. Solo lay curled up against the bulkhead nearby. Scott Montgomery wasn't on it.

Major General Daly looked at the man leaning against the tree before he left. "Son, I understand you had a lot to do with stopping all this."

Scott shrugged, not really wanting conversation, much less congratulations, for what he had done. The general seemed unsure how to treat the man but could see the damage and pain etched on Scott's face. "Hell of a thing," he said, spitting a stream of black tobacco juice in the dirt. "Lot of good men lost today. Worst battle of my career." He looked back over the valley full of bodies and the smoking wreckage of military equipment. "Any idea why? Why did they do all this?"

"She wanted to save the world," Scott said softly.

"Seemed like just the opposite," the Marine said.

Scott shielded his eyes from the sun and looked up at the man. "It would have worked, her plan. Still might, in fact. She wasn't saving us from the blackout…she was saving us from what comes next."

"Eh?" the man said. "What would that be?"

Scott just shook his head. "Y'all took everything from the labs?"

"We did, everything that was undamaged and seemed safe enough to transport," Daly said.

"Good, they were doing some vital work there. The scientists will be able to help. There is a man on the Aquatic Goddess who should have the computer files from all the research going on. If humanity has a chance to survive what comes next, we will have to adapt. Sir, you have what you need to make it happen."

The general reached out a hand to help Scott up. "Walk up this hill and get on this bird with me, Montgomery. We need good people like you, we will need your help."

Scott reached up and took the outstretched hand but just shook it. "I'm done, sir, I've climbed my last hill." He gazed out over the smoke-filled horizon a long time before continuing, "There is also a chance I could become a danger to those around me. She…she did something to my genome. Besides, I've got something I have to do here as well." He glanced over at the covered bodies lying on the ground outside the cave entrance.

"A Pyric victory, Son—win the battle but lose the war. You know as soon as we're gone, the infected are going to be everywhere. Those sound generators your guys dreamed up are the only thing keeping 'em away. Batteries on most are starting to get weak already."

Scott nodded, "Its ok, sir. Please do one thing for me, though."

~

Harris Springs, Mississippi

Todd watched in disbelief as another load of evacuees landed and came streaming up the gangplank. Bobby and Angelique were coordinating the incoming crowds as best they could. "Cap?" DeVonte yelled from the entrance. "The infected are getting across."

"Shit." It was what they had been fearing. All day the crowds of infected on the far side had been growing. Many had tried to cross and drowned or been eaten by the numerous gators, but some had made it, then more and more. They had to protect the docks and the new arrivals. "Make sure everyone out there has a weapon. Don't waste ammo but keep them away from the ship. Ask Tahir if he can crank up the volume on the sound generator more."

"How far out dey is? the boy asked.

The convoy and many of the residents of AG were out there bringing in the last convoy of Patriots. "Ten miles last report, hopefully, closer now. They said it was hell going out, we lost several cars and occupants. Bartos said not to worry, though, coming back should be fine."

"How's dat?"

"No idea, kid, trust in the Cajun, though." He watched another chopper coming into view. This one he'd been told carried captured supplies to help feed all the new additions to the community. Tahir walked in looking pale. "What's wrong, Tahir?"

"Scott. He's not coming. I just got off the radio with a Marine general. Scott said for us to leave as soon as we could. Don't wait on him."

"What the fuck, man?" They'd already heard from Krychek and Nez about Skybox's death and what Scott had to do to defeat Gia. "The military said that place will be crawling with infected, worse than here even."

Tahir nodded and sat in the chair heavily. "I started going through the data from the labs there. There are teraflops of it, may take years to go through, but I learned a couple of things already." He looked out the bridge windows as the chopper came in for a landing. "First, we have to get ready for something even worse than the blackout. That is what they were working on, modifying plant and animal life to survive what is coming next. The Gulf Stream is slowing to a halt. It will make weather more extreme, and much of the planet will be uninhabitable."

Todd shook his head trying to absorb what he was hearing. "God-damn...and the second?"

Tahir sighed and stood up. "I looked at the medical records, Dr. Colton had a file on Scott. He didn't receive just the treatment the rest of us did. The changes to his genome are more...significant. In time, he may become like those," he pointed across the Intracoastal Waterway. "Or, he could just be a carrier, infecting us with a new strain. We already know the antiviral may not work long-term."

"So, he knows this...and that is why he can't come home?" Todd said, rubbing his eyes.

Tahir nodded, "I discovered one other thing in the medical records," he said. "Something about Gia." Todd gave an instant look of disgust.

"Not sure I give a good holy fuck about anything to do with that woman," Todd said.

"She was never pregnant, couldn't have children, in fact. It was a massive tumor. The cause seemed to be the result of exposure to an ancient pathogen when she was much younger. She fought it all her life, much of her research centered around it, but in the end, it was killing her."

"Scott thinks he killed his unborn child," Todd whispered. His heart ached for his friend. He longed for a way to tell his friend that one bit of news.

The handset beside the ship's helm crackled to life with the familiar sound of Bartos. "Hey, lugnuts, lower the bridge, we are coming in hot."

Todd smiled grimly, looking inland and seeing a dust cloud coming off the road, and keyed the mic. "Make it fast, Cajun, we are starting the old girl up now." He pulled the binoculars to his eyes and looked at the fast-approaching convoy. "Bartos…is that tanks I see escorting you back?"

"Hell, yeah, we made some new friends out here. They want to take a cruise, too. You ain't gonna believe this shit."

Todd radioed down to Scoots to lower the bridge but to keep the infected off best they could. He saw Solo darting across the dock below. The dog hadn't wanted to stay in the ship while Bartos was still out there. Trish and Bobby walked hand in hand with Jacob and Sylvia playing tag right behind. DeVonte was directing new recruits to fire on the infected coming out of the water, but he kept stealing looks back at Angelique who was helping offload supplies from the chopper. Porter's adopted son, JD, was up with several others on the descending draw-bridge, AR-15 at low ready waiting on Steven and Pam who had been out with Bartos. His dog, Elvis, was eyeing Solo warily, but he'd already seen the two dogs playing chase with each other earlier.

"You ok, Todd?" Tahir asked coming up and placing a gentle hand on the big man's back. Todd's body shook with racking sobs of grief, but he nodded remembering Scott's mantra, 'We fight, we live, we love.' He turned two levers and pushed the green button starting the big diesel engines. "Life will go on," he whispered. *Thank you, my friend.*

EPILOGUE

Scott smoothed the dirt over the grave. The soft forest soil had been easy to dig, once he found the body bags he was looking for. He was also starting to get used to all the infected around. Some would get too close and even bump into him. Occasionally, one would growl, but they generally just seemed to ignore him. He was ok with that, he wanted to be ignored. He'd said his goodbyes to Skybox, then turned to the other hole nearby. He'd unzipped Gia's body from her bag. Even in death, she was the most beautiful woman he'd ever known. The rictus of death was already making her body stiff, but he leaned and kissed the top of her head. He placed a hand on the bump of her belly, idly thinking it seemed too firm to be just baby, but he had no frame of reference for that.

"I don't understand the cruelties in your life that made you this way, Gia. I choose to remember the other you. Whether it was false or not, she was a good person. She tried to do good, maybe to offset some of the bad that was going on in the other half of her life." He placed her, uncovered, down in the hole and began raking handfuls of dirt over her body. "I love you, Gia. I wish you peace from the torment in this world." His eyes stung, but the tears didn't come this time. His body refused to let go of any more of its moisture for his losses.

~

Adrift in the middle of a dazzling blue-green Caribbean Sea, the California bobbed with the gentle waves. The presidential yacht was anchored thirty miles off the Costa de Mosquitos, or Mosquito Coast, of Nicaragua. The oppressive sun beat down unmercifully on the deck and occupants. The luxurious boat with its rich finishes and luxurious textures was now swathed in blood, gore, and the remains of much of the Coast Guard crew.

Madelyn Chambers sat in her stateroom, unwilling to make a sound. The creatures outside the door of the suite kept banging it or looking through the single round window. While she was injected with the treatment and immune from the Chimera virus, her crew had not been so lucky. She had carried the infection on-board, and in doing so, brought about her own end.

The engines had gone silent three days earlier. The lights and air conditioning stayed on for several hours before fading to a stop. The temperature in the cabin was well over a hundred, and the sun hadn't reached midday yet. Behind her suite was a warehouse of food, fresh water and other supplies, including her wardrobe and makeup. She looked down through the tears at her battered hands, the bruises and cuts from where she'd beat on the porthole glass the previous two days. Like most of the room, it had been retrofitted to be bulletproof. She couldn't get out, couldn't get fresh air.

The smell of raw feces overwhelmed her senses as the toilets had ceased to function as well. She eyed the useless 'football.' The launch codes for the nation's nukes, as well as the access to orbital bombardment weapons, were all offline. *That damn Levy had canceled them*, she felt sure. She quietly moved to the stateroom door and peered up and out the small round window. A line of angry, hungry looking creatures met her stare and began charging the door again. Her crew, all infected, were now her captors. The boat bobbed again as a gentle swell rolled underneath.

She looked around the room for the hundredth time for a way out.

There was only one, she knew that now. Her fingers unclasped the box on the shelf with the presidential emblem. Reaching in, she removed the commemorative nickel-plated pistol. It had an American flag imprinted on the ivory grips and a solid-gold eagle on the barrel. She looked at it a long time, sweat dripping off her and ruining the designer dress she wore. Sadly, she pulled the slide back like she had seen done in movies, remembered to click the safety off and placed it against her temple. She closed her eyes and pulled the trigger. A dull click sounded. "Fuck!" She threw the gun against the wall.

Several hundred miles to the east, the Aquatic Goddess sailed past en route to Costa Rica. The almost 6000 occupants of the AG anxious to get a fresh start. Someone looking down that day would have seen Captain Todd holding Jack's Bible in his hand as Roosevelt escorted a very lovely Angelique toward a beaming DeVonte, and Bobby Montgomery escorted his daughter Kaylie forward, handing her off to a very nervous DJ. The double wedding would be the first of many the captain would perform.

The remnants of the US military were aboard numerous Navy ships heading to Guantanamo Bay. They had also asked Cuba for temporary asylum. That island country's isolation and more basic infrastructure had protected them somewhat. They had not yet encountered the infected but had suffered great losses since the blackout. Commander Garret and General Daly had promised any assistance possible in helping the country remain free of the pandemic in exchange for allowing safe harbor.

It would take years for the infected to finally die off. Until then, the epigenetic treatment pioneered by Dr. Gia Colton would become routine and widespread, and all descendants from the groups of survivors inherited the immunity. Her alternate identity and other more ruthless pursuits would be lost to history, yet benefits to mankind from the work at Thunder Ridge would benefit everyone in countless ways over the years to come.

~

The hordes of infected were long gone as they were in most places he'd been. They'd kept moving westward, migrating packs of predation in search of new hosts. A few still wandered the streets but not many. Not a day went by that he didn't think of his friends and family, or Gia, for that matter, but he was dealing with it. He'd spent weeks searching through the bombed-out labs in Tennessee finding several even more amazing discoveries. He'd looked for Tommy, and several times felt as though someone was watching, but never saw the man. *We are the last of the living, both of us ghosts among the dead,* he thought.

In a remote hangar there, he'd found row after row of the sleek LSV Spider vehicles. He'd strapped spare fuel, batteries and a trailer full of supplies he'd found and finally headed off the mountain. He made a stop at Graceland where he slept for weeks in a bed supposedly belonging to Elvis. His leg wound healed remarkably fast before then heading toward Little Rock where he visited the old Sanderson place where Bobby had met Jacob and his mom. After a long stay at a small cabin on the Pearl River near Jackson, he headed to the coast.

The gas ran out about a hundred miles from Harris Springs, the electrical motors on the LSV carried him on to within twenty. From there, he'd walked, his limp barely noticeable now. He passed the entrance to the old dam and saw the sleek but abandoned HondaJet Tahir had landed sitting off the side of the road on Highway 50. The sides of the road were littered with the now familiar sight and the smell of thousands of decaying corpses. The infected had been thick here. He hoped with all his heart his friends got away unharmed.

It was over three months after the final exodus, when Scott Montgomery walked across the lowered bridge into what had been Harris Springs. Not seeing the Aquatic Goddess in its familiar mooring place as he approached the town was jarring. He wove his way past the marina. Todd's fishing boat, the Donna Marie, still sat bobbing in its slip. He moved down the main street past the dilapidated buildings. He thought of his walk months earlier with Jack. He felt closer to the man now than ever before. He paused on the old raised sidewalk thinking of the day of the event, seeing the preacher that morning in that garish shirt crossing the street toward him. Those guys had saved him, and he'd tried hard to return the favor. He rounded the corner and walked toward the docks they'd built for the AG. The space was empty save for something large covered by a canvas tarp on one corner.

He removed the tie downs and pulled the tarp back to reveal his Jeep Wrangler. On the back, in its familiar spot, hung his Trek Domaine bicycle. A note sat on the driver's seat along with what appeared to be a map. His lips fought against gravity and months of depression to form the tiniest of smiles.

-End-

MESSAGE FROM THE AUTHOR

Thank you for reading my novel "Ghost Country". I hope you enjoyed it. If you would be so kind as to take a moment and leave a review, I would be very grateful. Unfortunately reviews and referrals are the only real ways for self-published authors to compete with the big-name writers, and it sure would be nice to make it out of the crowded, dark and dusty aisles of Amazon.

If you do write a review, please email me at author@jkfranks.com and I will forward you a special bonus chapter featuring 'Bartos' story' from the end of the book. It also offers a few hidden facts and a surprise (re)appearance. I thought this would be a fun way to say "Thank you"

ABOUT THE AUTHOR

International bestselling author JK Franks once again offers a look at an alternative America in his latest book—Ghost Country. This is the gripping story of a country at war with itself and a group struggling to maintain their humanity in this concluding chapter to the epic Catalyst Series. The prior novels of this post-apocalyptic series have been hailed as some of the best in the genre including American Exodus which became an International #1 Bestseller early in 2018. "Post-apocalyptic fiction are cautionary tales that should scare us but also, even more importantly, they should make us think."

His stories are not only fast moving, each has regular and amazing characters who must make life changing decisions, all while the earth is experiencing an apocalyptic event unlike anything imagined.

Franks and his wife now live in West Point, Georgia. He is currently working on a new story, not involving the end of the world. No matter where he is or what's going on, he tries his best to set aside time every day to answer emails and messages from readers. You can visit him on the web at www.jkfranks.com. Please subscribe to his newsletter for updates, promotions, and giveaways. You can also find the author on Facebook or email him directly at media@jkfranks.com.

OTHER BOOKS BY JK FRANKS

The Catalyst Series

Book 1: Downward Cycle

Life in a remote oceanfront town spirals downward after a massive solar flare causes a global blackout. But the loss of electrical power is just the first of the problems facing the survivors. In the chaos, that follows. Is this how the world ends?

Book 2: Kingdoms of Sorrow

With civilization in ruins, individuals band together to survive and build a new society. The threats are both grave and numerous—surely too many for a small group to weather. This is a harrowing story of survival following the collapse of the planet's electric grids.

Book 2.5: American Exodus Novella

This companion story to the Catalyst series follows one man's struggle to get back home after the collapse. No supplies, no idea of the hardships to come; how can he possibly survive the journey? Even if he survives, can he adapt to this new reality?

Book 3: Ghost Country

Since the Solar superstorm and CME almost two years ago, the Gulf Coast town of Harris Springs, Mississippi has suffered from gang attacks, famine, hurricanes and battled a crusading army of religious zealots. Now, they face their greatest challenge. Outsmarting a tyrannical President and escaping an approaching pandemic.

Connect with the Author Online:

** For a sneak peek at new novels, free stories and more, join the email list at: www.jkfranks.com/Email

Facebook: facebook.com/groups/JKFranks/

Amazon Author Page: amazon.com/-/e/B01HIZIYH0

Smashwords: smashwords.com/profile/view/kfranks22

Goodreads: goodreads.com/author/show/15395251.J_K_Franks

Website: JKFranks.com

Twitter: @jkfranks

Instagram: @jkfranks1

CPSIA information can be obtained
at www.ICGtesting.com
Printed in the USA
LVHW092147200319
611355LV00006B/21/P